Bad Choices

LUCY VINE

ORION

First published in Great Britain in 2021 by Orion Books,
an imprint of The Orion Publishing Group Ltd
Carmelite House, 50 Victoria Embankment,
London EC4Y 0DZ

An Hachette UK company

1 3 5 7 9 10 8 6 4 2

A CIP catalogue record for this book is
available from the British Library.

ISBN (Mass Market Paperback) 978 1 4091 8091 3
ISBN (eBook) 978 1 4091 8092 0

Typeset by Input Data Services Ltd, Somerset

Printed in Great Britain by Clays Ltd, Elcograf S.p.A.

MIX
Paper from
responsible sources
FSC
www.fsc.org   FSC® C104740

www.orionbooks.co.uk

Dedicated to anyone who hasn't been able to
hug their best friend lately

Lucy Vine is a writer, editor and the e-bestselling author of novels *Hot Mess*, *What Fresh Hell* and *Are We Nearly There Yet?* Her books have been translated into ten languages around the world, with *Hot Mess* optioned for a TV series in America. She's also host of the podcast and live event series, the Hot Mess Clubhouse, celebrating funny women. Her writing regularly appears in the likes of *Grazia*, *Stylist*, *Heat*, *Fabulous*, *New*, *Now*, *Marie Claire*, *Cosmopolitan*, *Daily Telegraph*, *Sun* and *Mirror*.

By Lucy Vine

Hot Mess
What Fresh Hell
Are We Nearly There Yet?

Prologue

Present Day

Why do women cry in loos?

My theory is that it's because we're *needed* by so many people.

Our parents, our children, our partners, our siblings, our bosses, our co-workers, our pets, our friends, every fucker you ever met needs something from you.

And I'm going to say this next thing and I don't care if I'm not supposed to, so shut up: it is a female problem.

You think 90 per cent of those cis male, boat-shoe-wearing drones care if they're needed? You think they spend their days worrying about their friends and family's emotional load in the same way women do? Ticking off their mental lists and concerns and worries late into the night? Of course they don't.

I swear, that's how men got so much taller than women – they're not weighed down by all the emotional baggage.

We cry in loos because we have to. It's the only place we can escape all that fucking *need*. I cry in loos because I am sad a lot of the time, and I can't let anyone see that. Because how can you let yourself break when you're responsible for holding so many pieces – so many people – together? The loo is all we have, the only safe space we get, away from all the expectations.

Although – let's face it – anyone who's ever had a child in

their house knows the loo isn't always a private safe space either. Not unless you get a big fat deadbolt on that door. That's why I never thought I'd have a kid, but you can't predict what's going to happen in your life. I had no idea.

Crying in bathrooms – public and private – has always been a woman thing. A *me* thing. Which is why I guess I shouldn't be surprised that I'm sitting here on a loo today, on one of the worst days of my life, crying my eyes out yet again. Here I am, wearing this alien outfit from the back of my wardrobe, while so many people wait for me to – I don't know – *perform* out there. They all need me to be the star of this bleak theatre production with no punchlines and no ending. They're all waiting for me to go out there, get up in front of everyone and play the part of the brave, strong, fearless Woman. They'll even want me to cry a bit. But see, not like I'm crying now, right here. They'll want something moving and discreet. Slow, glistening, brave, feminist tears rolling – nay, *winding* – down my cheek. So they can shake their heads and swell with pity at my loss. They don't want these bathroom tears, full of snot and soggy tissue, and painful mascara blobs lodged in my eye socket. They don't want the loud clogged sobs; the guttural noises; the mess.

So I'll do it here. I'll cry in a loo. For quite possibly the thousandth time in my life.

The worst thing is, it's all her fault.

So many people need me. They need me in so many exhausting, draining, soul-crushing ways. And sure, she needed me too, but in a way that felt recharging and energising most of the time. She was the only person in my life I could cry with – in or out of the loo – the only person who understood. And it's so unbelievably shit that she's not here with me today when I need her most.

2

Outside the toilet, someone starts banging on the door. They probably want to start, it's getting late.

I can't do this without her, I can't do this without her, I can't do this without her.

The banging continues, with an extra edge of urgency.

I just need to sit and cry a little bit longer. I just need to miss her for a little bit longer.

I clear my throat, resisting the urge to shout fuck off.

'GIVE ME FIVE MINUTES,' I shout, furiously, my voice unrecognisable. 'I'm just . . . just . . .' I trail off, searching for an excuse that will ensure a few more minutes of solitude and crying. 'FIVE MINUTES,' I shout. 'I'VE LOST A TAMPON INSIDE ME, OK?'

The knocking abruptly stops and the silence is deafening.

That excuse always works.

1

Twenty Years Earlier: 2001

ZOE

OK, fuck this.

If this girl doesn't shut the hell up, I'm going to lose my mind.

I mean, here I am with my pants round my knees and my forehead pressed against the shiny wall, trying to have a quiet little cry, and some dick comes in and starts bawling in the cubicle next to me.

Next to me, the wailing becomes even more dramatic.

This is particularly unfair because I never cry. I actually pride myself on being, I don't know, like, a dried-up husk inside? Dad said I never used to cry when I fell over as a kid. I was always the 'brave one', the one my little brothers could look up to as an example of how to keep it together. I didn't even shed a tear last year when everything happened.

So yeah, I really think I've earned this. I've earned some peace. I just need ten minutes alone with a fucking tissue. Ten minutes to get seriously dehydrated and headachey from sobbing too much. Ten minutes to lean my head against the cool plastic cubicle walls and be sad, you know?

I listen to the snotty sobbing next door for another minute, distractedly reading the badly spelled graffiti about a 'bitch' from year eleven called Andrea. I wonder if Andrea really is a bitch or whether it's just jealousy. At my last school there were loads of girls who called *me* a bitch and Mum said that was jealousy. Although she didn't really have an answer when I asked her what there was to be jealous of.

It's probably jealousy with Andrea, but I'm not totally discounting the possibility that she's being called a bitch because she really *is* a bitch. Sometimes that happens. At least 20 per cent of the times I was called a bitch at St Mary's was because I was being a total bitch.

Maybe the weeper next door *is* Andrea? Maybe we're meant to be friends? It is quite a coincidence that we're both in these loos crying simultaneously – maybe it's a sign from God or the universe? I don't know if I believe in God or the universe, but I might do. I haven't figured out if believing in a god would make me interesting or lame.

The sobbing shifts up another gear.

If it is Andrea, she's probably sad because of the graffiti. I could talk to her, tell her how awful it is, and then we'll bond over how jealous everyone is of her. Then I'll help her clean it up and we'll write over it with mean shit about other people.

Or maybe she's sad because she's been such a bitch to everyone today and it all got too much for her? I could sympathise with that, too. Anything for a friend.

I wonder if I'll end up with graffiti about me here? I wonder what it would say.

The sobbing gets louder still and I inwardly sigh, giving in to my curiosity.

'Andrea?' I say softly, hopefully, and the girl's sob catches. Imagine if I got that right, how cool would that . . .

'Did you just call me *Andrea*?' the voice sounds outraged. 'Like, Andrea Allen from year eleven? She's such a

B-I-T-C-H.' She spells out the word before continuing in an insulted tone, 'I am *so* not Andrea.'

'Er, no, no,' I am flustered and disappointed. 'I said, um, *ah dear*. Because, y'know . . . because you're crying.'

There is a long, suspicious silence and I feel a tear I was halfway through shedding slowly make its way down my cheek. I sniff, a little more loudly than I'd intended.

'So . . . are you OK?' I try again.

'No,' the short answer comes at last. 'I'm not.' There's more than a hint of martyr in there, and I cover a smirk.

Actually, I realise, the voice is a little familiar, which surprises me. I've not really met anyone at this school yet.

'Do you want to talk about it?' I try.

'Yes,' she says immediately, her voice breaking as she gives one last overly dramatic sob. 'But first, you tell me why *you're* crying?'

'I'm not cry—' I begin, instantly defensive, and then loudly sniff again. 'OK.' I hesitate, unsure how much I want to share. She's no Andrea, after all. 'Well, it's my first day here at this school and I . . .'

The crier interrupts me. 'You're the new girl!' She suddenly sounds cheerier. 'You're in my form – 9CL? Miss Cornelisse's class?'

That's got to be how I know the voice. But I can't find an associated face in my memory bank.

The faceless voice continues, 'Corny introduced you in registration this morning – what's your name again? It's a cool name, right? I can't remember.'

'It's not,' I say shyly. 'I don't . . . um, I'm Zoe.'

'No, no, your surname,' she says impatiently. 'It's, like, totally dramatic.'

'Darling,' I mutter, embarrassed. 'Zoe Darling.'

Through the plastic wall, the voice sighs happily. 'See? That's supercool. My name is Natalie Winters, which is soooo boring. Last year I tried to get everyone to call me Roxy but they wouldn't do it. Don't you think I seem more like a Roxy? I thought people might call me, like, *Foxy Roxy* if I were called Roxy. But they just laughed at me. Maybe they'd do it if I wasn't so fat but I don't think fat girls are supposed to call themselves foxy.'

'Oh, right.' I'm a bit flummoxed.

She pauses like she is waiting for something. 'You think I'm fat?' she says at last, sounding offended.

'I don't know what you look like,' I point out.

'Oh, that's right,' she says, sounding relieved. 'I forgot that. I'm just used to people automatically saying, "You're not fat!" when I say I'm fat. Even though I am quite fat. Actually, I wish they wouldn't say that, because then it makes me worry that being fat is the worst possible thing in the world to be, when I don't mind it. I really like food and I like my tummy. It's nice and round and I can hold it when I go to sleep. Plus, my mum's fat – so's her best friend Sue – and they don't seem to care. They just drink a lot of wine and eat Toblerones and laugh a lot.' She pauses to take a breath. 'The only thing is, I think the cool people in our year would like me more if I wasn't fat. And maybe they would've been up for calling me Roxy instead of boring *Natalie*. But,' she goes on happily, barely pausing for breath, 'otherwise I don't mind being fat. Are you fat?'

'I don't really know,' I consider it. 'My brothers call me fat, but I think that's just because they learnt it as an insult and want to upset me. I guess it depends what you consider fat. I knew a girl at my old school who said she was fat and she ended up in hospital for malnutrition.'

'God, that's so cool,' Natalie says, impressed for some reason. 'Did she die?' She doesn't wait for an answer before steaming on. 'Did you like your old school? Is that why you're crying? Because you hate it here?'

I shake my head. 'No, I just . . .' I trail off, wondering how much to share with this oversharer. I take a deep breath. 'I, um, started my period today – my first period. I guess it's, like, a big moment and I feel sad I'm on my own. Plus, I didn't know it would hurt like this or feel so fucking weird.'

She shrieks. 'No way! I just got my first period, too! That's why *I'm* crying. Oh my God, Zoe Darling, we're basically twins.'

'Really?' I laugh. 'That's so strange.' I pause. 'Are you OK? It's gross, right? Is yours . . . um, is yours a bit *brown*?'

'Uh-huh.' I can hear Natalie nodding. 'I thought I'd pooed myself a bit or something.'

I stop awkwardly, then add in a hushed whisper, 'Do you have towels or tampons or whatever?'

'No,' I can hear Natalie shaking her head. 'But I have some nice tissue if you want to use that? It's better than the crappy loo roll they have in here.'

There's some rustling and a small hand appears under the plastic wall. It's holding wads of Kleenex, crumpled but apparently unused.

'They're clean,' she says quickly. 'It was in my bra, but I don't mind being an AA cup again for the rest of the day. It's not like the boys look at me anyway.'

I take it, a little reluctantly. 'Um, thanks. Have you got enough for you?'

'Yeah.' She gives me a thumbs up under the wall and I giggle at the sight. She continues, 'I don't really know how to use tampons anyway. Mum bought me some a while ago

9

so I could practice but I spent ages trying to get it in before realising I was trying to force it into my bumhole. Really put me off.'

I have no answer for that.

'Don't you feel like we're the last people in the universe to get our periods?' she goes on. 'I feel like everyone else started when they were, like, eleven.'

'Yeah,' I say and nod. 'But I still don't feel ready.' I consider all the awful euphemisms about *becoming a woman* and feel sick. Being a woman sounds horrendous, I don't want to do it.

'So, you have brothers, huh?' Natalie continues seamlessly from bumholes to siblings, as I carefully line my stained pants. My heart beats harder at the sight. How will I hide these from Dad? I can't put them in the wash. Maybe I'll have to throw them away?

'*Three* brothers. They're dumb, I hate them,' I reply, distracted. 'I'm the oldest. I think Mum and Dad were trying to have another girl after me, but willies kept popping out.'

'There's *four* of you?' Natalie breathes out, awed. 'It's only me at home, it's so boring. Mum says one was special enough for her but I think she means I cried too much as a baby. I always wanted a sister – a twin sister.'

'Same. My younger brothers are twins though and they're the worst.'

'Oh my God, you have twins in your family!' she enthuses. 'Can they read each other's minds and feel pain when one of them gets stabbed?'

'Why would one of them get sta—'

She doesn't let me finish.

'Do you want to come to the cinema with me and my family tonight? We're going to see a film called *Shrek*. My mum says it's got Austin Powers in it and that actress lady from *The Mask*. We're also having sandwiches and cake at my house beforehand because it's my birthday. No one else is coming so it'll just be me, Mum and her friend Sue. And my dad,' she adds as an afterthought.

I look at the wall between us. 'Is your birthday actually today?' I say, surprised. 'It's *my* birthday today.'

'You're lying!' she shouts and I worry someone will come in to see what the fuss is about. 'It *is* today! See!! You're totally my twin!' She is still shouting. 'Do you think our parents had us adopted separately, like the start of *The Parent Trap*? God, I love Lindsay Lohan.'

'She's amazing. She's, like, *so* talented. I also really like Jennifer Love Hewitt – she was my favourite in *I Know What You Did Last Summer*.'

Natalie gasps. 'You were allowed to see that?' She moans in apparent agony. 'I wasn't allowed to! Mum said there was too much sex and violence, and more importantly the plot made absolutely no sense.'

'Yeah, I've totally seen it a few times.' I pause. 'And *Cruel Intentions*.'

She moans again and I feel smug. I've not seen either film but Natalie thinks I'm cool, and I'm not going to correct her.

A wave of pain ripples from my back to my front. So these are the cramps *Sugar* magazine told me about. Well, that sucks.

'Yeah, agreed,' I say and then add shyly, 'And yes, I'd love to come to the cinema, thank you. I'll have to check with my dad but I don't think he's got anything planned. He says turning fourteen isn't that big a deal.'

'I think it is!' Natalie says passionately. 'It's HUGE! We've been teenagers for a whole year and we, like, *get* it now, y'know? Plus, we have SATs this year and have to choose our GCSE subjects. God, it's, like, so much pressure being fourteen.'

'Right?' I say, getting caught up in her enthusiasm. 'Dad totally doesn't get it, he rolled his eyes at me when I said that thing about SATs.'

'Dads don't understand anything,' Natalie continues. 'Mine just sits in a corner reading the newspaper all the time. They've never been a teenage girl, they don't have a clue.'

Suddenly I feel a bit sad. She's right, Dad doesn't have a clue.

'Sorry it's not going to be a big birthday party.' She's still going. 'I did invite Simon Stan from our class – do you remember him from registration? He's *so* handsome – but he said he couldn't think of anything worse and then him and Romesh and Tom all laughed, and Janine threw a pencil at my head.'

'What a bunch of shitheads,' I say, loyally.

'Oh no, it's completely fine,' she says quickly, brightly. 'I actually love stationery, so it was a win for me because I got a free pencil. They're the most popular boys in our year – they even hang out with some boys from sixth form! – so I didn't think Simon would say yes, but I had to ask him because of my feelings for him.'

'Your feelings for him?' I repeat slowly.

'Yes.' She pauses dramatically. '*I love him.*'

'You do?' I am confused. 'But why, if he's so mean to you?'

'He's only being mean to impress the other boys,' she explains nicely. 'It's peer pressure. *Newsround* did a whole special about it. It's like bullying, but by your friends. It's normal, it happens all the time.' She sighs deeply. 'So I understand why he's mean to me and I don't mind. I think we're going to end up together one day and I want us to look back and laugh at the days when I'd ask him out and he had to pretend he didn't like me, even though he secretly did.'

I decide it's too early in our new friendship to offer an opinion on this.

She continues, breathlessly, 'And I can't wait to get married and take his name. Natalie Stan sounds so much better than Natalie Winters, don't you think?'

'I like Natalie Winters better,' I say carefully. 'Plus, Simon Stan is kind of a dumb name? Like, if you say it in a French accent, it sounds like semen stain?'

She gasps, horrified, and then giggles. 'Oh my God,' she hisses, still laughing. 'You are so naughty, Zoe! It does *not* sound like that!'

'It really does,' I insist, smirking.

'You are so funny,' she says. 'I can't wait for you to meet my mum, she'll love you. Do you want to dress up in double denim for the cinema tonight, like Britney and Justin?'

'No,' I say, alarmed. 'I definitely do not. They looked fucking stupid.'

She gasps again, still giggling. 'Oh my God, you swear, like, *a lot*. My mum would kill me if I used the eff word and you say it loads, like you don't even care. I'm too scared to use it even when I write in my diary in case Mum reads it. Doesn't your mum tell you off?'

I am quiet for a second, assessing the situation. I guess if we're going to be friends, she'll find out at some point. Might as well be now.

'My mum isn't around. She left my dad last year and we haven't heard from her since.'

'No way!' She sounds shocked, and I feel a weird combination of humiliated and powerful.

'Yeah,' I nod stoically, feeling very alone in my cubicle. 'It was pretty awful. She ran off with my old babysitter, Mr Chapman, who lived down the road. It was mad. Actually, my dad's still a fucking mess about it.'

There is a long pause and I feel intensely ashamed. Ashamed of my Ricky Lake family, ashamed of my mum. Ashamed of my dad for not being good enough to keep her. Ashamed of my broken family. This was too much to say on a first meeting. Too much through a cubicle.

'Oh my God, that is so ...' there is another long pause. 'That is so COOL!' Natalie says the word delightedly. 'Your life is so *dramatic*, Zoe.' She sighs and I can almost feel her hot breath on the wall between us.

'Excuse me?' I'm reeling from her reaction but she misses my change in tone.

'You are so lucky, Zoe Darling!' she says. 'My life is so dull. Nothing cool ever happens to me.'

'It's not *cool*,' I spit. 'It's not cool at all.' OK, now I'm furious. I can feel it bubbling up inside me, fireworks of anger in my belly at this faceless girl's shitty insensitivity. 'It's actually been horrible – *really* horrible!' I explode. 'How can you say that to me? You think it's cool that my little brothers haven't got their mum around any more? You think it's cool that I'm sitting here bleeding on a loo, without any idea what to fucking do because my mum should've been around to tell me how it works? You think it's cool that I'm having to restart my stupid life in an ugly new house, at a whole new school because my dad couldn't stand to be around our old home any longer? You think it's *cool?*'

A shocked silence descends before Natalie finally answers. 'Well ... kind of cool?' she says at last.

I stand up abruptly, yanking at my pants, now rammed

full of tissue paper. Pulling angrily at the lock, I slam the door open and then slam the door shut behind me, hoping to convey the full, furious extent of my rage. What an idiot, what a stupid, stupid little idiot.

Without another word, I storm out of the toilets, only waddling slightly because of the tissues.

Stupid fucking Natalie Winters! What an insensitive little cow. Maybe I should write some graffiti about her on the walls – she'd definitely deserve it. Natalie Winters, ugh. With her stupid loud sobbing and her oversharing dumb information about her trivial stupid little life. She's made an enemy for life here today. I can't believe I thought she might be a friend for me in this crappy place. I always make such bad choices.

Let's hope I never have to see or speak to that weepy, whiny little drama queen *ever* again.

2

Four Years Later: 2005

NATALIE

'Smoking is cool and you know it.' I nod authoritatively, attempting to blow a ring into the air and failing.

'You know you're my BFF, Nat, but you look like a fucking idiot,' Zoe tells me, rolling her eyes. 'And *Friends* is over – it's dead and done – can you please stop quoting it.' She pulls uncomfortably at the ringlets the enthusiastic hairdresser has given her, then jabs a finger at me as I lean further out of my window, almost falling into the willow tree in my back garden. 'And what's *this* really about anyway?' She scowls on the word *this*. 'Are you smoking because Semen Stain smokes?'

I sigh heavily. 'Please don't call him that, Zo. But yes, that is correct. I figure I can follow him outside tonight and strike up a conversation about how sexy I look while smoking.'

'As you erotically blow cancer all over each other?' Zoe is being max-level sarcastic but I don't care.

'Exactly right.' I nod emphatically. 'And then he'll finally realise how amazing I am after all. He'll get on the stage in front of everyone and announce to the year how great I am and also how not fat I am, while Romesh and Tom and Janine all nod in the corner, agreeing that they have been fools all these years to ignore me. And then Simon and I will go back outside to have sex in that bike shelter by the science block, before returning inside for the final dance of the night.' I take a long drag of the cigarette and try to hold it in my mouth, like they tell you to. I feel lightheaded and try to swallow down a cough. I have to seem like I know what I'm doing. Zoe cannot be correct.

'What a beautiful picture you paint,' Zoe says. 'And then you'll live happily ever after together, sitting side by side in the oncology ward, getting chemo, real sexy-like.'

'If that's what it takes,' I tell her solemnly. 'And when did you get so preachy? You're usually the one telling me to relax and stop following all the rules.'

Zoe rolls her eyes again. 'When I said that, I meant, like, stop worrying you'll get caught leaving the sixth-form common room during free periods, not take up an expensive and gross lifetime habit. It's stupid and it won't even work.' She pauses, then asks in a slightly nicer voice, 'Has Simon accepted your friend request on MySpace yet?'

'Oh,' I say, excitedly. 'Let me check.' I stub out the fag on the windowsill and stand up on my own bed. Then I laugh and jump up and down. 'Hey Zoe,' I say, waiting for her attention so I can do my hilarious joke. She looks up expectantly and I shout, 'I'M IN LOVE,' before jumping off and kneeling. She doesn't react. 'I'm Tom Cruise on Oprah's sofa? You saw it, right?'

'I know, I get it,' she deadpans. 'Literally every single person in our year has done that bit.'

'You're no fun,' I say, sitting down at my computer and opening MySpace.

'You checked five minutes ago.' She squints at me as I re-arrange myself, tucking the large skirt I'm wearing awkwardly underneath me.

'Yes.' I sigh impatiently. 'But how can I truthfully answer

your friend request question if I don't check again? Sure, he hadn't accepted five minutes ago, but he might've done by now.' There is no flaw in my logic.

'Nat,' she says, a bit more nicely, 'if he hasn't accepted it in the last three weeks, I doubt he will have in the last few minutes.'

'You don't know,' I say, waiting for the screen to load. 'It's prom night. It's our last few weeks of school before we all go our separate ways, into the great big unknown world as grown-ups. If there was ever a time to feel kind and friend-accepty, it's now.'

'I don't think Semen Stain has a kind bone in his body,' she mutters, as if I won't be able to hear it.

'OK! Well, who else can I have sex with tonight then, ZOE?' I raise my voice, frustrated, as I finally log in and see Simon is still pending. I have very few friends on there; pretty much just MySpace Tom, Zoe, a few random girls from drama club – I was Buttons in *Cinderella* at Christmas – and a couple of other fake accounts I set up to stalk Simon with. 'Because – I'll say this again, Zo – it's PROM night.' I'm shouting certain words for emphasis because sometimes I don't think Zoe takes me seriously enough. 'I'm EIGHTEEN today, and if I don't lose my virginity tonight I'm going to literally kill myself. And I don't mean that like when Jodie Meads from 12WT announced she was going to do it in maths because Brad and Jen split up, and then scratched herself with a compass; I mean I really will do it. And then you'll have to die with me, Zo, because you know I can't do anything without you. Also, how would you cope without me? You might as well come with me.' I throw my hands up, furious at the world. 'No one's even seen my boobs, Zoe! This is a crying shame because they're great and I've been trying to get someone to look at them ever since they finally turned up that summer when I was fifteen. And having big, soft, pillowy boobs is the best thing about being fat. Plus, they're only going to get worse after this. They're going to be saggy and stretch-marky by the time I'm, like, twenty-five, so I need some boys to see them right now. Quickly. Like, *now*.'

'I think saggy boobs are pretty cool, actually,' Zoe says contemplatively. 'I mean, what's so good about perkiness anyway? Boobs are just sacks of yellow fat in skin, so why does it matter if they're under your chin or down by your belly button?'

'Don't you like boobs?' I'm surprised.

'Oh God, yeah, I love them,' she says earnestly. 'They're amazing in all shapes and sizes. But I think saggy boobs probably get a bad rap. Surely they'd actually be more fun than the others? You could throw them about a bit and, I don't know, like, bury your face in there and get lost?'

I consider this. 'I don't think Simon would like me with saggy boobs,' I tell her a bit sadly.

'I don't think Semen Stain would like anything outside of what *Nuts* magazine has told him to like,' she sneers. 'He doesn't have the imagination. He's probably never seen an actual woman naked, he wouldn't have any idea what to do.'

'Simon Stan,' I say automatically, but I don't mind.

'I'm practising my French accent,' she says mildly. '*Semen Stain*.' She says it louder.

'Please be nice about my one true love,' I plead. 'And you're not in France yet, Zo. You don't even leave until we get our A-level results, stop trying to abandon me sooner than you have to.'

'Argh!' she squeals, throwing herself down on my bed, somewhat crushing her ringlets. 'I can't wait though! I can't wait to get out of this place. It's going to be so great. I was in a chat room the other day with these experienced travellers and they were recommending some amazing spots to visit in France and Italy. And then – I've been thinking about it a lot – I reckon I'm going to do three months in India, teaching English to monks. There's a gap year scheme you can apply to and it sounds great. Oh, and I think I might go to Australia for a bit after that.' She pauses. 'If Dad will lend me the money.'

He will, he's loaded. And he always gives Zoe anything she wants.

She sighs dreamily, adding, 'It's going to be epic, don't you think?'

'What I think is,' I take a big breath, feeling mournful, 'that you're going to get so much sex. Like, SO, so much sex. You'll meet all these cool, sexy women in foreign lands, and all of them will just want to scissor you or whatever.'

'I don't think scissoring is actually a thing.' She narrows her eyes but I can tell she doesn't really know either.

'Whatever,' I say, jealously. 'I'd take scissoring or anything at all involving genitalia right now.' I throw myself down next to her on the bed. 'Ughhh, I can't go to university as the only virgin on campus. They'll laugh at me, and I won't have you to be nice and tell me I'm not a freak.'

'You're not a freak.' She puts a comforting hand on my head and strokes it. 'Plenty of people wait to have sex. It's better to wait and do it with someone nice.'

'That's lame, grown-up advice and you know it,' I say into my duvet. 'And I don't want someone nice, I want sexy Simon.'

Zoe's not listening to me any more. 'You know, in an Australian accent, Simon actually sounds like salmon,' she says, testing it out loud. '*Salmon*. Simon, salmon? How have I never thought of that before?'

'That's not an Australian accent,' I sniff, feeling emotional. 'That sounds more South African. And screw Australia, it's much better here.' I pause, trying to think of literally any reason why it's better here. 'Like . . . oh!' I say, inspired. 'You know you're going to miss the next series of *The X Factor* if you leave in August? You might not even be around to buy Steve Brookstein's next album. You won't get to see him become the huge star he deserves to be.'

'I think I'll survive,' she says dryly, before softening her tone a little. 'Nat, don't be grumpy, I promise I'm coming back. The UK is my home, and you're my home. Of course I'll come back. You don't have to worry. Plus, you're going to be too busy to miss me anyway. But I'm not being shitty about stupid fucking uni or stupid fucking London, am I?'

I perk up a bit at the idea of university. A new adventure, new boys, new friends. Hopefully.

'Are you excited yet?' she adds.

'Yes, no, I don't know,' I shrug. 'It feels a bit unreal still. I haven't even heard which halls I'll be in yet. And what if I don't get the results I need? It's only a conditional offer. If I mess up our exams, I'll be stuck here forever, drinking cheap wine with Mum and Sue, and trying to steal the remote control so I don't have to watch any more *Big Brother* repeats.'

'You totally won't mess up,' she says confidently. 'You've been revising like crazy and you're so far up the teachers' arseholes, they'll have to take laxatives to get you out in time for the end of term. And it doesn't matter what halls you get assigned, it'll just be a bunch of fun people getting drunk all the time.'

My heart does a little flutter at the prospect of new people. 'I hope I can make friends,' I say quietly. 'I'm really scared about that. I mean, I literally don't know *anyone* in London.

Mum says she and Sue will come visit, but can you imagine anything worse when I'm trying to make friends than those two drunkenly teetering around my halls in their high heels, brandishing bottles of red wine?'

'I actually think that situation would attract all the right kinds of friends for you,' Zoe nods, somehow managing to apply yet another coat of lipstick over her lipstick. 'Everyone will love you. Will you be going by Natalie while you're there? Or Roxy?'

'Actually, I'm thinking about having a whole rebrand for uni,' I say chirpily. 'What do you think about the name Nicki Chair?'

'That's *very* cool!' she says encouragingly.

'Thanks.' I beam back. 'I got it from a sofa in a Daniels' department store. I just think people in London will *get* me more. And there are so many boys, I'm bound to get laid on a constant rotation!'

'Bound to,' Zoe says agreeably, moving to the mirror and staring critically at her hair.

'You look very nice,' I say as enthusiastically as possible.

'I'm not sure about this hair,' she says for the tenth time. 'It's a bit . . . ringlety?'

'Well, they *are* ringlets?' I say, carefully, before adding hastily, 'But they're lovely. Very prom-like. You really do look great.'

She really does. But she always does. I try not to be jealous of Zoe, but she's so pretty and slim. Not, like, very slim, but definitely smaller than me. She's probably my goal weight, except she won't tell me her weight. She says she doesn't weigh herself, which is obviously a lie. Is she even a girl if she doesn't weigh herself and then stand in front of a mirror making mental notes about everything she'd have fixed if she had the money and bravery for plastic surgery?

Zoe puts on more lipstick.

I bet everyone's going to ask her to dance tonight. A few boys asked her to be their date tonight as if the lesbian thing wasn't relevant. Obviously she said no, but I wonder if she would've asked Harriet from year twelve – the only other 'out' girl in sixth form – if I wasn't around.

I know I hold Zoe back. She never says it and she never acts like I do, but I know it's true. She'd probably be cool if it wasn't for me. Sometimes I feel selfish being her friend, because I know we're not really equals. She's way, way better than me. But I also don't know how I'd survive without her. I feel a pang of emotion thinking about how different my school life would've been if Zoe hadn't turned up in year nine. How much worse my life would be without her. How much worse it *will* be.

'Do you think I should've hired an escort for tonight?' I say contemplatively, trying to distract myself. 'Like, as my date?'

'Then who would I have gone with?' Zoe cocks her head at me in the mirror.

'Ugh, you could've *easily* found a prom date.' I wander back over to the computer. The screensaver pops up and pictures of Zoe and me from the last few years fade in and out – sleepovers, cinema visits, weekend park jaunts, joint birthday parties – all taken on her pink Olympus digital camera.

'Do you think it's too late to hire someone?' I move the mouse and our faces disappear. 'Imagine me turning up at the rec centre with a sexy older man on my arm and telling everyone he's my boyfriend. Maybe that would get Semen – I mean Salmon – I mean *Simon's* attention.'

'And he'd probably offer extras for the right price,' Zoe suggests. She's joking but it's genuinely a good idea.

'Maybe I *could* hire someone!' I say, feeling inspired and typing 'male escorts' into Ask Jeeves. 'It would be perfect to lose my virginity to an expert. Not only would I get that first time out of the way, but it would also be way better than some clueless fellow virgin fumbling about with my G-spot.' I pause to think about this. Is G-spot the right term? Do I even have a G-spot? Andrea Allen at school told everyone she didn't have one so maybe I don't either? 'And,' I continue, 'a professional could make sure it wouldn't hurt and he could show me all kinds of tricks, so I would be like a sex ninja when I finally got to do it with someone I actually like.' I wait again. 'OK, Ask Jeeves is showing me a lot of what looks like porn. Maybe it's a bit short notice for a sex escort. I mean, where would they get a tux in under an hour anyway?'

'Maybe stick with me as your date, eh?' Zoe leans over and exits the screen – just in time as Mum's head appears at the bedroom door.

'Are you girls nearly ready to go? Zoe, your dad's here with the pink limo. He looks hilarious in his little chauffeur hat.' She steps in and properly takes the pair of us in. 'Oh my goodness, you two look so . . . so . . .' Her eyes travel up and down my full-length, full-skirted lilac princess prom dress and then Zoe's green slinky number. Then up to our matching ringlets. Her eyes fill with tears.

'Sue, SUE, get in here, come look at these two,' she shouts out the door. 'They look like absolute ANGELS.' Mum looks like she's going to weep as Sue joins us in my cramped bedroom. She smiles at us, but, to be honest, she looks more amused by our outfits than emotional.

'Well, then,' she says a bit dryly. 'You certainly look like you're ready for the prom.' Her eyes widen at my dress in particular and I pull myself up to full height, feeling proud.

I look so regal in this dress. For my birthday last year Mum took me and Zoe to London's West End, to see *Les Misérables* at the Queen's Theatre. It was the best thing I've ever seen and I knew right then that I wanted a dress like Cosette wears for my prom. All big sleeves and big bows. Zoe hated it, of course, but she's not really that into theatre stuff.

'Are you excited?' Sue says, quickly adding, 'Ooh, do you want a drink? Maybe we should have something special?' She looks at Mum for permission and I feel a flash of dread that she might finally open that posh vodka we drained and refilled with water two years ago. 'Debs, was there any wine left? How many bottles did we drink last night?'

Mum makes an awkward face. 'A lot? But Bryan said he had a couple of bottles of champagne in the limo for the ride. Shall we go get it?'

'We probably shouldn't.' I look nervously at Zoe. She knows how messy I get, even after one glass. 'I really want to remember every second of tonight. I think it's going to be super special.' I picture Simon's handsome face bobbing in front of mine as we dance together. And then I picture him putting his willy in me. I wonder what that'll be like. I've heard it's horrible and painful the first time, but I'm ready for that. I can totally take pain if it means I can finally lose my V-plates. But maybe if it hits my clitoris, it won't hurt so much? Is a clitoris the same as a G-spot? Do I *have* a clitoris?

'I don't give a fuck about remembering anything,' Zoe says sounding blasé. 'Can I have a glass, please?' Sue obligingly scuttles off to retrieve the drink and Mum continues to stare at the pair of us as we fiddle with ourselves in the mirror. She looks intensely emotional but repeatedly declares that she is 'not going to cry.'

It's all right for Zoe. She's already had sex, with a girl she

25

met on holiday over Christmas. She went skiing with her dad and brothers – can you imagine anything less sexy? – and still managed a holiday romance.

When Sue returns, she's with Bryan, who is red-faced under his hat.

'Hi, Bryan!' I say shyly and he smiles nicely back. I really like Zoe's dad, even though he's a bit of an arsehat. That's Zoe's word, not mine. She really loves him, I know that, but she says he's a bit ... I don't know, *useless*? I think she ends up doing a lot of stuff around the house. They have a cleaner who does the washing and hoovering, but I think Zo mostly does all the cooking, tidying and putting laundry away. Plus, looking after her little brothers – who are all so, so annoying. But I don't think Bryan even realises how much she does, he's always so preoccupied with his work. I like him, though, he's nice to me. Although I'm not sure Mum and Sue are keen; I've heard them slag him off quite a bit and Sue loves taking the piss out of him whenever he's over here with Zoe.

'Well, well, don't you look like a princess, Natalie!' Bryan says, grandly.

'Is that a question, Bryan?' Sue mutters, sniggering behind her hand. She definitely doesn't like him. Mum hushes her, trying not to smile.

'And you look nice, too,' Bryan adds a bit less enthusiastically to Zoe.

They had a fight about the dress. It's a little, er, *clingy* and *modern*, according to Bryan, and he said she should wear a more traditional prom dress, like mine. But in the end he bought it for her and he hasn't given her that much of a hard time about it since then, to be fair to him.

'Saw you on TV again today, Bryan,' Sue says, still smirking, as she pops the bottle and liberally pours me the glass I didn't really want. Oh well. I take a long swig and then run to check my make-up isn't smudged.

'Oh yes?' Bryan's chest puffs out a bit and Zoe turns away, embarrassed by her semi-famous dad. Beside me, she picks up a brush and starts trying to drag it through her hair but the hairspray has turned everything crispy and stiff. The brush gets instantly lodged in place and she tuts at her reflection in the mirror.

'Yeah, can I have your autograph?' Sue continues, and everyone but Bryan knows she's being snarky.

'No problem, love, do you have a pen?' he says, all grandiose like. Sue runs out to find one, delighted with her prank. This is nowhere near the first autograph she's asked Bryan for, but he doesn't seem to remember that fact.

Bryan's a weatherman. Zoe says that before they moved here, he was a more boring meteorologist but then he got a job on local radio reporting the weather. Then he started getting 'telly aspirations' and worked his way up the food chain – in weather terms – until he bagged a twice-daily weekday slot for the BBC a few years ago. It's apparently pretty good money – Zoe's house is big and he's paying for her round-the-world gap year when school finishes in a couple of months – but I'd say 90 per cent of his time seems to be spent signing his name on bits of paper for middle-aged mums.

Zoe hates her dad's job. She actually kept it secret for a while after we met, but then someone in our year put it together. The family have a kind of distinctive surname and Zoe was listed on Bryan's Wikipedia page under the 'personal life' section. She asked him to take her off it but he said he's not responsible for the page, even though we all know he wrote it himself.

At the time, the news of Zoe's almost-famous dad was

massive at school. Simon and Janine – along with some of the other popular kids – actually started talking to her a bit at lunch and I think they even invited her to one of their big, cool parties. I was really terrified she was going to dump me to hang out with them, but I should've known better. She told them to stick it.

I don't know if I would've been that brave if that lot had suddenly started being nicer to me. I think I would've been hypnotised by the offer of popularity. Seduced by their inexplicable charisma. I would've run into their collective arms, licking them like a faithful dog.

But Zoe's always been a better person – a stronger person – than me. Either way, within a few weeks, the popular kids realised being a weatherman is actually not as cool as you might think and doesn't get you invites to literally *any* BRITs after-parties. So they lost interest.

And it went back to being just me and her.

I don't want to be mad-overdramatic or anything, but Zoe's been my whole world these last few years. She's not just my best friend, she's like the other half of me. She makes me a better person and a happier person and I can't imagine not having her to talk to every day. Which is what makes this coming year so scary.

My heart skips a beat a bit at the thought of what will happen after this summer.

In September, I'm going straight off to university in London to study geography. I begged Zoe to come with me – her exam results are on track to be better than mine, even though I worked ten times harder – but she's never been that into school. She can't wait for it to be over and honestly, I'm not sure she'll go to uni at all. She only agreed to stay on for A levels because she didn't know what else to do and I made her stay. But no amount of wheedling could persuade her to stick around for more education this time. She's going travelling and calling it a gap year to appease her dad – who I think really wants her to follow in his footsteps with, like, weather? – but I wonder if she'll even come back at all.

What if she doesn't? What if she moves to France or Italy? Or – even worse – *Australia*?

A lump forms in my throat at the thought and I stare over at where she's standing by the mirror, still trying to force the brush through her curls. Brute strength is not working. She'll tear her hair out at this rate. I go over to help.

'The forecast is looking bright for tonight, ladies,' Bryan booms from the doorway.

'Oh, Dad.' Zoe rolls her eyes. 'Please, no more awful weather puns.'

He smiles widely and then winks at me. 'No problem, love, I'll save them for a rainy day.' He giggles and I catch Sue elbowing Mum in the ribs.

'Dude, sorry about Mum and Sue teasing your dad,' I whisper to Zoe.

'Don't be, it's funny,' she sniggers. 'And he *is* an arse. He could do with being taken down a peg or two. Not that he's aware enough to even notice he's being mocked – what an idiot.'

'Yeah, that's fair,' I say agreeably. 'Probably why your mum left.'

'Who could blame her?' Zoe nods.

'Are you ready to go, girls?' Bryan approaches, hovering as I finish up with Zoe's hair and down the rest of my drink. 'Or are you—' smirk '—still *shooting the breeze*.' I laugh at this, realising the alcohol, along with the cigarette, has gone straight to my head. I feel loose-limbed with anticipation and ready to say something stupid to Simon.

'Yep, ready,' Zoe says as I smile excitedly. She looks a little nervous, which surprises me. She's usually so fearless.

That's OK; I can be the brave one this time. Just this once.

ZOE

'Do you think it would be weird if I asked Nanny Surrey about sex?' Natalie whispers into my ear. She sloshes her champagne over the seat as we awkwardly turn a corner in this lumbering, ugly car.

Dad insisted we get a pink limo to travel to prom and I didn't make the fuss I would've liked to, because I knew this was Natalie's big dream for tonight. It's exactly how she always pictured us travelling to prom night. Except, y'know, obviously Semen Stain would've been on her arm in the dream scenario, gazing at her adoringly. Instead of me.

You should've seen her face when she saw the pink car and my dad in his chauffeur hat – the thrilled vibes coming off her were palpable. And then you should've seen *my* face when I realised Nanny Surrey was driving to prom with us. She's such a fucking bitch, always around to ruin my good time.

'Because, y'know,' Natalie hisses, and it's clear the booze is already going to her head. 'I've asked you about sex plenty of times but – no offence – there's only so much you can tell me about what to expect when you don't get penises involved.'

'And you think Nanny Surrey is the best person to ask?' I whisper back, raising an eyebrow.

'Who else?' Natalie says a little too loudly. 'I can't talk to my mum about it, and Sue wouldn't tell me anything when I asked her, except to say that all men are pricks and I should avoid them at all costs.' She pauses. 'Besides, Nanny Surrey is like a hundred, so she's probably had sex with loads of people, right? I mean, we know she's definitely had sex at least once.' She gestures at my dad and I gag a bit. 'More – you have uncles and aunts, right?' she adds, lightly spitting on my ear.

I nod. 'Yeah, she's got four sons, including Dad. Boys run in my family. I'm the anomalous girl, that's why she hates me so much.'

'She doesn't hate you!' Her eyes widen in shock at the idea of anyone in a family not offering unconditional love. As an only child, Natalie is the centre of her mum and dad's world. She has only known pure, sweet, unadulterated love, and she's so sheltered because of it. She doesn't hear the poison in literally everything Nanny Surrey says to me.

'The other day,' I whisper. 'She told me I was "really confident" for someone who looks like I do.'

'That's a compliment,' Natalie insists, rolling her eyes affectionately.

'It's really not,' I roll mine back. 'But sure, ask away. I'd be delighted to hear her answer.'

'Nanny Surrey,' Natalie calls across the car sweetly, her voice high and girlish. 'Can I ask you a question about your, um, life experiences.'

Nanny Surrey turns around in the front, her moustache twitching. Her badly-applied purple-pink lipstick shines like a bruise.

'Yes, dear?' she says faux-nicely, her lips pursed.

'Well,' Natalie considers how to phrase it. 'Have you . . . do you . . . um, how young were you when you started d-dating?'

'Do you not have a boyfriend then, dear?' Nanny Surrey

doesn't wait for an answer before adding, 'No, of course you don't, you wouldn't, would you?'

Natalie shakes her head, agreeably.

'I was eighteen when my parents introduced me to a respectable young man in the RAF and allowed me to wed,' she says proudly. 'So you should be looking for husbands now you're of age, really.'

'Oh!' Natalie looks reassured. 'So it's normal to have waited until now to be with someone?'

Nanny Surrey smirks. 'Unless you want to be the kind of whore that gets written about on bathroom walls.'

Natalie leans forward a little more. 'And what if I do?' she says, genuinely curious.

'Well,' Nanny Surrey titters nastily. 'Well then, God shall judge ye. You know your ten commandments don't you, my dear?'

'Of course I do!' Natalie says firmly, eyes wide. 'There's the one about adultery, and then the one about the right to bear arms, and free speech.'

'I think *some* of that was the American constitution,' I murmur helpfully, taking another long sip from my champagne flute.

Nanny Surrey tuts in my direction. 'What about you, Miss Know-It-All? Do you have a prospective husband lined up yet? You don't want those eggs shrivelling up – and they are, you know. Every single day.'

'No, Nanny Surrey,' I say as patiently as I can. 'You know I'm gay. I like women. If I were to get married it would be to a woman.'

Nanny Surrey exaggeratedly makes an amused face. 'Ah yes, I forget you have these little *phases*. Of course, in my day, gay meant something quite different. I really don't see why you young people have to ruin perfectly good words.'

'We live to ruin things,' Zoe says mildly. 'That's what they teach us at school these days.'

Nanny Surrey smiles benevolently. 'This is why too much school for girls is only ever a bad thing – you're just going to learn to be dissatisfied with your lot in life. Especially when you're not even being taught the basics of being a woman any more. Where's the needlework? Where's the cooking? And I still don't understand why on earth you wanted to take *music* at A level. A husband doesn't need a pianist, Zoe dove, he needs someone to take care of his offspring.'

I'm silent at this, because I don't know why I took music, either. I never know why I make any of my shitty choices. I guess I thought, since I wasn't that into school – if I was going to keep doing it – I should at least study something I actually like. But she's right, it's stupid. It's not like I'm talented or deluded enough to think it's something I could use in real life as an adult, so it was kind of pointless.

Nanny Surrey turns back around to face front, and starts barking orders at my dad about his driving. In the mirror I see Dad's scared face. He's terrified of his mum.

'OK,' Natalie looks back at me, a bit embarrassed. 'Maybe she wasn't the best person to talk to about sex.' She hesitates, regarding me sideways. 'I'm sure she didn't mean that thing about a phase, or about your music. I love your music! Different generation, isn't it?'

'I don't think generational differences excuses twattishness,' I say, used to it. 'I'm sorry we don't know enough other sexually active women for you to consult with.'

'It's all right,' Natalie says and sighs dramatically. 'I have the internet and *Cosmo* magazine. I know the basics.'

I give her huge, floofy dress a reassuring pat, feeling a bit guilty.

Nat thinks I lost my virginity at Christmas with some girl on our skiing holiday.

Duh, of course I didn't.

But it's kind of Natalie's fault she thinks that! When I got back from the trip, I started to tell her about this hot girl I'd met one evening in the lodge, and she started shrieking that I'd obviously had sex with her and she could tell just from looking at me and how cool it was and how jealous she was. I didn't really have a chance to tell her the truth. Which was that I totally bottled it and only spoke to the girl in question for a few minutes before running away.

But honestly, how she thinks a night of virginity-losing passion was possible on a holiday with four male family members hovering around me at all times is beyond me. I was sharing a room with my brother Matthew, for fuck's sake.

The truth is, I've barely gone even, like, halfway with anyone. I'd explain in bases, but I don't understand how the analogy works. I assume first base is kissing, right? And I've definitely done that. Like, loads of times. And then second base is, what, feeling each other up? Third base is presumably oral, then fourth base must be penetration ... is it? Then home base is when you string someone upside down from the ceiling, blindfolded, ball-gagged and then put vegetables in every hole.

Something like that.

Anyway, I've only really felt girls up. I've touched seven and a half boobs now and they've all been fucking magical. I could've gone further with a couple of those girls but, I don't know – it's fucking scary. I have these feelings and urges or whatever, but I'm also so nervous about actually doing any of

34

it. About someone touching me in that way and me touching them like that.

When I was talking to that girl in the ski lodge, all I could think was, what if I don't work down there? What if I look different to other women? What if I'm broken, somehow?

And it didn't help that I knew my dad was watching us from the table across the room, while my brothers probably giggled like idiots.

I mean, my dad knows I'm gay, and he's fine about it. He's more upset about me not going to uni. He was all, 'But where will you learn about meteorology?' and I was all, 'Nobody gives a fuck about meteorology, Dad, make one of the twins follow in your footsteps – because if you keep harping on about this, I will start telling people I believe in astrology.' That shut him up. He's pretty into science, my dad. Natalie once started talking about us being Geminis and how that was even more proof of our twindom, and Dad went white and had to leave the room.

Anyway, I don't know why I haven't told Natalie the truth.

Maybe it was because she was so excited about it and it felt kind of cool being the grown-up; having this thing she was so impressed by.

Or maybe it was because of what's coming next in our life. We've been so entwined in each other's lives these past four years. And I love it! I love Nat so much – she really is my sister – but we're about to be separated. We're both on the verge of starting brand-new lives, heading down new paths. We're moving in totally opposite directions in a few months, and I think maybe a part of me was trying to prepare myself. Trying to keep a secret, knowing she soon won't be around to share everything with in the same way. I guess I was trying to wean myself off Natalie. I don't know.

I realise we've pulled up outside the rec centre, the sound of Destiny's Child booming, and nerves fill my stomach.

'Here we are,' Dad shouts, tipping his hat at me in the mirror. 'Time to make hay while the *sun shines*.' He leaps out, laughing at his joke, preparing to open the door for us.

'Shall we go in?' I say after a moment.

'Zo?' Natalie takes my hand, looking serious. 'Happy birthday.'

I smile at her. 'Happy birthday, you fucking idiot.'

'Wait,' she says feeling a bit panicked. 'Do you think this might be the last year we get to spend our birthday together?'

'No!' I frown, although I've had the same thought. 'Why would you say that?'

'I don't know.' She looks into her lap. 'It just feels like maybe things are going to change after this year. Everything will be different. You're going travelling, I'm going to uni, what if we drift apart?'

'We won't!' I shake my head fiercely. 'Don't be a dick, we won't.'

'Promise me we'll spend our birthday together every year?' she says, pleadingly, and I feel a rush of fear. She continues before I can reply, 'I know I sound pathetic, Zo, but I don't want to lose you. Can you promise me we'll always spend our birthday together? Like, you will come back next year, right? Even if you come back and then leave again for more exciting travelling and scissoring, you have to promise me you'll be back for our birthday. You are my sister and we were meant to be friends. We were meant to spend our birthday together. Please promise me.'

'I promise,' I say seriously. We look at each other a bit fearfully.

I'm scared of this next year. Everything's changing and I don't want it to. Our friendship has always been the one constant in my life. And it's been easy because we had school – we had to see each other even when we were annoying each other. Now . . . now what? What's going to happen? Everything's going to be different.

The door opens and Dad's voice says, 'M'ladies?'

In the front seat, Nanny Surrey turns around. 'Have a nice time, you two,' she titters. 'But not whoreish fun. Remember, you're *ladies* first and foremost.'

'Come on,' I say loudly, grinning at Nanny Surrey as I pull Natalie out of the car behind me. 'Let's go see if you can lose your virginity to Semen Stain.'

* * *

AIM>new chat window>Zoe Darling

1.40am
Zo?

Zoe?

Zoe, I can see you're online,
you must be home.

Can't believe I had to
be home by 12.30, my mum
is such a B-*-T-C-H

1.55am
Do you think I can still

37

ring ChildLine even though
I'm 18 now? ☹

I really feel like
Simon would've got off
with me if I'd had another
half an hour to hang out
in his eyeline ;)

2.03am
I know he was snogging Fran
and Jess and Janine but I
think I would've
been up next if I could've
stuck around :/

2.10am
Zo? You there? ☺

I rang ChildLine and they
were really nice but
said Mum is in the right
which is so unfair ☹

2.25am
OK, I'm going to sleep now
I miss you ☹☹☹

2.48am
Nat, you still online?

Sorry, Dad was still awake

when I got home, got
another dress lecture ☹

2.52am
Simon also snogged Bex
and the cloakroom attendant
from year ten. Sorry ☹

2.55am
Stop ringing ChildLine

3

2006

NATALIE

'I really feel like the shoe and sock industry are in it together, don't you think?' she's staring intently at her feet. 'Like, why haven't they invented shoes that don't need socks? That's right, because it's a scam to get you to pay for two different things to put on your feet.'

'What about flip-flops?' I point out, taking a drink.

She looks up at me, aghast. 'Flip-flops do *not* count as shoes. They are, like, the opposite of a shoe. They protect your foot from no element. NO ELEMENT, NATALIE. In fact, they *encourage* elements; water, earth – what other elements are there?' She pauses, looking confused. 'Do you know how many tiny stones a flip-flop will scoop up to stab your foot with? It's absolutely outrageous and I cannot believe you would have the audacity to bring flip-flops into this conversation on our special night.'

I attempt what I think is a nod but my head is too heavy. 'OK,' I slur a bit. 'What about high heels? You don't tend to wear socks with high heels, right?'

'Oh?' she says exaggeratedly, flapping her hands furiously. 'You mean the evil patriarchal agents that you can only wear for fifteen minutes at a time and, even so, immediately get blisters, corns and sweaty feet?' She lifts her leg in the air, resting one trainer on the edge of the tablecloth and leaning back dramatically. 'Trainers are the only way I can physically keep up with men, but I resent paying for two things. See the problem?' She waves at me, trainer still on the table. 'See, you don't need two hats when you want to wear a hat, do you?' She narrows her eyes as she thinks about this. 'You don't even need to wear a hat to wear a hat. Like, you have hair, don't you?'

I'm vaguely aware she's started to shout.

'It's a CONSPIRACY, NAT! THE SHOES AND SOCK INDUSTRY ARE SCREWING US. MEAN-WHILE THE GOOD PEOPLE OF THIS WORLD IN HAT PRODUCTION ARE JUST LIGHTLY SUG-GESTING WE CAN WEAR ONE THING ON OUR HEAD OR NOT EVEN ANYTHING IF WE DON'T FEEL LIKE IT.'

'Yeah, but heels make my bum look nicer,' I murmur, feeling like a traitor to my gender.

'Shhhhh!' She presses her fingers hard into my lips; they smell nice.

'I'M GOING TO START WEARING A LOT MORE HATS,' I yell supportively, deciding to be a better feminist. Hats are the way forward. Fourth-wave feminism is all hats. Zoe tries again to pass the coffee flask of warm white wine under the table and I swat at her hand.

'Get it away from me, I don't want it,' I hiss across the table. 'I've already had too much.'

'SHHHH,' she says, even louder.

'Stop shushing me, you always shush me when you're drunk,' I half-shout, giving in and taking the drink from her. I duck down, half under the table, half-buried in tablecloth and take a small sip of the wine. It's horrible and I make a face before handing it back to Zoe.

She shakes her head at my lameness but she knows all too well that we have vastly different alcohol constitutions. Zoe can stomach a lot and still stay conscious, whereas I am liable to pass out onto my plate after one and a half glasses of wine. I've definitely had at least that much and urgently need to pace myself. Meanwhile Zoe's probably had most of a bottle all to herself already.

A supercilious man seated one table across peers over his glasses at the pair of us as Zoe accepts the flask back from me. 'Er, girls?' he tells us in a scolding tone. 'You know you're being really loud? And also really obvious about sneaking your drinks under the table?'

'Fuck you, we can't afford these posh wine list prices,' Zoe tells him, leaning almost too far towards his table. I catch her by the elbow and she rights herself.

'You know, Zoe,' I say conversationally, realising I have dipped one boob in the bread basket. 'Maybe we could actually pay for the restaurant drinks, just this once? It is a special occasion after all.'

'SHHHHHHHHH,' she says again, spraying saliva across me and my one boob. 'Shut up, Natalie, you have to stop talking so loudly in fancy restaurants.'

'This is a Pizza Express,' the man beside us blinks aggressively.

'It's all right for you,' she says to him, brandishing her flask and pausing to take a long swig. 'We're only just adults, we don't have any money. And we probably won't have any money for at least another fifteen years, thanks to fucking boomers like you.'

He looks affronted and turns back to his Calabrese muttering about obnoxious young people. What an old loser – he must be at least thirty! Gross.

'It's our birthday,' I shout over at him, happily. 'We can be obnoxious if we want to, right, Zo?'

She shushes me again, fondly, but I know she doesn't mean it. 'Happy birthday, Nat,' she adds, raising the flask for a cheers before making accidental eye contact with a waiter across the room. He frowns over at us and we both quickly look away.

'Shall we make this a tradition, too?' I ask.

'What? Being annoying?' she giggles, clearly into that idea.

'No, no, Pizza Express!' I explain joyfully. 'Y'know, getting drunk with wine in a flask from your handbag. And eating a lot of pizza before we go to whatever party we have planned?'

She scrunches up her nose. 'Let's not commit to that,' she says carefully. 'I feel like as soon as either of us are earning any money, we might want to try something a little nicer. Maybe even, like, a Strada one day? I feel like I'm a person who probably likes the finer things in life.'

'OK.' I look askance at her. 'But how likely are we to be earning any money in the near future? Or ever, really? I'm a pathetic penniless student, pursuing a completely useless degree that has no vocational point, and you're a pathetic penniless ... um,' I trail off. 'What do I call you now? Are we still pretending this is your gap year? Or is that done with now you're back home and mooching off your family?'

She glances around the room furtively, even though there is no chance her dad would be here. 'We're still pretending I'm on my gap year,' she confirms in a low voice. 'And not even because I think my dad would be angry. It's more that I can't deal with the what-next questions. I refuse to think about what I'm supposed to do with my life while I still have a tan. I actually think it's a violation of a person's basic human rights to worry about your future when you have a tan this glorious.'

I nod seriously, feeling a little more sober. 'That's fair.' After another moment I add worriedly, 'But you're really all right? You're not freaking out about being back and what's going to happen?'

'I'm not you,' she says, smiling nicely. 'I don't worry as a by-product of breathing.' I giggle because this is infinitely fair enough. But then she sighs and picks up a fork, looking at it thoughtfully. 'OK, maybe I'm a little worried.' She sighs again. 'How do people go from being a kid to being grown-ups? I don't have any clue what to do with my life.'

'What about your music?' I cock my head at her, because it seems so obvious to me.

'What about it?' she replies, looking confused.

'I mean,' I say carefully, 'you've been playing the piano and whatever else since you were – what? – six. You took music at GCSE, AS and A level. You play all the time and you're constantly at gigs for boring indie bands in east London that no one's ever heard of. Don't you want to do something with that?'

'Music isn't a job!' She rolls her eyes. 'It's a hobby. People don't *work* in music.'

I laugh. 'Of course they do! You could play in a band, get discovered and be famous!'

'Yuck,' she makes a face. 'That's definitely out, I don't want to be famous. And I don't have a sad enough life story to get me an *X Factor* audition.'

'Sure you do!' I'm getting so into this. 'You can use the mum abandoning you thing, and the semi-famous weatherman-dad stuff. They'll eat that up.'

'Absolutely not.' She looks a bit pissed off at this idea. 'And

I really don't want to perform publicly, it's not for me.' I start to interrupt and she puts on her sternest face. 'I'm not just saying that, Nat, I really hate being on stage. You know I throw up every time I've tried to do it seriously.'

'OK.' I know I look disappointed – I would totally love having a famous musician best friend. 'Well then, producing, writing, marketing, talent discovery – those are all music type things, right?'

'Yeah, I guess so.' She's hedging, looking embarrassed. 'OK, actually, before I went away – while I was still thinking about what to do in my fake gap year – Dad did kind of say he could get me some intern work experience at a record label – y'know, through his media contacts.'

'Woah!' I sit back in my chair. 'That's huge! And you said no? Why would you say no? That's dream job stuff!'

'I felt stupid about it,' she says in a frustrated tone. 'I don't want my dad to get me a job. It's, like, nepotism or whatever.'

'Duh!' I try not to laugh at this. 'How else do you think anyone gets a job in media, you idiot.'

'I wanted to go travelling, anyway,' she says firmly.

'Well,' I raise my eyebrows, 'what about now? Couldn't you ask your dad if it's still possible? Just *imagine* how cool it would be, Zo! Working for a real-life record label! You'd be hanging out with bands all day long, getting drunk with them, helping them write music, having sex with them. It would be amazing. And I could tag along on tours and also have sex with them.'

She takes a long swig of the flask, clearly stalling for time, then passes it to me under the table. I fake drink and she lets me. She knows I don't want to turn up to this party too wasted. Tonight is going to be maybe quite odd. There are a lot of random elements coming along for drinks – family

45

and friends who haven't met before or might clash. Too many people whose judgement I fear. That's why I don't want to be too drunk and, funnily enough, I think it's exactly why Zoe *does* want to be drunk.

'Yeah, maybe.' She shrugs at me, closely examining her nails. 'I'll talk to Dad about it.' It's clear the subject is closed and I feel a bit awkward suddenly. I only want to help her. I don't want Zoe to get left behind.

'I can't wait for you to meet my uni friends at last,' I say quickly, filling the silence.

'Yeah . . .' her reply is unenthusiastic and I feel a stab of worry. She has been ever so slightly funny about my new friends whenever I've brought them up over texts and emails. But what did she think I was going to do? Stay friendless at uni? Wait by the phone every night for her calls? I mean, I did actually do that a bit, but I also had fun. I know it's strange, seeing each other start other lives, without the other. But this is what happens, isn't it? And she should be happy for me that I'm actually having fun at uni – finally going to parties and being included. It's a first for me.

She looks up and I can see she feels bad because she suddenly smiles brightly. 'It's going to be lovely putting faces to names,' she says nicely. 'Who's coming tonight?'

I beam back at her, relieved. 'So, I think a few girls from my halls are coming: Laura, Devinder, Emma, Lydia and Julia. Then there's Choi, Other Zoe and Pete from my course.'

'Oh, Pete!' she says, recognising the stand out name in the line-up. 'He's the one you keep trying to seduce?'

'I think it's going to happen tonight,' I say determinedly. 'I really need to get laid, and I know I've said that ten thousand times, but this time I really mean it.'

'Then you probably shouldn't have invited your family?' she suggests mildly.

'I didn't mean to,' I whine, desperately. 'Mum asked me how I was celebrating turning nineteen, and then she and Sue got all excited when they heard you were back in the country. So my mum rang your dad and he said we were having a party at yours and she immediately invited herself. You know what she's like.' I pause. 'But it's fine because you have a big house, so I can sneak off with Pete to one of your spare bedrooms when he finally relents.'

Zoe looks at me quizzically. 'Dude, you can't rape him. No means no.'

'I know that,' I say nodding haughtily. 'But I really do think he wants to. We kissed at a party early in the first term and I think he would've had sex with me then but Other Zoe let slip that I'm a virgin. So then he said he didn't want the responsibility of taking my flower and when I went to kiss him again, he turned away and I snogged his ear.'

'Fucking *Other Zoe*,' she mutters, looking hateful.

I ignore it, but the fear of them meeting pulses again. 'So that's that,' I say breezily. 'And now I'm literally the last person in the world to have sex.'

'You're not, I promise,' she tells me, attempting a reassuring tone. 'Everyone's pretending to have done it, same as I did. Everyone's lying. And most people who did it early regret it because it was rubbish.'

'Bullshit,' I proclaim loudly. 'Andrea Allen from school did anal in a Café Rouge for her first time and she said it was amazing.'

She side-eyes me. 'I don't think that rumour was true, Natalie.'

'Oh my God, it totally *was* true,' I shake my head at her.

'You weren't even around then, it was in year seven.'

'Year seven? When she was eleven?' Her tone is sceptical.

'Definitely.' I pause. 'Don't look at me like that, Zoe, it's 100 per cent true.'

'Well, if it helps' – she lets me have that one – 'I had some terrible sex on my trip.'

'You did?' I sit up a bit straighter, looking hopeful. She's been a bit cagey about her sexcapades on the trip. She told me about that first time in France – after finally admitting she'd lied about losing her V-plates the year before – but since then I think she's been too worried about me getting jealous. Which I would've been, and very much still am.

Nodding, she picks up her napkin to wipe her face. 'Yeah, stranger sex can be so awkward. There was this one girl in Italy – she was going down on me and kept looking up *during*, like she was expecting something from me. And I didn't know what to do, so I waved at her.'

'You *waved* at her while she was inside your vagina?' I am delighted.

'Yeah, and she seemed to like it, so I kept waving.' She's nodding a lot. 'And this other time in Australia, this girl asked if I wanted to sixty-nine, which I'd obviously never done and never want to again. What is hot about being sort of upside down next to genitals?'

'Oh my God, it sounds brilliant – all of it!' I am completely engrossed.

'Also,' she continues, getting into the stories, 'that sixty-nine woman said *downside-up* instead of upside down – what the fuck is that? Is that an Aussie thing? Because they're upside down? I got out of there so fast.'

'You are my hero,' I sigh, happily.

'Hmm . . .' She suddenly looks a bit sneaky. 'And don't judge me, but I also had text sex a few times with Ms Redwood.'

'Ms REDWOOD?!' I shout this and our disapproving friend on the table next to us glares over again. 'The sixth form student PE teacher? Holy mother, Zo, that is so hot and wrong and bad and cool. And, wait, you still call her Ms Redwood?'

'Yeah, I don't know her first name.' She giggles, then stops abruptly. 'I feel like she might be someone I feel weird about later in life.'

'Probably.' I squint at her. 'I think we're meant to feel weird about a lot of the sex we have, aren't we? I mean we, as women. Women are supposed to be uncomfortable about a lot of the times they say yes.'

'I don't think *supposed to* is the right term.' She closes one eye at me, looking concerned.

'Oh, OK,' I reply, uncertain. 'I mean we probably just *will do* because we're women, right? But Jordan the glamour model doesn't care, does she? And she seems *super* happy. She and Peter Andre are the dream couple, they're totally going to make it, whatever *Heat* mag says.' I pause to swallow some food. 'Was there any really good sex while you were away, or was it all just awkward?'

She stops to bite off a broken nail. 'Actually I . . .' She looks annoyed and fiddles again with the nail.

'What?' I'm waiting expectantly.

'Well,' she starts slowly, finally looking up. 'I don't know what you'll think of this but I-I had sex with a man.'

'*What*?' I say again, feeling baffled. 'Seriously? Wait, what, hold on, I'm not sure I understand . . .'

'That makes two of us,' she says, looking nervous. 'I think, um, to be honest, I think I might be – maybe – bisexual? Or possibly just the tiniest bit straight in amongst all the gay.

Like, maybe 90 per cent gay, 10 per cent straight – is that a thing?' she stops short, realising that she's rambling. There is a shocked silence between us and she stares at my face anxiously.

'Are you OK?' she says at last, looking fearful.

'No.' I shake my head, looking down at my plate.

'Fuck, do you hate me?' she says quickly. 'It's not like I've been lying to you, it's just that I didn't know. It's all been so jumbled in my head and fancying this guy, it came as a shock to me, too – believe me – and it only happened a few weeks ago, just before I came back and—'

'No, no!' I interrupt her quickly. 'God no, don't be silly, Zo. Being bisexual – or, like, 10 per cent straight if you prefer – that's fine. That's completely not a big deal. Thanks for telling me. I'm just knocked down because I keep thinking I know you inside out. I sometimes feel like I share everything I think and feel with you, and you hold so much back.' I stop myself – I'm always saying too much – and then smile cheerfully. 'Plus, I know it's selfish but I can't believe how unfair it is. I mean, all the cool stuff happens to you! Someone will probably make a film about you one day and I'll be the bit-part sidekick everyone feels sorry for. You're the cool hero with big, exciting life stuff going on, and here I am, a plain Jane clueless virgin, who's stuck fancying men who have no interest in me – like Pete or Simon Stan.'

'Semen Stain,' she says automatically, but then adopts a more supportive tone. 'Don't be so down on yourself, Nat. I mean, you're moving in the right direction. Semen Stain was an awful wanker *as well* as not being interested in you. At least this Pete dude sounds like he's a *nice guy* who's not interested in you. That's something, isn't it?' She laughs so I know she's kidding, but it's also true.

50

'I guess that makes sense,' I admit. We stop to eat silently for a few seconds before I can resist no longer. 'So,' I say casually. 'Was it good? With the man, I mean?'

She considers her answer. 'Yeah, it was, actually. Strange, and completely different to women, but it was good. Seven out of ten, would recommend.'

'At least I can ask you for sex tips now,' I say, looking at her a bit hopefully.

'Hmm,' she grunts through a garlic dough ball. 'I don't know about that. I still definitely prefer women. This was just an aberration or an experiment. Whatever, let's not talk about it.'

She looks away, signalling the end of yet another conversation I desperately want to have. I watch her carefully for a minute, chewing slowly on her pizza.

'I bet you had loads of pizza in Italy,' I comment at last.

'Of course I did,' she laughs. 'I ate pizza and pasta every day for a month. It was the best.' She cocks her head at me, sensing my jealousy. 'It doesn't mean I can't appreciate a good Pizza Express Romana base, though. It's a totally different eating experience.'

'That last line made you sound like a dick,' I tell her kindly.

'Yeah, I know.' She nods sadly. 'I heard it, I know. But I have tried really hard not to be a dick about the travelling and it's too hard. I mean, Nat, you get so smug! You meet so many random people, who are all trying to outdo you with their fucking cool fucking stories of backpacking in the outback and trying local drugs. You get into the habit of competing and trying to show off. You have to let me do it a bit.'

'Well, I bet the fancy home-made pizza restaurants in Italy didn't let you order off the children's menu,' I say cheerfully, grabbing a fish finger from my side plate.

'That is very true, they didn't,' she agrees, picking one up, too.

'Did you really do drugs while you were away?' I ask, curiously.

'Not really.' She shrugs. 'A little bit of marijuana here and there. Everyone was doing it and I didn't want to be left out, but I barely inhaled. And this other time a super-hot girl offered me coke so I put some on my gums. It was quite fun, like getting numb at the dentist, but I don't think I'm going to be a drug addict. I've considered it as a career path but it's not for me.'

'Yeah, being a drug addict doesn't sound *that* fun.' I nod, then I smile knowingly, ready to tell her my big secret. I've been saving it up for her, specially. 'So, Zoe, I did some marijuana while you were gone.'

'Fuck off, *did* you?!' She is so shocked, I can tell. I bask in the glory for a moment.

The truth is, I'd always been such a goody two shoes when it came to drugs. I always wanted to be brave but the one time we went to a club and someone actually offered us a pill, I screamed LEAH BETTS and ran away to hide in the loo until Zoe came in to reassure me the drugs had gone away.

'What happened?' She scooches in close and I smile widely, delighted to be the one with the exciting anecdote for once. I've been so desperate to tell her. 'When was this? Who did you do it with?'

'My friend Choi – I told you about him, right? He's on my course and he made me some edibles at his house share one weekend.' I shrug, trying to sound as nonchalant as possible. 'Honestly though, it had, like, zero effect on me. I kept waiting for something to happen and Choi kept asking me if I was OK, but I felt nothing. I was just staring at the ceiling for a couple of hours. Then I freaked out a bit and sat up all night, ready to ring an ambulance, just in case, but it was fine.' I am immensely proud of myself, and Zoe is looking at me like she's proud, too.

'That's very cool, Nat.' She smiles at me. 'What kind of edible was it? A hash brownie?'

I laugh a tad condescendingly. 'Um, Zo? I think you mean hash browns, actually.'

She frowns. 'Wait, you had hash browns? He put hash in potato breakfast food?'

I return her frown. 'What do you mean?'

'What do *you* mean?' She looks puzzled. 'Tell me exactly what happened.'

I sigh, feeling frustrated and drunk. 'So, we were studying at Choi's and we stopped for lunch. He asked me if I'd like some eggs and hash brown, because he was going to have some. I thought, why not! I'm at uni and if I don't experiment now, when will I? But I wasn't very impressed with it.'

'Nat,' she says slowly and carefully, 'hash browns and hash brownies are very, very different things. You did not have drugs, you had potato.'

'Shut up, what?' She's *definitely* wrong.

'This is like when you thought house wine was a brand name,' she points out, laughing, and I feel my face redden. I join in, but the humiliation of being the loser with no life experience – yet again – burns.

A tinny version of 'Ridin'' by Chamillionaire starts blaring from Zoe's phone. She's changed the ringtone while she's been gone. We used to spend hours together, selecting the coolest ringtones for our phones. Yet another thing that's changed this past year.

'Yes, yes, no problem,' she squeaks into the phone. 'Sorry,

we're on our way.' She hangs up and waves the waiter over for the bill. 'That was Dad,' she says breathlessly. 'They're all waiting for us, we better run.'

ZOE

The cold air immediately goes to our heads making us staggery drunk as we roll into the party at my dad's house.

Dad and my brothers moved again while I was away and I'm still not used to this oversized, exaggeratedly gaudy place with too many rooms, that includes a – for some reason – games parlour.

We don't talk about money in our family – I guess that's because we have it – but I don't think money is why Dad likes to move house a lot. I think it's because he gets scared of memories being made, if that makes sense? Like, when Mum left, it shook him up so much because he'd got complacent; too set in his ways, too used to the way things were. And then it all got taken away. He never wants to feel that way again. He never wants to let himself feel content again in case the rug gets pulled like that. Once he starts to feel settled and familiar in a home, the fear sets in, so he moves us all again. At least I only had to change schools once, though, that was hell.

I can't wait to move out and then actually stay living somewhere for more than a fucking year.

Nat and I get slightly lost looking for the living room and are on the verge of giving up when we finally find the party. The room shouts surprise and I nearly fall over in my drunken attempts at pretending to be shocked. Which is weird and unnecessary because I helped arrange this. I smile hazily around at all the faces, counting off the familiar ones – Nat's mum, Debbie, her friend Sue, a few other family friends and relations. My brothers are all here, along with a few of their mates from school and they make up an awkward-looking bunch; half-grown children dressed up semi-formally for the occasion. Dad is standing by the food, smiling widely next to Nanny Surrey, who is regarding the buffet with pure disdain. He waves a bit desperately, obviously hoping I'll come rescue him from his mother. He can get fucked.

Dad has aged a bit since I've been gone. He has new lines on his face, new grey hair at his temples; it's weird. I think losing the only woman in the house – i.e., me – is the reason, but I also think this past year has been somewhat good for him. He's learned to use the washing machine at long last and my brother Matthew said he's actually been cooking real food. I mean, not just cheese toasties, which is what we lived on for two years after Mum left.

Beside me, Natalie squeals and runs off towards a shy group of about seven or eight people, huddled together towards the back. They must be the infamous new university friends. Ugh, I hate them already. Look at them wearing their stupid oversized hats and scarves indoors, even though it's almost June. I wonder if fucking *Other Zoe* is there. She's probably that cool-looking, tall one at the back. I bet those glasses are just pointless frames. Fucking students. I hate them.

Matthew approaches, smiling, and pulls me in for a hug. I feel a surge of affection for the brother closest to me in age. He's seventeen now – eighteen in August – and he's changed a lot this past year, too. He's really grown up. When I left for France last September, he was just like the other idiot boys in my house – all shoving each other and squeezing spots and having annoying fights over the PlayStation 3. Now he stands tall – taller than me – and hasn't even shoved me once today. The acne's still there, though, and I'm glad. I don't want him growing up too fast – I like him being my sweet kid brother.

Matthew was always the nicest of my siblings. Always fairly quiet; a kind and sensitive soul who checked in on me when I seemed moody or hadn't left my bedroom in days – which was most of the time, because being a teenager is hard. I like him the most out of my family, but it's hard to compare anyone to my twin brothers, Ben and Jacob. They're fifteen but could easily be eleven. They don't talk to anyone but each other and just snarl at people who try to make small talk with them.

'Shall we do Nanny Surrey duty?' he says, grinning and I groan but follow him.

Reluctantly, we join Dad, who gives me an awkward birthday pat on my shoulder. Nanny Surrey scowls at my outfit.

'Darling!' Dad says jovially. 'We're so happy to have you back home. I'm on *cloud nine*, aren't I, Mum?' He guffaws and then glances nervously down at his four-foot-nine mother. She gives him a sugary smile back.

'Of course we are,' she says in an exaggerated voice. 'And doesn't she look *well*, Bryan? Very *healthy*. I'm so glad you're not *thin* like you used to be, my dear.'

I nod stoically, taking the usual shit without complaint. My failure to rise to it only baits her though, and she goes in harder. 'And it's so *brave* of you, my dove,' she says then pauses, clearly enjoying herself, 'to keep wearing the same clothes you used to, even though they clearly don't fit any more.' She stops for a small titter. 'So *bold* a choice to make.'

'I haven't!' I protest, slightly. 'I didn't – I mean, there was a lot of pizza in Italy but . . .'

She interrupts me. 'Oh my goodness, it's a *compliment*, my dear!' she says faux-surprised. 'Some men even quite like the *bigger* girls. I hear there's a fetish. I'm sure you can find a husband in those internet chat rooms or whatnot.'

'I'm not sure it *is* a compliment,' I mutter, feeling defeated.

She dramatically rolls her eyes. 'For goodness sake,' she says breezily. 'I can't possibly control what you choose to think of as a compliment or not. I'm just trying to *help* you, my dear. And *I* love you, no matter what anyone else says about you behind your back.'

'Thanks, Nanny Surrey,' I say robotically. There's no point in engaging.

She's always been like this – walking acid – and she's only got worse since Grandad died about ten years ago. Dad is terrified of her, but also clings to her obsessively, for some reason. Actually, she's the reason we moved to this area when I was fourteen. When Mum left, I think Dad thought his mum could take over as some kind of maternal figure for us four. But all she's ever done is passive-aggressively (and sometimes just aggressive-aggressively) put me down and dismiss my feelings and accomplishments. Especially since I came out a few years ago. When and if my gayness comes up, she mostly just pretends not to understand, but otherwise she'll refuse to acknowledge it, making constant snide comments about me needing a husband and babies. She's nicer to my brothers – because obviously boys are better than girls – but I'm weirdly grateful for that. *I* can handle Nanny Surrey's nastiness – I'm not sure my brothers could.

Having rinsed me dry, she turns to Dad.

'I hope you're not drinking, Bryan,' she keeps her tone light but dangerous. 'I'll need a lift home when this – what would you call this thing? – *gathering* ends.'

Dad looks caught out, glancing down fearfully at the beer in his hand, but luckily a distraction arrives in the form of Natalie's mum, Debbie who gives me a happy squeeze hello.

'Hello, you lot,' she says cheerfully, swigging from a plastic beaker of orange juice. 'I'm not drinking tonight, Nanny Surrey, I could drive you home?'

'What!' Sue joins us, overhearing and looking outraged. 'Why aren't you drinking, you stupid bitch!' Debbie giggles in response and playfully swats at Sue.

I love these two together, they're hilarious. Always side by side, always laughing, always teasing. I really couldn't tell you if Sue actually has her own home, because she's always with Debbie whenever I'm around. But then, maybe she thinks the same about me and Nat? I look about for any sign of Natalie's dad, but nothing doing. Actually, I'm not sure I've ever really seen him out of his armchair?

'Goodness, Zoe love, look at the time,' Dad says quickly, afraid Nanny Surrey is about to launch into her usual tirade about women drivers. 'We better have a *rain* check on this conversation and get some presents opened, eh?'

Debbie agrees loudly, ushering me towards a table at the back featuring a pile of brightly wrapped gifts. Natalie joins me, smiling widely at the table before us. She's surrounded by her new pals who are all watching on eagerly. I try to subtly assess them individually but they all merge into one annoying gaggle of friend-stealers.

'Shall I introduce you around?' she whispers at me, gesturing at the group and giving my hand a squeeze.

'Um, maybe after this?' I hedge, nodding at the presents in front of us and avoiding eye contact.

'Oh.' She looks disappointed, but rallies quickly, nodding. 'Sure, OK. Let's do this!'

It's not that I don't want to meet Natalie's new friends. It's just that I really, really don't want to meet Natalie's new friends.

I mean, I was so excited to come back here; to see her after so many months apart. But all she does is go on about these new friends she's made.

I'm not jealous. I'm really not. Except I am sooo jealous.

I suddenly feel a lump in my throat and swallow hard, knowing there are a bunch of waiting eyes on me. It's hitting me now that so much has changed while I've been gone. I thought I was the one who was meant to go on a journey – literally and mentally. I'm the one who was meant to come back all tanned and sexually experienced, with loads of adventures to tell and photos to show. I should be the one here tonight with the exciting new international friends, not Natalie.

I mean, I did have plenty of fun while I was away, don't get me wrong, but what have I got to show for it? I still haven't got a clue what to do with the rest of my life and most of the people I met travelling live abroad. There was one girl I got on really well with – Hayley Wilson – who lives in England, but she's away for a few more months. So we'll probably forget each other by the time she's back. And there was that unbelievably sexy girl in Italy, Giulia, but I haven't heard from her since I left the country. Basically, I have nothing to prove I was even away, apart from some fridge magnets I thought were charming and realise now are ugly as fuck.

'PRESENTS! PRESENTS! PRESENTS!' Natalie's uni mates start chanting confidently as they join us. I know there are presents, you dipshits – what do they think I'm doing? Would it be out of order to tell them to get the fuck out of my house? Possibly.

It's just that there's this whole new part of Natalie's life I don't know anything about. The 'University Natalie', the one I've never even met. And these people surrounding her now know *that* person. I feel pangs of jealousy every time she mentions them. Who are these people? Are they good enough for her – will they take her away from me? They've had Natalie most of this past year. They've reached milestones together, they'll have in-jokes about lecturers and their halls of residence. Things I can't understand and never would.

We open presents loudly, thanking people as we go and making suitable ooooh noises.

What if Nat and me can't get over this disjointed stage? What if we don't ever reconnect? What if Other Zoe becomes just Zoe, and I eventually become the *Other Zoe*?

I have a new phone – a Sony Ericsson K800i – from Dad. It looks expensive and he puffs his chest as I give him a thumbs up, ripping open the box to admire the shiny black metal. Maybe it's a hint to keep in touch more? To be fair, I barely contacted him while I was away – the odd email once a week from an internet café – but now I'm back in the house, back in my old room, he seems keen to revert to child rules. I am supposed to let him know where I'm going, who I'm seeing, when I'll be back. It's driving me nuts. I'm not a kid any more.

As the party resumes around us, Natalie and I get drinks and sit down to review our gifts. Reading my mind, like she does, she nudges me.

'You haven't told me, how are things living back with your dad?'

'Shit,' I acknowledge, grimly. 'Dad put all my stuff in storage while I was away and I can't find anything. I had to masturbate over the Bible because there was nothing else available.' Natalie gurgles her wine, choking, so I continue. 'To be fair, that Jezebel chick sounds so hot.'

'I always thought I'd quite fancy Noah from the ark?' Natalie says contemplatively. 'Like, y'know, he has a cool beard, his own boat, and he's really nice to animals. Plus, you could totally have *any* animal cuddle you wanted, night or day, at the drop of a hat, depending on your mood.'

'Your mood?' I enquire.

'Yeah, like if you really wanted a slow, sweet hug, you'd go find a koala. If you wanted a dangerous cuddle, you could locate a lion. Or, if you really needed, like, a massive bear hug, you could look for, well, a bear, I guess?'

'You've thought about this a lot, haven't you?'

'Of course! I think it's weird that you haven't.' She pauses, eyeing her friends across the room. 'Hey, are you ready for introductions now?'

I clear my throat awkwardly and she holds my hand. 'I really want you to like them, Zo. I know they look like an odd bunch, and in all honesty they *are*, but they're also great. And you know how hard it is for me to make friends. It took me years just to find you.'

I nod enthusiastically, feeling like an idiot. 'Yes, of course, I'd love to meet them. Sorry.' I swallow again. 'I'm just nervous to meet your other life. I've missed you so much.'

She hugs me, hard. 'I have, too,' she says into my shoulder. 'And you know no one will ever replace you. You're my number one. If we were on the ark, you'd be the animal I'd want to cuddle most.' She pauses. 'Even over and above the pot-bellied pigs.'

'Thanks,' I whisper, feeling tearful.

It turns out they're nice enough. Fucking Other Zoe wasn't even there, for God's sake. The girl in – probably real – glasses is called Lina and she's from Germany. She's nice. They're all nice.

But they still feel worlds away from me.

I leave them to it and work the room, getting drunker and drunker. What am I going to do next with my life? I love my music, but that's never seemed like a realistic goal for work. Performing makes me sick with nerves and attention makes me uncomfortable. How else do people use music to make money? I could write, I guess? Maybe I *should* ask dad about that work experience.

The night wears on and I only get drunker. People are having fun, I think.

I start dancing with Lina. She's pretty. Her body moves awkwardly under loose clothes and I wonder what she'd look like naked.

I better not have sex with Natalie's friends; she'd be upset. Friend rules, right?

I should be with Nat, really. It's our birthday and we have a pact. Maybe she can tell me what I should do with my life. She always has a plan. She's so much surer of everything than I am.

I look around me, realising I haven't seen her in a while. I want us to talk about next year and what I'm going to do. I feel lost and scared. I want her to tell me I can move in with her and her friends at university, even if I'm not one of them. I want her to tell me I *am* one of them.

I find Debbie and Sue drunk-dancing in a corner.

'Debbie, have you seen Natalie anywhere?' I sound very drunk, yelling over a terrible, sappy song about someone being high on a subway and seeing a girl they fancy. A drippy man is singing about smiling at her even though she's with another man, and how beautiful she is. It makes absolutely no sense. Everyone here seems to know the words, though, and I'm suddenly glad I've been gone a year.

'What?' Debbie screams at me, clearly wasted, too. So much for not drinking tonight. She and Sue continue dancing fast, even though it's a slowsong.

I spot Dad, putting on his coat and leading Nanny Surrey towards the door.

'Thanks for tonight, Dad.' I stage whisper for some reason.

'You're very welcome, my love,' he says and smiles, looking tired. 'Please don't stop partying, I'm just popping your grandmother home. I'll be back in a bit, but I'll head straight to bed. I think a few of your friends are going to feel *under the weather* tomorrow.' He high-pitch giggles and I roll my eyes.

'OK, Dad, we get it, you're a weatherman.'

'Meteorologist,' he corrects a little haughtily.

I nod. 'Drive safe, meteorologist.' He gives me a quick hug and turns to go. I grab him. 'Oh, by the way, have you seen Nat?' He waves me in the direction of the loo. I nod my thanks as he leaves.

I stagger out into the hallway, thinking about my well-meaning, easily frightened, and oh-so vulnerable Dad. I wish he could meet someone. I wish he could trust people again. I wish he could tell his mother to shove it.

In front of me, the bathroom door opens.

It's Natalie, she's dishevelled and flushed in the face, yanking at her skirt as she emerges. I look down, her tights are off.

Has she? No way.

'Natalie?' I say from a few feet away and she stops dead, her hand still on the toilet door. Behind her, out comes a man, his hair all messed up and his tie missing.

They've been having sex. Natalie's just had sex.

'What the *fuck* did you just do?' I scream.

Nat sees me and all the colour drains from her face.

Because the dishevelled man coming out of the downstairs loo is my little brother Matthew.

4

2007

NATALIE

'Why is it considered sexy when *women* don't wear underwear but super unsexy when *men* don't wear underwear?' It's a question I've been pondering all day, and now seems to be a good time to ask.

'SHUSH,' Jamie hisses furiously at me, pressing her boobs into my right side. She shifts a little and someone on the other side of her groans at being elbowed.

'It's probably fine to talk,' someone else, unidentifiable, whispers into the dark. 'I think I can hear most of them downstairs; they can't hear us.'

'That's not the point,' Jamie spits, furious. 'They might come in at any second and everything would be ruined.'

'It's just a game, Jamie,' I say as nicely as I can. 'This isn't Al-Qaeda.'

The cupboard falls into silence again and I sigh.

Why have I agreed to play this uncomfortable thing?

Oh, that's right, because I want to have sex with Mo tonight, and he was the one who suggested playing sardines. I was going to counter with spin the bottle, but then Jamie got excited and said she'd never lost a game of sardines before, so I got all competitive.

So that's how we've ended up here, with, like, five – maybe

six? – people squished in this bedroom cupboard. And none of them are even Mo. So, duh, of course I'm talking out loud, I *want* him to find us.

Not that there's any room for him at this point. I'm currently sandwiched between Jamie, who – for the record – also blatantly wants to have sex with Mo. And Mike the other side, who, yep, also wants to have sex with Mo. Basically, everyone wants to have sex with Mo because he's so dreamy and clever. But I know I'm going to win out. I will win through sheer willpower. I will not stop until his penis is inside me – this I vow before king and country. I *will* win this sex race. I elbow Jamie a bit, out of spite, but she doesn't react. She will be my fiercest competitor; the girl has spirit. But I have flavoured condoms.

You know what's funny about uni? Smart, weird people are suddenly the most fuckable. It's the absolute opposite of school, where everyone's trying super hard to blend in and desperately sandpapering out any strange edges from their personality. University is like a loser paradise for those of us who never felt like they were worth anything at school. And since realising that fact in my second year, I've been getting laid like a maniac. You can be whoever you want to be, and the more outlandish and ridiculous you get, the *sexier* it gets.

To be honest, my studying has really taken a backseat this year. I was pretty diligent with my Geography course in the first year. I treated it pretty much like school; did my coursework, attended all my lectures, tried to suck up to the professors. But I've settled into a routine now and embraced the freedom of uni. Me and my friends have moved into a house share together and we're all bonded, there's no more shyness and fear and awkwardness. Instead, there's free-flowing alcohol and a whole lot of mad boning. Occasionally we remember to go to seminars and write some essays, but mostly it's about the drinking and boning.

It's fantastic.

And things are about to get even better, because Zoe's moving in.

She's taking Lucas's room, which is next to mine, down the hall. The bedroom we're hiding in currently is Choi's, and then Other Zoe, Lydia and Julia all have rooms on the second floor, upstairs. It's a big place.

I shift and stumble a bit on what feels, under my feet, like a dildo. I pray to God this isn't Choi's sex cupboard. I kick it towards Jamie, hearing her grunt in response.

I still can't believe Zoe and I are actually going to be living together! It'll be amazing; all-night chats, all-night parties, all-night laughing. Ooh, maybe we can learn Morse code and pass messages through the wall at night! Or I guess we could just text? That might be easier. Either way, I'm so excited, I can't wait to have her here with me all the time.

And let's face it, she needs me right now. She's been a mess since Giulia dumped her to move back to Italy – I've never seen her like this before. She's always so strong and in control so it's kind of freaky seeing her so broken. But I guess she'd never been in love before. They met in Italy when Zo was travelling, and hooked up a couple of times, but I don't think either of them thought it was more than that. Then she showed up in London, not long after Zoe got back, and they started dating. I really liked Giulia, but she was quite old – twenty-five – and wanted to move back to live nearer her parents. So they broke up, and Zoe's been crying on my floor for the past two weeks. It's been non-stop and I've been so worried the rest of the house might change their mind about her moving in. I mean, I wouldn't *totally* blame them for not wanting someone around the house who cries all the time. Luckily she's mostly kept it together in front of them, only breaking down in front of me and in the loo.

'I'm just saying, it's definitely not actually sexy when women don't wear underwear,' I begin again, into the hush. 'It's all, like, sweaty and stressful.'

'Are you not wearing any underwear?' someone asks politely.

'I am,' I say and nod. 'But it's got a big rip in the front so I feel very exposed. It made me think.'

'SHUT. UP.' Jamie's spitting mad and I fall silent again.

I wonder what it's like to fall in love and then have it torn away? I can't imagine. I don't even know what the love part is like – unless you count Semen Stain. Which actually I kind of do? I know nothing ever happened between us, but I think I get to call it love because I really thought it was at one point. I think that's allowed. Love comes in lots of different forms, doesn't it? That's what my mum says. And unrequited love is just one of those forms. But I hope one day I find a love that is requited. I bet that's quite nice.

For the record, though, I'm not in any major hurry. Not while I'm having all this casual sex.

'There you are, you bunch of cunts!' Mo flings open the cupboard door and a rush of sexy endorphins flood me at the sight of his face. God, he's hot.

'Mo, get in!' I shout joyfully and Jamie shushes me again. 'Move over, Jamie,' I say even louder and give her a little shove in the dark. Someone whimpers and I feel a wave of fury coming off Jamie in the dim light. Mo throws himself into the mix, pushing his way in delightedly and someone falls over the dildo again. He pulls the door shut behind him and everyone shuffles around, giggling and shushing each other playfully. I think Jamie might lose her shit soon if people keep making noise.

Beside me, I feel Mo's warm breath on my face and it makes me tingle.

Mo's a friend of one of my many housemates. He's at the same uni as me, but he's studying medicine – so he's, like, a *real* student, unlike me. In the dark, I try to make out the outline of his face. He's not conventionally handsome, but he is incredibly attractive. He's always happy and loud and silly, and – God – is there anything more unbelievably sexy than a happy person?

I imagine having sex with him would be a happy experience. Like, you'd laugh a lot, and he wouldn't mind the mess or make a face when your vagina makes a funny noise. He would probably smile and try to make his penis do the same noise. I think it would be good sex with Mo. To be honest, it would be really nice to finally have some good sex, y'know? I've done the deed a lot this past year, and I'm not saying it's been *bad* exactly. Like, it's super great that I've finally ticked sex off my life list. And it's a really great way to make men like you! You can distract them from all kinds of stupid things you might say or do by just quickly having sex with them. It's a good counterbalance to my personality. Because, let's face it, I'm never going to be any guy's first choice, am I? But if I'm the one at the end of the night still hovering at your elbow, more than willing to put out, then I win, right? Being up for sex makes up for the rest of *me*, I think.

But maybe with Mo – just this one time – it could be more about me than him. It could be great.

Actually, the only time I've had sex, where it felt like it was more about *me* than *him* was, um, that first time.

With Matthew.

Oh God, even just thinking his name makes my cheeks hot with shame. Blood rushes to my face and I'm suddenly so glad no one can see me in the dark. There's no way I'd be able to hide these feelings.

It's been a year this week since it happened and the memory still has the same effect on me: shame, humiliation, slight horniness. It's all still as fresh as the night it happened. Honestly, I wish I'd been blackout drunk so it wasn't all so clear the next day.

The night comes flooding back again now. The good bits; laughing with Matthew, kissing him, the awkward, fumbling but lovely sex. And then the terrible bits; getting caught, the furious row with Zoe, the drunken apologies, the sober apologies.

God, I was mortified. I still am.

I still don't really know how it happened.

Of course, a big factor was how very drunk I was. But I can't blame that entirely, because I can also see – in hindsight – that I was in a strange mood that night. It was my nineteenth birthday, I had my best friend back after so long apart, and then all my uni friends were there, too. It was an odd collision of worlds, all in Bryan's huge, unfamiliar new living room. And so, when I bumped into Matthew in the kitchen, I guess I was already looking for some kind of escape. He said hello as I liberally poured myself a drink and I did a double take. I couldn't believe it was him. I hadn't seen any of Zoe's brothers since she'd left for France – nine months or something – and God, he'd changed *sooo* much in that time. Like, he didn't look like a kid any more, he looked like a man. A really gorgeous man. And he seemed so happy to see me! We hugged in the kitchen and something in me felt strange as we held on for maybe too long. Then there were shots together, lots and lots of shots. And talking, so much talking. Then there was laughing, and then ... then kissing. I don't know who started it, but I do know there was tongue.

And it felt wrong and bad and for a moment I stopped it because: Zoe. But then he looked at me with this intensity and I didn't care any more, because I wanted him so much. He pulled me out into the hallway and into the loo, where he started kissing me again. Then I saw his willy and that was really nice, and then we were doing it and that was weird and great. It was really uncomfortable and then good and then uncomfortable again, and I didn't want it to end.

And then Zoe saw us.

She was so angry. Which I totally understand. I would've been too. I mean – her *little brother*? I had sex with her baby brother – her Seventeen. Year. Old. Baby. Brother – how could I do that? What's wrong with me? Seriously, I'm asking. Who does something like that?

Zoe was screaming at me and I was crying and saying sorry and that I wished I could take it back. And then Matthew looked at me really sadly and I felt guilty about him too. But in the moment, Zoe was the only thing that mattered, Matthew's feelings were irrelevant. I was so worried she'd never talk to me again. I don't think I could've handled that.

So then Mum and Sue came out to see what the shouting was about. They calmed Zoe down and took all of us into Matthew's room. The three of us sat on his bed and I stared over at his new Nintendo Wii, still paused on a game of tennis, and I realised I was basically a paedophile.

I felt so ashamed and said sorry to Zoe again. She got really quiet and then made us promise we'd never do anything like that again. I started crying and swore we wouldn't. I never,

ever would, I told her, it was a total drunken mistake. I said sorry a thousand more times, and she forgave me.

I couldn't even look at Matthew, and I haven't since. I expect he's in therapy, talking about the predatory older woman who took his virginity and left him unable to love. Oh God, I hate myself so much. I hate to think he might hate me, but we should never have done that. *I* should never have done that. It was so stupid and thoughtless and hurtful. I'm still so ashamed of myself.

But at least I'm not a virgin any more?

'What are you doing?' Zoe opens the cupboard door, peering inside at all of us and looking puzzled. Her phone is in her hand. 'I was about to ring the police,' she continues, relief in her voice. 'I thought there was a burglar or maybe a rapist in the cupboard.' She pauses. 'What is this, like a sex thing? Are you having an orgy?'

'If we were, would you join in?' Mo jokes from beside me and I feel a pang of jealousy. Everyone always fancies Zoe.

Zoe cocks her head at this, vaguely amused. 'Is Natalie in there with you?' she asks dryly.

'Present,' I say, trying to put my hand up, but it's trapped between bodies. 'Sorry Zo, I didn't realise you were here. We're playing sardines. I didn't think you were coming back tonight.'

'Dad gave me a lift with some of my stuff,' she says, amused. 'I know I'm not moving in until Thursday, but I thought I could start bringing over a few boxes in the meantime?'

'Of course!' I again try to move but again cannot.

Jamie suddenly loses patience with us. 'No offence, but can you fuck off please, Zoe?' she says from just behind me. 'Or get in if you must, but you're ruining the game right now.

71

The others will be able to hear you and find us.'

'Who will?' Zoe says innocently. 'My dad?'

'No,' Jamie scoffs, spitting ever so slightly on my ear. 'Not your dad, the rest of the house who are currently looking for us. Don't you know the rules of sardines?'

Zoe looks like she wants to laugh. 'There's no one else here, Jamie,' she tells her, kindly. 'You're all in there already.'

There is silence in the cupboard.

Oh. Oh right, someone really should've taken a head count.

'Do you need help with the boxes?' I ask Zoe when we've all finally un-wedged ourselves from inside the cupboard. The rest of the party has moved back downstairs for drinks, and I'm determined to get a spin the bottle going in a minute – but I also don't want to abandon Zoe with her stuff if she needs help.

'You're very kind,' she says, grinning. 'But don't worry too much, there aren't that many and Dad's got it. He keeps telling me how he's on a diet right now, so could do with the extra calorie burn of lifting my stuff.'

'A diet? Your dad?' The idea makes me smile.

'Yep.' She nods, opening the flap of a box and peering inside. 'He says turning fifty next year is finally the push he needs to get in shape. But I think it's because he joined Twitter and saw what people were saying about his TV paunch.'

'Twitter's the one with the white eggs, right?' I squint at her. 'I was going to try it, but our neighbour changed his Wi-Fi password on us again, the selfish git. I will get it again one day, you'll see.'

She laughs and a sweaty Bryan staggers into the room carrying two piled up boxes full of DVDs.

Poor Bryan, he does have a tiny bit of a belly these days.

But he's still a handsome man. I always think it must be so much harder for good-looking people to age. Like, they have to deal with so much more, as people stop staring and complimenting them in the way they once did. I realise Matthew looks a bit like his dad, and then feel super dirty, like I need a shower.

'Where shall I put this, love?' Bryan huffs and Zoe waves him over to a corner. 'Hello, Natalie,' he adds, heaving the DVDs to the floor and standing up straight. 'How's your family? Please send them my best wishes.'

'They're very well, thanks, Mr Darling.' I beam up at him. 'How is, um, the weather?'

'Oh! Thank you for asking!' he says, glancing over at Zoe reproachfully. She rolls her eyes in response. 'It's going to remain wet and windy, I'm afraid, Natalie.' He's using his TV voice, which is deep and knowledgeable. 'The temperature's unlikely to get above eight degrees this week, with humidity at 92 per cent and rising pressure. Expect strong winds from the north, as well.' He looks at me expectantly, so I nod enthusiastically.

'Wow,' I tell him solemnly. 'That is so useful to know. I better take my brolly with me to lectures tomorrow.'

'Always a sensible idea,' he tells me authoritatively. 'By the way, I get given a *lot* of free umbrellas, so if you ever need one . . .'

'I know where to go,' I finish for him.

'Indeed you do.' He smiles widely, heading out the door to fetch more boxes.

Zoe grunts after him. 'God, he's embarrassing,' she mutters.

'Do you want to come and get a spin the bottle game going?' I whisper to her excitedly.

She crinkles her nose up. 'Ugh, students. You guys are

73

supposed to be the nation's next great hope, and all you seem to do is drink leftover snakebite and play kid's games.'

'I don't understand where the problem is with what you're saying?' I say blankly and Zoe laughs. 'Is that a no, then?'

She considers it. 'Maybe,' she says, then looks a little sad. 'But I don't know if I'm really ready to kiss anyone else. It just makes me think about kissing Giulia.'

'You could get off with Julia from upstairs?' I suggest hopefully. 'That's almost the same name?'

She frowns and then looks even sadder.

'I'm sorry,' I add as nicely as I can but I feel a bit tired. Honestly, I was so excited having a fun, silly evening with my uni mates, and sometimes Zoe can be a bit . . . I don't know, grown-up? She's been temping for most of this last year and working in an office with people in suits seems like a world away from my student life of sleeping until midday and turning up to seminars still drunk. We have endless chats about what she might want to do with her life, and she seemed to enjoy the various work experience placements her dad got her at that record label – but they came to nothing. When I suggest applying for jobs, she gets a bit hostile and says it's impossible to get a foot in the door. She can be a bit defeatist at times. Personally, I still think she should've come to university with me – and she still could? – but it seems less and less likely to happen.

Don't get me wrong, I'm super excited to have her around, of course I am! But I guess there are moments when it's awkward with my uni friends. I think they annoy Zoe a lot of the time, and I worry they don't really get her dry sense of humour. I don't know how to integrate them, but I'm hoping us all living together will help with that. I just want to have fun and enjoy myself. And I want Zoe to do the same.

'Sorry,' she says suddenly, catching maybe the edge of my frustration. And then I feel bad. I want us both to be happy, because *I* am! So happy. I want her to be here with me, on the same level. That's all I've ever wanted for my best friend.

'No, *I'm* sorry!' I say, adding reluctantly, 'Do you want to stay up here and talk about things? You know that's fine, I can go grab us some wine and . . .'

'No, no!' She shakes her head determinedly. 'Don't be silly. I'm not going to be the party pooper. I've just decided to be a fun person again. Let's go join in the games. That was Mo, who just left right? Let's go get you some sex from Mo. I'll distract that rude girl who was all over him.'

'OK, great,' I enthuse, discreetly breathing a sigh of relief. Zoe's going to be fine. She's totally fine. She's looking so much happier already. And a wild night of silly games is just what she needs.

'I'll just pop down and say bye to my dad,' she grins. 'And then let's have some FUN!'

See, she's totally OK.

ZOE

You know when *you know* you're being an absolute downer? When you know for a fact that you're depressing everyone around you? When you walk into a room and the mood in there sinks into the floor? People stop being silly, they stop laughing, they stop enjoying themselves. All because you're there. And they hate you for it. They want to be happy and live their life but you're there now with your black cloud of misery hovering around everything, ruining it for them. But you still can't pull yourself out of it.

That's how I've felt for months.

Even before Giulia dumped me, I felt like that. And I don't really know why.

I just feel so pulled down by life lately. I'm so miserable and bored and uncertain. I move from job to job, temping and feeling isolated. I feel sick and tight in my chest all the time. And either I'm pretending to be fine – which makes me feel even worse – or I'm talking about how shit I feel, which everyone is so over.

I feel intense guilt over how much I've been putting on Natalie. But I also feel angry with her because I can feel her boredom with it. I can feel that she's sick of listening to me crying; of me moaning about my life and my break-up; of me complaining about not having a purpose. She tells me to apply for jobs, in a slightly impatient voice, but she doesn't know that of course I fucking have been. For a year I've been applying for every job going in music. And nothing. I've done my work experience – I've done a lot of it – and nothing. It feels like it's never going to happen. I'm stuck in a vacuum of endless applications and rejections.

Honestly, I don't blame Natalie for being sick of it. She's sick of me being the buzzkill. She's sick of me, the outsider, standing on the edges of her friends, barely trying to fit in. She's sick of *us*.

And now I'm moving in and I don't know if it's going to make everything better or worse.

'That's your lot, Zoe, love.' Dad shuts the car boot with a loud thump. 'I'll bring the rest on Thursday.'

'OK,' I say listlessly. 'Thanks for your help.'

He looks at me for a moment. 'Are you all right?'

'Ugh!' I throw my hands up in the air, frustrated. 'I wish people would stop asking me that. Yes! I'm! Fine! And maybe

76

I would be even finer if people would stop asking me if I'm all right constantly.'

Dad raises his hands in surrender. 'OK, OK!' he says, trying to keep his tone light. 'I'm sorry, Zoe. I just worry, you know. It is my job as a parent to worry, I can't help it.' He looks sad for a moment and I feel guilty.

More guilt.

'Sorry, Dad,' I sigh. 'I don't mean to take it out on you.'

He grins. 'Hey, what kind of pants do storm clouds wear?'

I indulge him. 'I don't know, Dad, what kind of pants *do* storm clouds wear?'

'Thunderwear!' he booms, laughing and I titter politely until we both fall silent.

'Are you sure you want to move out?' he says urgently after another moment. 'You know you can stay in your room at home as long as you want! You never have to move out if you don't want to. You don't have to pay rent, and you don't even have to work! We get along pretty well, don't we, love?'

I laugh, but not unkindly. 'Sure we do, Dad,' I say agreeably. 'But you know the twins drive me nuts. And I can't keep relying on you for everything. It's not right. I need to grow up and earn my own money and pay my own way. I'm twenty this week, I need to get my act together. Even Matthew's moved out. It's my turn.'

He nods, silently, swallowing hard, and I realise this isn't totally about worrying if I'm OK. I take a step closer and lean against the car beside him, resting my head on his shoulder.

'Will *you* be OK?' I say quietly. 'Without me there?'

He clears his throat and straightens up. 'Of course!' he says brightly. 'I have my work and the twins to keep me busy and ...' He trails off before adding in an unreadable tone, 'And my mum, of course.'

I make a face he can't see.

'You're not – you're not too lonely, are you, Dad?' I say softly.

He laughs, but then stops short. 'Maybe a little,' he says eventually. 'But I'm not ready for anything more in my life than I already have. I'm busy and I wouldn't want to disrupt the boys' schooling or . . .' He trails off again. 'Most of the time I'm completely fine. I'm fine, I'm really fine.'

'Good,' I say, head still on his shoulder. 'Then we're both fine, aren't we?'

5

2008

NATALIE

'Lower, LOWER! Oh my God, that feels so good,' Zoe moans in pleasure and I want to laugh, but it hurts too much.

'Now, you do me,' I croak, unable to raise my voice above a husky whisper. 'Everywhere. On my face.'

'No, no, Nat, not yet. Please don't stop doing me yet,' she whimpers, looking at me pleadingly. 'I'm literally begging you, just a little bit more. Come on, you know I need it more than you.' She starts to cry for no reason and so I start to cry, too. But then I realise no actual tears are coming out. I'm too dehydrated.

'No, it's my turn,' I wail bitterly and she relents, still weeping softly.

With all her strength, Zoe leans forward, reaching for the garden hose and aiming it at my face.

Oh my God, the sweet, sweet relief. The joyful, cooling effect of the freezing cold water immediately obliterates all other feeling. All other bad feeling. I lie there on the cool grass, soaking wet, feeling nothing but the cold water blasting my face. And nothing has ever been better. Ever.

For those few blissful seconds, my bloodcurdling, mind-altering, monster hangover has gone.

'Can you do me now?' Zoe begs again, lowering the hose.

'That wasn't a full minute!' I shout, immediately furious. Then I wince because the searing head pain returns with full force.

'You two are going to get legionnaires' disease,' Mum's dry voice says from somewhere nearby and I try to look up but it's too painful to move my neck. 'Natalie, you know we haven't used that hose in years.'

'Oh, Mum,' I mumble. 'Thank God it's you. You have to help us. Save us, please.' I start to cry again. The emotions are all too much. 'Please, please can you spray us both with the water? We're in such a bad way.'

'It looks like your twenty-first was fun, then,' she says wryly, and I can hear the smile even though I can't open my eyes just yet. 'What are you even doing out here? Tell me you two didn't sleep in the front garden?'

'No, I don't think so?' Zoe's voice is cracked and confused. I squint over at her, lying prone beside me on the grass. She looks like I feel; completely wrecked. She has last night's clothes on, but her skirt is backwards and one leg of her tights is off. There's lipstick on her forehead and I think – although I don't want to make assumptions willy-nilly – that is sick in her hair.

'I'm pretty sure we slept on the floor in the living room,' she continues. 'But it was so hot in there when we woke up, we had to get out. We crawled outside and found the hose. It helped a bit.'

'Plus,' I add trying to make my voice sound like my voice, 'the living room smells like tequila for some reason, and I was going to vomit again being around that for any longer.'

'The reason,' Mum sounds a bit miffed now, 'it smells like tequila, is that you two little fuckers were playing drinking games when you got in at four o'clock this morning and spilled alcohol all over my sofa.'

'Oh shit,' Zoe moans loudly. 'I'm so sorry, Debbie, I honestly am. And I really, really want to tell you we'll get up and clean it right now but this is the worst hangover of our lives and if we move, unfortunately we'll definitely both be sick again.'

'She's right,' I say tearfully. 'And I can't stop crying either, Mum. You know how emotional I get on a hangover.'

Mum sounds more sympathetic when she speaks again. 'I do know, and I understand,' she says nicely. 'Sue and I have certainly been there before. You stay out here cuddling the hose. I would stay and spray you with diseased water, but we're off to Tesco. Do you need anything?'

'Yes,' we both reply immediately.

'Does Tesco do, like, hot chicken wings or spicy wedges?' I ask desperately. 'Or anything else hot and carby. I need it so much, you have no idea.'

'Same,' Zoe says eagerly. 'And I also need Lucozade Sport. A lot of it. Like, Debbie, you'll think you have enough Lucozade Sport in your trolley, but it won't be enough Lucozade Sport. Get *a lot* of Lucozade Sport.'

'I'll see what I can do.' Mum nods, still sounding amused even though this is not a laughing matter. 'I'll put you a pizza in the oven when I get back and there's Berocca and Nurofen in the cupboard if you can get to it.'

'Thank you *so much*, Mum,' I say, starting to cry again. 'You're the best mum who ever lived, honestly. I really, *really* love you.'

'OK, dear,' she says kindly, but not sounding totally convinced. 'I love you too. I'm sorry about your hangovers but try not to vomit on the flower beds. Your dad would be very unhappy.'

'God, your mum is just *the best*,' Zoe says as we watch Sue and Mum drive off, cheerfully waving as they go. 'She deserves, like, so much happiness, y'know?'

'She really *is* the best.' I nod sincerely. 'Although I think our enthusiasm might be booze-fuelled. We probably have to factor in how hungover and still drunk we are right now.'

'That's true.' Zoe rolls over slightly, sighing happily as she lands in a puddle of muddy wet grass left over from the hose. 'And we both get very loving and intense when we're hungover.'

'Oh God!' I cover my face. 'I've got such bad hangover paranoia, Zo. Was I a nightmare last night?'

'Of course you weren't!' She sounds outraged. 'You were amazing. I think I was the one being a dick. I can't remember much but I keep getting flashes of this look on Other Zoe's face when we were in the bar. But I can't remember what I said.'

'I don't know,' I lie, remembering very clearly how Zoe spent all night deliberately getting Other Zoe's name wrong. She kept calling her Audrey and then passive-aggressively going, 'Oh, is that *not* your name? Sorry, babe, Zoe is just really hard to remember.'

'Can you sit up at all?' she says, trying to do likewise. 'I need to inspect my legs for drunk bruises. There are always at least five or six I can't account for.'

'I'll help,' I say, managing to get up, and then immediately lying down again, adding, 'No, actually I can't. Can you check me while you're up there.'

Zoe examines herself while I lie still, trying to piece together the evening.

OK, OK. My breathing shallows as I work through the night's events.

I remember the birthday pre-drinks at our place with the

housemates. And I remember doing way too many shots for a person who didn't have any dinner.

I remember getting emotional about the fact that I'm moving out, and crying on Julia and Lydia as I pointed at packed boxes and demanded they take me on a 'final tour' of their bedrooms.

I remember drunkenly knocking on our neighbour's door to tell him I would miss him 'most of all', even though we didn't actually meet in the two years I lived there. I also remember apologising for continually trying to steal his Wi-Fi and then I remember drunkenly inviting him out to the bar with us.

I remember getting to the bar, finding our reserved area, and then immediately getting on a table to perform 'Popular' from *Wicked*. I remember trying to make Zoe get on the table with me so she could be my Idina Menzel, and then explaining to the bar staff that I've seen the West End show four times, so it was OK. I remember I had some trouble pronouncing Kristin Chenoweth's name and then I remember getting up to perform 'Defying Gravity' as my encore.

I remember that's when Zoe's brothers all turned up and I remember that is the moment I made eye contact with Matthew.

I remember trying to play it supercool when I later actually spoke to Matthew – who was there with his girlfriend – and carefully avoiding all mention of the last time we'd seen each other a couple of years ago. I remember telling him loudly and without him asking, that I had a boyfriend now who I met in Italy and then I remember I couldn't think of a name, so told him the Italian boyfriend was called Rome. I remember that he looked amused – and so did his stunningly pretty girlfriend.

I roll over, so my face is in cool wet grass and let it take the heat of my humiliation.

'Oh God, Zoe, why did you let me get so drunk?' I wail into the ground.

'Why did *you* let *me* get so drunk?' she replies, sounding outraged. 'Look at my phone. Look how many times I texted Giulia. She's going to think I'm a fucking psycho.' She jabs her phone towards me. 'LOOK AT IT, NATALIE. AT ONE POINT I JUST TEXTED HER THE ALPHABET, LETTER BY LETTER. THAT IS TWENTY-SIX TEXT MESSAGES AT TEN PENCE A PIECE.' She shakes her head. 'Ten pence for a W.'

I grimace, cringing internally for both of us. 'You should just blame your weird new iPhone for being mad,' I suggest smoothly. 'Say it's just something Apple phones do, she won't know.'

'No, I can't text her again,' she laments. 'I can never message her again. I have to pretend she doesn't exist from here on out, or the shame will be too much.'

'Or I could text her the alphabet now, too?' I offer helpfully. 'That way, she might think it's a mobile glitch thing? I'll send the alphabet to everyone in my phonebook to really make it believable. I mean, who would ever do something that weird and stupid, unless it was a software error?'

'I'm never drinking alcohol again,' she says grimly, ignoring my genius suggestion.

'Don't say the A word,' I moan, catching a whiff of pure booze coming out of my pores.

'Crap!' Zoe sounds alarmed. 'Nat, do you remember getting off with Pepe in front of everyone?'

'Who?' I sit up straight, having no memory of this Pepe person.

'The neighbour!' she says, sounding exasperated. 'You invited him along and he turned up at, like, midnight. You were dancing together for ages. You don't remember?'

'Noooo!' I shriek, covering my face. 'Not at all. And I kissed him?!' I am horrified. Not only is Pepe known as the creepy neighbour, but he must be well into his forties. And I'm pretty sure he deals crack?

What will my friends think? What will Matthew think? And what will my fake boyfriend, Rome, think?

'You were definitely snogging,' Zoe confirms helpfully. 'And then you came over and handed me a Wi-Fi password on a piece of paper. I think you'd written it down in eyeliner. You said it was your parting gift to me, to celebrate us having lived together for a whole year. You said you'd got off with Pepe in exchange for his Wi-Fi password, so that I'd always remember you in that house, even when "some other cow" had taken over your room.'

The memory floods back all of a sudden. The taste of his cigarettey mouth on mine; how proud I was of achieving something so worthwhile.

'I did it for you,' I whisper. 'I got you that password at long last, even though I don't need it any more. It was for you, because I'm so sad we're not going to live together any more. Because I'm going to miss you so much. I can't believe I have to move home; I really don't want to leave you.'

'Don't say that!' Zoe says, welling up again. 'We will live together again one day! When you've got a job, or some money.'

'I will never have any money,' I wail loudly. 'I'll never be able to afford to live in central London anyway, even if I do.

And if we, one day, find a way to live together again, it won't be in *that* house,' I let out a little sob. '*Our house*. It won't have that weird, glittery wallpaper in all the bedrooms, and it won't smell like damp in the living room. We won't have that dickhead landlord who told us we had to keep the windows open all year round to air it out, and we won't have light fittings that fall on us in the night. And we probably won't get to sleep in rooms next door to each other. We won't be able to tap on the wall when we're hungover and bring each other coffee. We won't be able to text each other from bed at night and hear the beep through the wall. I won't be able to listen to you having sex and feel weirdly turned on—'

'OK, that's one step too far,' she warns and I sigh, feeling so, so tragic.

'Fine,' I say, sniffing loudly. 'But I really am going to miss living with you like crazy. I loved it. But at least I was able to do this one thing for you before I left. At least I got you free Wi-Fi for the rest of your time living there without me.'

'It was a noble sacrifice,' Zoe says, giving my back a grateful pat. 'But, babe, we got a two-hour night bus home to your mum's at two in the morning and woke up on your living room floor without any coats, bags or shoes. Do you really think I've still got that scrap of paper?'

'Ugh.' I dry heave. 'You better get the hose or I'm going to be sick again.'

ZOE

Two hours later and we have finally made it inside and onto the tequila sofa. Our hangovers have abated ever so slightly, with the help of a liver-damaging number of pills, eight cups of coffee, and all the toast and crisps we could find. We even raided Debbie's secret carb stash in her bedside table and felt too ill to feel bad about it.

'Do you think Tiffany will come back, too?' Natalie is asking me a question she knows I don't understand.

'Who?' I say vaguely. She also knows I'm not totally listening but this is how at least 60 per cent of our conversations go; her talking in a stream of consciousness, while I make the occasional 'hmm' noise. It's fine, though, we both prefer it this way.

She jabs with a finger in the direction of her mum's TV screen – the same TV Debbie's had the whole time I've known the family – where *EastEnders* – I think? – is playing.

'Bianca's back!' she says enthusiastically. 'Patsy Palmer, she's back! After years of trying to find another acting job, she's returned to her most important role ever. To the most important role anyone's *ever* played. Bianca, you know?' She pauses, then yells, 'RICKAAAY!'

'I have no clue what you're talking about,' I say, my brain squeezing with pain again. I reach for more Nurofen, even though it's been nowhere close to four hours since my last overdose. 'I don't watch soaps, you know that.'

'Screw you, then,' she says conversationally and then leans in to examine the device distracting me. 'They're too complicated, no one's going to buy them,' she sniffs dismissively at it.

I put down the new iPhone Dad bought me for my birthday. 'I think I fucked it last night,' I sigh. 'I remember dropping it, like, six times. And then throwing it at Pepe because he was trying to sell my friend Hayley some crack.'

'Was that before or after I kissed him?' Natalie asks, looking a bit jealous.

'I'm not sure,' I say absent-mindedly, trying to find an on/ off button on this weirdly smooth, oversized phone.

'I will always prefer my flip phone,' Natalie says smugly. 'Why would you need the internet on your phone anyway? How pointless is that?'

'*Your* phone doesn't even text or take calls,' I observe dryly. 'It will again one day!' she protests. 'Once I can afford to top up my minutes.' She gives an exaggerated sigh. 'Ugh, it's so unfair. You've got a cool new job, a nice house to live in and a fancy new mobile from the fruit computer people. Meanwhile I'm flat broke, in massive debt and moving back to *this* miserable place, with my mum and dad. I mean, I'm going to have a *degree* in a few months – an actual degree, Zoe! – but is that going to help me get a job? Not a chance. I can't believe I'm finishing uni just as the world collapses in on itself financially. What am I supposed to do?'

She throws herself into the sofa cushions and I bite my lip. 'It's really shit,' I say simply.

'Hey!' She sits up, looking inspired. 'Do you think they'll pay off my student loan while they're bailing out the banks?'

'You could ask?' I suggest nicely.

'Ooh, maybe you could get your dad to do a bulletin on the evening news?' she continues excitedly. 'Y'know, about how the government should save students before they save dumb Abbey National.'

'He's still only a weatherman, Nat,' I say and raise one eyebrow. 'I'm not sure what powers you think he has over national financial policy.'

'Yeah,' she is undeterred, 'but he could, like, totally have a word with the news anchors. They've all worked together for years, haven't they? They'd do your dad a favour, I'm sure.'

'HELLO! HELLO!' Debbie's booming voice interrupts us as she and Sue bustle in, Tesco shopping bags in tow. They dump themselves on the sofa opposite before Debbie spots the TV and gasps, 'Ooh, is that Bianca back?'

'Yes!' Natalie confirms triumphantly.

'Well, it's about bloody time,' Debbie leans in closer to the TV. 'It's where she belongs, really, isn't it, Sue?'

Sue nods emphatically. 'Absolutely, *'Enders* hasn't been the same without her.' She pauses and then shouts, 'RICK-YAAAY!' Just like Natalie did. These people are weird.

'How are you two feeling?' Debbie glances briefly away from the screen. 'Any better? You've both got a bit more colour on your cheeks.'

'I had a shower,' I say proudly, omitting the part where it was in my clothes and it was because I was covered in sick.

'Well done you!' Sue says nicely.

'I was going to shower, too,' Natalie says sadly. 'But Zoe wouldn't let me get in with her and I was afraid I might pass out if I got in there on my own.'

'Oh love,' her mum says sympathetically. 'Want me to help you? You do have quite a lot of the front garden on you.'

Natalie looks surprised and glances down at herself. She's still in last night's clothes, baked in mud and other mystery meats, whereas I've at least made it into a dressing gown.

'No, Mum,' she says dismissively. 'I am a grown-up, you know? Just because I'm moving home doesn't mean you and Dad get to treat me like a kid again.'

Debbie looks a bit embarrassed and turns to me. 'Well, how about you, love?' she says kindly. 'Hangover aside, how are things? Natalie tells me you've got an exciting new job!'

My chest swells with pride, because it *is* super exciting.

As of two weeks ago, I am the new marketing assistant for Harrier-Hawk-Hitchins Records. It's a music label that I did some work experience for last year, and one of the managers there sent me the advert when the job came up. To be honest, I wasn't going to go for it. I've applied for so many, and I know how many people go for jobs like this. They'd all be better qualified than me, with a degree and stuff. But Nat basically tied me to a computer until I agreed to try. I had a couple of interviews where I babbled about how much I love music and talked about the gigs I've been to recently, and – unbelievably – I actually got it. The money is awful and it's very entry-level stuff, but it's also absolutely dream-job stuff, and I'm struggling not to boast about it to everyone I know.

I mean, I technically already *did* boast about it quite a lot, because I posted about it on Facebook and Twitter and added the job title to my email auto-signature. Plus, my dad sent out a mass family newsletter to everyone he ever met.

But still, I haven't been stopping people in the street to tell them about my new job, so I deserve some credit for self-restraint!

OK, so I *did* stop a couple of people on the street, but in my defence, I had only just got the call and I was very drunk and the strangers seemed very happy for me.

I nod happily at Debbie. 'It's brilliant!' I tell her, leaning forward excitedly. 'I'm working with some of the biggest artists in the UK and I'll be helping create, like, multi-million-pound campaigns for their music! As marketing assistant, I'm going to be part of media strategy campaigns, which means hanging out with radio pluggers and music journalists. I'm pretty sure they'll start sending me out with stars, too. I reckon it won't be long before I'm best friends with, like, Beyoncé.'

Debbie and Sue stare at me in awe and Natalie looks part-proud, part-jealous. I beam back, so thrilled with myself.

I mean, so far it's mostly been tidying the photocopy area

and taking stuff to the dry cleaners, but they're just easing me into the big stuff, I'm sure.

'That's wonderful, my darling!' Debbie enthuses. 'You've earned it. Soon you'll be running the company. I bet your dad is so proud of you. How is he?'

I know she's just being polite. She and Sue still aren't the biggest fans of my dad. 'He's fine, thanks,' I say, even though she's already half turned back to the TV and the Bianca/Ricky person.

'Good, good,' Debbie says vaguely, absorbed in the screen. 'And your brothers? Are they all well? What are they up to these days?'

I glance furtively at Natalie. We don't really talk about my brothers that much. Not since MatthewGate. I mean, I'm totally over what happened, it's fine, and I even invited him and his girlfriend Sami to the party last night.

Obviously, my best friend and my little brother having – nope, I can't even think the word – was a massive shock at the time. But I understand how things happen when you're drunk, and we talked it out back then. It's all good. And I'm pretty sure Natalie's totally fine about it now, too. I saw her chatting to him and Sami a bit last night. It didn't look awkward.

But it's still kind of a tense subject for us.

Nat stares blankly at the TV screen, pretending not to be listening. But her ears and cheeks are pink. Maybe I shouldn't say this next thing? I don't want to lie and she'll probably find out sooner or later anyway. It's not like Matthew's her ex or anything, they just had one stupid encounter two years ago.

'Yes . . .' I begin slowly. 'They're all really well, thanks for asking, Deb. The twins are doing their A levels and expect to get decent marks. And Matthew . . .' I clear my throat. 'Actually, Matthew got engaged a few weeks ago.'

This gets their attention and the three women turn towards me.

'Wow, engaged?' Sue leans forward, fascinated. 'But he must only be – what? – eighteen?'

'He'll be twenty this summer,' I say a little defensively. 'He's only about fifteen months younger than me.'

'Woah,' Natalie says softly and I search her face. There's no sign of sadness, just surprise. She cocks her head at me. 'That's huge, Zo. To the girl I met last night? What's her name again? How did it happen? I had no idea!'

I smile nicely at her. 'Her name is Sami and they went to school together. They went out for a bit in year ten, I think, but they weren't serious. Then they bumped into each other again last summer and hit it off. Things got intense pretty quickly.' I take a breath. 'I know they're young but they're both pretty level-headed people. And they're going to have a long engagement, I should think.'

'That's so romantic . . .' Natalie breathes out, looking dreamy. 'So you approve? You like her? She's very pretty, I remember that much from last night.'

I nod happily. 'I do. She's really sweet and they seem to make each other happy. I know a lot of people will think they're going too fast, but who gets to decide what works and what doesn't when it comes to love?'

Debbie looks down at the floor at this point and I wonder if she's judging my brother. I keep talking, feeling defensive.

'I know the odds are stacked against them, but I believe in them. I have a feeling they're going to be one of those adorable couples sitting together in their garden in their eighties, holding hands and telling a whole bunch of grandkids how they've been together sixty-plus years.'

'Well, that's lovely,' Sue declares, smiling. 'Shall we have a celebratory wine?' she looks around the room hopefully and Natalie and I pale. 'Come on, you two,' she says and stands up. 'Hair of the dog! We need to raise a toast to Matthew and Sami, as well as you two turning twenty-one. I can't believe you're all grown-up – how did that happen? You can drink in America, so you should definitely drink two days in a row.' She smiles brightly and then adds. 'Oh, and we need to cheers to our girl Natalie moving home, too.'

Natalie scowls.

'Oh God, we can't,' I bury my face in my hands, feeling vommy again. 'Please no.'

'And I shouldn't,' Debbie says, looking sad. 'I'm trying to be good. I've been drinking so much lately what with *the situation*.' She stage whispers this last bit, glancing around as if John might suddenly leap out from behind a sofa.

Debbie's husband John – Nat's dad – lost his job recently. I don't even know what he does – did – for a living and it's one of those things where it's probably too late in our acquaintanceship to ask. I've known them all for, like, seven years now; I can't casually ask for personal details at this point. Actually, I've never really had a proper conversation with John. He's always about, but not engaged. He's generally reading a paper in a corner somewhere, gardening, or doing a crossword while ignoring us. I could probably count on one hand how many words we've exchanged over the years.

'Being good is for suckers,' Sue says mischievously. 'And you've heard the expression *bad things happen to good people*, haven't you? You don't want bad things to happen to you, do you, Deb?'

'Very good point,' Natalie interjects like it's the wisest thing anyone's ever said.

'I think you might be interpreting that saying wrong,' I say, but I stand up anyway. 'Fuck it, I'll get the wine.'

'Am I too old to join The Facebook?' Sue is asking Nat when I return.

'I think so,' Natalie nods solemnly. 'But if you want to mock old school acquaintances, they might be on Friends Reunited?'

'Can you set me up?' Sue looks excited. 'I hated literally everyone in my school, so obviously I want to talk to them.'

'How did you two meet, then?' I ask Sue and Debbie curiously. For some reason I always assumed it was at school.

Debbie looks a bit wistful and Sue laughs. 'You don't know this story? We shared a boyfriend.'

'Excuse me?' Natalie looks appalled and I realise she doesn't know either.

'Don't make it sound worse than it is,' Debbie scolds her friend, trying not to laugh. 'We didn't know we were sharing him.'

'OK, fine,' Sue smirks. 'So, his name was Edgar, which should've been our first clue something was off with him.'

'But we were both seventeen,' Debbie interjects. 'We had no kind of idiot radar back then.'

'I still don't,' Sue mutters, picking up the story. 'I met him in a local café where I was working and I'd been going out with him for about six months when a girl I didn't know came into the café and accused me of trying to steal her man.'

Natalie gasps and points at Mum questioningly. 'Was that you?' she says in a high pitch. Debbie nods, looking embarrassed.

'Yes, I'd met him in a bar about five months previously and things got serious very quickly. I thought we were going to be together forever and get married – until I found this picture of another woman in his room.'

'Me!' Sue jumps in delightedly.

'So I confronted him,' Debbie explains, getting into the story. 'And he told me it was his ex and she was obsessed with him. He said she wouldn't go away and kept leaving notes and pictures on his doorstep. He said the best thing to do was to ignore the "psycho stalker", and he would deal with it.'

'But she didn't,' Sue adds gravely.

'Of course I didn't,' Debbie confirms. 'Psycho stalkers didn't scare me. I was seventeen and I *was* a psycho stalker. So I figured out where this slut worked and went to start a fight.'

'I was delighted,' Sue says proudly. 'This scary woman with a resting bitch face storming in and terrifying the customers.'

'It's not a resting bitch face,' protests Debbie. 'It's very much a wide-awake bitch face, believe me.'

Sue nods agreeably. 'I calmed her down, got the story out of her. And then I explained that actually *I* was dating Edgar. I got the café boss to come out and talk to Debbie, he confirmed Edgar still worked there part-time and that we were indeed an item.'

'I cried a lot,' Debbie says grimly.

'She did,' Sue adds. 'And I didn't. I was too angry. Anyway, we both went over to his house, where he lived with his mum, and we told on him.'

I burst out laughing. 'You dobbed him in to his *mum*?'

'Big time,' Debbie confirms. 'We told her everything and asked her to tell Edgar he was double dumped. She was furious with him.'

'My only regret is that we couldn't stick around to see him getting spanked,' Sue laments.

'And then we decided to stay friends with each other,

mostly to piss him off,' Debbie says with relish. 'We'd see him out and about in town occasionally and he always looked terrified to see the two of us together. He'd run in the opposite direction.'

'Oh my God!' Sue cries, looking inspired. 'I need to see if *Edgar* is on the internet.' She turns to Natalie. 'Take me to the online immediately and show me this Friends Reunited thingy.'

The pair of them scuttle off to the corner computer and talk in hushed tones as the internet slowly kicks into life.

Debbie and I sit in companionable silence, drinking wine and staring at the Bianca woman on TV; she's gesturing wildly at someone working on a market stall.

'You're probably wondering what I meant earlier,' Debbie says suddenly in a low voice. She's staring over at Natalie who is hooting with laughter at something Sue's said.

'Oh?' I don't know how to answer this because it sounds important but I have no idea what's she's referring to.

'When I mentioned *the situation*?' she explains, quietly.

'Right, you mean about John's job?' I say, slightly confused but matching her low volume. 'I'm so sorry about that, are you—'

'No, no.' She shakes her head. 'Actually, um, I meant John and me.' She looks down at her lap, then takes a long gulp of her drink. 'I haven't spoken to Natalie about this yet. She's such a sensitive soul, I don't know how to tell her. John and I have split up. He left last night. He's gone to stay with his sister in Durham until we can figure out what we're going to do.'

'God, I'm so sorry!' I say, genuinely meaning it. I reach out and touch her shoulder a little gingerly, lost for words.

I've never really seen Debbie and John interact much – I've

never seen John interact with anyone – but I thought that was just how they were. To be completely honest, I thought that's what marriage was; just sort of ignoring each other most of the time. But, to be fair to me, I didn't exactly have a sterling example back home. Even before Mum left, I don't remember her and Dad being particularly romantic or affectionate with each other.

'It's fine, it's really fine,' Debbie says quickly, glancing worriedly at Nat. 'It's been such a long time coming, but him losing his job has brought everything to a head. We lost the love we shared many years ago, and now we don't even have anything in common any more. We don't talk, we don't touch each other.' She breaks off but looks worried more than sad. 'I'm just concerned about telling Natalie. She loves her dad, she's going to be so upset. Especially with her finishing uni and moving back here for a while. Things are so up in the air for her right now, I think this might devastate her. I have no idea how to tell her. What if she blames me? What do you think?'

I've never really been spoken to like this before by an adult. I mean, as one adult to another. Debbie is asking me my opinion as her peer. Is this what being twenty-one is like? Because I'm not totally sure I like it.

I open my mouth and then shut it again because I have no idea what to say. Natalie *will* be upset, that much is sure. She gets upset about most things. And this is a raw time in her life right now, when she's feeling extra lost and directionless. Honestly, sometimes with Nat it's hard to know what to take seriously in amongst the drama and hysterics, but I do know she's genuinely struggling. She's finishing her degree and she still doesn't have any idea what to do with her life. All the friends she's made in the last three years – Choi, Lydia, Julia,

Devinder, Laura, Mo, Other Zoe, and even Jamie – are all spreading out across the country. No one can afford to stay in London and no one can find a job in this mess of a financial climate. It's miserable and depressing and I totally get it. The last thing Natalie needs is her dad leaving her right now.

But there really is only one right answer.

'You just have to talk to her,' I say at last and Debbie's frown deepens. 'You have to be honest with her, that's all you can do. You're right, Deb, she probably will be upset, but she has you – and Sue – and it'll be OK.'

She sighs deeply. 'I know you're right,' she says at last. 'Sue says the same. I wish I had the same bravery I had at seventeen. I find difficult conversations so much harder, the older I get.'

'I'm really sorry about you and John,' I add softly.

'Thank you,' she says sincerely and then takes my hand. 'I'm glad Natalie has me and Sue – and you, as well.' She smiles, patting me nicely. 'She's very lucky to have a friend like you, Zoe. I've always thought that. I was so scared for her at school with all those idiots around her. Some of them were so cruel, posting things on her MySpace page about her being fat – all that mean bullying nonsense. I hated it and I hated that I couldn't help her without making everything worse. You saved her, my darling Zoe Darling, and I can never thank you enough for that.'

I feel a bit tearful and lean over to give Debbie a hug. She smells warm and familiar and comforting. I haven't had a mum for a long time and she's the closest thing I have to one. I guess I'm lucky in a lot of ways; some people don't even get that much.

'And you've turned into such a wonderful young woman.' She pulls away gently, still speaking emotionally. 'I'm so pleased about your new job, it sounds like the perfect place for you. I know you've always loved your music. They're very lucky to have you.'

'Thank you.' I nod, trying not to let this intimacy get to me. Deb's eyes are shiny.

'No, thank *you*, love,' she says, picking her wine glass back up. 'Thank you for listening. I'll do what you said, I'll speak to her this evening,'

'In that case, I'll get another bottle,' I say, getting up before she can see that my eyes are wet too.

* * *

TEXTING: ZOE DARLING

Tpped up my py as u go!

Well, that's 10p of it gone

Nat?

Srry, ws jst rplyng 2
all the txts Ive bn ignrng :)

Tkes ages 2 chck it's lss
thn 160 chrctrs

What? Are your
vowels broken?

No! It's txt spk, 2 sve mony & tme

Ugh jst got an alert -
nearly usd up all my top up alrdy :(

Damn, Nat, can you top up again?

Nat? You really should get a contract,
I get 250 texts a month

She's gone.

Good job you learned
text speak to save so
much money

6

2009

NATALIE

'How much exercise do you think I would have to do to get Michelle Obama's arms?' I ask, squeezing my hands into fists, looking for any hint of bicep muscle. Nothing happens.

'Is that the question you want to ask, since the first African American President was elected to lead the free world?' Zoe is being wry.

I consider this. 'Yes,' I reply with confidence.

'OK,' she says, nodding. 'Probably, like, fifty press-ups every morning. Then maybe another fifty before bed?'

'That sounds doable,' I say, making a mental note.

'How many can you do currently?' she asks nicely.

I roll off my sunbed to the pool edge and attempt one. With all my might I lower myself down but I can't get myself back up. Crap.

'So, half of one?' she says, sounding amused as I collapse on the hot tiles.

'I'll work on it,' I mutter, sweat forming over one eyebrow. I pull myself round into a seated position and dangle my feet in the pool. 'It's so hot, shall we get in?'

'I just have to finish this chapter,' Zoe says, turning a page.

While she's still absorbed, I shimmy as subtly as I can out of my shorts, side-eyeing the people around me for anyone who might be looking. It's all clear and I slip my T-shirt off in one move, simultaneously sliding towards the pool.

I don't *really* mind if Zoe sees my thighs or belly – I mean, she's seen them before and I don't think she judges me – but I would still rather get in the water while she's distracted.

We're on holiday in Portugal in honour of our twenty-second birthday and it's been a glorious few days so far. I mean, the actual destination is sort of irrelevant because we've just been lying by the hotel pool every day and then going into local bars and getting drunk every night. But it's warmer than it would be in the UK.

I launch myself through the water, causing a nearby kid with armbands to squawk and his mother to shoot me a dirty look. I think again that we should've chosen a child-free hotel. Every morning at the breakfast buffet we've had evil stares from harassed-looking parents as we slope in with minutes to go before breakfast ends, stinking of booze, with eyeliner all over our faces.

I do a couple of laps before getting bored and returning to the edge by Zoe. I can't get out yet, though, that takes too much psyching up. I look around at the other women by the pool, in all shapes and sizes. It blows my mind to see those who look like me, who don't seem to care. I watch them parade around in bikinis, all sorts of fleshy flesh rippling in every direction and they don't seem to mind. I don't understand how they can *like* themselves so easily; how they can laugh and smile and chat, while their bodies are so visible. I burn with jealousy. But I also pity them, because they'll feel so foolish when they eventually realise how wrong bodies like ours really are. Either way, the water is safe. Everyone looks distorted and rippled under the water. Water is the great equaliser.

The problem is getting in and out. That exposed few moments when you have to remove layers and hurry into the pool, without looking like you're hurrying. Looking like you're hurrying only draws attention to yourself.

I rest my arms on the surface and watch my boobs bob up and down on the water's surface before me. My sun-creamed arms sparkle in the sun, reflecting off the chlorinated water and I marvel at the effect.

'Do you think I look like a vampire?' I ask Zoe, who is still reading. She ignores me. 'Zo. *Zoe*?' I say louder until she sighs and lowers her book. 'Look at me sparkling! I'm like a Cullen.'

'You fucking better not be talking about *Twilight* again,' she warns, picking up her much more literary novel to shield her face.

'Er, no, not *Twilight*,' I hedge. 'The Cullens are a different thing that you don't know about.' I change the subject. 'What time is it anyway?'

'It's nearly six,' she says, checking her watch. 'We better go or we'll be late for the show.'

'Plus,' I say reprovingly, 'we had a formal agreement to drink every day from five at the latest.' Zoe puts her book down at last, picking up her towel, and I jump on the chance, quickly clambering out of the pool and pulling on my shorts and T-shirt.

Zoe collects the rest of our stuff, casually tying a see-through sarong around her stomach. No cover up for her. I wonder again how she finds that confidence. How does she just not care what people think of her? She is not so much smaller than me, but she doesn't mind. How is it possible?

Being so naked was the one thing I was afraid of when my parents offered to help pay for this trip out of divorce guilt. I kept suggesting cold places we could go – somewhere I wouldn't have to be semi-naked or sweating through leggings – but Zoe said we should be chavs for a week, lying in the sun with cocktails by a pool. I wanted to want that, but I've spent the weeks leading up to this in an absolute state of anxiety. I tried crash dieting and crash-exercising – if that's a thing – but nothing worked. So then I bought sixty-five different swimming costumes on my credit card and returned all but an ugly black one-piece that pulled me in and up in ways I didn't completely loathe.

The thing I don't get about swimwear is that men – the gender who don't even get judged on their bodies in the same way women do – are allowed to wear big, floaty, baggy shorts in the pool. Shorts that go down to their knees! Meanwhile, women – even women who have problem cellulitey, blobby thighs they hate – are expected to wear something that is essentially underwear around the pool. And they're expected to do so proudly, without shyness or self-hatred. Or else they're 'part of the problem'. It seems so unfair.

I've pretty much always been this shape, and I've pretty much always been unhappy about it. There were a couple of weeks last year when I felt a bit thin, just after Mum and Dad split up. For the first time in my life I didn't really think about food that much. I just wanted to lie around, feeling miserable. But that wore off within a few days and then I ate six Magnums in a row. Living with Mum, too, makes it impossible to diet. She makes the most amazing potato and pasta-based foods, and the chocolate cupboard is always full. It's the best and the worst part about living back at home.

I really need to get out of that house and take control of my life, but I'm still so broke. There's no way I can afford rent in London, not even sharing with half a dozen people again, like I did at uni.

On the plus side, I finally have a job. It's a shit job I hate, working in HR for an internet start-up, but it pays OK, and I might finally be able to start paying off some of my overdraft or my credit cards. There's even the remote possibility that I could one day afford to move out of Mum's. Imagine such a thing.

Zoe and I make our way to the hotel bar, where the evening's entertainment is starting. We're a few minutes late, so order our drinks quickly and find the only remaining table, which is – unfortunately – right up the front.

Which, of course, means we are immediately picked on.

'You go up,' I hiss at Zoe, who scoffs.

'Fuck off, no chance, *you* go up,' she retorts through gritted teeth.

'No *way*,' I say too loudly.

'I shall decide for you, ladies.' The creepy dude on stage sidles up to our table and hovers over us, his moustache twitching.

He regards each of us carefully, before offering a hand to Zoe.

I'm relieved but also feel the tiny sting of rejection. Zoe's always chosen.

The room erupts in cheers and encouragement, leaving her no room to refuse.

'I'm pretty sure I can't even *be* hypnotised,' I hear her mutter to The Great Hypno as he rounds the room, selecting a few other delighted volunteers.

'You five,' The Great Hypno booms dramatically, 'are my chosen, lucky few. Those intelligent and intuitive enough to be hypnotised. And you will now fall under my spell.' Turning to the audience The Great Hypno tells the room of his definitely-real expeditions to the Middle East, where he learned his trade from also-definitely-real magical gurus. I catch Zoe's eye and she discreetly mouths, 'I hate you' at me. I give her a happy thumbs up.

'You will now SLEEP,' the hypnotist shouts and all five heads on stage bob forward. Even Zoe's.

One by one, The Great Hypno gets his volunteers to do dumb stuff. One guy plays the air guitar, flipping his hair back and forth. Another barks like a dog on all fours. It's funny and stupid, and it's pretty obvious most of them are just going along with it out of embarrassment. Or possibly because of liquor. When he gets to Zoe, though, she looks genuinely out of it. Her face is slack and vacant, like she's not even really in there. The Great Hypno looks delighted and turns back to the audience.

'Let's put this subject to the test with some personal questions,' he says and waves his hands as if performing tricks. I try not to laugh, because – I'll be honest – he is not the most convincing stage performer. 'Any suggestions from you, lovely audience?'

'Ask her—' a hopeful young man with a deep sunburn yells out, '—who she fancies most in the room?'

'The barmaid,' Zoe replies blankly, with barely any hesitation.

The room turns towards the bar and a beautiful blonde freezes, midway through polishing a glass. She goes beetroot and a few people around the room titter. An older couple on the other side of my table glare furiously at me as if I'm ruining their evening. The woman, in her late sixties, leans towards me.

'People like you need help,' she hisses. 'Choosing to live the way you do is disgraceful. There are children here in this hotel.'

It takes me a moment to understand? Did I knock into her? Spill her drink? Kick her in the pool earlier?

She glowers up at Zoe now and oh, I understand. Zoe fancying a woman. She thinks we're a gay couple.

I feel a lump form in my throat, I'm so angry I might cry.

'You think being gay is a *choice*?' I ask, my throat constricted.

'Of course,' she sniffs, by way of reply.

I lean in. 'That's fascinating,' I say, innocently. 'So, when exactly did you *choose* to be straight?'

She scoffs. 'Don't be absurd, I didn't choose to be straight.'

'But I thought we got to choose our sexuality?' I feign confusion.

Her husband leans in. 'It's against God's will,' he snips.

I laugh, too loudly, missing another question for Zoe from the audience. 'I think you two are proof that sexuality can't be a choice,' I tell them. 'Because, let's face it, no one would ever *choose* to date either one of you, so it has to be biology.' The woman angrily narrows her eyes at me, so I keep going. 'And I definitely wouldn't choose to date men if I had a choice. I fancy men and it's the saddest thing in the world, believe me. If I had a choice, I'd fancy women every time.' I pause dramatically. 'Now please fuck off, you bigoted, homophobic morons.'

They get up hurriedly and leave, shooting me livid looks as they go.

I smile to myself, feeling proud of all the cool swearing I did.

Up on stage, Zoe is talking in the same blank way.

'I hate it,' she's saying calmly. What does she hate? What have I missed? Damn the idiots, ruining the show. She keeps going, 'It's awful and no one knows how I feel.'

The room oooohs like this is a big revelation and I look around, hoping for a clue. What don't I know? What does she hate? Is it me? What if it's me she hates and I had no idea?

The Great Hypno giggles in a high-pitched way and quietens the audience.

'A round of applause for the young lady and the rest of my volunteers,' he shouts and I want to ask what I missed, but it's too late. He's clicking the group out of it and the room is cheering. The dazed group staggers off stage and Zoe is back with me, looking embarrassed.

'What is it?' she asks, catching my facial expression and looking afraid. 'What did I do? Did he make me cluck like a fucking chicken?' She looks mortified. 'Please tell me he didn't. I don't remember what happened, it's all blurry.' She looks at me searchingly.

'Um,' I hedge. 'No chicken noises. Some guy barked, though.' I glance over at the man in question. 'It made him cuter; is that weird?'

'Yes,' she says then sucks on her cocktail straw. 'So what did I do? It's weird, I felt so fuzzy and far away.'

'You . . .' I begin carefully, 'you talked about the thing in your life that you hate.' I say, trying to keep it vague.

'Oh fuck!' she gasps. 'I did? Oh my God, I'm so embarrassed. I told the entire room about my job?'

My mouth falls open. This is news to me. Zoe is meant to be the success story around here; the one who has her career trajectory sorted. She's been working for HHH Records for over a year now and honestly, as far as I knew, it was the dream gig. She gets to hang around producers and musicians. She goes to fancy events and meets celebrities. She's helping the label make music – it's awesome! Everyone we know thinks it's the coolest job in the world. Her Facebook friend requests from old school enemies have shot through the roof since she was papped with George Sampson from *Britain's Got Talent*. I thought she was loving it – it's everything we ever dreamed for her. It's everything.

'Tell me what's going on,' I say softly, putting a hand on her arm.

She looks down, then shrugs. 'I was just in a dumb trance, I didn't mean it!' She smiles up and over my shoulder, trying to sound enthused. 'Why wouldn't I love my work? It's an incredible job, right? Working with pop stars, helping create music, making money doing something I love. A thousand people would kill to be in my position.' She pauses. 'I mean that literally – we had an intern recently who tried to poison an admin assistant so she could apply for her job. It's the dream.'

'That doesn't mean it's your dream,' I say gently. 'Talk to me, Zoe.'

She shakes her head. 'No, really, it's great, I'm fine, I ...' she trails off as she finally looks me directly in the eye.

Then she starts crying.

I scooch around with my chair until we're side by side, then put my arm around my crying friend.

'I know I *should* love it, I *should* be happy,' she whispers, despairingly. 'I don't know what's wrong with me. I'm so lucky and this is everything anyone could want. But I hate it. I wake up full of dread about going into work.' She wipes away a tear. 'I thought I'd be part of something magic. I thought I'd actually be able to see music being made and help – or at least help with the campaigns – but I'm not even allowed to talk to the head of marketing, never mind the producers or musicians.'

'Oh, Zo, I'm so sorry,' I say quietly, trying my best not to start crying, too. It hits me so hard seeing her emotional like this, but I'm trying to let her have her moment to be sad without taking over with my own histrionics.

'Do you know what I did last week?' she says between sobs. 'I spent all of Tuesday taking costumes from a music video to the dry cleaners and then all of Wednesday getting them back. On foot. My boss wouldn't even pay for me to get on the bus, never mind a taxi, so I had to walk. There were seventy-two backing dancers in that music video, Nat. Seventy-two costumes. By the end of Wednesday, the dry cleaner invited me to her wedding.' I pat her and make soothing noises as she keeps going. 'And that was actually a nice break from my normal routine, which is almost entirely spent tidying up after people, booking taxis for artists, and making endless cups of tea for Spotify reps. Spotify reps that I'm also not allowed to talk to, of course.'

'What's Spotify?' I crinkle my nose, but she ignores me.

'And I told you I was with George Sampson on the red carpet that time I got papped. But I wasn't. I was just walking past him at the event, dropping off shoes for one of our artists. She not only demands extra Christian Louboutins be on hand for her at award shows, but she insists that they've been "broken in" for her in the hours beforehand. Then I didn't even get to stay at the awards, they made me leave. And all the comments on the *Daily Mail* were calling me a predator because I was apparently looking at George funny in the picture.' She takes a deep breath, tears rolling down her cheeks. 'And obviously it's not really about the celebrities, Nat, I don't care about hanging out with celebs.' She swallows. 'But of course I do! I want to hang out with all the cool celebrities and become friends with Beyoncé! I promise I won't dump you for Bey, but she could hang out with us sometimes, right?'

'Of course she can,' I say generously.

I rub her back, waiting for more, but she seems to have run out of steam. We sit quietly for a few minutes, watching the other holidaymakers wandering around us, holding brightly coloured drinks, wearing brightly coloured clothes.

'It's funny, I thought you were all sorted and it was just me without a clue,' I say at last.

Zoe shakes her head. 'I have no idea what to do with my life.' She uses the tablecloth to wipe the corners of her eyes, but the tears have gone. 'If I don't like this job, what if I don't like anything? What if I'm just not suited to working in an office? Does that make me an entitled little cunt? If I don't ever want to work in my life?'

'Well . . .' I pause, then say, 'Yes. But I think most people feel that way.'

She laughs a little. 'I really thought this was it. I thought this job was going to make me happy. I should be happy.'

'Maybe you just need to find something else,' I say thoughtfully. 'Just because it's someone's dream job, doesn't mean it has to be your dream job.'

She sniffs sadly. 'Would you still love me if I wasn't a cool record label marketing assistant though?'

I hug her fiercely. 'Zo, I would love you if you were a self-service checkout machine.'

We stay there for another minute, holding on to each other.

'Shall we get very, very drunk?' she says at last, sounding more like herself.

'Indeed we shall,' I say grandly, releasing her. 'We have work to do this evening. Where are we on the tart chart?'

'You're winning. You got ten points for giving that boy who looked like Heath Ledger a handie last night.'

'RIP,' I say solemnly. 'Why don't you start by chatting up the sexy barmaid over there?' I suggest, biting my lip.

She looks at me in wonder. 'How did you know I fancied her?' she says, confused. 'It weirds me out when you read my mind.'

'I'm considering a career in stage magic,' I say authoritatively. 'Get me another cocktail while you're at it. If we don't end the night dry humping a unicorn pool float, we haven't tried hard enough.'

ZOE

It turns out it's actually quite difficult to dry hump a unicorn pool float. Particularly the dry part.

It's three in the morning and Natalie and I are illegally in the hotel pool, trying our very best to climb on the floats for a race. Alas, too much alcohol has been consumed and we're mostly just getting carpet burn from the squeaky plastic as we repeatedly slide off our respective inflatables.

The barmaid I've been snogging all night – name still unknown – let us in the pool area and is now asleep on a sunbed across the way. As is Richard, a random guy Natalie briefly kissed several hours ago, who's been trailing around after us ever since in the hopes of a blow job.

We're all an absolute mess, soaking wet and steaming drunk, but we're having the very best time.

'OK, I am actually on this time,' Natalie shouts, clinging for dear life to her unicorn. Its neck bends at an odd angle and suddenly she's sliding forward and off again, screaming loudly as she goes into the water.

It wakes Barmaid, who sits up with a start.

'Oh my God.' She looks around, bleary-eyed. 'What time is it?'

I swim over, laughing at her sweet confusion, and pull myself out of the water.

'It's gone three,' I tell her, leaning over to kiss her cheek. 'How do you still look so great at this hour?' She smiles hazily and pulls me in for a proper kiss. She tastes like chlorine and I realise that's probably me, not her.

'I'm a mess,' she replies, pulling away at last and laughing as she hides her face behind her hands.

She really is beautiful.

'Will you two stop being so adorable?' Natalie shouts from the pool. She's back on the float and seems to have finally found some kind of balance. 'It's not fair, you guys being that cute, while that idiot over there, who belongs to me, is snoring his head off.' She points at Richard, who is open-mouthed wheezing on his sunbed, the noise rumbling around the pool. Barmaid snorts and picks up her handbag.

'Are you working all this week?' I ask, as she hunts for her phone. 'I really want to see you again, but we leave on Saturday.'

Barmaid grins. 'I've got tomorrow off,' she says and reaches to tuck some hair behind my ear. It's such an intimate thing to do and it makes me feel amazing.

'Oh great,' Natalie yells joyfully. 'I love being the third wheel. It'll be great watching you two snogging each other's faces off for the rest of this holiday.' She's laughing, happily. I can tell she likes Barmaid. And I do, too. I really like her. She's sweet and cool and kind. And suuuuper pretty.

Now I just need to figure out her name.

'Oi, Richard,' Natalie's shouting from her unicorn. 'Richard, wake up please. You and me are going to have to hang out some more this week so Zoe can snog her hot new friend.' She pauses. 'RICHARD WAKE UP, I'M READY TO GIVE YOU THE BLOW JOB NOW.'

He does wake up at this and looks around in a daze, like he has no clue how he got there. 'Did someone say blow job?' he slurs, wiping dried dribble off his chin.

'Yep,' Natalie says. 'Might as well, eh.'

He stands up, suddenly wide awake. 'Great, shall we do it in the pool?'

Natalie laughs. 'Sure, we can give it a go and see who drowns first. If you can catch me on my great steed.' She starts paddling away and he leaps into the water, fully clothed. She shrieks with laughter as he starts swimming after her.

Barmaid giggles at the interaction, but seems distracted by her phone.

'Everything OK?' I ask, a little concerned.

'Oh yeah,' she says, smiling. 'It's just Silvia, she's super mad at me for not coming home tonight.'

'Silvia?' I scan my memory banks for any mention of a Silvia. It doesn't ring a bell. 'Is she your flatmate?'

Barmaid throws her head back and laughs. 'No, she's my girlfriend, silly.'

'Your what?' I feel cold.

'My girlfriend,' she repeats a little impatiently, and strokes my hair. Her hands no longer feel good touching me and I resist the urge to slap her away. 'But don't worry, she doesn't have any idea where I am. She just thinks I'm working late. She's not going to come find us and beat you up or anything!' She laughs again and I stare at her with new eyes.

She has a girlfriend. A girlfriend who apparently has no idea Barmaid is out with another woman, kissing and making plans. She's not sweet or cool or kind, she's a cheater.

'Do you have, like, an open relationship or something?' I ask carefully, moving away from her and grabbing a towel to wrap around myself. I realise I'm trembling a little bit.

'No.' She shakes her head, still looking amused. 'But we barely ever have sex any more and she's such hard work. She's always on my case about something. I'm allowed to have fun, aren't I?'

I turn on her, immediately furious. 'You're a fucking cheater!' I shout and the pool suddenly falls silent. 'What is wrong with you? That is disgusting.' I'm almost spitting I'm so angry.

Her face goes white. 'Woah,' she says, still trying to smirk a bit. 'I was just having a bit of fun. It's really none of your business how I live my life or what I do in my relationship.'

I am red hot with rage. 'It fucking *is* when you drag me into it! You made me an accessory to you treating your girlfriend like shit. There's seriously something wrong with you.'

'Hey,' Barmaid attempts to sound more conciliatory, 'don't be like this, Zoe, we can have some fun. What she doesn't know won't hurt her.' She stands up and takes a step towards me.

'Get away from me,' I say and my voice is dangerously low. 'I mean it, fuck off. Go home to your poor girlfriend, I hope I never see you again. And I hope she dumps you and finds someone who doesn't treat her like she's nothing. You are the lowest of the low.'

Barmaid makes a humph noise. 'Whatever. *God*,' she says as she picks up her stuff, 'who knew you'd be such a drama queen.' She leaves without another word and I stand there, watching her go, shaking with fury.

'Are you OK?' Natalie whispers in a worried voice, after a minute. She's made her way over to my side of the pool and now lifts herself out. I slump down next to her.

'Can you believe her?' I ask furiously. 'I hate cheaters so much. If you're not happy, just fucking leave, y'know? End it. Don't cheat, there's no reason for it. I hate that I just got used. I hate that I got pulled into something that could really hurt someone else, and I didn't get a choice in that. It's really uncool.'

We fall silent again, but I'm still breathing hard, my chest feeling tight.

'Is it because of your mum?' Nat says at last, in a soft voice. 'I mean, is it because she cheated on your dad? Is that why you get so angry about it?'

I stare at the ground. 'Maybe,' I admit, watching an ant make its way across the tiles on the edge of the pool. 'I don't know.' I pause. 'But you saw me back then, you saw my dad. The whole family was a wreck after what she did to us. And Dad is still on his own and scared to trust anyone. I just don't understand how a person can do that to another person. And that barmaid didn't even seem to feel bad! She could be ruining someone else's life and she didn't care. I'm clearly not the first; I bet she cheats on her girlfriend all the time. There's no excuse for it, none.' I take a deep breath. 'Sorry, I just feel so sucker-punched. I thought she was a nice person.'

'She might've been a nice person,' Natalie says slowly. 'I mean, in some ways! Sometimes we get messed up and we mess up. Maybe she's been doing it for so long, she's forgotten how unfair it is. When we feel guilty about stuff, sometimes we have to put it in a box, or it would kill us. Maybe she puts her cheat-guilt into a box and is nice in all other parts of her life.' She throws her hands up in the air. 'Or maybe she's a total sociopath who delights in causing pain – what do I know? I just don't want you to let what your mum did affect how you see people. Sometimes we do things we shouldn't, or even *become* something we shouldn't. But I think there's a lot of grey in life.'

'Not with cheating,' I say harshly. 'That's black and white. You just don't. If you want to be with someone else, then end your relationship.'

'OK . . .' She nods supportively and I realise Richard's still standing awkwardly in the middle of the pool, trousers round his knees.

'Read the room, Richard,' Natalie says, sighing loudly. 'The blow-job window has closed, it's not going to happen. Off you go.' Richard looks a bit sad, but nods resignedly and wades towards the edge of the pool.

'Bye, Richard,' I say feeling slightly bad for ruining his good time.

He gives a forlorn wave as he gets out, fully clothed and dripping wet as he exits the pool area.

'Parents fuck you up, huh?' I say after he's gone, giving Nat a small smile.

'Oh sure.' She grins. 'I've become extremely fragile since learning I'm from a broken home. But I have to say, my parents have been *quite* generous since Dad moved out. And – to be honest – I've never seen Mum happier. She and Sue spend all their time giggling and watching *Big Brother*.' She pauses. 'I mean, they did that all the time before, too, but I can tell Mum feels freer without Dad in the house. He could be quite an oppressive presence, even from the armchair in the corner.'

She shrugs before adding sincerely, 'And I guess we wouldn't be here without our parents.'

'That's so wise,' I say, wide-eyed. 'You're right, we should be thanking them for giving us life and existence! Without them, what would we be? Floating around this universe as formless souls? Or would we be *other people*? We wouldn't be anything without them!'

Natalie looks a bit awkward. 'Oh, er,' she hums. 'I actually meant here on this holiday, y'know, since they paid for us.'

'Right.' I nod, trying to sober up a bit. 'I get it. Sorry I'm such a mess.'

'Oh Christ,' Natalie half-laughs. 'Don't apologise for that. So, you're a mess – I'm a mess, too. Literally everyone's a mess at twenty-two, aren't they?'

'But people keep acting like I've got it sorted!' I sigh, frustrated. 'They look at me like I'm a grown-up, and I don't feel like one at all. When is adulthood meant to kick in? When do I stop feeling stuck and sweaty all the time? I feel really lost, Nat, honestly.'

'Well, so do I!' She looks suddenly alert. 'I live at home in my old kid-bedroom with my about-to-be-divorced mother. I work in a temp HR job, where my work is mostly disciplining male managers for Googling porn on their office computers. Oh, and as if that wasn't crappy enough, I've also never been in love and am too fat to be fanciable.'

'Oi!' I'm cross again. 'Please stop calling yourself names. Fat is a natural thing your body makes to fuel the body and insulate you. It's like moaning you have fingers on your hands, or hair on your head. Everyone's got fat. Some people have more, some have less. Who cares? There's no point in hating yourself over something so arbitrary and pointless. And you'd never be mean to someone else over their looks, so stop doing it to yourself.'

Natalie pouts. 'Like it's so easy to ignore a lifetime of conditioning.'

I sit back down so I can see her better. 'You can reprogramme yourself, Nat,' I say softly. 'But you have to start by being kinder to yourself. Treat *you* like you're your own best friend. You wouldn't call me names or insult my appearance, would you?'

'Of course not!' She looks shocked. 'But you're my best friend, so I'll have to be my own second-best friend. Does that still work?'

'Sure,' I say, nodding, confidently and we sit quietly for a few seconds before I speak again. 'Hey, Nat, do you ever think we're friends mostly because everyone else in the world is so awful?'

'Hmm.' She looks a bit sleepy. 'Maybe. But I'm pretty sure I'm awful, too. Humans are all awful. Apart from Barack Obama who is a sexy, sexy saint.'

'I hope he doesn't turn out to have molested a White House intern,' I muse.

'Shut your mouth!' She looks outraged. 'He would never.'

'Quite right,' I reply, lying back on a sun lounger. 'Thanks for always setting me straight, Nat. I'm having the best holiday, cheating barmaids aside. And fuck her, I don't need anyone but you, anyway.'

She lies down next to me. 'OK, that's really nice.' Her eyes are closed. 'But I do need more than just you. I really want a boyfriend.'

7

2010

NATALIE

'When you had sex with that man, that one time,' I begin and she cuts me off.

'Ew, please don't remind me.' She visibly cringes.

'No, no, come on,' I say, side-eyeing her. 'You liked it, remember? You definitely did. Don't pretend you didn't.'

She makes a disagreeable noise but doesn't actively deny it. I know she doesn't like to think about that night. She identifies as a lesbian and I think it confuses her too much to think about what happened when she was eighteen. Plus – as I often say to her – who would have sex with straight men if they didn't have to?

'So,' I repeat determinedly. 'When. You. Had. Sex. With. That. Man.'

She sighs deeply. 'Yes?'

'What did you . . . like . . . do?' I finish lamely.

She narrows her eyes at me. 'What did we *do*?' she says, perplexed. 'What do you think we did?' She pauses. 'Wait, are you rebranding again, as a virgin? Because you spent a fucking long time trying to shake off that label. You can't tell me you're starting again.'

I pick up a pretty blue bra, rubbing its knotty, lacey material. And then I drop it when I see the labels. The nice ones are only ever available in sizes up to a D. I wander further down the aisle, looking out for the large, ugly boulder-holders that will cost twice the price and be half as nice.

We're emergency bra shopping ahead of tonight's party. We were doing a fashion show over at Zoe's flat, trying on birthday outfits, and I realised the slutty dress I wanted to wear urgently required a strapless bra. They're not usually my friend – ending up somewhere around my belly button within an hour – but Zoe insisted M&S had sturdy ones that would work.

I shake my head hard. 'No, I'm not starting again with sex, but it's different with Joe.' I wait for a nearby woman to move off along the aisle before I continue, pleadingly, 'With other boys it didn't matter that I only know two moves, because I was just in it for the short-term wee-wee—'

'Please don't refer to a penis as a wee-wee,' she interjects. 'If even I – a woman who doesn't really like them – can say penis, you can say penis.'

I pull a face. 'Ugh, it's just so clinical,' I complain. '*Penis*. Ugh. Willy sounds too silly, and knob or dick just sound insulting. What else do I call it?'

'Urethra sausage roll?' she offers and I consider it.

'Too much of a mouthful.'

'No pun intended,' she points out dryly and I nod. 'Pig in a blanket?' she suggests next.

'That just makes me hungry.' I shake my head. 'And being hungry and horny are not a great combination. Plus, Joe says we shouldn't have sex after eating because he worries I might get farty near his wee-wee.'

Zoe says nothing and I feel a beat of anxiety pulse through me. I can tell she's on the fence about Joe, even though she hasn't even met him yet. That's happening tonight and I'm so incredibly nervous. What if they don't like each other? What would I do? Because I'm really, really into Joe. He's ridiculously handsome and clever. It blows my mind that he's interested in ugly, stupid little me.

'So, wait, what are you asking me about sex?' She gives up on the wee-wee debate.

I sigh. 'I just really want to be amazing at it,' I explain earnestly. 'Like, see, most of the time – with the others – I just lay there making noises. Or maybe sometimes I got on top if they let me keep my T-shirt on, but I know there's a whole ton of other positions out there and I want to keep Joe interested in me. I really like him, Nat. I've never felt like this before.'

'I might be the wrong person to ask about sex with men,' she says kindly. 'But, that one night—' resigned sigh '—I guess I just went with whatever felt good. Same as I do with women. It isn't a choreographed dance, you don't have to go through certain positions and finish with jazz hands. I think you just have to let go and do what feels good for you both.'

'Zoe,' I make a face, 'that speech was really "sex ed with Miss Cornelisse".'

'Yeah, sorry.' She looks embarrassed. 'I guess what I'm trying to say is: if you're both having a great time and you can lose yourself in the moment, then it's probably going to be good sex, whatever position you're in.'

'How do you *lose yourself*?' I am amused. 'What the hell are you talking about?' I adopt a mocking tone. 'Oh yeah, I'm always losing myself in moments. Oh, those moments, they're always lost and I can't find them, it's so cool. Where are you, moments? I've lost you again.'

'Fuck you!' She says and laughs. 'OK. Well, clichés aside, I don't think you should overthink sex. It's meant to be fun.'

'It's not fun,' I say determinedly. 'That's a lie sold by, like,

Ann Summers and *Cosmo*. Sex is nice but it's not fun. There's too much to think about. Like, do I have the energy in the first place? And who's going to initiate it? Then it's the worry about who's going to suggest a condom and at what point in the proceedings? And, of course, what to say when he *doesn't* suggest wearing one, and how to stay sexy when he then says he'd rather not wear it and that he can't get a hard-on with one on. Oh, and then you've got the awkwardness of the act itself, where you're under pressure to act like you don't care what you look like naked. I have to pretend I'm fine taking all my clothes off in front of someone else, when I don't even like doing it alone. Then I have to act like my tummy isn't bouncing around, slapping into *his* tummy when we're doing it, and all the while having to pretend it's all super sexy and that I'm lost in *the moment*. And that's even before you get to the bit where you have to either pretend you had an orgasm or when he says, "You came, right?" decide whether to lie or awkwardly say no and then deal with his look of disappointment. And it's not even disappointment with himself, it's disappointment in *my* failure.' I pause to address the look on Zoe's face. 'Before you say it, yes, I have tried telling men beforehand that I don't orgasm during sex but weirdly, that just makes them think they don't need to bother with foreplay, which surely is the opposite of what I'm saying?'

'I worry about you, Nat.' She shakes her head. 'Is there any point in me saying yet again how beautiful you are? And reminding you that, honest to God, no decent man gives a shit about your stomach?'

'Lies,' I say conversationally, picking up a plain black bra and holding it against myself in the mirror. I'm unconvinced it has the structural integrity required. 'Of course they give a shit. If *I* care, they must care. But that's not the issue at hand,

Zoe. I just want you to tell me what the sexiest positions are that also hide my tummy. Positions that he'll like so much, he'll stay with me despite everything I'm not bringing to the table.'

'Does it matter if you actually like these sex acts?' she questions dryly.

'Not really,' I say sincerely. 'Sex is mostly for him anyway.'

'That's incredibly fucked-up thinking, Nat,' she tells me sharply.

'Is it?' I am genuinely surprised.

'Shall I lend you the *Kama Sutra* or something?' she says, a bit exasperated. 'Is that what you're asking for here?'

'Maybe not that extreme,' I muse. The other shopper is back, touching up that blue bra. I lean in closer to Zoe, speaking in a conspiratorial whisper. 'I stole this book from my mum's bedside table the other night, and it is totally shocking. By someone called Louise Bagshawe – and oh my God, Zo, there's so much boning. The women in those books all like being strung up from the ceiling and spanked with whips and told to effing shut the eff up. Do you think Joe would like that kind of thing?'

'You super need to move out of Deb's house,' she points out, knowing full well I still can't afford to. 'And no, I don't think you should be suggesting bondage this early on with Joe. How many dates have you had so far?'

'Six,' I say proudly. 'I think he's going to ask me to be his girlfriend soon.'

'And how's the sex been with him so far?'

'Great!' I say, in a slightly brittle voice. 'I mean, lots of the normal stuff but also . . . um, he really likes doggy – I mean *really* likes it – which is fine but I do have to go to the loo afterwards to cry because doggy makes me feel really weird. I know it's stupid, but I feel like he doesn't want to look at me and that I'm an animal or just a hole to bang himself into.' I pause before adding quickly, 'But that's totally on me, that's my issue, because I know doggy is a popular one.'

'Maybe you could ask Other Zoe or Jamie or someone else about doggy?' she bites her lip, looking sorry for me. 'Straight sex sounds kind of awful and I don't know what to suggest. I like looking at faces, so I can't imagine turning away from each other in sex. Most of the best stuff is on the front.'

There is a silence as I consider what she's said. To be honest, I have already had this conversation with Other Zoe and Jamie. And Choi and Mo. I like to have the same chat with several different people, to compare notes and advice. Then I can pick and choose the parts I want to listen to. Although, to be honest, they mostly all said the same sort of thing.

'Well, either way,' she says cheerfully, 'I'm really looking forward to meeting him. What time is he joining us?'

'I'm not sure,' I admit, checking my watch. 'He said he'd pop down at some point, super casual. I told him there was no pressure. You know, it's a big deal, coming along to our birthday drinks and meeting all my friends, I don't want to put him under any pressure at all.'

'I'm sure he'll want to meet everyone,' she says encouragingly. 'And we'll be nice, I promise. Who else have you invited? Are any of your other new workmates coming down?'

'No, I don't think so.' My brow creases into a frown. 'Am I allowed to fraternise with the team, do you think?'

She shrugs. 'You're the HR rep, you tell me. And, I mean, you're dating one of your co-workers. I guess if that's allowed, so is friendly drinking?'

Shit, will I get fired for dating Joe? We've been keeping our romance on the downlow in the office, but I thought that was just while we were still trying to figure out if he liked me or not. What if it's against the rules? This company doesn't really seem that into firing people. We had a guy in the HR cubicles the other day who'd been bombarding female employees with requests for photos of their feet. But he said a foot fetish is a medical condition so he was let off with a verbal warning.

Maybe I should get into feet? It seems pretty popular.

Seeing my worried expression, Zoe puts her arm around me, laughing. 'I'm sure it's fine, don't worry! You're definitely allowed to socialise with people. It sounds like a pretty fun company. Are you enjoying it?'

'I guess so.' I feel a little unsure of my answer. 'It's nice to be earning some money at long last and it's probably a good thing, having a bit of structure to my life. But I really never thought I'd end up working in HR. I only meant to do it as a placeholder job for a bit, y'know, to ease into office life while I tried to think of something I actually really wanted to do. And I definitely didn't picture myself doing HR for some random new internety messaging company based in America. It'll probably shut down in five minutes.' I gasp as a thought occurs to me. 'Oh God, what if I have to fire the whole team when this business *does* fail? Or what if they want to move the whole team to the US and Joe wants to go but I don't?'

'Maybe try not to overthink it?' she says nicely, picking up a simple strapless bra in my size and holding it up to me. 'Hey, this one would work?'

'I'll try it on.' I take it from her and we look around for the changing rooms sign. 'Hey, remember when we went bra shopping that very first time?'

She laughs. 'When we were fifteen?' She nods at the memory. 'Isn't it weird how bra shopping changes as you get older? Like, that trip back then was about finding the most padded bra possible. We wanted our boobs to look the biggest they could. These days it's about finding something that keeps them still, doesn't hurt your back and avoids angry strap burns on your shoulder.'

'Do you remember those silicone, chicken fillet insert thingies?' I wince at the memory of the feel of them; cold, blobby gel that seemed doomed to burst if a boy put his hands anywhere near them. Not that any boy did.

'Of course.' Zoe grimaces. 'And I also very much remember one of mine falling out at the Valentine's Day disco in year eleven, and not noticing until Semen Stain, Romesh and Tom discovered it over by the food table.'

'Oh yeah!' I'm delighted by the traumatic memory. 'They played catch with it for twenty minutes, and then demanded the girls all line up in a row so they could see whose boobs were uneven.'

'Thankfully most boobs were uneven at sixteen,' she breathes out, reliving her relief.

'Mine still are,' I confirm, as we join the changing-room queue.

ZOE

It's nearly midnight – the time when people are starting to peel away for kebabs and last tubes – before the elusive Joe finally shows up.

Standing at the bar, I clock him immediately, recognising his face from the hundreds of Facebook photos Nat's shown me these past few weeks. He glances around a little awkwardly at the remaining drunk stragglers and I feel a pang of pity. It must be terrifying walking into something like this – meeting all these people already connected to each other, all waiting to judge him. But the pity is quickly followed by irrational hatred. Who does this guy think he is? He better be fucking amazing if he's dating my Natalie.

Make an effort be nice make an effort be nice make an effort be nice.

I take a deep breath and steel myself to go over for introductions.

'OH MY GOD! CHOI AND LYDIA ARE SNOG-GING!' Natalie is suddenly in my ear, breathless with the latest news from the drunken frontline.

Of course those two are snogging; they've both been doing shots all night and both are newly single and vulnerable.

'Gross,' I say casually as a thrilled Natalie points an excitable finger over at the bar where Other Zoe, Jamie, Devinder, and my travelling friend, Hayley, have formed a circle around the oblivious couple. There are tongues and glasses of green booze flying everywhere.

'Hey,' I nudge Nat, 'Joe just got here.' She looks up at me, wide-eyed; the Choi and Lydia spell broken.

'What?' she shrieks and I nod at the door where Joe is still looking around, nervously hopping from foot to foot. Nat's whole face lights up.

'JOEEEEEEEEEE!' she screams at the top of her lungs, throwing herself across the room. 'You're here! Come, come and meet everyone.'

Clinging to his arm, she guides him back towards me.

'This is my best friend in the whole universe!' she declares proudly and he swallows hard, looking overwhelmed and wincing from the grip on his bicep.

'Hi, Joe!' I say too loudly. 'I'm Zoe.'

He nods seriously. 'Hello,' he says in a low voice that

sounds fake. Like he's going for a Christian Bale Batman vibe.

Up close, he's handsome enough, I guess, if you're into penises. Lots of hair that he obviously attends to with loving care, and small blue eyes that peek out under curtains that haven't been cool since 1999.

'Nat talks about you a lot,' he continues, a type of fondness in his voice, and I soften slightly.

It's the first time since Semen Stain that I've seen Natalie actually really into anyone and I so want him to be a decent guy. I want to like him, I really do. I want us to be able to hang out together as a three, without any awkwardness or third wheel comments. But more than that, Nat *deserves* someone amazing; someone who adores her and looks after her, and reassures her even on those days when she's really anxious for no reason. She deserves someone who challenges her and comforts her. Someone who laughs *with* her, not at her, when she gets Craigslist and *Schindler's List* confused.

Maybe it could be Joe?

'To be fair, I talk about her a lot, too.' I laugh as nicely as I can. Natalie beams at me, clearly delighted with this minimal exchange.

'I would introduce you to the others, Joe,' Nat stage whispers, leaning in, 'but they're all KISSING each other!' She jabs over at the rest of our friends, who are collectively hypnotised by Choi and Lydia's increasingly frantic PDA.

'Oh?' Joe looks a bit nonplussed.

'OH MY GOD!' Jamie has now arrived. 'DO YOU GUYS KNOW CHOI AND LYDIA ARE KISSING?' she slurs, slumping an arm over my shoulders.

'OH MY GOD, I KNOW!' Natalie shouts happily back.

'Who's this guy?' Jamie squints at Joe, regarding him critically.

'This is *Joe*,' Natalie says proudly, standing taller.

'Oh,' Jamie says and grins. 'Joe. The infamous *Joe*-Joe. You're here at last; we didn't think you were going to show up.'

He shrugs, looking uncomfortable again. 'I had another thing I had to go to.'

'No, it's fine!' Natalie says quickly, sounding panicked and shooting Jamie a warning look. 'It's more than fine. I'm just happy you're here.' There is a pause and Natalie rushes to fill the silence. 'Jamie's my friend from uni. Most of that lot over there are.'

He nods, disinterestedly.

'So you guys met at work?' Jamie jumps in, and Joe nods.

'Yeah, I've been there a couple of years now,' he confirms, his voice proud. 'I'm a project manager.'

This is a title I've heard a lot since I became a grown-up, and I still don't know what it means. Same with 'consultant'. It really feels like only men have those job titles.

'Joe just got promoted!' Natalie interjects, sounding proud. 'He's now on the bonus scheme and has a company car.'

'Ew,' says Jamie, screwing up her nose. I agree with her; bonus schemes and company cars – it all just sounds so adult and seedy.

'CHOI'S BEING SICK.' Devinder joins us now, holding her drink aloft and swaying slightly.

'Do you think it was Lydia's tongue?' Jamie sniggers and Natalie giggles. Joe looks horrified because he's not one of us and fuck him.

'Are you Joe?' Devinder acknowledges the stranger and he nods, exhausted.

'Do you LOVE Natalie?' she continues and I elbow her.

'Don't be a dickhead,' I hiss at her knowing Natalie will be mortified, but she smirks. It's possible that introducing Joe to this group of idiots after a heavy night of boozing was a mistake. I can see the same thought occurring to Natalie now and she fake-laughs a little hysterically.

'We've only been on six dates!' she says in a high pitch, not daring to look at Joe.

'Um, project manager sounds, er, cool, Joe?' I try to save the conversation. 'Does that make you one of Natalie's bosses?' He looks amused by this.

'No, she's in the HR department, nothing to do with the work I do,' he explains, just as we're interrupted again.

'Has anyone seen Choi?' Lydia bundles into our circle, eyes barely open and her dress done up wrong at the back. 'He was being sick in the ladies' loo but now he's gone? I think I love him.'

'You *don't* love him!' Jamie rolls her eyes.

'Most of the time you don't even *like* him,' Devinder snorts.

'I FUCKING DO LOVE HIM,' Lydia shouts back, stumbling a bit on the spot. 'Also, he said he was getting me a drink and I don't have any money, so I need him.'

'Um, hey Joe, have I told you what Zoe does for work?' Natalie interjects frantically, trying to distract from the collective hot messes around us. 'She works in music!'

'Oh?' He turns to me, looking more interested. 'What kind of thing?'

'She *was* working in music marketing,' Natalie continues, not waiting for me to answer. Next to us, Lydia and Jamie are shouting at each other about oxytocin and blood-alcohol levels. 'But she's now in Artist Relations, which means she works directly with the musicians. She makes sure they're happy, gets them anything they need and organises parties for them and stuff. She gets invited to literally every bar, hotel and club opening ever! It's so cool.'

'Do you get VIP Glastonbury tickets?' Joe moves closer and I internally roll my eyes. Everyone I know – and everyone I don't know – wants fucking Glasto tickets from me.

'Um, yes,' I say slowly. 'But the job is more about keeping our artists content, so it's a lot of event organising and sending champagne.'

'It is *super* awesome!' Natalie enthuses as Lydia starts vomiting into an ice bucket at a nearby table.

'It's been quite a tricky transition though,' I add quickly. I don't want this man to be impressed by me. I know it's unfair, but I don't like him.

'Oh yes.' Natalie pulls a sympathetic face. She turns to Joe again. 'Zoe had a bit of a rough time getting here. She was so brave, quitting her previous job – her nan was so mad! – but she knew it wasn't right for her and she was unhappy. So she took a leap and changed career paths within the music industry. Don't you think that's brave?' He nods half-heartedly.

'I don't know about brave,' I add awkwardly. 'But yeah, I had to admit that what I thought was a dream job, er, really wasn't. I was pretty miserable. It was a tough decision but I didn't want to lie in bed every night for twenty years, dreading the next morning.' Natalie looks at the floor and I feel bad for hitting what I can see is a nerve. 'Anyway,' I add quickly, breezily, 'it wasn't easy, but I'm glad it happened.'

'Scars remind us where we've been, they don't have to dictate where we're going,' Joe says, looking sombre.

'Wow, that's so wise,' I say politely. 'Who said that? Was it Anne Frank?'

'David Rossi from *Criminal Minds*,' he nods.

'That dude with the goatee in the serial killer show?' I am hesitant.

'That's right.' He slow blinks.

'Anyway,' Natalie says quickly, 'Zoe's amazing for figuring it out, because most of us still are, right? But that's what being young is all about! Making those bad choices, owning up to them, and trying to get things right next time.'

'Experience is the most brutal of teachers but you learn, my God, do you learn,' Joe says in the same guru tone of voice.

'Is that David Rossi, too?' I ask politely.

'No,' he scoffs. 'It's C.S. Lewis, actually.'

'Right!' I'm impressed. Maybe Joe does have other levels to him after all.

'Yeah,' he nods. 'They quoted it on an episode of *Criminal Minds*.'

'Oh.'

There's an awkward silence until Lydia loudly throws up again beside us. 'Maybe I should take her to the loo,' I say at last, when no one else volunteers.

'Ugh,' Jamie grunts. 'I guess I'll come help.' We take an arm each and stagger towards the loo, Lydia a dead weight between us.

'Are we going to find Choi?' she asks us sleepily as we queue for a cubicle. Jamie tells her to shut up and we lug her in before taking a seat on the sinks.

'He seems like an idiot, doesn't he?' I say at last as Jamie examines her mascara.

'Who, Choi?' She rifles through her bag.

'No,' I say impatiently, 'this Joe guy. What the fuck was that David Rossi shit?'

She shrugs. 'I don't know, I've never watched *Criminal Minds*.'

'Well, I have,' I say huffily. 'And I can tell you, that character's main contribution to solving the crimes is telling everyone he's been married loads of times. Why would you pick him to be your hero?'

'I dunno.' She shrugs again. 'But he doesn't seem that bad. He's all right looking. Bit quiet and boring, maybe. But we're very loud, so he—'

'I think he seems like a prick,' I interrupt decisively and she stops applying lipstick and smirks at me in the mirror.

'Well, you would,' she says. 'No one would be good enough for your friend. Plus, you're probably worried he's going to steal her away from you.'

'Shut up,' I say defensively. 'That's not it at all. I want her to be happy and she's wanted to find a boyfriend for as long as I've known her. But she's too eager to please him, too puppy dog around him. Did she tell you she's joined that stupid Twitter website thing? It's because he told her to.'

Jamie scrunches up her eyes. 'What, that dumb hundred-and-forty-character social thing? What is even the point of it?'

'Exactly!' I say, feeling validated. 'Natalie's always said she'll live and die Facebook. When Twitter started she swore hot vengeance on its "pointless" existence. But apparently Joe told her Facebook is for "mums and losers".'

'He's not wrong.' Jamie nods at her reflection.

'I hate him,' I mutter petulantly.

'DO YOU LOVE HIM?' Natalie suddenly bursts into the loos and I jump a foot in the air. 'You love him, right?' she continues breathlessly and Jamie smirks at me again.

'He's . . . fun,' I say as genuinely as I can. 'It's great to see you happy, Nat, just really . . . great. Great.'

'I hope we haven't scared him off with our drunkenness.' Nat pulls a face as Lydia starts retching in her loo cubicle again. 'We can be quite intense as a group, can't we? Do you think he minded? Do you think he likes me? I can't believe Devinder asked him if he loved me, oh my God, right? I'm going to kill her.' She is breathless with excitement.

'Look, Natalie,' I say impulsively, turning to take her hands, 'let's move back in together, huh? My rental contract is up at the end of next month, so we can find a little two-bed flat to rent together. I loved living with you when you were at uni, and you really need to get out of your mum's house.'

'Are you serious?' She looks blindsided. I am a little bit, too – I didn't know I was going to say it until I was saying it. But I really want this to happen. I feel like I'm losing her already and she's not even properly dating this Joe guy. 'But . . . but . . .' She is frowning. 'I can't afford it.'

'I can subsidise your rent a bit,' I say quickly. 'Until you start making better money. My income is OK and you know my dad gives me a bit every month as well. I can cover the deposit, too.'

'Oh my God!' Nat is scrambling but then looks up, shiny-eyed. 'Oh my God, YES! I loved living with you, that would be amazing! Yes yes yes!' She beams at Jamie, who looks amused. 'A boyfriend *and* a new flat! Maybe this is finally adulthood!'

'Doubt it,' Jamie mutters.

* * *

WHATSAPP

To: Zoe Darling

Hey, it's me!!

Oh man, do I really have to use this app?

Yes.

Don't be grumpy about technology,
you sound like Nanny Surrey

But why is it any different to
text messaging?

It's free, and you can send pics etc

Just go with it

It'll never take off. What's even the point.

What are these blue ticks about?

But OK fine

Oh, just to warn you, someone took a shit
on the communal stairs in our new building.

OMG WHAT!

What do you mean someone?

You mean a person? Please tell
me you don't mean a person?

It's under investigation

It might be a dog

I hope it's a dog

I'm so happy I moved in with you.

8

2011

NATALIE

'Wait, stop, I can't breathe,' I wheeze, and even saying those five words is too much. 'Please, Zoe? ZOE! Zoeeeeeeeee.' She doesn't hear me and I'm losing her. She's going, gone, off into the distance. Happy and oblivious to what's happening to me.

I keel over, bent double, trying to get my lungs to cooperate but they hurt too much. They feel like they're bleeding inside me.

So, this is what it's like to die.

I always wondered. And I always knew I'd die young.

I guess, at least it'll be dramatic? The *Daily Mail* will probably write about me – I'm young and middle class enough for them to care. Although the comments section will call me fat. People will cry, my friends will cry, everyone will cry. Zoe will feel terrible she left me – *abandoned me* – in my moment of need. She'll be wracked with guilt. But then I'll return to her in a dream to reassure her that I don't blame her and let her know she can move on and forgive herself. Of course she won't be able to.

My parents will be devastated. Maybe they'll even be united in grief? They'll lean on each other, realise their love was buried under there all along and get back together. And this time Dad will care and make an effort – he'll do more than sit in his chair. My death will be the making of them. In fact, it'll be the making of everyone I know and love. Pete, Choi, Hayley, Other Zoe, Mo, Lydia, Laura, Devinder, Jamie, Julia they'll all be so sad. Pete and Mo will regret not having sex with me when they had the chance. Even our old neighbour, Pepe, will wonder why we never gave things a proper shot. Joe will wish he'd married me the moment we met. He'll regret ever wasting the moments we had together. But it's too late now, I think sadly. Too late.

My breath shortens again. This is it, then. Goodbye cruel world. I had so much left to do, so much to figure out, so much more sex to have. It's not fair. I never got to find my dream job, never got my wedding to Joe, never even got the proposal I think he's planning. But I've lived a good life, I've lived well. I've eaten some super nice food and I've laughed a lot.

I think about how much Zoe and I have laughed and a warm feeling spreads through my chest as I let go. This is it. Goodbye.

'What the fuck are you doing?' Zoe is back and she's standing over me looking disapproving.

'I can't do it,' I say simply, my breath finally returning to normal as I stand back up straighter. 'It's impossible.'

'I thought you trained for this?' she says, eyes narrowed. 'You said you were training every morning. I asked if you wanted to train together and you said I couldn't match your epic stride.'

'I was going to Millie's Cookies,' I say sadly. I wish I was eating a Millie's Cookie right now. 'Running just isn't for me, Zoe, I gave this my very best shot.'

'We've been running for exactly three and a half minutes,'

she says a tad patronisingly, gesturing at the joggers passing by in their stupid shorts and vests and their 'proper' trainers. Apparently my Converse trainers are not really appropriate. Zoe tuts. 'It's only a 5K charity run, Nat; we can walk if you really, really want.' She looks at me sternly 'But you can't quit.'

I kick sulkily at the dirt and then mentally apologise to my immaculate blue and white shoes.

'Fine,' I say, petulantly. 'Ugh, but please have your phone ready for when you have to ring nine-nine-nine after my LUNGS COLLAPSE.' A few joggers look at me sympathetically as they pass.

'Will do,' she says cheerfully and then loops her arm through mine. I limp a little dramatically for a few metres before realising I'm not actually in any pain and the bleeding lungs have returned to normal.

'How long does it take to walk a 5K?' I ask innocently.

Zoe shrugs. 'Not sure, maybe forty-five minutes? An hour? But your mum and Sue are at the finish line, ready to cheer us on. So we can't quit. Especially not after you so aggressively made everyone sponsor you.'

'I think some of the uni lot are coming down, too,' I say, determinedly, picking up my pace. 'And Joe said he'll be in the crowd near the end.' Zoe doesn't say anything to this so I keep talking and I can hear the defensive prickle in my voice. 'He had a massive work thing to finish first – it's really important – so he couldn't be there at the start,' I'm speaking a little loudly; I know what she thinks. 'But he *is* coming down.'

'That's cool,' Zoe says neutrally.

I know what neutral means though and I can feel her judgement. 'Actually, I think he's planning something nice – a birthday surprise,' I say, nodding. More runners pass us by, but we're nearly at the back of the pink crowd now. It's mostly fellow walkers with us at this point. I smile brightly at a woman in her seventies, before noticing her T-shirt, imprinted with the face of a much younger woman. I stop smiling.

'Actually,' I turn back to Zoe, intent on getting her approval even though I totally don't need or want it, 'I think he's going to propose, isn't that wild?'

Zoe stops short, forcing me to stop, too. 'Are you serious?' she says urgently. 'Why do you think that? You're not even living together; wouldn't that come first?'

I giggle, enjoying the drama. 'Yeah, maybe.' I give Zoe a gentle pull and we start walking again. 'But Joe's actually pretty traditional. His parents got married young and he's said a few times recently that he'd want to do it like them.'

'Is that it?' Zoe sounds relieved. 'He hasn't dropped any other hints?'

'Well, you know he finally met Dad a few weeks ago?' I continue. 'I did leave them alone for a few minutes before dinner and when I came back, Dad looked so weird. I think Joe might've asked him for permission.'

'Do you think he's spoken to your mum, too?' Zoe says faintly.

I shake my head. 'Nah. You know he doesn't really like my mum, says she's too much of a busybody. And, like I said, Joe's traditional, he would only ask my dad. He says tradition is super important and that this "PC culture" is stupid. Anyway, it's just a guess, so I might be wrong. I don't want to ruin the surprise by asking too many questions.'

'Wow,' Zoe says softly, and we walk in silence for a minute before she speaks again, hesitantly. 'Don't you think you're maybe . . . a little young? We're only twenty-four this week.'

'Well, yeah,' I say casually. 'But we could have a long engagement. I'd like to save up for a really massive big day.

Don't worry, I won't be moving out of our flat for a long while yet.' Zoe is silent again, so I add a little defiantly. 'Plus, your brother got engaged and married young, and you thought that was fine.'

Matthew is still kind of a taboo topic for the two of us but I'm feeling cross enough to use him to win this point. She was super supportive of her favourite brother marrying his childhood sweetheart in September, and I'm older than them, so I know this is just about her not getting on that well with Joe. And sure, that makes me sad – I wish they were close – but not everyone can like everyone. Joe says she's jealous of our relationship, which I guess makes sense. Zoe has been single a while now.

'To be honest,' Zoe says carefully, 'I'm not sure Matthew and Sami are doing all that well. Since he started his nursing training, and she's working all hours with law school, they've been struggling a bit.' She pauses. 'But you're right, of course. I'm being a hypocrite. I just want you to be sure. Because this is your first love, your first big relationship, y'know? Don't you want to fall in and out of love a few more times before you settle down?'

I say nothing.

Zoe seems to realise she's crossed a line and adds quickly, 'I just want you to be happy. You *are* really happy with Joe, right?'

I nod emphatically. 'Oh yes, very happy,' I insist, picking up my walking pace and feeling my breath quicken in response. 'You know, we have our arguments, but that is mostly because I'm so annoying – don't say anything, Zo, we both know I can be very, very annoying, but I'm working on it – and he's so patient with me. Plus, since he changed jobs, he's been *so* busy, sometimes he even has to sleep at the office! Poor thing is so stressed out. It's hard for him because I'm doing something I find pretty boring, while he's passionate about what he does. So of course he gets impatient with me moaning. It would get to any couple.'

I think again about this morning's fight at his place. We'd had a nice evening together, I'd made dinner and managed to keep a lid on my dumb stories. Then this morning we were lying in bed together after sex and I ruined it. It was my fault. I was telling him about this guy at work who's been boasting on social media about having sex with interns on the manager's desk. I thought it was a funny anecdote, but Joe thought I was complaining about work again. Even though – as he says – I have it so much easier than him with my job. But I really wasn't complaining! Or maybe I was. It must be so hard for him to have to listen to me. And either way, I know I was being boring, so I totally understand why he blew up at me.

'OK, well, for the record,' Zoe says nicely. 'I don't find you annoying.' She pauses. 'I mean, I do occasionally, but I find *everyone* annoying. Your annoyingness is still the best annoyingness around and I love it.'

I beam, feeling a bit cheerier as we keep walking.

'And, er, congratulations, if he is proposing,' she adds at last, a little unenthusiastically. But I appreciate it.

I know Joe and Zoe are very different people, so it's to be expected that they don't get on. Joe is more of a man's man, y'know? He has this big group of boy mates and they go out and get plastered several nights a week. But that's just lads being lads, isn't it? And it's me he comes back to at three in the morning. It's *my* bed he crawls into. It's me he holds onto. I know some people don't totally understand our relationship, but that's almost what makes it so special. Joe and I are the only ones who get it, we know how much we love each other, and I know how much he needs me. He tells me all the time how no one will ever love me like he does and how important I am to him. And that's really something. No one else has loved me unless they had to, if that makes sense. Like, my mum and dad *have* to love me, don't they? And Zoe's known me for ten years, so she has to love me, too. Joe found me by accident and he chose to love me, even though I'm fat and disgusting and annoying. I'm lucky, I'm *so* lucky. It makes me sad Zoe doesn't see that.

God, this race is exhausting. Maybe I should ask Zoe if we can get a taxi the rest of the way? No one would mind, would they? It's about charity, not the actual run bit. And we could be at the finish line in, like, five minutes flat if we just hopped in a taxi. At this rate, we're going to be last anyway.

Suddenly Zoe stops short. Thank God, she's had enough, too.

'What the fuck?' she mutters and she's staring into the crowd.

'What is it?' I ask, scanning people lining the side. Maybe Joe's here! After he'd finished shouting this morning, he said he forgave me and would do his best to pop down. Maybe he's here already?

She shakes her head, looking dazed. 'No, nothing. I don't think ... I thought it was ... no, nothing.' She shakes her head again, and snorts at herself. 'Stupid,' she mutters, smiling, and starts walking.

'Did you see a ghost?' I ask, intrigued. 'I just read this thing about ghosts online and they are definitely, definitely real.'

'Yeah!' She snorts again. 'Yeah, I thought I saw a ghost, but I'm going mad. I'm definitely going fucking mad. Shall we go a bit faster? We should try not to come literally last. There are elderly people in this race.'

We half jog, half speed walk for the remaining thousand or so miles, me feeling resentful the whole way. Zoe does all the talking because I can't breathe very well and, as we turn a corner, the finishing line comes into view.

'Let's sprint for this last stretch!' Zoe shouts, pulling me with her.

I pick up my pace but Zoe lets go, shooting off into the distance. God, this is horrible! Why do people do this? The blood-filled throat and lungs are back.

I squint through sweaty eyes into the distance and make out Mum and Sue holding a banner and shouting for us. There's some of my uni friends over there, too. I scan the crowd but there's no sign of Joe anywhere.

It's fine, it's fine, it's fine. He's very busy; he has so much going on. I can't expect him to drop everything for my stupid race. Maybe he's even using this time to prepare for a romantic birthday proposal. You don't know.

Up ahead of me I can see Zoe punching the air as she approaches the finish line, but then she suddenly stops short, with metres to go. Other racers meander past her and Mum and Sue stop cheering, looking concerned. I'm close enough now to see her properly and I feel a stab of fear. I've never seen that expression on her face before, not in ten years. Is she having a heart attack? I shouldn't joke so much about death, this is my fault. I always knew she'd die young, I knew I'd lose her. So many people will cry, this will . . .

I pull up next to her, breathing hard and sore. 'What is it?' I manage to get out, grabbing her arm. She doesn't look at me, just continues to stare off into the crowd up ahead with that same scary look on her face. I follow her eyes but can only see anonymous faces, people hugging sweaty pink-wearing runners.

'Talk to me Zoe, what is it?' I beg, feeling stronger now. 'Should I call an ambulance? What's wrong?'

Zoe slow-blinks and at last turns to face me, her face still unreadable.

'It's my mum,' she says in a low voice. 'My mum's over there. I think she's waiting for me.'

ZOE

'I wasn't sure you'd recognise me.' The woman brings a cigarette to her mouth and takes a long drag, her fingers shaking.

Not *the woman*. Mum. She's my mum.

'I mean, I was thirteen when you left,' I point out, looking down at the ground. 'I wasn't a baby. I remember plenty.'

She clears her throat. 'Could we go somewhere to talk?'

'We *are* somewhere and we *are* talking,' I say petulantly. I'm not feeling particularly cooperative. I'm not really sure what I'm feeling at all, actually.

'I know. What I meant . . .' she trails off and then gestures around her at the field. A banner lies near us, discarded, while organisers clear up. A few people are still shouting for the stragglers coming across the finishing line. Some are still hugging, some are crying. There suddenly seems like too much pink around me for this moment.

'How did you even know I was here?' I say, still not completely sure if this is real.

'Matthew,' she says simply and I realise he's been weird with me lately. Cagey, uncommunicative, not returning my messages. I thought it was because things were rough with

Sami but it was this. He's been speaking to our mother and he didn't tell me.

'I know you must hate me,' she begins, a bit desperately.

'Please don't presume you know anything about me,' I say coldly. 'I don't have any feelings about you. Why would I hate you? I don't even *know* you.'

She looks wounded and I suddenly feel terrible. I'm being so cold and mean to this stranger, who isn't a stranger. Anger is bubbling up inside me but I don't want it to leak out. I don't want her to know she's hurt me, I want her to think I never gave her a second thought.

'I get it,' she says quietly, taking another long drag on the cigarette. 'And I'm not here to make excuses.'

'Excellent, here come the clichés,' I spit. 'It's a shame, actually, because I'd really love some excuses from you. I'd love an excuse as to why I've not heard a word from you in ten years. What *is* your excuse for leaving your four children to have ten birthdays without a mother? A terrible car accident that left you in a decade-long coma? Harold Bishop-style amnesia that meant you started a new life as someone called Ted? Were you in witness protection after giving evidence against high-level members of the mob? Please do tell.'

There is silence and I watch her swallow hard. Her throat is deeply lined, horizontally, and her face is a little sunken. She must be a similar age to my dad, but she looks older; more worn out by life. Her dyed blonde hair is styled neatly away from her face and she's dressed like someone who couldn't decide what to wear.

Her face is the hardest to look at: alien and so familiar. I can't look directly at it for more than a second. She turns away to push her hair out of the wind. I notice it's started to lightly spit with rain.

'I . . .' she begins. 'I don't have anything like that to give you, I wish I did. Nothing can excuse what I did, but I was unhappy, very unhappy, and your father . . . he wasn't the easiest man to live with, never mind your grandmother.'

'Oh, I see, you're going to blame my dad for you abandoning us?' I laugh, genuinely amused. 'For you leaving four children behind without a thought and not getting in touch for ten years?'

'There was a lot of thought, actually,' she says quickly, without anger. 'A lot. The thoughts – they never stopped. Constant thoughts, never-ending thoughts. I thought about you four every single day.'

I'm silent at this. I thought about her every day, too.

'Look . . .' She stops again. 'Please can we talk somewhere? Out of the rain?'

'If you want to talk to me,' I shake my head, 'it's now or never. Say what you want to say.'

Silently, we stay standing across from each other in the field. People all around us are laughing and smiling, shouting about going to the pub or getting food. Normal stuff.

'I understand,' she begins again, haltingly. 'I'm so sorry. That's what I came to say, really.' There is another pause and I look at her, arms folded tightly across my body. She starts again. 'When I left, I felt that I had no other option. I knew it was wrong, even then, but it was as though I couldn't stop myself. I didn't know the person I'd become, I felt so completely lost and broken. But I'm better now, I've been working with doctors – therapists – in the last few years and I know now I was suffering with very bad depression.' She pauses before adding quickly, 'Again, this is not an excuse, Zoe, but I want you to know I didn't leave because of you or your brothers. Not because of your dad, not even because of Nanny Surrey. It was because of me. The world got too big and too loud and too scary. I didn't feel like I could cope with any of it and I thought you'd all be better off without me. I convinced myself of that.' She looks at me searchingly. 'And then, the more time that went by, the more I knew you must hate me. I mean, how do you apologise for leaving your family – your *children*! – and then how do you apologise for being gone a year? Then two years? Then five? It felt like a bigger and bigger transgression than I could never truly say sorry for.' She swallows again. 'And I'll admit, I was afraid, I was a coward. Owning up to what I did and seeing you all again was too terrifying for a long time. But then it got too terrifying not seeing you. The weight of it was too much. I had to face you and tell you I never stopped loving you.' She cocks her head. 'I know that must sound so stupid after what I've done to you, but it's true.'

I so, so badly want her to be here. And I so, so badly want her to go. I want to cry and scream and fight and put my head on her shoulder and have her hold me for hours. It's all too much.

I swallow hard. 'And what about Mr Chapman?' I say at last in a husky voice. 'You cheated on Dad, you ran away with my fucking babysitter. Who does that?'

'I'm so sorry,' she whispers again, looking it. 'He was an escape. He was nice to me and gave me an outlet for my fears. I didn't have to think or be myself with him. But we're not together any more. He's long gone.'

'It doesn't make it OK,' I tell her harshly. But I can feel something inside me unfurling. Like a tight knot in my stomach slowly releasing. One I didn't know was there.

'I know that.' Her eyes are shining. 'There's nothing I could say that would make what I did OK.' She wipes her face with a tissue. 'But I had no one growing up. I don't know if your dad ever told you that. My parents were drug addicts and I was in foster homes throughout my childhood. I never knew my real family. When Bryan came along – and then the four of you – I thought it was everything I wanted. But it also scared me so much, being responsible for all of you; all of your lives and happiness.'

I didn't know this. I tried so many times to talk to Dad about Mum but he always walked away. I suddenly feel angry with him, too. Why do I know so little about my own mother? 'I'm sorry you went through that as a kid,' I find myself saying and she shakes her head vehemently.

'Don't,' she tells me sternly. 'I don't deserve it. I should've dealt with my issues, not run away from them. It's something I'm working on; I've always run away from my problems. And when I did that to the only family I'd ever known . . . I don't know, I couldn't cope with what I'd done. I wanted to reach out so many times – I wrote thousands of emails and letters – but the longer it went on, the harder it got. And suddenly you'd grown up without me.' She stops and gives me a small, sad smile. 'You're a grown-up. And you're beautiful.'

I bite my lip, the emotions welling up again.

'I've followed your career,' she says, hopefully. 'I saw you in the *Mail* a few years ago with that boy from *Britain's Got Talent*. I was so proud of you.'

That hits me in a weird spot and I'm suddenly angry again.

'You don't get to be proud of me!' I snap. 'I understand you had your reasons for leaving, I understand life can be hard and it can get too much. But you still did it. You still left me when I needed you most. You left my brothers when *they* needed you most. You broke us and now you come back ten years later with a sob story? What do you want from this? Do you think I'll forgive and forget and we can go back to being one big happy family? Is it that easy for you? You don't get to be proud of me, you are nothing to do with who I am now.' I only realise I'm shouting when I feel a hand on my arm. It's Natalie.

'Are you OK, Zo?' her kind voice gently interrupts, bringing me back down to earth.

'Yeah,' I say, nodding and turning to her. 'I don't want to do this, actually. Can Debbie take us home?'

'Of course.' Natalie takes my arm, glancing curiously over at the woman who gave birth to me and we walk determinedly away.

'Matthew has my number,' the woman calls after me. 'If you're willing to talk more.'

I don't say anything and I feel Natalie look sideways at me as we trot towards the car.

'So, your mum, huh?' she says simply.

'I don't want to talk about it,' I say shortly.

'OK, but . . .' She stops me, still a few metres away from the car, where her mum and Sue are waiting discreetly. 'I just want to say that I hope you're all right, Zo. I can't imagine what you're going through right now, and if you want to talk about it, I hope you know you can.'

And then I take it out on her.

'Well yeah, you *can't* imagine,' I say sharply. 'Because how could you? You've always had a really great mum, who would've done anything for you – still would. She'd never – not in a thousand years – consider leaving you, not for a moment. Same with your dad. And I know you think you've seen, like, *difficult* times now because your parents are divorcing, but, really, you have no idea. You could never get it. That woman left us!' I jab a finger in the direction of my mum, who is walking off into the distance. 'She *abandoned* us, when we were just kids. Who the fuck does that? Only monsters. You could never know what it feels like to be rejected like that, Natalie.' She nods sadly and her understanding about my horribleness makes it worse. 'And yet, you're the one who's fucked up!' I say exasperated. 'You make terrible choices and can't see it. You've been working for years in this dead-end job you hate and – worst of all – you hate yourself. Why are you so messed up, Natalie? What excuse do you have? What has even really happened in your lovely, sheltered existence to make you so complicated?'

She takes a deep breath, taking my shit, and the dark place in me knows it's because she says worse things to herself every day.

'I know nothing that bad has happened to me, Zo,' she says slowly, at last. 'But isn't life enough to fuck you up?'

We get in the car and we drive back home in silence to our flat.

9

2012

ZOE

'If you're watching this, it means I'm dead.' Natalie's sombre face fills my screen and I gasp at the recorded message, sitting back heavily into a chair. 'I wanted to record this message, to be distributed in the event of my demise, because I want all my loved ones to know how much I love them.' She pauses, eyeballing the camera and I start shaking. The phone in my hand quivers in response as Natalie's voice continues. 'I lived a very happy life and I want you all to know that. I promise I won't haunt any of you, but just know that every time you see a butterfly, it's, like, me, or something. No, wait, not a butterfly, maybe a dove? Doves are a nice symbol of peace or green leaves or something, right? Hold on, do we have doves in England?' She looks confused before remembering she's on camera. 'Anyway, please remember that I love you all and everything will be OK.'

She pauses and then adds, 'I will be sending this to the executor of my will, Zoe Darling, for safekeeping until I die, and she will distribute it to you all then. Goodbye one and all.' She pauses before leaning a little closer to the camera phone to whisper. 'Make sure the *Daily Mail* uses a good picture of me from Instagram. One with the Valencia filter. No pictures from Facebook where I'm super drunk – I don't want to be cross-eyed in my obit. And definitely nothing before 2009, ugh. OK, that's it. Mum, please don't read my old diaries and if you do, I didn't mean any of it.' She reaches forward to turn off the record button and her freeze-framed face hovers close to the screen. I stare at it for another few seconds.

Wait. So she's sending this to her executor who apparently is me?

'Oh, Natalie!' I say out loud, realising she's probably not dead.

A few people in the bar glance over at my exclamation and I feel myself turn red. They already think I'm weird, sitting here alone in this dark bar.

'Yes?' she says from over my shoulder and I leap up out of my chair to face her. She's smiling widely, oblivious to the effect her video's had on me.

'What the fucking fuck is this?' I say, holding up my phone to show her the video I just received. 'You scared the shit out of me.'

'Oh!' Her face falls as she realises I'm genuinely angry. 'Shit, sorry, I meant to add an explanation to the video. I'm not *actually* dead. I just thought I'd like to have something ready to pass around for when I am.'

'You're mad,' I say, the adrenaline fading. I sink back down into the chair and gesture at the table. 'And hello. I got you a drink.'

'Ooh, thanks!' she says, delightedly picking it up and taking a long sip from the straw.

'You know it's super weird and creepy how often you talk and think about death?' I point out, feeling a little drained.

'Oh yes, I know,' she's nodding. 'Joe says that too.'

I bristle at the comparison. I don't want to have anything in common with that man.

'I can't help it though,' she continues. 'I've always thought about death a lot. I just have this feeling that I'm going to die young, y'know?' She looks at me reflectively. 'Or maybe you will? I don't know, but definitely someone very important to me.'

'Oh cheers,' I say rolling my eyes. 'I look forward to it.'

'Does death bother you?' she asks, looking interested.

'Er, yeah, duh,' I reply. 'Doesn't it bother everyone? It scares the shit out of me. Not knowing what's going to happen. What if it's like locked-in syndrome and everyone thinks you're dead but you're still in the dead body going, "Argh, I'm in here, don't burn me!"'

'I don't mind the idea of death.' She shrugs and looks away for a moment. 'We've all got to go someday, haven't we? I think it might be quite nice to just sleep and sleep and sleep.'

'I do like sleep,' I say agreeably, feeling pinpricks of worry along my spine.

'What do you think you would do if I died?' she says, dreamily. 'Like, would you be devastated? You know in films, when someone dies, the characters always lie on a floor crying for ages, but I think I'd be secretly thinking quite mundane thoughts. Like, oh no, I'm supposed to be at the dentist to-morrow, should I cancel? And wondering how much work I'd have to miss. Because, like, you can't go back to work *too* soon after someone close to you dies, can you? Everyone would think you were heartless.'

'Maybe you're a bit of a sociopath?' I suggest.

'I don't think so,' she says, shaking her head. 'I think I'd be really sad, as well. I feel everything very deeply. Too deeply, I know. I'm way too emotional; it's something I need to work on, because crying is emotional blackmail.' She speaks this a bit robotically, like it's something she's been told many times.

'I think you're allowed to have feelings,' I say aggressively. 'And you're allowed to express them. They might not always be rational, but we're human beings and humans aren't particularly rational.'

She doesn't look like she's listening, so I keep going. 'And I think if you care about someone, it's not important if it's rational but it's important that you listen and empathise with them being sad.'

I frown as she continues to stare off into the distance.

She looks so different these days, every time I see her it's a shock. In my head – when we're not together – Natalie still looks the way she's always looked. Big hair, happy colours, soft body, always smiling. But in the past year that's all changed – *she's* changed entirely. For one thing – the *big* thing – she's lost at least three stone in weight. She says she's really got into the gym, but it looks more like the not-really-eating kind of weight loss? Like, I can't see any muscle mass in her thin arms as she reaches for her drink again. And – even though I bet everyone's telling her she looks great for the weight loss because that's what people do – she doesn't. Not really. I mean, it's *OK*, it doesn't look awful, but she doesn't look like herself any more. Her cheeks and eyes are much more hollow and grey. She seems sadder and listless. A tiny bit – I don't know – *lifeless*. And what is this black drapey thing she's wearing? She's not wearing colours like she always used to, or smiling like before.

But it's not just her looks that have changed this past year; she's much more withdrawn, less silly, less emotional. She shares so much less. And I don't see her nearly as much since she moved in with Joe. She still messages me a lot, as much as ever, but when I ask about meeting up or even FaceTiming, she too often has an excuse for not seeing me. I can almost feel him hovering over her in those moments, telling her I'm a bad influence. I know, from speaking to Deb, that she hasn't been going home much lately, either.

It's all down to that dickhead, Joe, I know it is. All of this – the weight loss, the disconnect, the shearing down of her personality – it's him taking away pieces of her. Breaking her down with every sneer and every putdown. I haven't been around them together in ages – not since she moved out of our flat at Christmas – but I know he does it. I know he makes her feel less than. She's also stopped talking about their sex life, which is massive. Sex used to be all Nat ever talked about, but now, when I ask her anything like that, she looks worried and says it's inappropriate. I worry what exactly is inappropriate in their sex life.

'Happy birthday, Nat.' I raise my glass and realise she's already finished hers.

'Oops,' she giggles. 'Let me get another one and I'll say it back.' She stands up and I can see her clothes hanging off her at odd angles. Her boobs and bum are gone and it makes me sad. They were lovely.

When she returns, she's bought us shots, too.

'Birthday tequila!' she says, delightedly, and it's almost my Natalie. 'This is great.' She looks around approvingly at the dank, dark little bar. 'Although, I'm sad we're not in Pizza Express or a Little Chef. I can't believe they shut down all the Little Chefs! Where will I get two slimy fried eggs and rock-hard chips now?'

'Let's raise a tequila to Little Chef.' I clink her glass sombrely, careful not to spill, 'You were greatly loved in your time.' We both down the liquid. It's burning hot in my throat but good. Familiar. It's like when you smell someone wearing your teen crush's perfume and it takes you back to an intense memory. Tequila has featured prominently in mine and Natalie's friendship over the years.

I stare at her now, feeling emotional as the alcohol goes straight to my head.

Her phone beeps and she reaches for it, looking a little scared.

'Who is it?' I say carefully.

'Um,' she looks up at me nervously, 'it's just Joe, nothing to worry about.' I look at her quizzically and she adds, 'He's wondering where I am. I didn't actually tell him I was coming to see you tonight.'

'Why not?' I probe.

'Oh, no reason really,' she hedges, her tone deliberately light. 'It's just that, um, he's so busy with work right now and he really needs me at home. But I wanted to see you – it's our birthday tradition – so I left him a note.'

I don't understand this – why would she need his permission to go out? And why would he forbid it?

'Are you going to reply?' I don't know what else to say.

'Er, not right this second,' she says, throwing her phone back into her bag and doing up the zip decisively.

We fall into silence, listening to a woman playing her guitar on stage for open mic. I get invited to so many fancy places with work. I have to recce new venues – everything from subterranean vaults to museums – hunting for sexy new party venues for our artists. It's rare I get to hit up dive bars and listen to bad music. My job is a blast, but I miss the occasional shitty pub. And this one is particularly shitty.

'Do you fancy a go?' I say cheerfully, nodding at the stage and trying to lighten the mood. 'We could sing something stupid and piss off all the wannabe professionals?'

'Nah,' she says, looking a little sad. 'I don't think I should put anyone here through something like that.'

I regard her carefully. Natalie used to love performing. She'd be the first to admit she doesn't have any actual talent for singing or acting, but it never stopped her before. She's dragged me to countless bloody West End shows over the years, as well as random touring theatre shows, Shakespeare on the Green – even local pantomimes – and every single time she would scream-sing the songs and recite the monologues all the way home on the night bus.

I can't hold my tongue any more. 'I feel like you wouldn't have cared what anyone else thought a couple of years ago.'

She swallows and looks away. 'Things change, Zoe,' she says faintly. 'I've grown up a bit. We're twenty-five, it's halfway to fifty. I'm just trying to make better choices and tone down some of my more annoying traits.'

'They were never annoying, though,' I say, feeling intensely frustrated. 'Who says they're annoying? Joe? Is it Joe? Because it's not fair of him.'

I'm choosing my words carefully. I want to say he's a cruel piece of shit and that anyone who's in a relationship with Natalie should worship the ground she walks on. They should love her sillier side, celebrate her loud narration of life as it passes by. A relationship should be mutual adoration, a shared appreciation of each other's weirdness. I want to point out this isn't how love should make you feel.

But I'm afraid of scaring her off. This is as close to a real conversation as we've had in a long time about this – about Joe. I know one false word will send her running away and I need to keep her here until I can get through. I need her to hear me.

'He's trying to help me be better,' she says helplessly. 'He used to love me like mad, he'd buy me flowers and choco-lates. He was so romantic. I just need to be a better version of myself, so we can get back to that.' I stare at her and she keeps going, not really looking me in the eye. 'He's super stressed with work, Zoe, you have no idea. And he's got his gaming commitments, which takes up a lot of time. I don't want to add to his stress. I am hard work, don't say I'm not, Zo, because you know I am.' She breaks off, then adds weakly. 'When he's in a good mood, it's great, he's so good to me.' She pauses. 'He doesn't mean it and it's my fault anyway.'

'He doesn't mean what? What's your fault?' I say urgently and she doesn't reply.

She looks up at last and her whole demeanour has changed. 'Let's talk about you. Is work still great? How are you?' she says brightly, shoulders back. 'It feels like forever since we got to hang out.'

I sigh, debating whether to press the issue. She stares at me unblinking and I can feel her pleading with me to drop it.

'Everything is good,' I say at last and she breathes out. 'I had a date last night, actually. Her name's Vanessa. Funnily enough, she works in HR, too. She started at our company last month, I think she mostly does recruitment.'

'That's so exciting!' she squeals. 'Show me a picture. Do you really like her? Is she The One?'

I laugh, scrolling through my phone for a selfie we took together last night. 'I don't know about "The One",' I roll my eyes jokily. 'It's only been one date, Nat, don't get carried away. But I do like her.'

'She's beautiful!' Natalie exclaims, staring down at my phone with an unreadable expression. 'You look so good together.' She pauses before continuing, 'I used to do more recruitment at work, but then I asked someone in an interview if they'd read *Fifty Shades of Grey* and we talked about the red room for thirty minutes.'

'I hope she got the job?' I take a sip of my drink.

'No.' Nat makes a face. 'My boss said her email address was a dealbreaker. Apparently circlejerk69@hotmail.com isn't acceptable.' She pauses. 'I think he disapproves of Hotmail.'

'That makes sense.' I hide a smile. 'Oh hey, guess what?' I sit up straighter. 'Would you believe I'm having lunch with Mum tomorrow – *and* Dad!'

'God, seriously?' Natalie looks shocked. 'For real?'

'Yep.' I nod enthusiastically. 'AND Nanny Surrey. It's going to be tense as fuck. I'm almost excited to hear the passive-aggressive comments Nanny Surrey's going to be dishing out.'

'But how did this happen?' Natalie is flummoxed. 'I thought Bryan refused to have anything to do with your mum?'

I nod. 'Apparently they had a long chat on the phone last week, after the twins asked Mum to be at their graduation this summer. Dad said he didn't want to get in the way of us having a relationship with her.'

'Do you think they might get back together?' Natalie gasps dramatically.

I laugh at this. 'No way,' I say definitively. 'She's been dating this bloke, Jack, for years now. I haven't met him yet, but Matthew says he's a good guy. It's really not like that between Mum and Dad – it never would be again – it's just an attempt at civility, I think. Y'know, so we don't all have to avoid each other at important moments like graduations and birthdays.'

Natalie nods solemnly and then asks quietly, 'Do you feel like you've properly forgiven her?'

I take a deep breath. 'I don't really know,' I say at last. 'It's been very up and down these last few months. Some days I feel like I'm just trying to be civil – same as Dad – so I don't ruin this new relationship for Matthew and the twins. But other days I cry for hours because I want her to be my mum again so badly.' I break off for a moment and Natalie holds my hand. I squeeze it, feeling stronger. 'So I don't know,' I continue. 'I was really angry for so many years, I'm not sure I'll ever be able to fully work through that. But I guess it's nice to be on all-right terms, for now. It's a work in progress and maybe one day I'll even be able to give her a hug without also wanting to stab her. For now, it's enough to know I have another handy kidney should I need one.'

'That *is* reassuring.' Natalie smiles. Inside her bag, her phone starts ringing. She stares down at it and I stare at her. I can tell who it is from how tense she just got. Her whole body just went into rigor mortis.

'Tell me the truth, Nat,' I say quietly, as the phone continues to ring. 'Are you really, truly happy? Honestly? Does Joe make you happy?'

She takes a big deep breath in, holds it, then lets it out in a rush.

'C'mon,' she says, determinedly. 'Let's go sing.'

NATALIE

I experience a brief moment of shame as we rush the stage and the man singing a heart-rending and ultimately extremely boring rendition of 'Careless Whisper' stops short.

'You're not getting a record deal,' Zoe shouts delightedly in his face. 'So fuck off the stage, it's our turn.'

He looks crestfallen and I put a hand on his oversized shoulder pad as Zoe plugs in her music. 'Dude, don't be sad,'

I offer nicely. 'You can sing with us if you promise to stop using that creepy falsetto?'

'My mum says it's my USP,' he wails, running off the stage clutching his manbag and shouting, 'This was my chance to be famous, my talent was finally going to be recognised. Mummy says I'm still young, I'm only forty-fourrrrrrrrrrr!'

'HELLO, NEW YORK,' Zoe shouts into the mic and the feedback shrieks. The room groans and Zoe grins at me, offering up the second mic.

'HELLO, NOT NEW YORK,' I yell, delighting in the ludicrous. 'DON'T WORRY, MY FRIEND ZOE KNOWS YOU'RE NOT NEW YORK, SHE'S JUST BEING FUNNY.'

The room groans again and Zoe presses play on the music.

'This isn't fucking karaoke, you idiots,' someone yells from the back as we launch into a shouty version of 'Somebody That I Used to Know' by Gotye featuring Kimbra. But we ignore them as we begin screaming words into the mic. I spot the 'Careless Whisper' dude in the corner, sobbing into the phone – probably to his mum – and I give him a big thumbs up. He sobs harder.

Zoe hits a particularly bum note and I catch a woman in the front row muttering to her friends that we are, 'stupid bitches'. I smile beatifically over at her.

I truly don't care what she – or anyone else – thinks, and it's an amazing feeling. I used to feel like this all the time.

Beside me, Zoe is dancing as she sings the wrong words. I feel the tequila warm in my chest and she cracks on another high note, sending me into hysterics again.

This is so much fun. So stupid and silly. I haven't had that in so long.

We high-five over the next line and lean further into the

mics as a few people boo loudly. This is what you get for venturing into east London: there's no sense of humour in this room.

I can't leave him, I can't leave him, I can't leave him.

I try to push away the thoughts and enjoy this moment. This isn't about my relationship with Joe, this is about me and Zoe enjoying our birthday.

What would I be without him? Nothing. He says that all the time and he's right. Who else would put up with me? No one would love me, I'd have nothing, I'd *be* nothing. If I left, I'd be all alone. Being alone is worse than being unhappy, isn't it? The same words I hear and say every day parrot in my head.

He's a good boyfriend! He's good to me. When Joe's in an OK mood – when I've cooked the right food, when his team's doing well at gaming, when he's had a successful day at work – things can be wonderful between us. He's sweet and loving. He strokes my head and says he loves me. We have nice sex and sometimes he even looks in my eyes. I live for those moments.

It's just the rages I don't like. The rages that seem to come more and more frequently.

Zoe beams over at me, sweaty from the bright lights and the shouty-singing. I grin back, focusing all my energy on her face, blocking everything else out. I force out a stupid laugh and it works, sending happy hormones to my brain. I'm enjoying the growing boos around the room. Someone throws a handful of nuts at us and I pick up a few from the stage floor as Zoe takes the solo. Yum, salted peanuts.

'DELICIOUS!' I shout into my mic, and ten more people throw their food at us. It only makes Zoe and me laugh and sing harder.

This is what it's all about, *this* is what a Friday night should be. I just need to spend more time with Zoe, *that* will make everything better.

God, I've missed her so much.

We still talk a lot on WhatsApp, but it's been harder and harder to make time to see each other. I can feel this growing distance between us and I know it's because of me. I'm jealous. I'm jealous of the cool, fun job she loves, and the cool, fun life she lives. She gets to be happy, while I'm stuck being me, in this dumb HR position I hate. I was hoping that the next time I saw her, I'd be able to boast about my new promotion, but I heard yesterday that a junior on the team – a man who's only been working in HR a few months – got the role instead. They said he had the right attitude but I think he had the right gender.

The biggest reason for our distance, though, is Joe. I can feel her judgement about him every time I see her. I don't want to feel her dislike or her disapproval. I don't want to hear her silent dismay when I mention things he's said – things I didn't realise were bad until I see it on her face. It's easier not to see her.

Plus, Joe doesn't like me going out too much, especially not with Zoe. He's not a big fan of hers. He says she puts ideas in my head and is trying to sabotage our relationship. I don't think she is, but it's so hard to know what the truth is. I feel foggy a lot of the time these days. I do know she doesn't like him, but that's because she doesn't understand us. She doesn't believe me when I tell her how nice he can be. Some of the time.

I love her, though, and I need her. I feel *less than* without her.

This song is nearly over but I can see door security have

arrived from outside, and the bar staff pointing in our direction. More food flies at the stage and Zoe reaches out, taking my hand. A hefty guy with an eyebrow scar makes his way over, beckoning wearily for us to get off the stage. We ignore him, singing the last few lines even louder. The song ends at last and the room cheers because we're finished.

But I don't want it to be finished.

'Fucking get off the stage!' someone yells and the security guy waves at us more frantically. Zoe and I hug joyfully, both a bit sweaty. We break apart and she looks so happy, grinning nuttily. It reminds me of so many happy times we've had together over the years. She's laughing and I'm crying.

'That's enough now, girls,' the bouncer says sternly and Zoe looks at me, eyes glinting.

'Shall we sing another one?' She grins and the front row starts booing again. The beleaguered security guy – now very much out of patience – launches himself up onto the stage and Zoe and I scream and dodge in different directions. We make a run for it, more nuts flying past our ears, and head for the exit, hand in hand again.

'GET BACK 'ERE!' shouts the security guy but we're out the door. We're out and we're in the cold fresh air, light rain on our faces as we run. We keep going until we are around the corner, before we finally stop, breathing hard.

'That was amazing,' I gasp, bent double, trying to get my breath back. I realise I'm still happy-crying, and we're still holding hands. I don't want to let go. 'I think the crowd really loved us.'

'They really did,' she crows delightedly. 'Let's head over to Lucky Voice next! They have feather boas and hat props.'

'Yes, let's,' I say, looking at Zoe and suddenly feeling very sober.

All my life, I've wanted a boyfriend. Always. I thought a boyfriend would save me from myself. I thought he would make me a person I could finally be happy to be. I thought he would love me enough for the two of us. I thought he would lift me up and help me belong in a world that rejects me. I thought he would – to use the cliché – complete me. But Joe doesn't do that. Maybe no boyfriend can do that? Zoe does that.

This is love, this is love, this is love.

Not sexy, romantic love – but something better. A love that matters, and I've abused it and ignored it, yearning for a dream man who probably doesn't exist.

'We'll go to Lucky Voice,' I continue casually, like it's the easiest thing in the world. 'And then I'm going home to break up with Joe.'

10

2013

NATALIE

'And then she asked me what my weaknesses are and I was like, OMG, where do I start? I talk too much, I overshare, I am incredibly co-dependent and I sort-of hate men like 90 per cent of the time? But I also desperately want them to love me, which is really shit. And then she looked at me like I was mad and said she meant weaknesses in a work context, so I said I have been known to use the office photocopier when I get drunk to see how big my bum is.'

'So it went really well?' Zoe nods, helpfully.

'Best job interview ever,' I say confidently. 'I feel like I don't even need to wait for the email, I'm already spending the pay rise on Asos as we speak.' I look up from my phone and laugh so Zoe knows I'm joking and am fine with being a mess, even though I'm not.

'Did you actually really want the job anyway?' she says, nicely.

I shake my head. 'Nah, not really. It was just more of the same boring HR stuff, just with better money. Honestly, I hate it, it bores me to tears. But it's too late to change now, isn't it? I'm officially in my late twenties, I can't change career paths at this point. I'm stuck hating my life choices, just like everyone else in the world.' I smile brightly. 'It turns out I'm not special, I'm not different. I'm the same as everyone else out there, falling into something they can't stand and ultimately spending their weekends dreading Monday morning and obsessively playing the lottery.'

'You *are* special,' Zoe says loyally. 'And it's not too late to do something else. Lots of people change their mind. I was just reading an article about it: we're the generation who got screwed over by the previous one. We can't buy houses, we can't find a job, we can't have unrepressed sex, it's the worst.'

'You have unrepressed sex?' I say a little resentfully.

'Yeah, but I'm lucky,' she says and shrugs. 'I'm gay.'

Zoe and I are snuggled up under a blanket on the sofa, eating ice cream out of the tub and watching *Twilight* for the thousandth time. This is my happy place and, I think suddenly, feeling delighted: I *am* happy. It's a nice feeling.

Although, I think, looking down at the two-thirds-gone tub, I hate that I'm back at my pre-misery weight.

For those first few weeks and months after I left Joe, I barely ate anything. I lost even more weight and found that I enjoyed the numbness I got from starving myself. It was like I was watching myself from above, desperately miserable, trying to regain some semblance of control in my life any way I could. But all things must pass, as Joe would say because *Criminal Minds* said it once. And as the numbness and misery lost its hold over me, my weight gradually crept back up.

It is nice to wear all my old clothes again, though. I couldn't fit into anything while I was skinny and Joe wouldn't let me get anything new. He said he preferred me in baggy clothes. Ugh, what a prick. And what a prick I was for believing him.

When I told him I was leaving he didn't take it very well. I was afraid to do it in person, so Zoe and I went to pack up my things when we knew he was at work, and then I sent him a message explaining we were done.

He exploded. He left me all kinds of awful, nasty, vicious voicemails for days, demanding I come back. Saying how I was lucky to have him and I should be grateful he was willing to lower his standards to settle for me – how dare I leave him. The sad thing was that I completely believed that. Listening to his voicemails berating me, I believed him entirely. Zoe found me one night, listening to the messages in her spare room, tears streaming down my face as I packed up a bag to go back to Joe. She listened through the messages, listened to everything he'd been saying. And watching her listen, seeing the expression on her face . . . I've never seen someone go so white, so quickly. She looked genuinely frightened and I suddenly realised how not-normal and not-OK it was that Joe would speak to me like that. That my partner would use words like that when talking to me. It was – to use a horrible cliché – a massive wake-up call. Soon after that, the charming Joe of old returned. Instead of insults, he left sweet, romantic, darling messages for me instead. He sent gifts and cards. It was like the early days of our relationship.

'He's a malignant narcissist,' Zoe explained. 'And narcissists are charming. He's a controlling, abusive shithead who is trying to manipulate you into going back to him. He sees you as an object that belongs to him. An object he's spent two years crushing into a small, compact space that he had full ownership over. And he can't believe you have the strength to leave. But you do, Natalie, you are fucking strong and beautiful and wonderful and kind. You deserve to be happy.'

I didn't believe her at the time, but I believe her now. A bit. Like, sometimes.

*

I glance over at her now, stuffing a huge spoonful of ice cream into her face and I grin happily.

'Thanks, Zoe,' I say, feeling a rush of love that may or may not be sugar related.

'Whaffor?' she says, mouth still full.

'For being so – for being so *you*.' She looks appalled by the cheesiness and throws a cushion at me, but then groans.

'Fuck, I got ice cream on the sofa,' she complains. 'That's your fault.'

'Lick it off?' I suggest and she does like a legend.

'Hmm, furry,' she says, rubbing her stomach.

'Do you ever eat so much that seven hours later, you still can't move?' I say conversationally, still shovelling ice cream in. 'Like, you feel OK for a few hours and then you feel much fuller later, like the food is expanding in your stomach?'

'Have you ever been tested for Crohn's disease?' Zoe asks.

'I need a poo,' I say, rubbing my stomach. 'Come with me?'

'Sure,' she says, struggling to stand up.

'You two are disgusting,' Vanessa says suddenly, from across the room. I jump a little because I forgot she was even here.

'What? Why?' I say, defensively.

Vanessa is grimacing. 'You poo together? You actually go to the bathroom together?' She looks absolutely appalled. 'Is there anything you don't do together?'

Zoe shrugs, then looks to me to see if I can think of anything.

'Oh!' I say, inspired. 'I don't sit in the room with you two when you're having sex.'

'She's got you there,' Zoe says, pointing at her girlfriend. 'She's never watched us when we're doing it, baby.'

Vanessa shakes her head, unimpressed. 'Yeah, but I bet you would let her if I didn't object.'

Zoe side-eyes me. OK, that might be true.

'And she comes into our room every morning and gets into bed with us,' Vanessa says, sounding a bit irritated.

'Yeah, but I always knock first!' I protest weakly.

'You're ridiculously co-dependent with each other,' she says, and I can tell she really means it. 'I'm getting a little sick of it.'

Vanessa's usually super laid-back and nice. She's never made me feel like a third wheel, even though it must've been rough for her, me moving in just as she and Zoe started dating. In fact, she was incredibly kind to me in that awful Joe aftermath, never making me feel judged or stupid for crying or talking about it for hours. And she never once turned up to see Zoe without bringing me biscuits.

But since she moved in a few months ago, I know this co-dependence thing has become more of an issue for her. She's brought it up before with Zoe. Who of course immediately told me because we tell each other everything. But that doesn't mean we're co-dependent!

I glance at Zoe, feeling a bit sheepish. I don't want to get in the way of their relationship, I really don't. I love Vanessa; she's fun and cool and sexy, and she brings out the best in my friend. I've tried to give them more space, but my favourite person to hang out with is Zoe. After what she helped me through last year, I feel intensely connected to her. I can never thank her enough. We've gotten so close again and I never want us to drift or be pulled apart by some dickhead man again. So I don't know what to do.

'OK, we won't poo together any more,' Zoe promises, pouting. 'And maybe, Nat, you only get into bed with us, like, every other day?' She looks to me and I nod encouragingly, feeling a bit put out. I really like getting into bed with them.

I miss sharing a bed with someone and morning cuddles are the best part of my day before I have to go to stupid work with my stupid colleagues.

'Ughhh, you two are impossible!' Vanessa lets out a frustrated noise and stomps out of the room. There is an awkward silence.

'I'm being an awful third wheel,' I say at last, hoping Zoe will contradict me.

'Maybe a little,' she admits, sadly. 'But I really like having a third wheel. Del Boy's van wouldn't have been nearly as cool without the third wheel.'

I sigh deeply. 'I'm sorry,' I say quietly. 'I really don't want to get in the way, or make Vanessa angry with you. Or me, for that matter. Maybe we do need more boundaries in this friendship.'

'Gross, who wants boundaries?' she says, attempting to lighten the mood. 'But maybe it's something to think about. I better go after her and see if she's OK.' She heaves herself up, discarding the almost empty ice-cream tub.

'Shall I come with you?' I say and she looks at me, amused.

'No, I think that might exacerbate the problem,' she says dryly. 'You go have your ice-cream poo without me. We should try to be more normal.'

'OK.' I sigh, sadly. 'It's probably not going to be very pleasant anyway. I'm very obviously lactose intolerant; I don't know why I keep doing this to myself.'

I watch Zoe leave the room and then launch myself up, too.

I really need to get a life, that's the problem.

On the loo, I scan through my phone, half-heartedly. Pooing is much more boring without a friend to chat to. Maybe I should download Tinder at last? Everyone else seems to be on this new dating app so maybe I could give it a go? But I don't want to. I might be lonely, but I'm also definitely not ready to meet anyone.

Upstairs, I can hear the hum of slightly raised voices. Vanessa and Zoe, arguing. I feel so guilty. Then I recognise Van's muffled laugh and breathe out. It'll be OK. Those two are so good together, nothing can tear them apart. Surely not mine and Zoe's toilet habits.

I open WhatsApp and – as usual – there are, like, seven hundred new messages from the uni group in the space of an hour. They're talking about tonight and want to know if there's a theme. I type quickly, telling them the only theme is how awesome Zoe and I are.

I haven't thought much about celebrating turning twenty-six. Maybe I don't want to, because what am I actually doing? What have I achieved in life? Apart from literally one relationship, and that was an utter shite-show.

I finish on the loo and wash my hands, staring in the mirror and examining my face for new wrinkles. It's all downhill from here, looks-wise, right? And dammit, I forgot to peak while I had the chance. God, I miss my early-twenties skin. The bags under my eyes are already starting to require ten times the amount of concealer, and I seem to have a sunspot forming on my forehead. The lines aren't too bad yet, which is the one thing I might be able to thank Joe for. When you spend two years not smiling, at least you don't get wrinkles. Ugh, I need some make-up on before my family gets here. Sue told me the other day that twenty-seven was when her face really started to deteriorate, so that's nice. One more year before it's over. I better make the most of it.

I sigh loudly at myself in the mirror.

As I leave the loo, Zoe is back in the living room. She looks upset.

'Vanessa's gone for a smoke,' she says, sinking back onto the sofa. 'She says she's OK, but I can tell she's not really.' She looks up at me, all big, worried eyes. 'She's not going to leave me, is she? She wouldn't? We're really happy.'

'Oh God, Zoe, I'm so sorry.' I cover my face. 'This is all my fault. I will give you guys space, I swear it.' I pause. 'Should I move out, do you think?'

'No, no!' She looks panicked. 'Please don't do that, I love living with you. And you know Vanessa loves you, too. I guess we just . . . I guess we should just consider being less involved with each other's lives? We are a bit intense sometimes. The bed thing should probably stop. And I don't need you to write your period dates in my diary any more or pluck my nipple hairs, for example. And I guess, like, we both don't need to be naked right now.' She smiles wanly at me. 'But you're my best friend in the whole world and I never want that to change. I feel like I nearly lost you when you were with Voldemort.'

I nod, resigned to the new rules. 'You won't lose me,' I say firmly. 'But you're right, I can't rely on you for everything. I'm sorry. I think I got too used to needing you after my break-up with Joe, and I haven't shaken myself out of that. You have been amazing, and so has Vanessa, but I want you to put your partner first – you *should* put her first.'

I offer her my hand to shake on our new agreement and she takes it.

'Do you think Vanessa wants us to cancel our joint birthday lunch and drinks tonight?' I say anxiously.

'No!' She looks alarmed. 'Of course not. She's not unreasonable, she just wants to spend time with me one-on-one occasionally. It's fair enough. And I think if I really show her I mean it about putting her first, she won't mind us having a co-dependent birthday together once a year.' She looks a tiny bit sad before adding, 'We better enjoy this while we can. Because, starting tomorrow, we have to start trying to be a tiny bit more normal.'

'Better start getting drunk now then,' I say.

'Absolutely,' she says enthusiastically, then lowers her voice. 'But first tell me how your poo was?'

ZOE

From my bedroom, I hear Debbie and Sue arriving, talking loudly as they let themselves in our front door. Vanessa's with them and I quickly fold away the costume I'd laid out for tonight as a surprise for Nat and me. I was going to suggest we dress as the twins from *The Parent Trap*, since it's still one of our favourite films and we think of ourselves as twins. But seeing me with it this morning was part of what pushed Van over the edge. I suppose, in hindsight, being two halves of a costume at a party that doesn't even have a dress up theme *could* possibly come across as co-dependent.

'I'm just saying, she was obviously an entitled little bitch,' Sue is telling Debbie and Van as she passes my room, heading towards the living room.

'She goes into someone's house when they're not there – that's breaking and entering – and then steals their food.'

'She was lost and scared!' Debbie argues furiously.

Vanessa loudly agrees. 'Exactly! Where else was she supposed to go, Sue?'

'Fine,' Sue still sounds outraged. 'But did she then literally have to eat all their food, get into their fucking beds and go to sleep? Only a white girl could get away with this shit. Anyone else would've been shot dead.'

'Who are you talking about?' I ask curiously, following them into the hallway.

Sue turns around. 'Goldilocks,' she explains, before turning back to start the argument again.

'Happy birthday, my darling,' Debbie says, giving me a quick hug, and returning to Sue. 'But she was lost and tired, what was she meant to do?'

'Er,' Sue rolls her eyes. 'She could try *not* eating three different meals she found in someone else's house. And then she could try not getting her sweat all over three different beds, climbing in and out of them. What was so bad about sitting on their doorstep and waiting for help? I hope they ate that bitch.'

'She was probably traumatised by her parents giving her the name Goldilocks,' Vanessa mutters and then turns to me.

'Sorry about the tantrum,' she says in a low voice, smiling shyly. 'You know I don't really mind Nat being around so much.'

'Don't say sorry, baby,' I say, taking her hand. 'It's my fault, and Nat and I spoke about it. We're going to respect the boundaries. I love you so much, I'm sorry.'

Van lifts my hand to her mouth and kisses the soft skin on my wrist. 'I love you, too.'

The front door goes and I head off to let Dad in.

Deb and Sue, along with my dad are taking us out for a birthday lunch today. My mum was going to join us, too, but she's been struggling with her mental health again recently. Her partner Jack messaged me and Matthew last week to explain the situation and said her doctor and therapist are working with her to find the right anti-depressant dosage. I totally get it and told him to pass along our love. I've talked to Mum a lot these past couple of years about her ongoing struggle with depression. It's really tough, and she's needed to take a step back several times. I think it's brave, admitting you need help and I don't blame her for focusing on herself right now. It's what she needs to do. This is something she's had to deal with her whole life – and will always – and I feel for her.

'Dad!' I shout happily as I open the door. But my smile fades when I notice who's with him.

'And Nanny Surrey . . .' I greet my grandmother in a re-signed voice. 'You came.'

Dad pulls a guilty face as he pulls me in for a hug. 'Happy birthday love, um, and sorry.'

'Of course I came, my dove,' Nanny Surrey titters. 'It wouldn't be much of a celebration without me, would it!' She leans in for me to air kiss her on either cheek. I oblige, wishing we could cancel lunch. Nanny Surrey is more than capable of ruining any kind of happy event and I really could've done with some warning she was coming. I need to be emotionally prepared for her onslaught.

'Mummy thought she'd join us, isn't that nice?' Dad says nervously.

'Horribly nice,' I say with feeling as I usher them in.

'Gosh,' Nanny Surrey says looking around the hallway. 'This is awfully, er, *cosy* isn't it? Can't you afford anything better? Maybe it's time you got a *real* job, my darling.'

'Er,' Dad jumps in nervously. 'What did the hurricane say to the car?'

'I'm very happy doing what I'm doing, Nanny,' I say ro-botically as we all enter the living room and three heads turn our way.

'Hi, Bryan!' Sue says loudly, adding quickly, 'Oh, hi, Nanny

Surrey, we weren't expecting you. Nice to see you again.'

Nanny Surrey peers at her, with a faux-confused look on her face, then pretends – like she does every time – that she can't remember Sue's name.

'What is it again, deary?' she says. 'It's something *plain*, isn't it? A working gal's name, I'm sure? Something rather common, am I right?'

'Sue,' says Sue, not giving a shit. 'And if we're slagging off names, what was with *Bryan*? That is so close to being Ryan – a cool name – and instead you went with *Bryan*. Ugh, it's like you wanted everyone in his life to suspect him of being a paedophile – no offence meant, Bryan.' She nods towards Dad, who nods cheerfully back.

'None taken,' he says, generously.

'It's a family name,' Nanny Surrey sniffs. 'We come from a strong line of Bryans – good genes – but I really wouldn't expect you to know anything about that.' She looks Sue up and down, before adding, 'I bet you're one of those women who goes by *Ms* aren't you?'

'Actually, I prefer Professor,' Sue looks amused.

'The answer was "Shall we go for a spin?"' Dad shouts.

'What?' Vanessa hands him a coffee, looking perplexed.

'I asked, "What did the hurricane say to the car?"' he explains awkwardly. 'Shall we go for spin!' Vanessa laughs politely but Sue and Nanny Surrey are too busy squaring off.

'Right, er . . .' Natalie steps in before things get physical. 'Let's move through to the kitchen for a quick drink before we head to the restaurant, shall we?'

'Oh my, Natalie!' Nanny Surrey peers over her glasses at her. 'I almost didn't recognise you, my dear. What a shame you've put all that weight back on. You were doing so well with your dieting. You *have* heard of diabetes, haven't you?'

'It wasn't really a diet,' Natalie mutters. 'More the wearing down of my emotional well-being by an abusive boyfriend.'

'Whatever works, my dear!' Nanny Surrey giggles as Nat looks down at the ground. God, I *hate* Nanny Surrey. In one fell swoop, she's undone almost a year of talking and reassuring and coaxing. Nat finally seemed back to being *Natalie*. She's nearly back up to her usual – happy – weight and even though she complains and says she hates it, I can tell she kind of doesn't. I think she likes being her again, as well as getting to wear her old, bright clothes and being able to laugh without being called annoying.

'So, does that mean you've been dumped by that lovely man of yours?' Nanny Surrey says conversationally as we hand around drinks. She knows what she's doing, but she doesn't care. 'But what a shame, he was such a handsome chap. I'm sure you're aware you were doing *quite* well for yourself there.'

Natalie swallows hard, as Nanny Surrey continues, 'And how sad that you're alone again. It must be very trying for you. What's a girl to do with herself without a man to care for?'

I glance over at Debbie who looks thunderous. She glares daggers at my dad, willing him to step in and stop his mother, but he continues studiously staring at the ceiling. I love my dad, but he's an absolute coward. His mum has always been a bully, one minute lavishing him with praise and attention – the next, taking it away without reason. It's messed him up.

'Wank a lot?' I say loudly, trying to break her stride, but Nanny Surrey ignores me.

'Oh, hey, Natalie, guess who sent me and your mum a Facebook message?' Sue says, brightly, trying to shift the mood of the room.

'Are we changing the subject?' Nanny Surrey asks innocently. 'Don't we *want* to help Natalie? Because she's getting to an age where she'll be seen as *used up*. Soon, no man will want her, especially looking so – so *unhealthy*. I'm just worried about you, my dear, that's all it is.'

'Edgar!' Sue shouts in a high-pitched tone as Debbie continues glaring expectantly at Dad. He starts to sweat, looking increasingly panicked. He's under pressure to do something – anything to shut down his toxic mother. But he never has before, so he has no idea how.

'Um, who's Edgar?' He leaps on Sue's outburst, eyes darting back and forth.

'He's an idiot Debbie and I dated when we were teenagers,' she says quickly, coming to sit next to Natalie, who still looks forlorn. 'He cheated on us both back then, and this week he found us on Facebook. He sent a message saying sorry for how he acted back then. He said he's changed and was a stupid fool when he was young. Isn't that hilarious?'

The room titters politely as Nanny Surrey continues breezily in her attack. 'Oh dear,' she says to Natalie. 'It looks like I'm the only one here who actually *cares* about you and your future happiness, my dove. Everyone else here is too busy using the internet to relive past sins.'

'Right, that's *enough*.' Debbie takes a step forward at last, her face and voice stone. 'You will *not* speak to my daughter like that. Not after what she's been through.' Her head whips around to Dad. 'If you're not going to stand up to your mother, I will, you coward.'

'*Excuse* me?' Nanny Surrey looks furious and I watch in awe as Debbie takes another step forward, standing strong and tall in my grandmother's personal space. I silently cheer her on.

'If you want to be here, in my daughter's home,' Debbie continues icily. 'And if you want to join us for this special, family birthday meal, you will kindly cut the shitty comments about Natalie and Zoe. They are clever, brilliant, hard-working and kind young women, who are doing their very best to survive in this difficult world. You have no right speaking to anyone like that, never mind people you profess to love. Is that clear?'

For a moment I think Nanny Surrey will fight back, lash out with yet more bile. But after a second, her mouth slams shut and she nods.

'Fine,' she says, slightly defeated.

'Good,' Debbie says, nodding like a boss. Sue cheers and I beam at her, so delighted with what just went down. No one's ever stood up to Nanny Surrey before and it was glorious to behold. The best birthday present anyone could ever ask for. Debbie smiles back at me, looking a little relieved. Dad even looks secretly pleased. Maybe he'll be inspired enough by it to stand up for himself occasionally.

'Right, shall we get an Uber to the restaurant, everyone?' I say and the room breathes out. The moment is over.

'Uber?' Nanny Surrey squints. 'Is that a venereal disease?'

'Only if STDs come with star rating these days,' I say, ushering everyone out the door.

* * *

To: Zoe.Darling@HHHRecordsLtd.co.uk
From: NatalieRoxyWinters@gmail.com
Subject: News

Zo, there's a new girl starting in my office today and you'll NEVER

GUESS what her name is!! Liz Anya. Like lasagne?!! They just introduced her around and my mouth actually started watering.

--

To: NatalieRoxyWinters@gmail.com
From: Zoe.Darling@HHHRecordsLtd.co.uk
Subject: RE: News

That's funny. A guy just started in our PR dept called Percy Magoo, and I cannot stop calling him Merci Beaucoup.

--

To: Zoe.Darling@HHHRecordsLtd.co.uk
From: NatalieRoxyWinters@gmail.com
Subject: RE: RE: News

That's an epic name. Adding it to the list for when I change mine.

PS. How do you smuggle sanitary towels to the toilet when women aren't allowed pockets on their clothes?

--

To: NatalieRoxyWinters@gmail.com
From: Zoe.Darling@HHHRecordsLtd.co.uk
Subject: RE: RE: RE: News

You want to be called Percy?!

--

To: Zoe.Darling@HHHRecordsLtd.co.uk
From: NatalieRoxyWinters@gmail.com
Subject: RE: RE: RE: RE: News

Imagine how much attention I'd get ☺

11

2014

ZOE

'Please, please, *please* can I have a go?' my friend Hayley is begging Natalie for her phone.

'And then me,' I say, as Vanessa laughs next to me and squeezes my hand affectionately.

'Me, too,' Van asks. 'Can you easily change the settings to show women to swipe?'

'Actually, I've got my preferences set to show all sexes already,' Natalie says smugly and I snort.

'What?' I splutter. 'Why?'

'I was hoping I might start fancying women,' Natalie says earnestly. 'If I can just stare at the pretty ones long enough, y'know? Like, train my brain into lust?'

Vanessa and I raise an eyebrow at each other.

'Er, Nat, as you've been telling bigots for years,' I tell her witheringly. 'Sexuality is not a *choice*. You can't just decide to be gay.'

'But sexuality is a spectrum, isn't it!' she says heatedly. 'Maybe I am a bit of a lesbian but just haven't explored vaginas enough to know.'

'That's slightly offensive,' Vanessa says kindly. 'Do you – or have you ever – fancied a woman?'

Natalie's brow furrows as she thinks about it carefully.

'Um, well, I was really, really into Solange Knowles when she attacked Jay-Z in the lift?'

'But would you like to fondle her boobies?' I ask nicely. Natalie's face betrays her and I add, 'That's a no, Nat. I know it's sad, but you're stuck fancying men.'

'Ughhhhhh,' she moans, throwing her phone at Hayley who delightedly looks through Tinder. She's been happily married to Richard for ages, but everyone loves a harmless, nosy swipe, right? I've had many a go on there, even though I love Vanessa and I'm really happy with where we are.

'I just want something exciting to happen in my life,' Natalie continues to wail. 'I am so lonely and bored with crappy dates and crappy work. Do I have to keep working forever, you guys? Do I really? Like, how much do I actually *need* money? Would it be so awful to be broke all the time and living at my mum's?'

'Yes,' I comment casually, taking the phone from an excitable Hayley. 'You do have to work.'

'But maybe you could take a sabbatical or something?' Vanessa suggests. 'You've been at your company for a while, haven't you? You could go travelling around the world.'

'Great idea!' I sit up straighter. 'I loved my gap year so much, and that's where I met Hayley, isn't it?' We beam at each other, both remembering those hazy, lazy, weird times in the sunshine, and bonding in Australia over our mutual Britishness.

'Oh,' Natalie looks alarmed. 'No, I don't want to travel. Too much danger, and that Ebola sounds awful.'

'Well yes, but that's pretty much confined to Sierra Leone and Liberia,' Hayley points out.

'It's just a matter of time before everyone gets it,' Natalie tells her gravely. 'I've been watching a lot of zombie movies lately and some kind of disease or virus is going to get us sooner or later.'

'Whatever.' Vanessa rolls her eyes, smiling. 'I'm ready for it. I'd be very happy to be locked up in a bunker with Zoe, living on canned goods. It's not like either of us can cook anyway.' We gooey-eye each other until Hayley threatens to throw her drink over us.

'Why have you been watching zombie movies?' I ask Nat, confused. 'You hate horror films.'

'I do, I really do,' Natalie confirms. 'But I thought it would make me sound cooler in my Tinder profile, y'know? I thought being a zombie fan who, like, drinks ale and smokes cigars would give me a niche. It has to be more appealing to men than a musical-obsessed wannabe *X Factor* star who loves pink Prosecco and farts in her sleep.'

The table nods but I want to reach out and hold her hand. She seems so vulnerable right now, and I know she's lonely. I resist the urge. We've been so much better with boundaries this past year, finally respecting each other's space. Of course we're still close but we are our own, distinct people a little more these days.

But I know Vanessa still keeps half an eye on us, waiting for us to slip back into our co-dependent ways.

'You know,' Natalie says dreamily, looking up. 'I once farted in my sleep next to Joe, and he woke me up to scream for three and a half hours about it. He said I was a disgusting pig and then he made me sleep on the sofa for the next two nights.' She pauses and her eyes look glazed. 'I stopped eating in the evenings after that, because I was afraid of doing it again.'

Everyone around the table looks a little uncomfortable. Sometimes these fun little titbits leak out of Natalie, I don't think she can help it. It's been two years since she broke up with that abusive fuckshit, but I think she's only really now starting to realise just how dysfunctional that relationship was. How cruel he was. He really messed with her head, but she's been so strong. I can't explain in words just how proud I am of her. How easily she could've slipped back to the devil she knew, but she stayed strong. It just proves the strength she has in there, underneath all the fear.

This time I don't stop myself, I take her hand and give it a squeeze. Her eyes come back into focus and she smiles brightly at me, like she's coming out of a trance.

'Let's find you someone lovely and kind, this time,' I say cheerfully, picking her phone up.

'Have you been on any actual dates?' Hayley asks, looking over my shoulder as I adjust the settings to exclude women.

'I've been on three dates,' Natalie says proudly. 'But they were not great. I mean, the first two were nice enough men, but the first one was so handsome I couldn't handle it. I wanted to roll over at his feet and expose my belly to him; submit like a dog. And he definitely didn't like me – he politely excused himself at nine o'clock, just when I was starting to get drunk. Then the second one seemed interested, but when I came back from the loo, he was literally sitting there on Tinder, swiping away on other women. That didn't seem like a great sign. I would've gone on a second date with him anyway, but he didn't text me back the next day. Then, I thought the third guy was a goer because he had a dog that he talked about a lot, which is always a sign of a good person. But when he went to show me a photo on his phone, a porn video that he was halfway through watching, popped up. The whole bar heard two Japanese pre-teens being spanked. Plus, he told me his mates all call him Herpes as a nickname. That's probably not a good sign, is it?' She sighs. 'I would just like to meet someone who *likes* me, y'know? I don't think my ex actually liked me at all.'

We all nod, and Vanessa mutters a few platitudes; he'll turn up when you least expect him and when you stop looking, while Hayley says she needs to put herself out there more and maybe try dating outside her usual type.

Natalie drinks in the advice, confusing and contradictory though it is, nodding enthusiastically.

'OK, so you guys pick someone for me,' she says excitedly, looking around for her phone, which has landed most recently in Vanessa's hands.

'I'm on it,' Van says, fierce determination in her eyes. 'And Zoe and I can be objective because we don't have a male type.' She laughs happily and I look away, hoping Natalie doesn't do that thing where she stares at me pointedly. She's great with secrets in theory, but she's also got no sense of subtlety at all. Things tend to leak out of her accidentally. And this is not the time and place for me to finally have the bisexual chat with Vanessa.

OK, so look, I know I should've told her ages ago. But at the start of our relationship I didn't tell her because I really didn't know how she'd take it. Then, the longer it went unsaid, the more it became about this big *secret*. You can't just casually reveal something like that years into a relationship, can you? When is the right time, though? First date? Third date? When you decide to be exclusive? When you say I love you? Whatever the right moment was, I didn't know, so I didn't say. Plus, only Natalie knows I'm bisexual, so it's hardly even real. Even my family are in the dark.

'Jesus!' Vanessa is swiping left a lot, looking grossed out. 'Why do so many of these men look like they have a half-written manifesto about "why women are bitches" on their computer?'

'I know, right,' Natalie sighs. 'My expectations are so low at this point, all I ask is that they have a bedframe and radiators in their house.'

'I'm going to get repetitive strain injury,' Vanessa complains, pausing to shake off a hand cramp.

'Clearly you're not working your hand muscles enough,' I say dryly and she snorts, playfully slapping at my leg.

We're being particularly lovey-dovey tonight and I know it must be irritating for everyone around us, but I can't help it. Van's made such an effort for my birthday, surprising me with a hotel stay by the seaside in Norfolk – and there were boat rides and presents and so much kissing. I know relationships have their peaks and troughs – and, sure, we argue plenty when the troughs are bad – but it just so happens this is a major peak. Everest, K2-type peak.

I squeeze her free hand again now, thinking: God, I'm mad about you. The way she moves, her facial expressions, how she laughs – it all makes me crazy. I never thought I'd feel like this about someone.

I was single for a long time before I met Vanessa and I was happy. But this is like a different kind of happy.

Of course, I'm trying really hard not to be an absolute twat about it in front of Nat. I know she really wants to meet someone.

'Right, *this* dude,' Van says confidently at last and Hayley leans in to inspect her choice. She reaches over to flick through the chosen man's pictures, nodding as she goes.

'Agreed,' she says. 'He's got a nice, friendly face. No tigers, no topless selfies, no weird bio about following his dreams. You should go out with Ross.'

Natalie smiles kindly, but I can see she is more amused than happy. 'You know, you can't just pick one profile?' she says slowly. 'You guys have been in relationships the entire time Tinder's existed, so you clearly don't understand how it works.' She rolls her eyes. 'It's a numbers game. You can swipe this nice-faced chap all you like, but I doubt he's even seen my profile, never mind swiped me back.'

'Oh, really?' Hayley looks disappointed. 'Do it anyway, we like Ross.'

Vanessa obliges and waits a beat before looking sad. 'OK, well he's bound to swipe right on you soon,' she says hopefully. 'Can I have a look at the dudes you've been messaging?'

Natalie hesitates a moment and I take the phone from Vanessa who heys me, looking annoyed.

'I'll look,' I say decisively and Natalie looks relieved.

'So, this guy and his backwards baseball hat wants to know if you would like to see his duck?' The table laughs, Natalie slightly less so.

'I'm replying,' I say confidently and read out loud as I type. '*You have a duck?? That is amazing, yes please, I'd love to see your duck.*' I press send and see the baseball hat come online. 'Oh my God, he's typing!'

'*LOL,*' appears on the screen, quickly followed by, '**dick.*'

'Gross,' I say casually, showing the group his reply. 'I'm going to block him.' I pause. 'Unless you lot do want to see his dick?'

'Not especially,' Natalie says, not looking as amused as the rest of us. 'You get sent a lot of unsolicited willies on there and it stops being funny after a while.'

Before I can reply, backwards baseball cap has sent me a picture of his sad, semi-erect penis. Yuck.

'Fucking arsehole,' I mutter. '*Why are you sending me a*

child's penis?' I write quickly. '*That is child pornography, I will be reporting you to the police.*'

'*No it isn't*', he instantly replies. '*It's mine.*' That's immediately followed by, '*Fuck you fat cunt.*'

I delete it quickly and block him. Natalie's right, this isn't that fun. I hand back the phone to Nat and head to the bar to order more drinks.

When I return, we've moved on, and Hayley is regaling everyone with hilarious tales from the frontline of teaching. She's a science teacher at a secondary school in south London and apparently teenagers are obsessed with Bunsen burners.

'It sounds like a nightmare,' Vanessa grimaces. She's not really a kid person, which is fine, because I'm not either. We're going to have a happy, sleep-filled life together with no shitty nappies.

Hayley smiles. 'It can be, I guess,' she says, head cocked. 'But mostly I really love it. The kids are so full of excitement and hope for the future, it makes me a more optimistic person being around them. I feel like they're going to save the planet when they grow up, they care so much.'

'It sounds brilliant,' Natalie says breathily and she does look transfixed.

'Have you ever thought about teaching?' I say suddenly to Nat.

'What?' She looks surprised.

'I think you'd be amazing at it,' I say, realising she would. 'You love helping people, you're energetic, you're a natural performer. You also have more empathy than anyone I know, Nat – you always see the complications in life, the greys. Which is perfect for teaching. You want to help even the most hopeless cases. And let's not forget how much you hate your current job.'

'What would I teach?' She looks unconvinced. 'HR skills?' she says and laughs. 'I've forgotten everything they taught me during my Geography degree. Not that I learned anything anyway, I was too drunk the whole time.'

I think about it. 'What about something like drama?' I suggest, feeling inspired.

'Yes,' gasps Hayley. 'You'd be so great at that, Nat! You love plays and shows – all of that stuff – you're always going on about some musical or play.'

'And you love life's drama,' I say dryly, discreetly rolling my eyes and thinking about all the new names and characters she's tried on over the years. All the drama she's craved in her life, her love of silliness – this could finally be a good outlet for it.

'We actually have a teaching assistant post being advertised in the drama department right now,' Hayley says excitably, pulling out her own phone to look up the job description. 'You can train on the job.'

'Do you really think I could do something like that?' Natalie suddenly sits up straight. She looks more excited than I've seen her in years. 'Surely you need a teaching degree or something?'

'Initially, you need a degree, which you already have.' Hayley is nodding authoritatively. 'Then you need to do some kind of postgrad course – a PGCE – but if you're already working as a teaching assistant, you'd be a shoo-in. And there are bursaries or grants – stuff like that – to help you train.'

'Think of all the character names you could come up with for your student plays,' I goad and she looks inspired.

'I just added Lois Price to the names list,' she says excitedly. 'I got it from a supermarket cashier who was telling me about the cheapest deals and I misheard him.'

'Good one,' I tell her. 'And you're welcome to Zoe any time.'

She makes a face. 'Maybe.'

'Oi!' I am affronted. 'I thought you loved my name! It was one of the first things you said to me when we met.'

'To be fair,' she says awkwardly. 'I meant your surname – Darling. And I assumed you'd be a Zoe with, like, a y on the end – Zoey – or, at the very least, a Zoe with one of those sideways colons over the e. Zoë.'

'And spend my life looking for the keyboard shortcut for the umlaut?' I'm outraged. 'You wound me, Natalie.'

Hayley grins, ignoring our back and forth. 'I think this is a good idea, Nat,' she says confidently. 'I can really see you in front of a class.'

Natalie sits in silence for another minute, considering it. My heart's beating faster; suddenly I'm so sure this is the path for her. She'd be an amazing teacher, she has an easy way of speaking to almost anyone. She explains things accessibly – if not concisely – and is passionate enough to inspire young people. I think back over all those moments of kind, quiet calm she's given me when I've struggled. How she's counselled me through my many crises – Mum, my Giulia break-up, changing my job, silly fights with Vanessa – she's endlessly patient. I think how she pulled herself through everything with Joe without it turning her dark inside. She has all the best qualities of every teacher I've known. This is *perfect*.

NATALIE

I leave the drinks feeling befuddled from booze and buzzing thoughts.

Honestly, I kind of love the idea of teaching, but is it mad? I'm twenty-seven this week, I can't just change my whole career now! That's stupid. It's too late for that, surely? And do I really want to start training again? Haven't I done enough of school – do I actually want to spend another year taking exams?

And yet . . .

I want it. I really want it. Suddenly, urgently, I want it.

Because what's the alternative? Am I really going to spend the next forty years of my life doing HR? A job that, on a good day, I barely tolerate. What would it be like *not* to wake up every hour on a Sunday night, dreading the coming week?

Ugh, it's too big a decision. Too massive.

But Zoe did it. She did. It was years ago now, but she changed her career plans. Not entirely, like this would be, but she burnt her bridges quitting a job just when everyone thought she'd figured things out. Oh, but Zoe is so much braver than me.

Maybe I need to get the rest of my life straight before I focus on my job situation. Like, I need to lose the weight I've put on, and I need to find a nice boyfriend who'll be kind to me. Then I can have a think about work. I need to fix *me* first.

I walk to the bus stop, feeling alone and missing Zoe. I really miss living with her since she and Vanessa moved into their own place.

I mean, in some ways it's great living on my own for the first time. I do love the freedom and doing whatever I want. Ignoring the world, eating what I want, watching what I want. And I just subscribed to this thing called Netflix that Jamie and Mo keep telling me is amazing. I feel a bit disloyal to LoveFilm but I'm so bad at returning DVDs on time.

I check the bus timetable, eight minutes until mine's due.

My phone vibrates with a notification from Tinder. I study the average-looking man and his average-looking gym selfies with a below-average amount of interest.

It was fun at first, being on Tinder. Like, people watching. But after a few months of it, and barely any actual decent dates materialising from it, I'm feeling tired. Bone tired. It is exhausting keeping the faith. So taxing to keep believing someone lovely is out there, when most of the evidence is to the contrary. It's draining to talk endlessly with guys who disappear for no apparent reason or turn up to dates looking like their own dad. It breaks me down when someone finally seems OK, and then he starts trying to sext before we've even met, like the rest of them. I'm worn down. I need a break from it all.

But maybe I'm being too judgemental. Maybe it's fine that men want to send me a picture of their willy? Maybe that's just normal and cool and maybe lots of women actually really love it? Maybe I shouldn't have let Zoe block that guy with the baseball cap earlier tonight – he was so good-looking. Maybe if I'd just nicely said no thank you to the dick pic we could've had a good chat and it might've been the start of something. Oh, or maybe I could've even said yes please to the picture, and then been polite about his willy? I don't really get why men are so proud of those veiny appendages that leak bodily fluid and get bits of toilet paper stuck to the end, though.

But maybe, just maybe, it could've worked out with base-ball cap.

And at least he wasn't Joe.

I feel a pulse of guilt there, thinking about how nice Zoe was to me earlier when I mentioned the farting in my sleep thing. I don't know why I said it out loud, I thought it would be funny. But then no one laughed and I didn't laugh either, so I guess it wasn't.

Zoe thinks I was so strong after I dumped Joe. She says that, whenever he comes up, how brave and awesome I was in the months afterwards. Even though I don't really think crying all the time and eating ice cream for three meals a day was particularly strong or brave. And she doesn't even know the half of it. Sure, I was brave for the first few weeks, but then he started being nice to me and I couldn't resist. She doesn't know about all those nights I slipped out of the flat and went to see him – for months after we broke up. Zoe doesn't know how we would have sex and lie in each other's arms and how Joe would be so sweet and loving and charming afterwards. How he would beg me to come back to him and say that he'd changed and how no one would ever love me like he did. And how desperately, desperately I wanted to stay and how much I wanted to believe him.

But I didn't.

I kept hearing Zoe's voice in my head telling me that this nice Joe wouldn't last. He'd be back to that mean, cruel guy who bought me underwear two sizes too small which he said was meant to 'inspire me' to lose weight. The man who never wanted me to see my friends or family because they would 'turn me against him'. Who read my texts and email, then said I was worthless and pathetic.

And so I ended it – properly at last – and blocked him in every physical and emotional way I could think of. I deleted the photos and the messages, and trained myself to remember the bad, not the good. It worked. Eventually.

But now everyone seems to have someone but me. Everyone is happy and settled and getting sodding married. I'm the last single person in the universe.

The worst thing is when Zoe and Vanessa are kissing and see me looking. I catch their pity and that boredom over my loneliness in their eyes. And they pull away from each other like I won't be able to cope with their dumb PDAs! I want to scream that I don't resent them for being in love and being happy. Or, if I do, I wouldn't let it show.

My phone beeps again – the Ross guy Vanessa and Hayley picked out has matched with me. That's a nice feeling; I am at least worthy of a finger twitch right swipe from a normal-seeming man.

I flick through his pictures. He does have a nice face. And his bio is OK. He altogether seems OK. Maybe it would be OK being with him. Maybe we'd have an OK life together, warding off the loneliness at night with OK spooning.

My bus is pulling up.

You know what? I don't want OK. I want more than that and I think that's allowed. I don't want to date Ross. People called Ross should only ever date someone called Rachel anyway. I'm going to lean into the loneliness and embrace it. I'm going to figure out how to make my life good without a stupid man to fill it. And I think I know how.

I exit Tinder and pull up Safari instead, Googling, 'how to become a teacher'. I feel excited and scared, and it's a really good feeling. This could be the start of something more than OK.

12

Present Day

Grief is a funny thing, isn't it?

I remember when my grandpa died – a long time ago now – and that feeling like I was on the outside of the grief I felt. I was on the outside, looking in at my tear-stained face and forlorn smiles. Watching that small, grateful nod I gave when people asked how I was doing. It all felt so performative – so fake.

The thing is, I *did* feel sad, I really did. I loved my grandpa a lot. He was kind and smiley and let me sit in his special armchair when I visited. But every time someone asked me how I felt, I put on the sadness. I wore it, so they could see it.

It's a bit like that thing we all do when we call in sick for work. We put on an extra ill-sounding voice, even when we really are feeling awful. But instead, I put on an extra sad voice.

Someone's back at the door, knocking again. I can't keep ignoring it, they'll be starting soon. I can't miss it. I have to be there, up the front. I have to speak. I fumble in my bag for the folded paper. Two sheets of notes; a life boiled down. I don't think I can do this; my tongue feels thick and swollen.

I've always felt like grief is an inside thing. I hate how much we're expected to make it an outside thing. My sadness is private, I don't want to share it with that neighbour I met once or the priest who does this every week. Today I want my grief to be my grief. I want to cry and laugh and smile and sob in here, but out there, they can't have it. They can't have my grief.

I think she would understand that.

I slowly pick myself up off the loo, inspecting my black dress carefully for errant toilet paper. This is not the kind of event for that.

'I'm coming,' I shout, trying to sound reasonable but my voice is strangled and unfamiliar, my tongue still thick. 'Sorry,' I add lamely, too quiet for them to hear on the other side of the door.

I'm going to have to face them all now. I don't know how to do this. Not without her. I'm too scared without her, I always have been. Too scared.

I head to the bathroom door, take a deep breath, and reach for the lock.

13

2015

NATALIE

We stare at each other.

'You go first,' she whispers across the table.

I shake my head furiously. 'No, *you*, you're great at openers,' I hiss back.

There is more silence. I gesticulate wildly at her and she mouths, 'What?' angrily.

'For fuck's sake,' Zoe says at a normal volume. 'This is stupid, we should've written a script.'

'No, no,' I say, fiddling with the buttons. 'The whole point is that it's super natural and chill. We're just two hilarious legends, chatting about pop culture and the world, and – I don't know – unsolved crimes or whatever.'

'You want us to casually chat in an unplanned way about unsolved crimes?' Zoe looks at me perplexed.

'OK, shush,' I find the button I need and restart the recording. 'Just introduce us,' I whisper still waving my hands.

Zoe rolls her eyes witheringly and then gives out a resigned sigh. 'Um, OK, fine. Um, hi, everyone out there, my name is, um, Zoe Darling, and this is, um, Natalie Winters . . .'

She trails off and I pick up the thread. 'And we are the podcast pussies!' I say too loudly into the mic in front of me.

Zoe stares at me blankly. 'We're the fucking what?'

'The podcast pussies,' I hiss. 'We need a name for the podcast. This is a brand we're creating, Zoe, don't be difficult.'

'I'm not being difficult! That is the worst name I've ever heard; why did we not talk about this before you started recording?'

'Because we're improvising!' I say desperately. 'We're ad hoc, we're free spirited. We don't need to *consult*.'

'We definitely fucking needed to consult on this. I'm not attaching myself to that name.'

'OK, *you* come up with a name.' I'm trying to find the stop button again.

'Right now?' She looks a bit deer in headlights. 'Er, how about, um, The Drunk Pod?'

Shit, that's good, that's really good. How does she just come up with this stuff on the spot? It's so unfair. 'No, that's terrible,' I say jealously. 'We'll have to figure it out later. We can record the intro later, let's just start chatting.'

'About crimes?' She raises an eyebrow at me.

'Not necessarily,' I say, a little haughty. 'I just finished reading *Gone Girl* though, we could talk about that?'

'I haven't read it,' Zoe says unhelpfully.

'OK, well it's really good,' I say firmly. 'And all you cool listeners out there should totally read it. There's a woman in it who's a total psycho. Oh wait – should I say spoiler alert? She's not a psycho until the second half, when we've finished her diary. And her husband is, like, kind of a bit of a psycho eventually, too – spoiler alert.'

'I'm so confused,' Zoe interjects.

I ignore her. 'So, that's a five-star reccy from your podcast pussies.'

'I thought we agreed we're definitely not doing that name?' She looks annoyed now.

'We need to have catchphrases!' I say, a little high-pitched with frustration at her lack of cooperation. 'Y'know, things we say in every podcast episode, so that we can then put out merchandise and make money or whatever?'

'Did *Serial* have catchphrases?' she asks me seriously.

'Kinda!' I say, reaching for something. 'Like, Sarah Koenig is always saying like, er, "It got me thinking . . ." or something.'

'Does she?' Zoe looks suspicious.

'You know what? Never mind,' I say hurriedly, returning to the mic. 'So, how about that Zayn Malik leaving One Direction, huh? Do you think he and Jon Snow will, like, form a splinter group for sexy people?'

'Jon Snow? From the news?' She sounds suspicious.

'No, silly,' I say, trying to keep things relaxed. 'Jon Snow, from *Game of Thrones*. He's totally dead. Which is probably a spoiler alert, too. I'm saying, they should, like, team up and do some kind of spin-off.'

'Spin-off from what? I have no idea what you're talking about.' She has one eye shut, like she's trying to make sense of this. I take a long swig of my drink. Look at us – this is already solid gold content. We are so hilarious together, like Laurel and Hardy. I knew this would be great. I think this is going to be *huge*.

I've been trying to persuade Zoe to make a podcast with me for weeks. Everyone else seems to be making them, and it looks so easy. We're so funny together, it would be depriving the world *not* to do this. She finally said she'd do it as her birthday present to me, but only if we were allowed to get drunk while we recorded. I said that was a genius idea because it's, like, *so* relatable, y'know? Who wouldn't want to listen to us chatting like this, while tipsy?

'I'm getting another drink.' Zoe hops off her stool. 'Do

you want another one of those?' I nod, then remember I'm a podcaster now, and say out loud, 'Yes please, Zoe! You're so very kind and I do love to drink alcohol with you.'

She looks at me oddly as she opens the fridge, retrieving the gin and ice.

'Are you still recording?' she whispers as she pours and I sigh at her.

'Yes, of course, this is all great colour,' I explain. 'It's like B-roll. We're giving our fans a little insight into our record-ing seshes. This is all going really well; it'll be super funny to listen back to, I promise.'

Zoe sits back down, sliding my drink across the table to me. 'How about you hit pause there and we listen back. If it's funny, like you say, we'll keep going and we can even go with that terrible podcast pussies name or whatever you said. But if it is – as I suspect – really fucking annoying and stupid, we'll give up, get drunk without recording it and then head on over to your mum's for our birthday tea? Deal?'

Fifteen minutes later and the mic is locked away for – as far as I'm concerned – the rest of my life. I never, ever want to hear the sound of my own voice again. What an amazingly awful experience.

'To being twenty-eight.' I raise my gin glass to Zoe's. 'And to being old enough to recognise a dumb idea when I have one.'

Zoe laughs and raises hers. 'To the realisation that we are still young enough to make stupid choices, but being old enough to accept they're stupid very quickly.'

'Cheers!' I smile, nervously. 'And to being able to forgive each other any stupid choices, right?'

She laughs. 'Of course. Always.' I breathe out with relief and then spot the clock on the wall.

'Shit, we have to get to Mum's,' I exclaim. 'She said tuna sandwiches would be ready at six.'

'Shall we Uber?' Zoe asks, mildly.

'All right, moneybags.' I smile. 'If you want to pay. Some of us are students again.'

She side-smiles back at me. 'But you're loving it right?'

'So much,' I sigh, dreamily. 'The paperwork is awful, but the kids are so great. There's a girl called Becca in my class who makes me cry laughing when she's acting. Even the naughty kids make me smile, but I have to pretend to be stern. They mostly laugh at me when I act cross, but I think they're laughing *with* me, so I don't mind.'

Zoe giggles, looking happy. 'I'm so pleased for you,' she tells me. 'I knew this was a good move. Hayley says you're brilliant with the kids.'

'She did?' I'm delighted with this news. 'That's a relief because everyone at school loves Mrs Wilson; if she decrees that I'm good, everyone else will agree. Maybe she'll even get me a proper teaching job there when I've finished my training.' I beam at Zoe. 'What about you – is work still great?'

'It has its ups and downs,' she confirms. 'It's mostly fun, but I'm working with a couple of absolute nightmare artists right now. One needs all his dollar bills and pound notes to be *ironed* before he'll use them. Another dickhead demands a fresh loo at every venue. And I don't mean a clean loo, I mean literally a brand-new toilet installed. Like he's the fucking Queen.'

'Don't make me think about the Queen on the loo, please.' I wince.

'And there's one guy who requests the craziest porn to be

streamed at whatever hotel he's staying at on tour.' She leans in. 'It has to involve werewolves, which is much harder to come by than you'd think.'

'It's clearly not hard for him to cum by,' I say dryly.

'Please don't pun.' She looks pained.

'Well, that all sounds very intense.' I nod gravely. 'But c'mon, it's also clearly absolutely brilliant. One day, you're going to write the best celebrity memoir, exposing all these fools.' Zoe raises an eyebrow than nods, like she's banking that idea. I change the subject. 'And what about Vanessa? How is she? I can't believe you're buying a flat together – I'm about seven hundred years away from being able to buy.'

'Well, you know I couldn't do it without Dad's help,' she says sheepishly. 'He's lending us the whole deposit. I don't have any savings, neither does Van.' She pauses, before adding in a guilty voice, 'And it's not even really in London; it's so far out I don't think it actually counts as a zone.'

'Don't play it down, it's really exciting!' I say, trying to sound enthusiastic. I really am happy for Zoe and Van, but I'll admit, I do feel the smallest pull of resentment at her being able to take this big, giant, grown-up leap. Especially when I'm so far away from anything like that.

No, wait: not *resentment* exactly – just, maybe, a little bit of sadness at the reminder that I will be renting for the fore-seeable. I'm poorer than ever, after a year spent on minimum wage as a teaching assistant, while I qualify as a teacher. I'll be on OK money once I start my full-time teaching job, but I'm unlikely to get out of my overdraft for years, never mind put away any savings. And even if I wasn't changing careers, buying my own home would've been out of the question forever anyway. The only people I know who have any pros-pect of doing it have either inherited a huge great wad, or have parents helping them out. I know Mum would lend me some money if she could. She's so kind and has done what she could for me this past year while I've been retraining, but she's mostly as broke as me. She and Dad divided up their assets when they split up and it really wasn't much in the first place. There's no way she could help me out in the same way Bryan does for Zoe.

But it's OK. I like my rented bedsit flat just fine. It's damp, smelly and tiny, but I really like living on my own. I'll admit it took some getting used to at the beginning, but it's great now. And even though it's made me poorer than ever – even with a grant from the government and my mum chipping in – I'm genuinely so, so excited for my new career. Working as an assistant has been awesome this past year. Of course it has its rubbish moments, just like everything. There are sucky days when you can't even see for the mountains of paperwork on your desk, or when some entitled, rich parent scolds you for trying to help their entitled, rich kid. But it's mostly totally wonderful. The connections you make, the progress you get to see. You're literally watching these kids turn into *people* – people you're going to send out into the world, who you've hopefully made better with your words and presence. And, OK, sure, drama's not going to change or save lives, but ohhh, it's fun. It's so much fun. I really love it. I feel excited about what I'm doing for the first time in my life.

Everything would be really great in my life, if not for *the thing*. It hovers over my days like a shadow. The secret I have to tell Zoe. And I know she's going to hate me.

ZOE

When we get to Debbie's, the party is in full swing. I blow a kiss at Vanessa, who's already here, dancing to Abba with Sue in the corner, along with all three of my brothers. They look ridiculous but they also look like they're having a blast. I pop my head in the kitchen to say hi to Dad and Natalie's mum, who are red-faced trying to arrange sandwiches on plates.

The doorbell goes and Nat goes to let in a few of her uni friends, who all chorus HAPPY BIRTHDAY from the front door. They shout it again as they come into the living room and see me. Hayley's arrived with them, too, and we hug, shouting over each other about how great her dress is – no, it's so old; no, it's so great; no, it's so cheap; no, it's so beautiful.

Debbie looks harassed when I return with drink orders and my dad smoothly volunteers to be in charge of booze, grabbing bottles from the counter and following me into the living room to set up a bar area there.

I help myself to a gin and feel the warm buzzy feeling of being nicely drunk, without going overboard. I'm glad we're not doing anything wild this year. I used to love nothing more than a big night out for our birthday, but I don't feel that need any more. I like having a quiet drink with my family and close friends.

OK, but maybe I'll get a *bit* drunker?

Debbie brings in the sandwiches and the room piles over to the food table. Sue turns Abba up and we stand around, chewing tuna sandwiches and trying to make small talk over the music.

Matthew comes over and gives me a big hug. He looks really happy.

'Where's Sami?' I say, glancing around in case I've missed her.

'Oh, she has to work,' he says, grimacing. 'She sent her love and apologies for missing out.'

'She is a workaholic, that one,' I say, smiling and not minding. I'm very fond of Sami, and I know she makes my brother happy, but she's not really the life and soul at gatherings like this. I'm not sure she feels like she fits in with this lot. I glance around at the people gathered here. They are an acquired taste, to be fair.

'How are you guys?' I say, sipping from my plastic party cup. 'How's the new place?'

'It's amazing,' Matthew says beaming. 'Having the extra space has been great and Sami's got the little study to work in when she needs.' I give his shoulder a squeeze feeling very proud of my little bro. Things haven't always been easy for him, I know. Mum leaving, Mum returning, Mum going away again in a smaller way several more times. But at least we all understand the why of it now. She talks to us when she needs time away, instead of disappearing, and we continually check in with her while she's struggling.

It's been a tough road for my brother and I reckon some might've used it as an excuse to go off the rails. But not Matthew. I know he's struggled at times – work has been up and down over the years – but he seems to be enjoying his job in intensive care at the hospital. He and Sami seem great now, too. I was pretty worried about them not so long ago. They seemed to be arguing a lot while she was training to be a lawyer and whenever I saw Matt he was pale and quiet. He didn't talk about it much, he never was a big sharer, but I knew things weren't too good. But ever since they moved into their new house last autumn, they've been so much better. And look at him today, shinier and happier than I've seen him in years.

'I'm really glad, dude,' I say warmly, squeezing him again.

Behind us, Debbie starts shouting that it's cake time and we need to gather round to sing. Or, in mine and Nat's case, be sung to.

We sit down as Dad lowers the lights and I try to embrace the childishness of the moment. Everyone sings, and I can hear one person – probably Mo – singing the monkey/zoo version.

Natalie and I giggle at each other as the room finishes singing and shouts at us to blow out the candles. We do so in two blows and everyone cheers. I look up and catch Debbie's eye.

I wonder if she will tell Natalie her big secret today. It's been so weird keeping something so huge from my best friend these last few months and I feel awful about it. But it's not my secret to tell.

NATALIE

So, *the thing.*

It started about five months ago, not too long before Christmas, when targeted ads kept showing me cutesy Christmas jumpers to buy 'your other half'.

I'm not blaming targeted ads for what happened next, but they have been to blame for most of my worries about 'belly fat' over the last few years.

It was a Saturday and I was at a very triggering wedding all on my own. Of course, I hadn't intended to go on my own – not to a wedding full of awful people, that would be madness. I was supposed to be there with Zoe and Vanessa. Then Zo rang on the Friday to say Van's brother had last-minute decided to elope to Vegas and they were going with them. She said I couldn't cancel, as well, it was too rude. So, I had to go on my own. Leaving me to face a bunch of terrible, terrible people we went to school with, all on my own.

I got to the reception late and headed straight for the loo, cursing Zoe's name and wishing we hadn't accepted the invite. Honestly, it was weird that we were even on the guest list. It's not like we spoke to any of these people back then. But we couldn't resist the self-harmy appeal of attending. Y'know, that delicious and horrible pull of seeing people you hated so many years ago?

I hid in the toilet for thirty minutes, trying desperately to conceive of a way to leave without being rude, but also without seeing or talking to anyone. Eventually I negotiated myself down to staying half an hour. One drink, one circuit of the room. So people could witness I'd been there. Maybe I could squeeze in one small bit of eye contact with the bride from across the room and a quick thumbs up to show appreciation. Then I could go.

But then I walked in and immediately bumped into him. Into Simon Stan.

ZOE

I'm drunker than I meant to be – like always – but I'm having a good time. I've been dancing with Sue, who's been telling me about a new squash club she's joined.

'I enjoy it so much,' she enthuses. 'Bashing the balls as hard as you can and pretending they're men I've dated.' She briefly does the robot dance move and I copy.

'You've probably never seen a man's testicle, have you love?' she says kindly and I side-eye the room, clocking Vanessa chatting to Matthew.

'No,' I lie and she nods.

'You're lucky,' she tells me, 'They're dreadful little things.' She starts doing the Gangnam Style. 'Is this move still cool, Zoe, love?'

'Sure is,' I lie again. 'Do you have a squash partner? Is Debbie playing with you?'

'No.' Sue makes a face. 'She hates sport.' She pauses for a second, looking a little lost. 'I don't know what's going on with her, she's been really distracted lately. I don't know ... She used to tell me everything but I'm not sure now. I think there's something up but I don't know. Maybe I'm imagining it.'

She doesn't know about the secret. I feel awkward and open my mouth to say something but nothing comes out.

Across the room, Debbie loudly clears her throat. 'We have an announcement,' she shouts to the room. Next to her, Dad is turning down the music.

Shit, it's happening, they're doing it. I'm glad – I'm really glad – but I'm also weirdly nervous.

I found out their secret about a month ago, when I came back to my dad's one evening without calling. I was collecting some documents I needed for the flat sale, and let myself in without a thought. I assumed no one was home and wandered around for a few minutes stealing food, like I always do.

That's when I walked in on them, in the utility room, *doing it*. Debbie and my dad.

I already needed therapy – for sure – but this was some next-level traumatising shit. I screamed. Dad and Debbie leapt apart, frantically pulling on clothes and shouting at me that they were sorry, sorry, sorry.

They admitted they'd done the deed a couple of times and didn't want anyone to know before they'd figured out if this was anything. I said I thought they hated each other, and Dad made a weather joke about how the '*frost had started to thaw*' a couple of years ago, when Debbie shouted at Nanny Surrey. He liked that and they became a bit friendlier. And then, well, they – puke – had sex.

And now, in front of everyone, it looks like they're ready to tell the world they're a couple.

'We ...' Debbie swallows hard and Dad looks nervous. I smile at him encouragingly and he picks up Debbie's thread.

'We wanted to tell you – the people we love – that we are not together,' Dad says, and immediately looks relieved.

Wait, what? Did he say *not* together?

'We know that you must all have guessed by now that we've been having a bit of a fling ...' He laughs heartily and waves in my direction. 'And I'm sure Zoe told you all!' I screw up my face because A, what the absolute fuck is happening? And B, oi, I can totally keep a secret.

'We had sex three times in total,' Debbie says loudly, looking around the room and making eye contact with every guest. 'It happened a bit out of the blue and we thought it might mean something.' She glances over at Bryan who nods encouragingly. 'But then we realised it was just because we were both a bit lonely and drunk. It turns out I am actually really repulsed by Bryan!' She says this last bit delightedly and he grins at her.

'And I'm also repulsed by Debbie!' he adds. 'We should've known that, but the trouble is—' uh oh, he's making his here's-the-science-part face '—when a penis and a vagina touch each other in an intimate way, there are all kinds of confusing hormones released and you can get all caught up in it.' They both laugh warmly like this is a fun experience for everyone. 'Especially when you've been through a serious *dry spell*, if you know what I mean!' He winks slowly at the room and I feel the life force drain from my soul.

'Anyway, we thought it was important we tell you all the truth, so there's no confusion,' Debbie says grandly, like she's done us a favour. The biggest, most unnecessary favour ever. 'We are not together and have no interest whatsoever in ever being together. Or doing it again.' She pauses. 'Right, that's it, enjoy the party, everyone!'

I glance around the room. Everyone looks sick. The twins are barging their way out the door, possibly to literally *be* sick. Matthew is frozen to the spot, staring at the ground. Natalie's uni friends are trying desperately not to laugh, while Sue is making no attempt to disguise her look of disgust.

'You had SEX?!' she shouts now. 'With that guy?! That guy we hate? THREE TIMES?'

Debbie looks bashful, but nods. 'You had a right to know, Sue, I'm sorry. I know he's the worst but it just happened.' Bryan nods expansively, fine with being the worst.

'Why didn't you tell me sooner?' Sue yells and Debbie moves towards her, looking ashamed. 'No!' Sue takes a step back. 'Don't *comfort* me, Debbie. I thought you told me everything – what happened to us? We used to *talk*.'

She's genuinely upset.

I mean, I'm also genuinely upset – I just had to hear about my dad's penis going in and out of my surrogate mother, Debbie. But Sue is *betrayed*.

There is an awkward silence as people around the room shift a little, uncertain what they're meant to do next. After another minute of glowering, Sue storms out and Debbie follows. Bryan awkwardly tells Alexa to put the music back on and low talking around the room resumes.

I glance around for Natalie, keen to see her reaction to the sex announcement, as well as her mum's argument with Sue. She looks shocked, so shocked.

Poor Nat, she needs a hug, I should . . .

And then I see it.

I see it, and I cannot fucking unsee it. Is it right? Am I hallucinating? I can't believe this.

Red-hot rage fills my vision.

NATALIE

'Hello,' I said to Simon, my heart thumping in my chest faster than ever before. Faster than it ever went during my brief flirtation with jogging.

'Hello,' he said back, pleasantly enough. And then I realised he had no idea who I was.

'You don't remember me, do you?' I said, too amused to be offended.

'God, sorry,' Simon pulled a face, looking a bit sheepish. 'I don't. But please don't take it personally, I have the worst memory. I smoked too much pot as a teenager.' He paused. 'Did we go to school together? Everyone at this wedding seems to be from school, it's quite a memory-lane trip.'

'Er, yeah, we did,' I said, nodding slowly. 'We were in the same form for most of it.'

'Hmm.' He scanned my face, eyes narrowed. 'Wait, don't tell me. You do look very familiar.' Then he smiled that old Simon Stan smile and my insides went to jelly as he twinkled at me and my mouth gaped open. 'You'd think I'd remember someone so attractive.'

'I'm Natalie,' I said in a hoarse voice, and suddenly all those old fantasies flooded back to me. Simon and me kissing, Simon and me having sex, Simon and me getting married.

Maybe this was the universe's plan all along? We needed this time apart to find ourselves and figure ourselves out. So we'd be ready for this moment – for this reunion ten years later – when we'd had a chance to grow up and become better, nicer people. People who don't throw rulers at other people during class. The prospect was so romantic.

'Natalie!' He snapped his fingers in recognition, his eyes widening. 'Of course! I remember now. You were pretty quiet back then, right?'

I nodded helpfully even though I knew for an absolute fact I wasn't quiet. He just didn't hear me when I talked. But that was fine, because he was hearing me now, and he was also drinking me in like he finally wanted to touch my boobs. God, how they'd yearned to be touched by Simon's hands back then.

'You look great,' he said, a flirty tone to his voice. 'So different. God, school seems like a million years ago now. But it's also so weird being a grown-up, isn't it?'

I giggled. 'Yeah, it is. I still feel like a big dumb kid who's somehow allowed to turn the heating on and off whenever I want.'

He laughed generously before asking, 'Do you still hang out with that chick, Sophie? Was it Sophie? No, wait, Zoe, right? Zoe Darling, with the newsreader dad?'

'Weatherman,' I said automatically, and then looked down at my feet, feeling guilty because it sounded like I was putting him down. It reminded me of when Simon and his friends teased Zoe about it.

But he misread my gesture. 'You guys fell out, huh?' he said then nodded. 'I lost touch with most of the kids from our year, too. I still speak to Tom from Miss Cornelisse's class occasionally, but he lives in Canada now. I actually think it's kind of weird to still be that close to people you went to school with anyway!' He laughed, like we were on the same team.

'Er, right,' I hedged, not sure how to correct him.

'That Zoe girl was a total freak anyway,' he said in a low tone, relishing the subject. 'Someone told me she was writing One Direction fanfic for the internet a few years ago.' He laughed loudly. 'Tom forwarded it to me on Facebook and we had such a laugh. It was absolutely fucking terrible.'

I nodded, my face heating up because I was the one who wrote 1D fanfic and I couldn't believe people here knew about it. People I went to school with were passing it around to each other and mocking me?

'Do you remember how Zoe used to cry in the loos almost every lunchtime?' he hooted, not noticing my discomfort, and I got quieter still. He was talking about *me* again. I think Zoe only ever cried once, that first day I met her. I didn't think anyone knew about my daily crying sessions in the loo, never mind that they were all laughing at me about it.

'And do you also remember what, like, a *huuuuge* deal . . .' He rolled his eyes at this point. 'She made about coming out as gay in year ten? Like, who cares, Zoe? No one even knows who you are!' He laughed joyfully again, completely delighted with himself. 'And I bet it was just for attention anyway. I bet she's married to some boring bloke she met on Tinder by now.'

That was it for me, that was too much. It was one thing him humiliating me and my embarrassing memories, but to say that about my Zoe – my darling, beloved, brave Zoe – was beyond anything I could take.

'That is bullshit,' I said slowly, my face filling with blood.

'Huh?' He regarded me with surprise then.

'Zoe was – and is – the bravest person I've ever known, Simon. And she *is* gay, but she didn't even tell you idiots. Your good pal Tom found out and posted it all over Myspace, then Janine wrote it on the school loo walls. But even then Zoe didn't cry – she never cried about anything you idiots did – that was *me*. That was all me. Oh, and I'm the one who wrote the One Direction fanfic.' I was enraged. 'But, for the record, it wasn't terrible; a lot of commenters said it was really well written and sexy, so there. A lot of people have asked for more sequels!'

He looked amused then and the old Simon Stan sneer appeared.

'Oh, yeah I remember you now,' he sniggered. 'You're right, you *were* the loser out of the pair of you. Fat, dramatic, and always hanging around like a puppy, trying to be friends with us. It was so fucking lame.' He paused, and smiled like an evil cat. 'You know, we actually tried to save Zoe from you a few times over the years? She wasn't so bad – pretty, y'know? And her dad was on TV – but I think she thought you'd kill yourself or whatever if she dumped you. Like, who else would even talk to you?'

'I don't, um, I don't know . . .' They wanted to take Zoe away? She stayed my friend because she felt sorry for me? I froze up completely then. Suddenly it wasn't Simon's voice speaking, it was Joe's. Telling me I'm worthless, telling me I'm ugly, telling me I'm pathetic. I tried to speak again, to defend myself, but I couldn't.

And then he was there.

'Hey, fuckhead, how about you fucking fuck off?' came a deadly voice from behind me. Unfreezing, I turned slowly to find Matthew there. Lovely, lovely Matthew Darling, Zoe's little brother. The sight of him, standing protectively over me was like drinking a long cold glass of water when you're deathly hungover.

'Who the hell are you and what's it got to do with you?' Simon snarled. 'We're having a conversation here that's none of your business.'

'It *is* my business when someone's being a wanker,' Matthew said, coming closer to Simon and lowering his voice to a scary, dangerous level. 'Especially about my sister and her best friend. And you are most definitely being a wanker.' He pauses and then adds, 'Once a wanker, always a wanker, *Semen Stain*.'

Simon's nostrils flared and he turned a bit purple, looking from me to Matthew and back again.

'Oh, whatever,' he said at last and stomped away, muttering about losers.

Matthew watched him leave, a dagger stare in his back, daring Semen Stain to turn around. He didn't, and when he was lost in the crowd at last, I finally took a breath.

'Are you OK?' Matthew turned to face me then, taking me by the shoulders and furrowing his brow as he studied me, a worried look on his face.

I tried really hard not to cry. I tried really, really hard, but sometimes it leaks out of my eyes without my permission. And so I cried. And Matthew took me to the loos and held me while I sobbed on him. He kept stroking my head and telling me not to be sad about Simon being the same cruel idiot he always was. And I couldn't speak for tears. I couldn't explain that I wasn't crying at the mean words, I was crying over Matthew's kindness. I was crying over the sweet, caring, considerate way he was looking down at me.

And that's when we kissed again, for the first time in ten years. Despite where we were, despite what had happened, despite Zoe, and despite his wife. We kissed for a long, long time.

And we haven't stopped since.

ZOE

'WHY ARE YOU HOLDING HER HAND?' I shout across the room and a separate part of me, a million miles away from this furious me, says to stop shouting.

Natalie and Matthew spring away from each other and the room falls silent.

'I SAID WHY WERE YOU TWO HOLDING HANDS?' I yell again and I can't help it. I'm moving towards them and people leap out of the way, like I'm holding a knife.

'Zoe, it's not . . .' Matthew steps forward, standing in front of Natalie and the protective instinct only makes me angrier. He's protecting her from *me*? What the fuck is happening? 'Just hold on there,' he says, looking like he is ready to disarm a terrorist. 'It's not what it . . .' He can't finish the sentence. Because it is what it looks like.

'Are you fucking each other?' I say, and I'm still half-shouting even though I'm standing in front of them now. From somewhere behind me, I hear Dad gasp. 'Are you?' I say again, and I move around Matthew so I'm looking directly at Natalie. 'Are you having sex with my little brother?' I ask her, trying and failing to speak at a normal volume. 'Are you having sex with my *married* little brother, Natalie? Is that what this is?'

Natalie looks like she is going to have a panic attack, or cry, or both but I won't let her. Not until she's answered my fucking question. Is my best friend – who once swore on her life that she would never do this again with my baby brother

– actually having an affair with Matthew? Is she ruining his marriage? Has she been lying to my face about this?

I hold Natalie's eye until a weird calm seems to come over her.

'Yes,' she whispers and there is a small ripple of gasps around us. At least I wasn't the last to know.

I look at Matthew. 'You're cheating on Sami? You're cheating? You unbelievable shit. You're having an affair, just like Mum did? You're ruining someone's life. That is *disgusting*. *You* are disgusting.' I look between the pair of them and my breathing is shallow and hot.

Something far away in my brain registers a hand on my arm – Vanessa's. She's at my side. 'Are you OK?' she says in a low voice. 'What's happened, baby?'

I ignore her, still staring Natalie and Matthew down. 'Both of you,' I say quietly. 'You're disgusting. How long has it been going on?' They don't answer so I scream it. 'HOW LONG HAS THIS CHEATING BEEN GOING ON, YOU LYING FUCKING COWARDS?'

'Um,' Matthew clears his throat, looking around at other partygoers, 'about five months.'

I feel like I've been slapped. All this time, all this time, all this time. All the appalling, insidious lies they must've both told me in the last few months. The lies they've told Sami, too. I thought I knew these people, but they're liars, the pair of them.

I feel Vanessa's arm around me, she's whispering it's OK, it's OK, it's OK, it's OK. But it's not, it's really not. I shake her off, turn on my heel and walk out of the house, away from my girlfriend, my family, my own birthday party and my best friend.

14

2016

NATALIE

'Would you wee on me if I got stung by a jellyfish?'

'I don't know.' Zoe contemplates it. 'I think I read somewhere that's a myth? Like, weeing on it doesn't do anything except get you covered in wee?'

'OK.' I look at her pleadingly. 'But would you?'

'Is this a sex thing?' She looks suspicious.

'No,' I say earnestly, 'it's not a sex thing, I just want to know if you're my best friend.'

Her face appears from the top bunk, she's smiling. 'Do you want me to be your best friend?'

'Oh my God, like, DUH,' I say, trying to sound brave. I feel like I'm asking someone out.

'I mean,' she is smiling even wider, 'we've basically spent every day together since we met last month, so duh back at you.'

'Best friends then,' I say satisfied with the label I've been afraid to ask for. 'Forever.'

'No matter what,' she says, her head disappearing back into the top bunk. 'And yes, Natalie, I would totally wee on you. I would *poo* on you, if you needed.'

'Wow,' I say gravely. 'You really *do* care about me.' There is a long silence in the dark. 'So,' I add cautiously. 'Would you wee on me if it *was* a sex thing?'

'No,' she says. 'I really love you and we'll be best friends forever, but I don't want to do sex things with you.'

'That's OK,' I say and sigh dramatically. 'Nobody does.'

I realise I've been staring at a freezer full of peas in the cold food aisle for probably close to ten minutes now, thinking about that first sleepover I had with Zoe. The memory is so bright and vivid, it feels like it just happened. But it also feels like a million light years ago. That was the night we stole booze out of my mum's cupboard and got tipsy for the first time. It was great, until Mum called us for dinner and we realised she'd be able to tell. We were so over the top, trying our best to be casual as we acted sober. I realise now that Mum must've known immediately. *Especially* when Zoe then projectile vomited pink wine across the roast potatoes. I told Mum she'd had some bad Chewits and she nodded nicely, as she got a J-Cloth. Later on, in my bunk beds, we got a second wind and decided to give each other fringes with a fruit knife. It was a super-fun night and we didn't regret it, even when the other kids in 9CL made up a song about our awful haircuts. A song they sang at us for months until our hair grew back.

I open the fridge door and stare some more at the peas. I always buy Birds Eye but now I'm wondering if the cheaper ones even taste any different. Do peas have that much of a subtle flavour that I'd be able to tell? I highly doubt it. Zoe always bought the own-branded versions of things and rolled her eyes at my extravagance. But I could swear £4 Nurofen works so much better than Tesco's 19p version. Even though – as Zoe pointed out – the ingredients are literally exactly the same.

I pick out one Birds Eye packet, one own-brand and throw them both into my trolley.

Maybe I'll spend my birthday doing a pea taste test – that sounds like fun.

I sigh heavily and a nearby shopper eyes me warily. I probably look like a lunatic, ready to open fire on my fellow consumers. I give her a nice smile, trying to off-set the pyjamas and unbrushed hair, but that seems to alarm her more. She throws down her potato wedges and hastily exits the aisle. I fight the urge to shout after her that I'm normal and not going to kill her.

My phone vibrates in my bag and I pull it out. WhatsApps from Jamie, Mo, Hayley and a few of the nicer teachers at school, all wishing me a happy birthday. Sue's messaged, too, and I decide to ring her later. Her and Mum are in a weird place these days, but that doesn't mean I can't still speak to her and love her, right? My phone vibrates in my hand, and this one's from Matthew, asking where I've disappeared to.

I feel bad. He left me in bed half an hour ago to fetch birthday coffee and pastries from the Costa over the road. But when he'd gone I suddenly felt so breathless and panicked. I needed to get out of the house. I needed to get away and find oxygen. I grabbed my bag and headed for the nearby Morrisons to stare at peas.

Fuck, I miss her. I really miss her. This is our first birthday in fifteen years that we haven't spent together and it feels weird and shit and sad and I hate it. That sleepover was one of so many amazing times we had together, did none of it mean anything?

Maybe I should send her a message? But I've tried that so many times. There have been so many unanswered texts,

WhatsApps, calls. I've tried emails, Facebook Messenger, Instagram DMs. I even tried showing up at her flat and ringing the bell fifty times until Vanessa came out and nicely told me to go. She said that Zoe didn't want to talk to me right now and to give her time. But it's been a year! How much time am I supposed to give her? Is our friendship really over? Fifteen years of friendship – just cancelled? Am I meant to just accept that? I don't understand how this is a deal-breaker. I don't understand how falling in love with her brother was such a hard, red line.

Except I do know. Because I didn't just fall in love with him, I had an affair with him. Every time he sneaked out of his house to see me, he was betraying his wife, and betraying Zoe. Every time we did that, we were doing what Zoe's mum did to her dad. She's always been so fiercely anti cheating – I've seen evidence of that so many times – and as far as she's concerned, I broke up her baby brother's happy marriage.

It doesn't make it OK, but he wasn't happy and the marriage wasn't a good one, hadn't been for a long time. They got married so young. Matthew was trying to fix a hole, I think, left by his mum leaving him when he was so little. He wanted to find stability and thought marrying Sami would give him that. But it didn't. And then she went to uni and law school and buried herself in work, while he did the same at the hospital. They'd drifted apart before I saw him at that wedding. They'd both changed so much – as you do when you're in your early twenties. Nobody has any idea who they are when they're twenty – I certainly had no idea who I was back then. I still don't, really, and I'm twenty-nine today. But I do know I love Matthew. I know that with every bit of me. Every cell in my body loves him. I love the way his face and body moves,

I love the way he smells. I love the way he smiles at me with such kindness and goodness. I love the small, romantic things he does for me and the way he looks at me like he adores me. I've never had a man who looked at me like this, who doesn't want me to change anything, or be anything different than what I am.

I always wanted love and craved it, but I never knew it could be like this. I always assumed love meant sacrificing at least some of who you are. Compromising pieces of yourself and trying to change to fit yourself around them and their life. But it's not like that with Matthew at all. I am my best self with him, and I am my worst self with him – I can be myself fully – and he loves me through it all. We can't get enough of each other, it's like a sickness. I love him so much sometimes I feel like I'm going mad.

But I also love Zoe. And I didn't realise that loving one would mean losing the other.

She still sees Matthew occasionally. They've been civil when they've seen each other at Bryan's house for family gatherings. They had Christmas together while I was with Mum and Sue. And they were both invited to the twins' birthday drinks, recently. Matthew said I should go with him, but I didn't feel right about it. I knew she wouldn't want me there and I don't want her to think I've stolen her whole family. Matthew's tried repeatedly to talk to Zoe about the situation but she cuts him off or ignores him. She won't hear it. She doesn't want excuses or justification. I know she's angry with us both, but it's me who's really betrayed her.

Some days I'm so, so angry with her about it. How could she just abandon us like that? Didn't I deserve more than to be cut off without a word? Isn't she sad? Doesn't she miss me?

Some days I feel like even if she reached out now, I'm too angry to forgive her.

But then other days I am filled with such guilt. Guilt so gut-wrenching I have to drink entire bottles of Gaviscon. Because I effectively chose a man over my best friend. I stole her favourite brother, her younger brother, and I caused him to leave his marriage. My life has been good in so many ways this past year, but there's a huge hole in it. Life is good, but it will never be quite as good as it *could* be with Zoe.

I'm still in the frozen food aisle and I can see the scared woman is hovering at the end, waiting for me to move on so she can retrieve her potato wedges.

I oblige, moving slowly through the alcohol section. Bottles and bottles of memories with Zoe. God, we loved getting drunk together.

Maybe I should give in and join the gang for drinks this evening. I said no several times – I just don't feel like it – but maybe I should force myself? It might be good for me, and Matthew did say quite nicely that I should probably stop mooning, just because it's mine and Zoe's anniversary.

In the queue for the self-service checkout, I pick up some deodorant on sale. Why don't we talk more about how shit deodorant is? Like, it barely ever works and half the time you end up covered in white powder stuff. Why haven't they invented something better yet? I shove it in my basket.

'Do you have a bag?' the machine asks me.

'Not yet you idiot,' I mutter.

'An unidentified item is in the bagging area,' it trills and I feel myself going red. I hate these things so much; why have they started appearing everywhere? What's so bad about a human person scanning your items?

'There's nothing in the bagging area,' I tell her, but she doesn't listen. A woman with a name badge that says Keira waves her magic lanyard and the screen reverts to normal. For one item.

'An unidentified item is in the bagging area,' it tells me again.

'How is it unidentified? I have just sodding identified it to you!' I shout. I move the peas away and then put them back again.

'An unidentified item is in the bagging area,' it says and I swear to God it sounds bitchier than before.

'IT IS NOT!' I shout and Keira comes back again, looking harassed. She fixes it again and I continue.

The voice is back, moments later. 'An unidentified item is in the bagging area,' it gloats, sounding delighted with my incompetence.

'I WILL MURDER YOU WHERE YOU STAND!' I yell now and look up for Keira – instead, making eye contact with the scared potato wedges lady. She gasps a little at the sight of me and makes a run for it with her wedges, without paying. Keira shouts after her to stop but she doesn't and I watch as a security guard and Keira give chase. The three run around the car park as I finish paying and head home to Matthew. I need a hug.

ZOE

'Happy birthday, my darling, Zoe Darling!' Mum sounds upbeat and I smile into the phone, feeling relieved. She's been so much better again in recent months. The medication she's on seems to finally be striking the right balance. She's been more like the mum I remember when I was little – the one who threw me in the air and laughed a lot.

'Thanks,' I say shyly. 'It's really nice of you to ring.'

'Are you doing something fun to celebrate? What are you up to?' she asks and I feel a pang.

'Actually,' I say tightly. 'Vanessa and I are off to a baby shower shortly. I'm officially now of an age where birthdays don't matter, it's all about other people's life choices.'

'A baby shower?' Mum sounds perplexed. 'Isn't that an American thing?'

'Unfortunately, cuntery is contagious,' I explain, opening my wardrobe and examining its contents for something suitable to wear. It needs to be formal enough for a fancy garden tea party, but also durable enough to survive a thousand kids running and screaming around my legs all afternoon.

'Who's pregnant?' Mum asks politely.

'Oh,' I wave my free hand dismissively, 'one of Vanessa's friends from work. She's in the living room right now, wrapping a present. I probably won't really know anyone at this party.'

'But it's your birthday!' she exclaims sadly. 'You should be surrounded by your best friends today. You should be the one getting attention and presents.'

There is a beat of silence as the phone line crackles. I don't really have that many friends any more. I've always been more into having a small, close circle than a big group. Or, at least, that's what I always told myself. But the truth is probably more that I actually don't make friends very easily. After we left school, Natalie was always the sociable one. It was her uni friends we always hung out with. I met Hayley travelling, but since she and Natalie started working together, they've been a lot closer as well. So who does that leave me with, apart from Vanessa?

My family?

Except Natalie's stolen them, too, hasn't she. She took my brother. I can't even go to family parties without feeling awkward and unwanted. I know they all blame me for what's happened. They think I'm overreacting and making a fuss over nothing. But they don't get it. They don't get the betrayal. Natalie broke a promise; she lied, she *cheated*. Not to mention how fucking creepy it is that my best friend started sleeping with my baby brother. He even looks like me! It's like she's dating the male me. It's weird. And even though she's the one who lied and cheated, she still gets to walk away with everything she could've wanted: my brother, a happy job I encouraged her to go for, a big group of friends intact. I bet she's out partying with them all tonight, not even noticing I'm not there. While I'm stuck spending my birthday attending yet another awful baby shower.

'It's fine, Mum,' I say cheerfully as Vanessa comes into the room. 'I don't like a big fuss. I got a cake and some fizz at work this week, which was nice. And I'm seeing Dad for dinner tomorrow night.' Behind me Vanessa takes off her top but then stops changing to wrap her arms around me. 'I love you,' she whispers in my ear, burying her face in my neck, and I think to myself '*You're enough. I don't need a hundred friends. You're enough.*'

'Oh dinner, that's good,' Mum seems satisfied with this. 'How is he? Do give him my love.'

'He's great,' I smile. 'And thanks, I will.'

It's bizarre how friendly Mum and Dad are these days. You'd never have thought it possible. But Dad's a different guy now. Maybe it was finally letting go of all his resentment towards Mum – realising we're all human beings who fuck up and that she didn't do what she did out of spite. Or maybe it's just semi-old age chilling him out. Whatever it is, he's much more down to earth and emotionally open. He takes the time to talk to people – not over them – and he's so much braver. I even saw him threaten to put Nanny Surrey in a home when she was being shitty at Christmas! He smiles and laughs all the time. He actually made a non-weather related joke during his weather forecast on TV the other day! His viewers couldn't believe it – the clip went viral on Twitter.

'I saw him a few weeks ago,' Mum comments casually. 'Jack and I went to meet him for a drink. Even Debbie and Sue came for a few – along with this new fella Sue's been going out with. I can't remember his name. Eddie, maybe?'

I gasp. 'Not Edgar?' It can't be.

'Oh, yes, I think that was it,' Mum confirms.

'Her teen boyfriend?' I am agog.

'Is he?' Mum sounds surprised. 'She didn't mention it. They seem very happy together anyway. Although I thought things seemed a bit strained between Sue and Debbie.'

'I can imagine so,' I say, dryly, 'if Sue's dating Edgar. They both went out with him when they were seventeen – he cheated on them with each other!'

'Ooh, really? How exciting!' Mum gasps. 'You can under-stand why things are a bit awkward, then. Each to their own.' She sounds like she's about to say something else and I wait. She waits, too.

'I also, um,' she begins carefully, 'I also saw Natalie and Matthew for lunch recently.'

I stay silent. I don't want to hear it.

She continues, 'They're also very well and happy.' Another long pause and then she sighs softly. 'I know it's not my place to say, Zozo,' she starts slowly, 'given everything I've put you and the boys through over the years. But my love, forgiveness is good for the soul. Holding onto something like this is very bad for you; it eats away at your insides until there's nothing but blackness left. Believe me.'

I'm silent, resentment building. I hate hearing this. As if I haven't heard variations of the same fucking tune over and over from everyone in the family this past year. I bet no one's telling Natalie off, scolding her like she's a child. Why does everyone think it's their business? I'm an adult; no one gets to tell me how to feel about my best friend betraying me. And it's a real slap in the face, hearing it from Mum. I have forgiven her for everything that's happened, and we've been over it so many times in group therapy. I know I can't throw it in her face every time she says something I don't like. But I so want to.

I say nothing and she continues, 'I just want you to think about it. You always had a hard time with forgiveness, even before I made it worse. As a child, you would sulk for days – like you'd never get over it – when one of the boys took your toys. It's hard to let things go, I know, and I know I don't deserve to be giving you advice, but I just want what's best for you.'

'Look, I have to go,' I say simply, trying to keep the anger out of my voice.

'Oh, no!' She sounds panicked. 'Please don't go, don't be upset with me. I'm sorry I said anything! You know I love you.'

'Of course,' I say, trying to sound kinder. 'It's just that I'm trying to get dressed for this party and can't find the handbag I need. It's the only one that matches these ugly, baby-proof shoes.'

'OK, sweet girl,' she says, sounding resigned. 'If you're sure I haven't upset you?'

I climb inside my own wardrobe, bashing my forehead as I go. Behind me, I hear Van laughing at me.

'No, ow, I'm fine,' I say, trying not to drop the phone. 'But I have to go.'

'Did you bang your head?' She sounds concerned again. 'Quick, how many fingers am I holding up? Who's the foreign secretary? Are you voting leave or remain?'

I laugh. 'I don't know, I don't know, and oh God! Enough about Brexit, please.'

I hang up and keep searching. It's here somewhere, I swear. I'm sure I haven't thrown it away, I never throw anything away. Vanessa accuses me of being a hoarder.

There! I spot a corner of leather and pull it out from beneath a pile of other barely used handbags I've accumulated over the years. There's a slightly damp smell as I unzip it, wary of the many gross things I may find in there. I empty out an old pen, three tampons, a mini pack of chocolate buttons that I'm going to eat – and at the bottom, along with random crumbs and a thousand hair grips, is a small piece of paper. Curious, I unfold it and read TXFF338792DF.

I frown at the jumble of letters and numbers, written in a shaky hand in what looks like black eyeliner. And then I remember.

The Wi-Fi code. From our old house. This is the code Natalie acquired from our neighbour Pepe at our twenty-first birthday. She kissed that old creep to get this for me, even though she was moving out.

My hand is trembling as I stare at the piece of paper for another few seconds. And then I screw it up into a ball and throw it back into the recesses of my wardrobe.

WHATSAPP

To: Zoe Darling

Today

I really hate that we haven't spoken today
message deleted

Please can we just talk?
message deleted

How many times do I have to say sorry?
You know I never meant for this to happen
message deleted

I miss you so much, Zo
message deleted

To: Natalie Winters

It's so weird spending today without you
message deleted

Do you think we could go get a drink?
message deleted

Fuck, I wish I could just get over this
message deleted

Stop messaging me creepy deleted messages

15

2017

ZOE

My pulse is racing as I go to settings and hit unblock on her name.

She answers after only two rings but says nothing. There are a few seconds of silence as we both breathe heavily into the handset, listening to the familiar sound of each other.

When we were teenagers, we would do this on our landlines during those few-and-far-between evenings when we couldn't hang out. We'd do our homework in silence, just being on the phone together from afar, occasionally complaining about the maths teacher who delighted in fucking us over with square roots. I know she got into trouble with her mum over the phone bill, but my dad never said anything about it.

Fuck, I miss her.

'I cheated on Vanessa,' I blurt out suddenly. The heaviness of weeks and weeks of shame empties out of me and into the phone.

The silence continues and I wonder if it's too late or this is too big. I am so, so ashamed of myself, so frightened by what this means about who I am as a person, so terrified that this means I am my mother's daughter after all. And I'm also so fucking embarrassed by my hypocrisy. Cutting off my friend and brother over something I've now done myself.

Until last week – until the test – I really thought Natalie and me were over. I thought our friendship was dead and buried, too mauled and kicked and punched beyond recognition to be revived at this point. But when that white stick did its thing and those lines appeared, Natalie was the only person I wanted. The only person I could call and the only person who could help me. But still, it took me days to work up the courage. I waited until the last possible moment.

'Oh, Zoe,' she says at last in a low, sad – and oh-so familiar – voice. But it is without judgement.

I let out a low sob that is more like a growl. 'I'm sorry to call you after all this time, I didn't know what else to do,' I say through hot, humiliated tears. 'I really, really hate myself.' I pause as tears roll down my face. Natalie stays quiet, so I keep going, readying myself to share the worst of it. 'And I'm so, so stupid, Nat,' I say, my voice breaking. 'And it's worse than that; it's worse than you're thinking. I'm pregnant, Nat, I'm fucking pregnant.'

There is another silence as she registers this. Registers that I must've cheated with a man. I'm a cheater and, worse than that, I'm a liar. I've been lying to myself, as well as Vanessa.

'Wow,' she says in the same soft, sad way. 'I'm really sorry, Zoe.' She's said those words so many times in the last couple of years – in every message and voicemail and email, but I'm only hearing her now. Carefully, she asks, 'What are you going to do?' and I look down at my shaking hands.

'I have an appointment,' I say shakily. 'For a termination.' The word sounds heavy and final, but somehow it's easier to say than abortion. 'Will you come with me?'

She doesn't hesitate. 'Of course I will,' she says simply,

easily. Like I haven't ignored her and treated her like she's nothing for two years. The shame beats down on me at her kindness. I forgot how kind she is.

'It's today, at four,' I say quickly, wiping my face. 'In north London, is that OK?'

Again, she barely misses a beat, although I know school must be busy with exam season ahead. 'I'll meet you there.'

NATALIE

As I hurry from the Tube station to the clinic, my stomach growls furiously. I'm so nervous that I haven't eaten anything today and I'm starting to regret it. What if I get hangry when I have to be my absolute nicest, most supportive self? Hopefully adrenaline will get me through. Or maybe they'll have a vending machine in there? Surely abortion clinics need a glass case of chocolate more than literally anyone else.

I check my watch; it's four already. I can't believe I'm going to be late to Zoe's abortion, that is so uncool. To be fair, she only sent me the address an hour ago. I was starting to think she'd changed her mind – but about the abortion or me, I wasn't sure. I'd already arranged cover for my afternoon classes, so was able to run straight out the door, but I'm still going to be twenty minutes late. I don't think they do abortions on time, though, do they? Probably not. I assume she's doing this through the NHS so, wonderful as they are, there's bound to be a wait.

I'm still trying to process the fact that Zoe called me. She *called* me. After all this time and all this hope, she finally called. And it was for something huge like this. It scares me a little that she's had no one to lean on this whole time. Has she been alone for all her big life stuff these last couple of years? I hope not. I've missed her – desperately – but I've also had people. I've had my uni friends, my work colleagues, and I've had my Matthew. Who does she have, really?

Her dad? Sometimes her mum? Vanessa?

But if Zoe got to a point where she slept with someone else, I have to believe things aren't great between them these days.

I mean, I'm not trying to excuse her doing what she's done. Obviously it's not ideal, but I'm not one to judge her, given my history with Matt. Honestly, I just think life is messy and difficult and stuff happens. We don't know what's really going on in anyone else's life or head. We make the choices we make, nobody can judge.

I'm sweaty when I arrive and ring the buzzer, ready to give an exotic fake name over the intercom, but no one asks. They just let me in and I make my way down a corridor, into a waiting area. A woman behind a protective glass frame looks at me enquiringly and I stammer, 'Er, I have a friend here?'

I glance around and spot Zoe in the corner. She's wearing a hoodie she had when we were friends and it makes me feel oddly better. I kind of had this idea that she'd be totally changed since our estrangement. That she would've thrown away any vestige of our friendship and life together the moment she walked out the door. She'd have a whole new wardrobe, and maybe she'd even have a whole new face, from extensive surgery. I know that's irrational, but it's how I felt.

She glances up and I breathe out. She looks exactly the same. She hasn't aged at all, and I feel shy, knowing I have. I suddenly wish I'd put more make-up on and then remember where I am. A full face of make-up would've felt a little inappropriate.

'Hello,' she says, half-smiling as I approach.

'Um, hi,' I say, and I find myself waving the tips of my fingers. 'I'm really sorry I'm late – the tubes were slow and Google Maps wouldn't load properly.' I'm rambling and she giggles nervously. 'Are you OK?' I add anxiously.

'Yeah.' She nods, looking a bit pale. 'I've just been in for the first bit.'

'Oh my God, and I missed it?' I say guiltily, taking a seat next to her on the plastic chairs. 'I'm so sorry, Zo.'

'No, no.' She shakes her head. 'Don't worry at all. That was just the first quick consult. She was a nice lady, she went through some questions. Y'know, to check I definitely want to do this. There are two more consults before I can leave, so it'll take a few hours I think.'

'Ah,' I say, unsure what to say. 'And – and that chat was OK? You didn't have any . . . doubts?'

'No,' she says determinedly, staring straight ahead.

I nod, and then keep nodding like an idiot bobble head as we sit silently.

'Have you noticed on telly, when characters get pregnant accidentally—' she begins suddenly after a few minutes of quiet '—they talk about the possibility of having a termination and they're asking their friends whether they should or not – all that – but then they end up having, like, a miscarriage or it turns out to be a false positive test. I think it's because writers are too afraid an abortion will make their characters unlikeable.'

'Maybe,' I say carefully. 'Are you afraid this will make you unlikeable?'

'Maybe,' she echoes back. 'I just always thought I was above this, y'know? Like, if this ever happened to me – although I didn't think it ever would, given my 90 per cent lesbianness – I figured I was feminist and intelligent enough not to be upset or feel bad. I would proclaim my abortion from the rooftops and let those who would judge me just fucking *dare*. I even kinda hoped there would be protesters or whatever outside the clinic I went to, so I could argue with them and show them that they didn't scare me.' She pauses and looks down. 'But it turns out I don't feel like that. I'm just fucking embarrassed. I feel like such a fool.' She lowers her voice and looks around at the few other nervous young women in the room. 'And I can't believe I'm *thirty* and doing this. These teenagers must think I'm a stupid old woman. This happens to teenagers who haven't had proper sex education, not me.'

'I get it,' I say slowly.

'I'm having to force myself to even say the word *abortion*, honestly,' she says. 'For some reason, it sounds so intense. I don't know, I thought I'd handle this better. I'm so sure I want to go through with this – I don't want kids and this was a terrible, terrible mistake that would ruin my relationship – but I'm also, well, I'm really ashamed.'

'You shouldn't be,' I say forcefully. 'This happens. We're human beings and we mess up. You're here, you're doing what is right for you and I think you're brave.' I pause. 'It will be OK.'

She takes my hand and squeezes it. It's our first physical contact in years and I fight back tears. This is not the time for me to be emotional. If anyone gets to cry, it's Zoe. There's plenty of time later for talking about the big things and being sad or happy.

A nurse opens a door and calls her back in.

'Shall I come with you?' I say quickly and Zoe shakes her head.

'No, I'm fine, honestly, stay here. I don't think it'll take long.'

As she gets up, I notice she's wearing Christmas socks. Christmas socks for a termination feels like a bold choice and I try not to laugh.

She is under twenty minutes and when she returns her clothes look a bit dishevelled.

'They did a scan,' she whispers, sitting back down. 'She showed me the inside of my womb and said the wall muscles are very strong and smooth, so I feel pretty puffed up by that. Might have another abortion just for the compliments.'

I laugh politely but I can tell she's freaked out.

'It's six weeks and one day,' she adds after a minute. 'How can they tell that so exactly?'

'I thought you slept with this guy only a few weeks ago?' I ask, interested.

She nods. 'Yeah, it's weird,' she explains. 'They date it from your last period, not from conception.'

'But that means you could literally be a virgin,' I whisper back, fascinated. 'A virgin who gets pregnant her very first time and you'd be classed as being pregnant before you ever had sex.'

'It's confusing.' She nods anxiously.

'It'll be OK,' I say simply and hold her hand.

'I took the first pill,' she goes on after a minute, a little shivery. 'That stops the pregnancy hormones. Then I take the second part tomorrow at home, which will make the product pass.' She pauses. 'That's what she called it – *product*. Strange, right?'

'Is Vanessa at home?' I say anxiously and she shakes her head.

240

'She's staying with friends in Cumbria for a few days,' she explains. 'I made a work excuse last minute, so I didn't have to go with her.'

We fall silent before Zoe sighs loudly. 'Now we just have to wait for the prescription to be approved by an external doctor. They said I can wait here, or go out and get some food. Come back in an hour or so.'

'What would you like to do?' I ask nicely, praying my stomach won't start growling too loudly.

'Can we stay here?' she says, looking a little wide-eyed and chewing on her top lip.

'Of course,' I say quickly. It's fine, I'm not *that* hungry. I won't die, waiting a few more hours to eat. On the other hand, passing out from hunger during someone else's abortion might come across as a bit melodramatic?

'I have a Dairy Milk in my bag if you're hungry?' she says, reading my mind and I try not to sound too grateful in my reply.

'That sounds amazing,' I say and smile. 'Thank you.'

She hands it over and I chew silently for a minute, knowing we have a while to go yet.

'While we're waiting . . . should we, um, talk about . . . the elephant in the room? And I don't mean me,' I nervously bark-laugh. 'I mean us. What happened?'

'Shhhh.' She smiles beatifically, resting her head on my shoulder and closing her eyes. 'Not yet. Later.'

ZOE

I wake up late the next day in bed, still in my clothes. Natalie is curled up on the end of my bed like a puppy. She's also fully clothed.

After we got back from the clinic, clutching a paper bag with pills, a hundred leaflets and two packets of enormous maternity sanitary towels, we sat up late, talking about silly stuff. Memories, mostly, from being teenagers. The sleepovers, sneaking out to the local park, the cinema trips, the late night talks about every minute detail of school and family. It was nice.

We still haven't talked about the big thing between us and the two-year silence. I guess we'll get to that, but for now we're still enjoying pretending nothing's changed.

I have to take my next pills later today – they go up inside me – and Natalie insisted on staying until it's over. I keep waiting to feel anything – pain, more guilt. But I don't. I'm just relieved. The last few weeks, since *it* happened, I've felt nothing but panic and fear and, above all else, so fucking stupid. But now it's done – or almost done – I feel so much better. Much lighter and easier.

Although, the nurse warned me this next part will be quite painful.

Natalie stirs at the end of my bed and blinks open her eyes. For a second she looks at me like I'm a stranger, her brows furrowed. Then she smiles.

'How are you feeling?' she says blearily, stretching out and yawning exaggeratedly.

I don't answer, instead asking, 'Do you remember that very first sleepover, where we got drunk and trimmed each other's fringes?'

'Yes.' Her smile is wide. 'I was actually thinking about that not so long ago.'

I laugh before adding, 'That was honestly the best haircut I've ever had. Do you want to trim my fringe again some time?'

'Sure!' she says excitedly and then giggles again. 'Zoe, did you know I kept a lock of your hair for, like, a month after that night, as a keepsake?'

'Dude,' I side-eye her. 'That is so massively creepy. Only serial killers and new parents keep locks of hair, and they are two sides of the same coin.'

'I know!' she says, delightedly. 'I was such a creep back then. But I was so obsessed with having a real-life best friend, I wanted to treasure every moment of the friendship in case you changed your mind and dumped me for someone better.'

'You idiot.' I shake my head. 'Who did you think I was going to run off with?'

'Well,' she says quietly, looking at me a bit penetratingly, 'I know you could've dumped me, many times over.' She pauses and stares down at the duvet. 'I bumped into Simon Stan a couple of years ago and he told me the truth about our schooldays. He told me you could've been one of them, that they regularly invited you out with them and tried to save you from me.'

'Why would I ever want to be *one of them*?' I shriek. 'They were awful! They were mean and unkind and so busy trying to pretend to be cool that they never even had any fun. I mostly felt sorry for them. It must've been terrible being popular at school – all that pressure to fit in and be cool.' She half-smiles, but like she doesn't really believe me, so I keep going. 'Nat, you don't seem to understand how brilliant you were – and are – and how much fun we always had together. You always act like I've done you a favour being your friend all this time – but I was your friend because you're amazing and silly and bring the sunshine wherever you go. I never had a bad day with you around.'

'Well, you sure did walk away fast enough when I did

something you didn't like!' A small hint of anger leaks out. 'You didn't give it a second thought.'

We fall silent again. I clear my throat, feeling like shit. I gave it plenty of second thoughts, and third and fourth. I was so angry for so long. And every time someone tried to gently tell me I was cutting off my nose to spite my face, it just made me more entrenched in my fury. It made me feel so ganged-up on. But gradually that faded and I just felt sad and lonely. I regret the way I acted so much, but how do I explain all of that? How can I say that now without it sounding like petty excuses?

'You know, I saw Sue last month?' I say softly, my heart beating quickly. 'I bumped into her in a Costa around the corner from my work.'

'Yeah?' Natalie sounds distracted.

'We ended up having lunch together.' I swallow, thinking about how thrilled I was to see her. How it made me realise how much I missed her and all of them – Sue, Debbie, Natalie, Matthew – even Natalie's silent, boring Dad, John. I missed the unconditional warmth. The laughing, the dumb soap operas and the Toblerones. They welcomed me into their family with open arms when it felt like I didn't really have a family of my own.

'She never mentioned it,' Natalie says, looking curious now.

'No,' I shake my head. 'I asked her not to. She gave me a lot to think about. Everyone's been telling me how stupid I've been these last couple of years, but she didn't say that. She wasn't judgemental and she didn't tell me off. She just made me talk about how you and me met and the things we've been through. What we've survived, what we meant to each other. She mentioned that she and your mum had a falling out over her new boyfriend, and how stupid it is. She told me how desperately she wants to say sorry but how it gets harder and harder. Especially when you get older. There are so many more excuses not to back down because you're so much more set in your ways. She said pride is a stupid fucker.'

Natalie stares down at the duvet and the silence stretches out between us.

'Do you want a coffee?' I say eventually and she nods.

When I return, she's typing on her phone.

'Sorry,' she says automatically, putting it down as I put her coffee down on the bedside table and get back on the bed. 'I was just texting Mam my mum.'

'It's OK,' I snort, pulling the covers back up over me. 'You can say his name. I know you're still together.' I pause and then add, 'And I'm happy for you both.' I stop again. 'I mean, *now* I am. I get it now and I'm really sorry. It took me a long time to understand it wasn't about me. I'm sorry. I realised how short-sighted I'd been. But by then it felt like it was too late to come crawling back, asking for forgiveness, y'know? I felt like I'd been an idiot but I had to dig my heels in and pretend I wasn't being an idiot. It became too big in my head to come back from.'

Natalie's face clears and she looks like a teenager again. I was so caught up with what was happening yesterday, I hadn't really taken her in. I do now, and notice the small lines starting to crease the edges of her eyes. It doesn't look bad at all – being thirty suits her. But I am suddenly sad, thinking some of those worry lines are probably my fault.

'Really?' she says, and she's smiling a lot. 'I thought you still hated me. I wish you'd called.' She sighs. 'I wish I'd kept trying, I wanted to. I never wanted to give up, but after a while I got too embarrassed and thought you might take out a restraining order or something. I felt so awful for taking Matt away from you, you have no idea. I've nearly broken-up with him a dozen times over this. I never wanted to lose you, but it was so much worse that I came between you two.'

'I was being a child,' I say, sighing. 'I was so staunch about my views on life and the world. I thought I had it all figured out and was being true to my *morals*. I guess it was partly because of what Mum did – I decided that cheating was the worst possible thing in the world. And I still don't think it's a good way to handle things, but I also understand that stuff happens and we all fuck up. I know that better than anyone now.'

There's a long silence as we both reach for our coffee. We take a sip, even though it's still too hot.

Natalie breaks the silence. 'Do you want to talk about what happened?'

I howl loudly and Natalie grabs my hand, looking agonised and apologising.

'No, no,' I say. 'I burnt my tongue.'

We both laugh a little awkwardly, and when I look up, she's staring at me without judgement. 'Yes,' I tell her. 'I really do want to talk about it. But I'm so embarrassed and angry with myself. This has been such a shitty fucking year. And it's all my fault. I sent my best friend away and pushed away anyone else who tried to talk to me about it. Your mum and my dad have wasted hours trying to convince me to forgive you and Matthew, and I was too butt-hurt and proud to admit they were right. So I even stopped going over there.' I sigh heavily. 'And things started getting bad with Vanessa, probably be-cause it got to be too much for her. She was the only person I had left and that's too much pressure to put on one person. A partner can't be everything, I know that now. I took my shitty resentment out on her and picked fights because it was easier than hearing about how crappy most of my choices have been lately.'

Natalie is listening carefully as she picks up her coffee and takes another sip. She's always had more of an asbestos tongue than me. I bet it was her brief smoking phase when we were teenagers.

'And there was this guy at work—' I break off because saying this out loud is making me feel hot with shame. This is my first time talking about it with anyone and I have no excuse. 'We were having a busy period in the office and I didn't want to be home with Van, so there were a lot of late nights. I was lonely and he didn't care what a bad person I was. He laughed at my jokes, he was nice to me. We got close, and one night, me and him . . . it just happened.'

I start crying. Natalie moves closer and puts her arm around me. She doesn't say anything and I'm glad. I don't want her to try to make me feel better about what I did. I don't want to hear that I'm a good person really, or excuses for why I might've done what I did. I need to – I *should* – feel bad about this, because it was a bad thing. You have to feel your feelings, good and bad, because otherwise you end up packing them in a box and pretending you're fine. You tell yourself you're in the right, that you deserve this, you're owed this, instead of dealing with the truth. It's what I've done for the past two years and it's time to confront what a piece of shit I've been recently.

I cry softly for a while longer on the bed, and Natalie stays where she is; arm wrapped around me. Eventually I sit up, feeling a thousand times better, and I drink my lukewarm coffee.

NATALIE

The pain started half an hour ago, and I can tell it is worse than Zoe was expecting. She can't keep still, continually marching around her living room and then sitting back down on the bathroom floor.

And it is worse than I was expecting, watching her go through this.

I put the central heating on about an hour ago because she described it as bad period pain, and now she's leaning up against the radiator, quietly moaning. I can tell it's not helping much.

'Can you pass me more painkillers?' she asks and her voice sounds hoarse.

'Of course,' I say, getting up off the floor and retrieving pills and a glass of water from the kitchen.

'I'm sorry, I'm going to need to poo some more,' she tells me, pulling down her leggings, her towel already full of blood after only a few minutes, and sitting on the toilet again. 'Pooing is usually one of my favourite things, but this isn't fun.'

'It's only a few hours,' I try to sound soothing, like a nurse on *Casualty*. I pop the glass of water on the shelf next to her. 'You can get through this. You're a woman, we're strong.'

'I always thought I was strong,' she says, sweatily. 'I assumed I had a high pain threshold, but I'm starting to re-consider. I can't believe women have babies. I'm just trying to pass an olive, I cannot imagine having to pass a nine-pound baby.'

I wince at this, but stroke her nicely, trying not to let Zoe see how much this is all getting to me. She takes the codeine from me, dry swallowing them; too tired to reach for the water beside her.

'You know, I thought about calling my mum for this,' she says suddenly.

'How are things between you these days?' I ask curiously, realising I've missed a whole year of ups and downs.

She shakes her head, her face pale. 'Not bad.' She pauses, 'But I also wouldn't say we were close. I thought if she ever came back into my life, we'd have our big emotional reunion, and then be super close – best of friends – once we reconnected. But it's quite up and down.' She falls silent for a few seconds before continuing. 'Then, when I realised I was pregnant and got so scared, it made me think about how scared she must've been when she got pregnant with me. Maybe she already knew she wouldn't be able to handle it. Because I knew right away. I knew I couldn't handle it. It made me feel sorry for her. She had my dad, she was financially stable, she had a home. To everyone else, she must've looked like she was ready and capable. Like, what could go wrong? But I'm financially stable, I'm in my thirties, I have a partner – and I don't feel ready. I don't think I'd ever be ready for that kind of responsibility.' She trails off again. 'I guess, what I mean is, that I wanted to ring her and tell her I get it a little bit more now. I didn't want her by my side – not like I wanted and needed you – but I felt like telling her I understand what she went through a tiny bit more.'

'Maybe you should?' I offer.

'Maybe I will,' she says simply.

I don't know what else to say, so I don't say anything.

'Can you distract me, please, Nat?' she says desperately, leaning her head into her lap. 'Talk to me about anything. Anything at all.'

'Sure,' I tell her, thinking fast. 'So, when do you think Trump will blow up the world? I'm surprised it hasn't happened already, but I guess he's only been in office a few months. I give him six months, tops.'

'He's bound to get impeached before he can start a war,' she says quickly through her hands.

'I don't know what impeaching is,' I say, feeling perplexed. 'Do they put you in jail? Didn't Bill Clinton get impeached?'

'Er, I don't know,' she says, and she must be in pain because she usually pretends to know about politics, even when we both know she's as clueless as me.

She changes her pad and I continue, conversationally, 'Genuine question. Do you think Trump would actually have sex with his daughter? Like, if he could get away with it and no one would know?'

'Yeah, I do,' she says, wincing at the pain and the question. It's bad again and she gets up off the loo and walks up and down the room, holding her stomach like she can force the discomfort back in.

'Shall I put some music on?' I say brightly, leaping up to get my phone to play Spotify.

A notification pops up. Matthew's messaged again to see how I'm doing. My heart aches for him, I suddenly miss him so much.

He doesn't know the specifics because I assumed Zoe didn't want me sharing this with her brother, but I have told him who I'm with. I said I was staying with her for a couple of days to talk things through and he was so happy to hear we've spoken. I know this whole thing has been really hard for him, too. The estrangement from Zoe has been like a dark cloud hanging over us and the whole family.

I send him a quick 'Love you, all good xx,' and then say loudly. 'Any music requests?'

'Anything,' she says, and now she's doing star jumps, her face focused. 'Anything – but make sure it's loud.'

I hit shuffle on a random playlist and 'Build Me Up Buttercup' by The Foundations comes on. Whoops, doesn't feel right for an abortion playlist. I hit skip and Destiny's Child 'I'm A Survivor' comes on instead.

Yes, that's much better.

'You doing OK?' I ask carefully as she jumps up and down.

'Yep,' she puffs. 'This is helping with the cramps, it really is. And it might shake out the clots.'

'Gotcha,' I say neutrally. 'Can I get you anything else?'

'Um . . .' She stops to catch her breath and then makes herself into a small ball on the floor. 'What else will distract me?' She considers it. 'Maybe we can watch porn? What are you into?'

'Ah, that's tricky,' I say. 'I'm very easily turned off by the wrong move. Like, I don't want to see anyone's anus and I don't want fake boobs. I need a penis in my porn, but I don't want too many penises, that's excessive. I like a kind of small ugly man, so I feel like I could overpower him easily, but I also—'

'OK, never mind.' Zoe's looking at me, half-bewildered, half-amused.

'Sorry,' I add, a bit shamefaced.

'No, no,' she waves her hand, 'it's good. I feel very distracted. I like a penis occasionally in my porn, too. But mostly not.'

'That sounds about right,' I smirk and she suddenly looks determined.

'I have to tell Vanessa I'm bisexual.' She sounds sure of it.

'You still haven't told her?' I say, realising there are a lot of gaps in our timeline. 'Are you going to tell her about all *this*, as well?' I gesture around the room as if it represents the cheating and the termination.

Zoe bites her lip hard. 'I don't know,' she admits. 'I want to, I want to be honest with her. But I don't know if that's selfish? It really was a one-time thing, and even when I was having sex with him, I realised I didn't want to. It was rubbish and just made me miss Van. I want to give us a shot and stop being a dick to her, but if I tell her about this, it's going to be in the relationship with us always. She'll always think about it and know I did that to her.'

'I don't think you should tell her,' I say slowly. 'I know that isn't necessarily the right or good answer, but if you're staying with Van and want to fix things – and you really have no intention of doing this again – I think it's kinder to her never to say a word. I won't say anything to anyone, you won't say anything, and she'll never have to carry this thing around with her.'

Zoe nods a little, looking sad. 'I never would've thought of myself as a person who could cheat. Never mind then lie about it. I guess you don't know how you're going to feel about something or a situation, until you're in it.' She pauses. 'I don't know if I can keep it from her. I did this awful thing. But if I'm only telling her to alleviate my own guilt, I should shut the fuck up, right?'

She winces in pain again and heads back into the toilet.

ZOE

'You know who would be great in this scenario?' Natalie says, staring up at the bathroom ceiling. 'Andrea Allen from school. You remember she had seventeen abortions in year twelve?'

'No she didn't,' I protest weakly. 'You believed everything you heard at school.'

'Oh my God, shut up, she did!' Natalie gasps. 'She told everyone she did.'

I smile to myself. It feels like old times.

'I feel like you deliberately timed this,' she says after a minute.

'What do you mean?' I say, looking over at her.

'What do you mean what do I mean?' She laughs. 'It's our birthday in a few days. Spending it together was our tradition.'

'Fuck, I'd completely forgotten,' I say, hand to forehead. I'm sweaty. 'Of course it is, that's so weird.'

'You haven't got a huge party planned, then?' she says, studiously casual.

'No.' I shake my head, looking down. 'To be honest, birthdays haven't been that much fun these last couple of years.'

'Same,' she says quietly and we fall into silence, lying side by side on the bathroom floor.

Guilt pulses through me. See, I was so angry for so long, but even when that faded, the pride stayed. My self-righteous, high-horsing kept me away from Natalie for so long that when I slowly started to realise that I missed her – as well as the closeness I'd had with Matthew – and understand that life can be complicated, it felt like it was too late.

'Can we go back?' I say softly. 'Can we forget this shit and go back to being best friends forever? Go back to stealing booze off our parents and trimming each other's hair and re-watching *The Parent Trap* and brainstorming new names for you. Can we, please?'

There is a long silence. Too long.

'I don't think I can,' Natalie says at last, looking desolate.

'Why not?' I sound panicked. 'I'm so fucking sorry, Nat, you have no idea. I know I'm a hypocrite and I'm selfish and I'm superior. I've been such an idiot but we can get it back, we can be close like before, I know we can!' I'm crying now, on the floor and I don't know if it's the pain in my stomach or the pain in what I'm saying. 'Please, Natalie, please. Can't we just try? Can't you just forgive me and let it go and we can try to make things right?'

'I don't know if I can. You don't know what's been going on, this is . . .' She is close to tears, too, as she trails off.

'But you can tell me,' I say desperately. 'You can fill me in on everything that's happened. I know it's my fault we missed so much, but it isn't more than we can overcome. Don't you miss us?'

'Of course I do!' She bursts into tears. 'I miss you all the time. I've missed you every day. But it's too much. We've got such different lives now. Matt and I are moving to the suburbs, you're in London. You've got all . . . *this* going on, and I—' She stops short again.

'Tell me,' I say urgently.

'We've been *trying* . . .' she says in a whisper. 'We've been trying to have a baby for a year. I've had two miscarriages; it's been so horrible, Zo.' She swallows hard and continues in the same whisper, 'The doctors can't find any problem, the tests have all come back pretty much normal. It's just not happening for us. We want this so much and it's not happening. And it's not even that interesting – so many people we know are having issues conceiving. It seems like everyone is bloody infertile! But at least most of them have a specific problem they can address. We're stuck just trying and trying, and losing babies.' She pauses to wipe her face with a tissue from the

254

loo roll above our heads. 'Meanwhile you—' She stops again, looking at me so sadly.

Meanwhile, I got pregnant from a one-night stand and made her come and watch me have an abortion.

There is no anger, no malice in her voice but I understand very clearly what I've just done. What I've just put her through. After two years of furiously punishing her, I ask her to do the hardest thing in the world – and she did it. She didn't say a word, she didn't try to talk me out of it, or judge me. She wouldn't even have told me about this if I hadn't pushed her for answers.

'I'm sorry.' I match her volume, knowing that sorry doesn't cover it and never will. 'I didn't know,' I add lamely.

'And there were problems with our friendship already,' she adds, hesitantly. 'I couldn't see it until we were apart, but there were. We were either completely co-dependent, or competing. I was so jealous of you for so much of our lives.'

'B-but,' I stutter, 'b-but we'd worked on the co-dependent thing, we got better.'

'It wasn't just that,' she says simply. 'You cut me off for lying to you about Matt, which I understand. But half of our relationship was you keeping things from me – mostly so you could feel good about yourself. You lied about your virginity, you lied about enjoying that marketing assistant job, you lied about my mum and your dad being together. You're always trying to win, Zo, and I've lived a life dazzled by you and grateful you were willing to be around me, which isn't right. It wasn't a relationship of equals.'

The truth of this hits me in the chest. She's right, she is. It wasn't deliberate, but she's right. I liked having someone hero-worship me. Part of me enjoyed keeping Natalie low so I could feel high.

We sit there in silence, knowing too much has happened. We can't come back from this.

'You better get back to Matthew,' I say standing up and desperately trying not to show the pain on my face. 'I'm feeling a lot better, the worst is over.'

She stands up. 'Are you sure?' she says, drying her face. 'I can stay, I don't mind.'

'No, really,' I tell her. 'You have no idea how grateful I am that you came, I was so scared. And I'm so sorry I put you through this.' I pause before adding, 'I mean through *this* today, but also, the last couple of years, maybe even the last fifteen years. I hope you'll forgive me one day.'

She smiles but it doesn't reach her eyes. We hold hands for a few minutes in silence, her warm fingers in my clammy ones, and then she turns away, picks up her bag, and leaves.

16

2018

NATALIE

God, I hate her, I hate her. Look at that dress, it's so beautiful and white and lovely. And she's so nice and sweet and
charming.

'Do you think she's really, honestly, that earnest?' one of
the NCT mums says cautiously. 'I mean, I really like her,' she
adds quickly. 'I'm just alarmed by how *nice* she is. Like, what
if she makes Prince Harry really nice, too? We don't want our
royal family to be relatable, do we?'

'Bloody hell, no!' Another mum – whose name I have
never known but it's too late to ask – looks alarmed. 'They're
the royal fucking family – we want them to be sneering and
snobby and occasionally dressed as Hitler or naked in a Vegas
hotel room.'

'You know, I never saw those nude photos of Harry?' I say
sadly. 'I was afraid I'd get arrested if I googled them. Does he
have a nice willy?'

'Ask Meghan,' Siobhan says and sniggers. 'And yes, I do
think she really *is* that nice. She's just American, they're earnest, it's a *thing*.'

'I'm not that sure about Americans, you know?' unidentified pregnant lady says. 'My Pilates teacher is American and
she says *pussy* way too much.'

'In what way?' I ask, trying to imagine doing Pilates ever, never mind at eight months pregnant.

'In a confusing way,' she says stroking her bump affectionately. 'Like she's trying to sound supercool and modern about it. She's like, "Pussies to the sky, ladies!" And then fist-pumps the air while everyone mutters at her to go fuck herself.'

I'm starting to quite like the sound of Pilates.

Siobhan makes a face.

I like Siobhan; she's the only one in this group who complains about being pregnant. Everyone else refuses to talk about the awful parts, insisting only that it's a 'miracle', like robots. That's what you get with IVF mums, I guess.

'I feel like pussies in the sky might be quite painful?' Siobhan glances downward, looking worried.

'Yeah, and then she *woos*, like it's empowering,' says unidentified woman. 'When did feminism become solely about being "empowered"?' She rolls her eyes. 'I have to keep pretending I'm an empowered woman at work when really I want to cry every day and hide under my desk with a plate of pasta.'

'Me too,' I say, warming to her. Is it Gwen? I think it's Gwen.

'I miss my pussy, I haven't seen it in months,' Siobhan says and sighs, looking forlorn.

'Ugh, please can you not call it that?' Maybe-Gwen cringes.

'What am I meant to call it?' Siobhan looks genuinely curious.

'Didn't we reclaim cunt?' a usually-quiet woman called Beth pipes up. *Hidden depths, that Beth.*

Siobhan nods. 'In theory, but I think most people still don't like it.'

Maybe-Gwen sits up straighter. 'I don't like it because I

feel like men are now saying it again,' she says loudly. 'Like, they got scared of saying it for a while, but now they hear women saying it, they think they can use it again.'

Siobhan waves her hands. 'That's unacceptable. It's *our* word to use or not use if we want. We're the subjugated ones. We're the ones who had that word used against us as hate speech for all that time. *We* get to decide if we use it now or not. But men never can, they're banned for life.'

'Agreed,' I say, trying to fit in. I shift in my chair, uncomfortably. Actually, I'm uncomfortable all the time. Every minute of every day. And today I have the worst heartburn, it's awful. It kept me awake all night, and I could barely eat my usual four slices of morning cake earlier. Terrible. Matthew kept asking if there was any chance I'm in labour, but I know it's not that. I know with absolute certainty that labour's going to be a thousand times worse. My mum told me in horrible, horrible detail how bad it will be, within an hour of me telling her I was pregnant. And then Sue googled labour horror stories and read some out. I left when she clicked on Google images. So that was great.

I feel like the world is divided between people who are obsessed with making out like your pregnancy is completely magical – who insist on stroking you without permission and drilling into you how lucky and miraculous you are. And then the other half of the population who are appalled and grossed out by every aspect of it. Who can't wait to tell you how horrendous pregnancy is and how much worse your life is going to be with a baby in it.

And if one more arsehole tells me to 'sleep now while you can,' I will get violent. How am I supposed to sleep, when I have a huge, squirming thing attached to my front end, regularly kicking my internal organs and sending the rest of my body's hormones into overdrive? Seriously, I now have hair where no human person should have hair and my feet are two sizes bigger than before.

But obviously I'm very lucky – and I know I have to keep saying that, or the universe or God – whatever – will smite me and my baby.

I had miscarriages before this one finally stuck. They were early term, but still, every step of this pregnancy has been scary. Every odd feeling sent me into a panic spiral. Every movement – or lack thereof – made me dial the first two numbers of 999. And the further along I got, the scarier it's been, in lots of ways. Because losing this baby now would be something I couldn't recover from. Not ever.

So – even though I haven't totally bonded with this NCT group – I am really grateful to them. They made me realise how normal it is for your body to be basically falling apart every minute of the day. I haven't worried nearly so much since I met Siobhan, Beth, maybe-Gwen and the others. It's been a comfort.

I feel bad for the husbands who don't have a group to share with. Matthew's pregnancy-anxiety has been even worse than mine. Poor guy has been quivering with fear every moment of the last eight months. In fact, he's been quite close to getting fired multiple times because every time I winced, he called in sick. He kept cancelling plans with friends, as well, too afraid to leave my side for more than a few hours at a time. I don't think he's seen any of his mates since last summer.

It's adorable and he is the sweetest, kindest man I ever knew. But I also legitimately want to kill him. Thank God he's away overnight in Liverpool for a training day with his team. I can finally relax for one night on my own and spread out across the bed, in all my humongous glory.

Oh wait, look at that, I have three texts from him checking up on me.

We finish our lame decaf coffees and head out into the bright sunshine, waving at each other as we head off in different directions.

I decide I like these women. They're mostly super nice and we have plenty in common, but every time I'm with them, it makes me miss Zoe that little bit more. I miss who she was intensely, but it's also about that history you have with someone you've known for a long time; the in-jokes, the sideways glances, the secret smiles when you know you're thinking the same thing. I miss her advice and her no-nonsense pragmatism, I miss her stupid laugh, I miss having wild nights out with her and quiet nights in. I just miss *her*.

I haven't seen her since last year and that difficult thing she had to do. I really needed space after those intense two days and for a while afterwards I struggled with what she'd done. It was worse than I thought it would be, seeing her do that and having to be unquestioningly supportive, all the while knowing my stupid womb wasn't working.

But then I got pregnant. And the closer I get to giving birth, the more I think I've been silly. I mean, why do I make these big, declarative statements? Why did I do the speech about never being able to go back! It's my dramatic side, I think. I'm always *so* convinced in the moment of feeling an emotion, that I will never feel a different way. Why couldn't I have just asked Zoe to give me a bit of time, instead of all that can't-go-back stuff and nonsense? It was *so* melodramatic.

The trouble is, a lot of what I said that day remains true.

We weren't equals a lot of the time. And I still don't really know how to forgive her for abandoning our friendship like she did. I had some of the best and worst times of my life in those two years she was missing. I really needed her, and she wasn't there. I don't know how to get past that.

I've been having some counselling these past few months. I realised I had a few things to sort out in my brain and a lot of it came up and out in a scary way when I got pregnant. I needed to talk to someone professional about what happened way back when with Joe, and also about my body issues. My therapist has been incredible and with her help, I've *not* been staring in the mirror every morning, calling myself names and crying over the huge changes my body is undergoing. It's really strange, rewiring a brain that's spent thirty years criticising, into a brain that instead says wow, look at what you and your body are capable of.

Recently, my therapist and I have started talking about Zoe. I really want to work through the sadness I feel about losing her. Even though I think it must be too late for us to get back what we had before. Too much has happened.

Right?

That *is* right, isn't it? You can't just blank each other for pretty much three years and then pick up where you left off. Can you?

Dammit, it's so hard to keep a thought in my head at the moment. I feel like crying constantly, I'm so emotional and hormonal, but God help anyone who says I'm being any of those things.

My phone rings; caller ID says it's Sue. I smile as I answer. I get one of these check-in calls every few hours from someone in the family. Mum rang just before NCT and now it's Sue's turn.

'Hello, baby machine!' she crows and I giggle.

'Thank you for that reductive title,' I scold and she scoffs.

'I called your mum the same thing when she got pregnant with you,' Sue laughs down the phone. 'She didn't like it much either. But I think you're both mad. Pushing a person out of your genitals, how can anyone believe in a God when that's how we make people?'

I laugh again, rubbing my tummy. Sue's voice always makes him or her squirm like mad. I don't know if it means they like her or not.

'So you won't want to be called Grandma, then?' I tease and she makes a gagging noise down the line.

'No thanks,' she says cheerfully. 'Sue will do me. Although Edgar's dying to be a grandpa.'

'How are things with you two?' I say, stopping to sit on a bench. I can't walk more than a few minutes these days without a rest.

'Oh love,' Sue's voice changes. 'You know the whole thing started out as a joke really? I only messaged him back to annoy your mum, after that whole Bryan fiasco.'

'You mean their weird, creepy, secret fling?' I shudder.

'Yep . . .' I can hear her nodding. 'Seeing Edgar again was only meant to be payback, to prove a point. But . . .' she trails off sounding dreamy.

'But?' I smile to myself.

'But, bloody hell, my darling,' she breathes into the phone. 'He makes me so happy. I never thought I'd be just another idiot in love. I'd sworn off men after my fourth marriage ended but I think he's It for me now.'

'Like a scary clown with a red balloon,' I mutter but she's not listening.

'I know your mum finds it strange,' she continues, sounding

a bit more serious. 'But she'll get used to it eventually.'

'Are things still a bit off between you?' I ask carefully and Sue sighs.

'I don't know,' she admits. 'One minute things seem to be back to normal, you know, the way they've always been. The next, it feels like we'll never get back to how we used to be – sharing every single thing. I know having Edgar in my life is hard for your mum, I understand that, but I really want us to get past it. I guess friendships have to change.' She pauses. 'You know that better than most.'

I swallow hard.

'But never mind, love,' she says breezily. 'There's plenty of time to get things back on track. And even if I don't see quite so much of Deb these days, you know I love you and I'm always here for you.'

'I do,' I say solemnly, vowing to talk to Mum. They just need a proper talk, a clear-the-air chat, that's all.

'So anyway,' she says, 'you're not in labour then?'

'Nope,' I say, laughing.

'Good.' She sounds satisfied. 'I better go then, Edgar's coming home early so we can spend some time in the Red Room. Have you read that *Fifty Shades* book, love?'

'Got to go,' I say in a high pitch. 'Loveyoubye.'

I hang up, feeling sick. My phone battery's almost dead. Another annoying problem with so many people constantly checking up on me.

I stand up, ready for the Herculean effort of walking.

Ow.

Shit, this heartburn is getting worse. I need to get home and lie down and/or eat more cake.

I turn the corner onto our road and almost double over with the pain. Oh God, maybe this isn't heartburn after all.

She opens the door and it takes me a moment to recognise her: she's like two Natalies glued together.

'Holy fuck, you're really pregnant,' I say aloud, and she laughs and then grabs her back and howls, all feral-like.

'Correction,' she says, huffing furiously after a second. 'I'm done being pregnant, I'm about to give birth.'

'Where the fuck is Matthew?' I ask, following her into the entrance hallway and glancing around curiously at the unfamiliar space. The walls are nicely painted – recently done – and I wonder if this was Natalie nesting. 'Did you ring for an ambulance?'

'Matthew's on his way back from Liverpool,' she says, panting again. 'But I don't think he's going to get here in time. The contractions are coming too quickly now.'

'But, but . . .' I can feel my breath quicken as the situation fully hits me. 'We should call for help then, shouldn't we?'

'I think it's too late for that,' she says, picking up an over-stuffed overnight bag, then putting it down again as another wave of pain hits her. 'And I was too scared to ring 999. It's for emergencies and I didn't know if this counted.'

'It fucking counts,' I say, feeling prickles of sweat under my arms. 'OK, let me take that bag, we need to get you into the car.' She nods determinedly, steeling herself, and I offer my arm. She looks at me as if noticing I'm really here for the first time and grabs onto me, smiling grimly. 'Let's go then. It's not far, it'll be fine.'

We slowly make our way out the door, her fingers vice-like on my arm, and I beep the car to open it. I let go to open the passenger side and she shakes her head.

'I better go in the back,' she says, nodding towards the messy backseat and I cringe, thinking about the half-eaten McDonalds and wrappers back there.

'Right.' I'm trying very hard to stay calm as I help her clamber in.

When she messaged me an hour ago, I misunderstood.

'I'm having a baby,' she wrote. 'Can you come right now?'

I thought she meant she'd weed on a stick, I thought she was emotional about getting pregnant after the miscarriages. I didn't know it would be *this*.

Matthew kept this from me. Why? And how did Dad not let it slip?

I guess I haven't been back home much these last six months, or even called much. Work's been busy and I've been so focused on making things better with Vanessa that everything else fell by the wayside. Yet again, I've been head down, selfishly hiding from the world and feeling sorry for myself.

I start the car, my palms sweating, and set the satnav with shaking fingers.

'Are you OK?' I ask a little redundantly, adding quickly, 'I mean, I know you're not. You're in labour and you're in the back of my car without Matthew . . .'

'Thanks for reminding me!' She bursts out laughing.

'Sorry,' I say lamely, pulling out of the road and praying the traffic won't be too bad. This isn't central London – they live in the suburbs now – surely it'll be OK. 'I guess I kind of meant generally? Are you OK? It's been a while since . . . Matthew, he never told me you guys were . . .'

In the back, she's breathing hard again, rubbing her stomach.

'I'm sorry,' she says, looking up and talking to my mirror. 'That was my fault. I was so scared for the first four or five months. After what happened with the other pregnancies. I didn't want to tell everyone this good thing was here, and then have to tell everyone a really bad thing.' She pauses. 'And then I so wanted to reach out and tell you personally, but I couldn't figure out the right moment or the right way. I wanted to speak to you properly and make it about *us*, not force you into a reunion because of this.' She gestures at her belly and then doubles forward again. These contractions are way, way too close together. Why didn't she call an ambulance? Or, at the very least, someone better equipped than me at dealing with this. I'm not even first-aid trained. They offered a course at work and I told the HR woman to fuck off and die. I'm so stupid, what was I thinking?

'I understand,' I say solemnly, eyeing my speedometer. My satnav says eighteen more minutes and I need to get her there faster, but I also cannot risk her by going any quicker – I can't risk either of them.

'And then there are so many classes and so many books you're meant to read, and I was overwhelmed,' she sounds tearful. 'All I wanted to do was lie in bed eating and crying. I wanted this so much but then it happened and it's such a big, scary thing that I don't know how to cope with. Am I really ready to be responsible for a human being, y'know? I'm terrified. My therapist says I am a catastrophiser, that I can't help it. My brain goes to the worst possibility too fast. She's given me some coping mechanisms but how do you breathe and tap through the idea that you're making *life*? A life that is going to grow up and know people and love people and hurt people.' She groans and undoes her seat belt to squirm around on the back seat. 'I've been in a state of terror for so many months. Then, suddenly I'm eight months pregnant and I haven't told the one person in the world I really want to tell most.'

We look at each other in the mirror. 'Me?' I say, my chest filling up with emotions I can't quantify. She's nodding hard and we're both crying a bit. I wipe furiously at my eyes, focusing hard on the road.

'I can't get emotional right now,' I say sternly, my throat dry. 'I want to talk and hug and cry a lot, but this is no time for a big heartfelt moment, Nat. You're having a fucking baby.'

She screams in a low, keening way and I grip the steering wheel that little bit harder.

'I think,' she spits through gritted teeth, 'this is the perfect time for a heartfelt moment, actually, Zoe. I'm having a fucking baby!' I laugh again as she continues. 'And I need to know if this kid has a godmother or not.'

I nearly yank the wheel as I glance back at her.

'Are you serious?' I say, eyes back on the road. 'Do you really mean it?'

'YES,' she shouts, climbing the walls of the car in agony. 'Of course I mean it. You've been my best friend since we were fourteen. And I don't care about some stupid, pointless estrangement. You were the person I wanted today, in the scariest moment of my life. I mean, Matt would've been good, too, but I think even if he was with me, I'd still have called you. I needed *you*.' She pauses to pant heavily. 'And I was the person you wanted with you last year, when you were scared. That means a lot. Being angry and resentful is a waste of our life, Zo. I want you in this life and I need you in the baby's life.'

I'm crying again; big fat, slow, hot tears pouring down my face.

'But you'll have to stop swearing so much once he or she starts talking,' she adds through gritted teeth.

I sniff hard. 'I guess I can try,' I say, my voice high with the emotion and I grin at her in the mirror. She starts to smile back and then she makes the most blood-curdling noise yet. It sends shivers right down my back.

'I think you're going to have to pull over,' she says when she finally stops screaming. 'I can feel it's coming. I have to push, I can't stop it.'

'But we're almost there!' I shriek. 'We're so close, can't you hold it in?' I am fucking terrified, but OK, probably not as terrified as Natalie. She's now on all fours in the back seat and she's so red in the face it occurs to me she might have a stroke. That's a thing, isn't it? Pregnant women have strokes? I'm sure I read that.

'I CANNOT FUCKING HOLD IT IN! I DON'T HAVE A CORK, I'M NOT A WINE BOTTLE,' she screams and I take a deep breath. She must be in a lot of pain if she's swearing, she never swears.

'YOU'RE GOING TO HAVE TO – AAAARRRGH-HHH—' The scream is piercing and I wince. 'YOU'RE GOING TO HAVE TO PULL OVER, ZOE. RIGHT NOW. THIS IS FUCKING HAPPENING, IT'S HAPPENING RIGHT NOW.'

I indicate and pull into the side of the road, my heart hammering. I look around us frantically, but there are no other cars or people around. Who lives so far away from anything? In the back, Natalie's still swearing like a trooper and I feel oddly proud of her.

I throw myself out of the car and pull open the back door, Fluid has soaked across the backseat and Natalie sees my reaction.

'Oh my God, I'm so sorry about your car,' she moans, looking panicked.

'Fuck, don't worry about that right now!' I say soothingly. It's Van's car. She's going to murder me.

'Oh Jesus, it hurts, it hurts so much!' She's crying and sweating and it's awful.

'What do I do, Nat? Tell me what to do?' The fear is in my voice and I try to breathe before speaking again. 'What can I do? What do you need? I don't have hot towels or, like, an epidural? I honestly don't even know what that is.' I look around the inside of the car frantically. 'Er, right, I have lube? Is that a thing that might help? Like, you know, let the baby slide on out a bit easier?'

'I don't know,' she pants, hair stuck to her forehead. I gently push it back for her. 'They didn't cover lube in the classes. Maybe?'

'It's strawberry flavoured,' I read the bottle out loud, wondering if there's a best-before date. Van and I haven't used this in at least a year, I thought we'd lost it. 'Does the flavour matter?'

She starts crying again. 'I don't want my baby to come out smelling like strawberry-flavoured lube,' she weeps quite fairly and I throw the bottle back down on the floor of the car.

'No problem, no problem at all, Nat, it's all fine,' I say calmly. What else? 'I don't have labour drugs but I think I have some marijuana in the dashboard; would that be useful?'

She ignores me, screaming long and hard again. I consider covering my ears but decide it would be rude. I hold her hand instead and wipe her sweaty face with my coat sleeve.

'Oh God, I think it's coming, Zo!' She is straining and breathing hard. 'You're going to have to check.'

Fuck fuck fuck. I reach down and pull her pants aside. Shittttttttting fuck, there's a head. There's an actual real-life fucking baby's head in my hand. How is this real life?

'Right,' I say trying very hard to sound calm as I pull off her underwear. 'Listen to me, you marvellous, strong little fucker, the baby's coming right now, and you really are going to have to push now. Push hard. Breathe too or whatever.'

'Helpful,' she says through gritted teeth, grabbing the headrest. She screws up her scarlet face and screams one more time, long and hard.

And then, suddenly, just like that, there is a baby in my arms. There's a real tiny, slimy baby, covered in all kinds of gook and it's looking up at me like I'm a long-lost friend. I guess I am, a bit.

It's a girl, I register dreamily, but everything seems far away. Maybe I'm in shock?

'Hello, baby girl,' I say at last, staring at her in awe.

'It's a girl?' Natalie says, collapsing onto the seat and trying to turn to see. I've never seen a person look so broken-down exhausted, but so excited. 'Is she OK? Why isn't she crying? Can I hold her?'

'I think she's OK?' I say, scanning the small thing as it squirms and waves; her face scrunched up as if she's miming the act of crying.

She looks like Nat. And – I think, swallowing hard – she looks like my brother. This is fucking magic.

'She seems great, actually,' I say confidently. 'Amazing.' I gingerly hand her over, wondering what to do about the umbilical cord. I sit back against the seat for a moment, breathing hard. 'Are we supposed to slap her or something?'

Natalie starts crying hard, cradling her little baby and then I lean in, so the three of us are huddled together on the backseat. Copying her mum, baby girl starts wailing loudly, and it's such a beautiful sound, I almost can't move. So I start crying, too. And we three all cry together for a few minutes, holding on to each other, sharing so much love and so much fucking adrenaline.

I have to pull myself together and get her to hospital.

'Are you, um, are you guys OK if I start driving again?' I remove my coat and help Natalie wrap up the baby in it. Nat can't take her eyes off its tiny face. 'You both need to be checked. We're close and I'll call ahead.'

She nods through her tears and wipes at her snot-covered, red, sweaty face. She looks so beautiful and serene. 'Yes, do,' she whispers. 'But I think we're OK, aren't we? She's breathing, and look at her, she's incredible.'

I climb back into the front seat and start the engine, my hands shaking as I grip the wheel.

I just helped deliver a baby. Natalie's baby. My niece.

'MAKE A U-TURN WHERE POSSIBLE AND PROCEED TO ROUTE,' the satnav suddenly shouts and we both start laughing as I swing the car round and dutifully proceed back to our original route. Back to where we're meant to be.

NATALIE

I feel so serene, lying here surrounded by loved ones and white sheets. Like a new mother you see in films, all calm and beautiful, holding her swaddled little newborn to her chest. I imagine I look quite goddess-like right now.

'Are you OK?' Mum says beside me, with a worried look on her face. 'You're still very red and sweaty.'

Oh right, maybe I don't look as serene as I was picturing.

'I'm wonderful!' I beam at her. 'I made a person.' She smiles at me, her eyes shiny.

'You really did,' she whispers and looks down again with wonder at her new grandchild.

'Natalie!' Matthew's voice bursts into the room with the rest of him. He's frantic, gripping car keys in one hand. 'Are you OK? Is the baby OK? What the hell happened?'

'Shussshh,' I say calmly, in what I hope is an earth-mother-type tone. 'I'm great, and she's great, too.'

'She?' he says quietly, reaching for my free hand and sinking down into a chair by my bed. He stares at each of us for a long time, a tear making its way down his cheek. 'I'm so, so sorry I wasn't there. I drove like a lunatic from Liverpool. I'm going to get so many speeding notices.' He shakes his head, looking intently at our daughter. 'I can't believe she's real,' he says with awe. 'She's so beautiful.'

'She really is.' Bryan nods, leaning over for another glance at the baby. He's so puffed up with pride, he looks like he'll burst any second. Sue and Debbie smile over at him, looking emotional. Maybe they'll all be friends one day after all. I grin over at Zoe, deliriously happy to have my whole family together; this is so wonderful.

In my arms, the baby starts grizzling and I ask Bryan to fetch a nurse to help me try breastfeeding again. Bryan, Debbie and Sue head off together and Matt leans in to peck me on the cheek. 'I'm going with them,' he says reluctantly. 'I haven't had a wee in five hours.' He looks down at me with so much love and affection. 'Our daughter,' he whispers again. 'Well done, Natalie, you are incredible. When all these people are gone I'm going to kiss you like you've never been kissed before.'

I narrow my eyes at him playfully. 'What do you mean by

that?' I ask. 'Because I've been kissed in loads of different ways – with tongues, without. One time upside down because I was trying to recreate the Spider-Man thing.'

'OK,' he says and nods. 'But have you been kissed like an actual spider before?'

'How do spiders kiss?' I reply innocently.

'I assume there is definitely something with legs involved, right? So just you wait.' He blows me a kiss and I watch him go.

Alone again, I budge up to make room for Zoe on the bed. She climbs on and we both snuggle into the baby.

'Have you thought about names yet?' she murmurs, sleepily, before her head pricks up. 'Oh my God!' Her eyes open wide. 'You finally have a chance to pick out the perfect, cool, *dramatic* name!'

I nod excitedly. 'I have a longlist on my phone. Can you get it? Let's check through them and see what she looks like.'

She reaches across the bedside cabinet to retrieve my phone and opens up my Notes app. There is a page with BABY NAMES underlined and she starts reading out the girl names.

'Meredith, Cristina, Miranda, Callie, Arizona, April—' she pauses. '—hold on, Nat, are these just characters off *Grey's Anatomy*?'

'Shut up,' I say conversationally, staring down at my baby, transfixed.

She returns to my list. 'Oh, OK, these next ones are very dramatic and not from any TV show that I've ever seen. Augustin Bizimana, Félicien Kabuga – they're both very cool names. Where did you get them?'

'They're soooo cool, right!' I declare excitedly. 'They're war criminals wanted for leading Rwanda's 1994 genocide.'

'Right.' She looks underwhelmed. 'How about Adolf?' she suggests and I laugh, but then I have to look down to double-check my daughter definitely doesn't look like an Adolf. Is Dolfy actually quite cute?

'Hey,' Zoe says, putting my phone down. 'Maybe becoming a mum, you could have a rebrand again yourself?'

'You know,' I say contemplatively, 'I'm actually pretty into "Natalie" these days. And now I get to take on one of the most common names in the world, and I couldn't be happier about it.' I smile at her before explaining: 'Mum.'

She doesn't say anything, just smiles back and circles her arm around me. We stare down at my daughter again. She really looks like her daddy – like all the Darlings. She has their trademark puffy bottom lip and upturned little nose. I can see Zoe in there, too.

'You know,' I say slowly, 'I think I know what she's called.'

Zoe looks at me questioningly and I smile.

'I want to name her after you.'

She draws back in shock. 'But,' she begins haltingly, emotion thick in her voice, 'you said ages ago that Zoe was kind of a boring name, didn't you? You don't have to do that, Nat.'

'Well, I think I'll put a Y on the end,' I explain. 'The Y makes everything sexier. Natalie would be fifty times the name if it was spelled with a Y, like *Nataley*.'

'You really want to do this?' She swallows hard.

I nod, tears pricking my eyes. 'I really do.'

'Hello, Zoey,' we both whisper down at the tiny person before us. She opens her eyes, looks up at us and, I swear to God, she smiles.

* * *

www.facebook.com/messages/NatalieWinters

Subject: My FB post

Friday 11.27

Natalie Winters
Dude, can you go like my post about Zoey?

Zoe Darling
What post? Why?

Natalie Winters
Hardly anyone has! I'm so offended!!!! I've spent ten years liking
every idiotic announcement post on Facebook from people I hate,
and now they're not returning the favour.

Natalie Winters
She does look cute right? I'm not biased, she's so cute, isn't she?

Zoe Darling
Unbelievably so. Next level cute. People are morons. I've liked it
and shared it on my wall. Maybe it's just that people don't really use
Facebook any more?

Natalie Winters
I know that! It's literally only for engagement and baby
announcements. But there's a code. A social media code of conduct
and my 761 friends are ignoring it. Furious.

Natalie Winters
I've messaged Matt, he's going to share it too. I can't believe people
aren't pretending to be more excited about my baby. So rude.

Natalie Winters
I'm going to delete them all as friends.

Natalie Winters
So upset.

Friday 11.33

Natalie Winters
Oh wait, I think I just needed to hit refresh. I have 260 likes. That's good.

Friday 11.49

Natalie Winters
Hmm, what about the other 500? I'm deleting anyone who doesn't like it. You do the same.

Zoe Darling
Happily.

17

2019

ZOE

'I have really big news,' she says as she opens the door.

'No, *I* have really big news,' I counter, feeling annoyed.

'Mine is bigger,' she says, eyes narrowing.

'No, *mine* is bigger!' I reply in a slightly petulant voice. I don't want to fight for attention over this, I want all of Natalie's focus on me this evening.

'OK,' she says, sighs and leans against her doorframe. 'How should we do this? Say both our news on three?'

'No, that's dumb—' I begin as she starts counting.

'One, two . . .' The numbers trail off as she clocks what's in my hand. There is a moment of silence, followed by realisation as my news sinks in. 'Oh,' she says and her voice changes. 'Maybe yours *is* bigger.' She reaches for me. 'Oh, Zo, I'm so sorry! Come in, I'll get the alcohol.'

See, that's better.

I follow her in, my hefty suitcase's dodgy wheel grumbling loudly over Natalie's doormat as I drag it in behind me.

She leads me through into the living room, before turning to regard me anxiously.

'So, who actually ended it?' she asks, waving me towards the sofa and heading for the fridge in the next room.

'Me,' I say simply, collapsing into the seat and burying my

face into the cushions. I suddenly feel so tired. So tired and so sad. 'I did it, so it felt like I had to be the one to volunteer to leave.'

'But it's your flat!' Nat says, returning with two glasses and pouring liberally from a bottle of wine, as she sits.

'Yeah, but I said I'd give her a few days to clear her stuff out.' I sigh, taking a sip. 'Is it OK if I stay here?'

'Of course,' Nat tells me earnestly. She takes a sip and makes a face. 'Sorry about the rank wine. I have Prosecco but it felt weird to give you a celebratory drink after a break-up.'

'What would be the right drink to mark the end of a seven-year relationship?' I wonder out loud. Natalie considers this.

'Tequila,' she says at last, definitively.

I nod. 'That's exactly right. Tequila is always exactly the right answer. Do you have any?'

She lights up. 'You know what? I think I do!' She leaps across the room to a cupboard, re-emerging with a slightly dusty yellow bottle. 'Bingo!'

She doesn't bother with new glasses, topping up the wine with the acrid liquid. We both grimace as we take a shot.

'So what happened?' she asks softly, after another moment.

'Fuck knows,' I say cheerfully and she head-tilts at me, waiting. Ever since she started therapy, she's become so good at that silent, patient stare. Just waiting for you to give into the awkwardness and tell her the truth of your feelings. It's awful. I'd much rather spend my life glossing over everything; laughing it off; pretending I'm all great and perfect. Fucking therapy has a lot to answer for.

'OK . . .' My voice wobbles a bit and I hate it. 'I just don't know if I can talk about it without crying and I really, really don't want to cry.'

'Why not?' The head tilt; the patient waiting stare.

'Fuck off, Natalie,' I snap. 'Don't therapy me. Everyone hates crying. I'm not weird for not wanting to cry, or never really crying. Nobody *wants* to fucking cry, it's horrible and embarrassing and—' I stop there because I am crying quite a lot and I can't speak that well through the tears.

She shuffles closer and holds me. Her warm, familiar smell makes me cry harder and I hate her for it, but I'm also grateful. I can feel the tightness in my chest unfurling and I already feel better.

'You know, crying is fine,' she says soothingly. 'It's good for you. We're literally designed this way – especially women. We have shallower tear ducts than men. Our emotions can't help spilling out. The world would be a much better place if men could cry more, too. They need the release just as much as we do, if not more.'

I nod into her jumper and do as I'm told, crying softly until I'm finally able to speak again.

'I know things have been shit for ages,' I sniff. 'But I kept thinking it would get better. Like, we both just needed to work less, or start having date nights, or be more thoughtful. *Something.*' I pause to take another shot. 'Then we'd have a good couple of days and I'd think, "See? I was right to stay, we can get back to how we used to be." But then we'd have another huge row and all the rows from before this row would come back up, and I felt like I was exploding with hatred and resentment and rage.' I stop again to wipe my nose on my sleeve. 'And yet I still didn't want it to be over – I still don't – but what else can you do? It feels like we've been going round in the same circle for months, maybe years. I'm so tired of it, Nat. I feel, like, broken-down exhausted by the same fights and the same anger. And every time we argue, she brings up the bisexual lie – how I kept it from her for so many years. She's never going to be able to let it go.'

Nat nods sadly, stroking my arm, and it makes me think how little Vanessa and I have touched this past year.

'So then, today, we were having lunch, and things were fine. We'd even had quite a nice few days, y'know? And then this advert came on the telly and it was this couple slow dancing. I thought to myself, "They seem so in love, but they're actors, they're just pretending." And I looked over at Vanessa and I realised we were just pretending, too.' I take a deep breath and Natalie tops up my tequila. I drink it, she tops it up again. My head swims.

'We sat on our bed and talked for a while,' I continue in a low voice. 'For once we weren't arguing, because I guess we both knew it was time. We agreed that we wanted to end things now while there is still some love. Because I'd be so, so sad if I lost her entirely, y'know? I want us to stay friends on some level if we can. Or at least have good memories and a fondness if and when we think about one another.' Natalie takes my hand and squeezes it. I take a deep breath. 'So then, of course, we had depressing, clingy sex for the first time in months and I packed my suitcase and left.'

'And here you are,' Natalie says simply.

'Here I am . . .' I shrug. I feel emptied out. She tops up my tequila again and we sit in silence for a few minutes. Drinking. Topping up. Drinking again.

'I called Dad on the way over to tell him,' I say after a while, enjoying the warm aftertaste in my throat.

She laughs. 'Don't tell me, he said, "This storm shall pass"? Or maybe, "It never rains but it pours"? No, no wait, did he go with the classic, "Every cloud has a silver lining"?'

'Actually,' I smirk. 'He just asked if I was OK. And then he said he loved me so much and if there was absolutely anything I needed, to just let him know. He said he would drop anything, any time or place to be there for me. He even offered me his spare room for as long as I might need.'

'Oh.' Nat looks put out. 'Well, now I feel bad for taking the piss out of him.'

'As you should,' I say primly. 'He really is so much easier to be around these days. So much happier. Did I tell you, he's even started dating? He's having the time of his life with the surplus of middle-aged ladies out there.' I pause to wipe my nose with my sleeve. 'Although, honestly, shallow weather shit might've cheered me up – sympathy is much harder to hear.'

'I'm glad he's happier these days, but I hope he doesn't stop with the weather puns and jokes *entirely*,' Nat declares, waving her glass around in the air. And that's when I notice her hand.

'You absolute fuck!' I shout, slightly slurring. 'Your news *is* bigger!'

NATALIE

Zoe forcefully grabs my hand to examine the diamond and I feel my stomach bubbling over with excitement. And then I feel bad. It's not the time to throw my happiness in her face.

Ugh, people being sad when you want to be happy is so annoying.

'We don't have to talk about this now,' I say, trying not to smile too widely.

'Don't be a dickhead!' she shouts, leaning forward a bit unsteadily. 'This is fucking wonderful news!'

'You really didn't know?' I ask gleefully. 'Matt didn't tell you he was going to do it?'

She shakes her head. 'No, the shithead. Where is he? Never mind *telling* me, he should've asked my permission.' She examines the ring again, her face full of genuine joy. 'It's so beautiful, Nat, congratulations. When did it happen? How? Tell me everything.'

I sigh dreamily. 'It was perfect.' Then I smile widely at her. 'I know when you've got a kid and a house with someone, marriage maybe doesn't matter so much, but I'm still so happy.'

'Of course it matters,' she says staunchly. 'If it matters to you, it matters full stop. Don't dismiss something that matters to you just *because* it matters to you.'

'I'm not sure I followed that,' I say, narrowing my eyes. 'But I've had a lot of tequila.'

'I just mean,' she looks impatient, 'that we all have a tendency to assume the things that are important to us are trivial and silly but they're not. And this definitely is important.' She pauses. 'So?'

'So,' I beam at her, basking in the story, 'you probably don't want to be reminded of this, but our birthday last week was the anniversary of the first time we, er, did the thing.'

'The thing?' Her face is cloudy. 'Oh! Gross, you mean sex. When we were nineteen! Ew. I don't think awkward, virginity-stealing of a 17-year-old in my dad's bathroom gets to be classed as an anniversary. Certainly not a romantic one.'

I snort. 'Maybe not. But we started talking about our life together, and marriage. We've talked about it loads of times in the past and Matt admitted he'd been planning to propose just before we got pregnant. He was going to do the whole bells and whistles thing—'

'Weird expression.'

'Anyway, he said he'd been planning it for ages. He was

going to do it in my classroom at school, surrounded by my friends and family, with the kids singing 'Can't Help Falling In Love' by Elvis Presley. He was even going to let them film it for YouTube because he knows how much I love a viral proposal video.'

'Ha,' Zoe laughs. 'He knows you so well. So much drama. He would've hated doing all that – he must love you like mad.'

I laugh, too. 'I know! And twenty-five-year-old me would've gone bananas for that kind of over-the-top proposal. But I realised, when he was describing it, it's not really me any more. I still enjoy drama from a distance – on telly or when Mrs Humphries from maths got drunk at the Christmas disco and put her hand down Mr Tandy from science's trousers – but I'm OK with not being part of it. I like my life to be boring these days. I like that I know where I'm going to be and what I'm going to be doing in ten years' time. I like knowing who I'm going to be with. I like my life being just like everyone else's.' I smile. 'So I told him that when he did propose – whenever it might be – I wanted it to be simple and private. Just me and him and little Zoey. Just the three of us.'

'You're going to make me cry again,' she says emotionally.

'And then,' I continue proudly, 'this morning, I woke up late to him bringing me breakfast in bed. He'd been up for hours with Zoey already, and she was beside me in bed, wearing her prettiest dress – the one you bought her at Christmas! He told me he loved me and had always loved me, and then he went down on one knee. He brought out the ring and he asked me the question—' I break off because I can feel tears welling up. 'I know it probably seems lame and boring, but it was perfect. It was exactly what I wanted and I honestly can't imagine anything more romantic.'

'It's better than perfect, it's fucking real,' Zoe says, voice slightly awed. 'And oh my God, you're getting married to my brother! This is what we always wanted – we'll be sisters!'

'Sorry about the timing.' I make an awkward face. 'It's so weird how life turns out.'

She contemplates this. 'Y'know, I'm actually pretty excited to be single again, Nat. Obviously I'm really sad about losing Van, but it's been so long since I was on my own. I'm looking forward to living by myself again. I can travel the world. Maybe I'll even move abroad! And I can *date*! So much has changed out there in the dating world since I've been with Van. I'm excited to try it.'

I grimace. 'Says every newly single person, ever.' I smile tightly. 'Just promise me you'll stay away from Tinder.'

'Gotcha.' She gives me a thumbs up and reaches over for a hug.

'You can always stay here if you get lonely or sad or scared of burglar noises that turn out to be radiators that need bleeding . . .' My voice is muffled against her shoulder.

'Thanks, Nat.' I can feel her smiling. 'I know you're just looking for a live-in au pair, though.'

I sigh. 'Busted. Oh hey, you'll be my maid of honour, right?'

'Yuck,' she says wearily. 'But yeah, of course. We're not spending five hundred quid per person on a hen do with butlers in the buff, though.'

'Err . . .' Nat looks sheepish. 'Is that a hard red line or . . .?'

* * *

INSTAGRAM

ZOE DARLING
Active 4h ago

Can I borrow your pink lacey bra?

Why? You're like three sizes boobier than me?

Also, it would be super creepy for you to
wear my bra for my brother

It's OK, it's for the #FeministChallenge
on here. I figure my boobs will
look magnificent in a bra that's too
small. They'll be bursting out all over.

Don't worry, I'm going to
nominate you for the challenge when
I've posted mine.

What the fuck is this now?

You have to post a super-sexy selfie in your
underwear, using the bunny Snapchat
filter, to prove you support women

In what way does this support women?

. . .

. . .

. . .

OK, I googled and apparently the challenge
is to help promote awareness of Saudi Arabia
not letting women drive. It's bad isn't it!!!!!

How does it promote awareness of that?

Well, I'm aware now

Oh God, I just checked my notifications,
I have 41 nominations

See!!!!

I do see. I feel so very much more feminist now.
With the power of my pink bra, you're
going to save all these Saudi women from
not driving

It's more about proving your feminism
and supporting other women

All these women in bras on my feed
are making me feel so very supported

OK fine, I just want to post a
hot selfie with the bunny filter,
can I borrow your bra or not?

Sure, girl. Me and my bra will offer you minimal
support in this venture

6 June 2019
6.56 pm

To my amazing female friend,
I hereby nominate you in the
#FeministChallenge. Show your
unwavering feminism by posting
a sexy pink bra selfie and then
nominating 300 other strong women
who all have to post their own selfie with

the Valencia filter and the hashtag.
If you choose to ignore this
nomination, bad luck will
follow you for seven years

BLOCKED

18

2020

ZOE

'IT'S AT THE BOTTOM OF YOUR FUCKING SCREEN!' I shout into the mic for the fifteenth time. 'Seriously, Nat, do we have to go through this every fucking time?'

After an eternity, she finds the unmute button and the noise of her household fills my laptop. Her face is red as she leans away from the camera. Her eyes are on the right, staring only at her own image in the corner.

'Sorry, sorry,' she says, flustered. 'I look fucking awful, I hate Zoom. I feel like I've done quizzes at least four times a day on it since quarantine began.'

'I did one last night with Hayley, Vanessa and Gilly,' I comment and Nat looks excited.

'What's Gilly like? Is she pretty? Does she look like you? Is it weird that Vanessa is with someone new? And that you all *hang out*?'

'Honestly, it's weirder that it's *not* weird,' I say considering it. 'It feels fine. We've been apart a while now and I'm just really happy we've been able to stay friends.'

'You absolute liar,' she huffs into the camera. 'You are jealous, don't lie, there's no way you're not jealous.'

I laugh. 'Maybe a tiny, tiny bit,' I concede. 'But probably only in the same way I'm jealous when all my friends fall in love. Not because I want to be in love – I really am happy single – but just because it means I get less of them. I'm a selfish shithead like that.'

Toddler Zoey suddenly appears on screen. 'Hiya, Zo!' she shouts and starts stomping up and down in front of the camera, singing and banging a small toy car into another small toy car.

'Fuck's sake,' Natalie mutters, trying to confiscate the car-cymbals.

'I love how much more you swear since you became a parent,' I tell her joyously as Matthew appears on screen.

'Can you grab her?' Natalie asks him, looking hassled.

'Sure,' he says, hoisting my god-daughter onto his hip. She squawks in protest. 'How are you feeling?' Matthew puts a kindly hand on his fiancée's shoulder, looking worried. Nat's had some symptoms this past week and she's officially in self-isolation. But I'm sure it's just hay fever.

'Not too bad,' she smiles nicely up at him and he smiles back, before taking Zoey off upstairs.

'Is it the screen's colour saturation or are you a bit feverish, Nat?' I ask, once he's gone.

She nods. 'It is me. I've been feeling hot all day. And I've got this fucking headache. Do you think I've got it? Boris came for a school visit right before all this happened. What if I got it from him and I've been incubating it all this time?'

'That seems unlikely,' I say dryly. 'It's two weeks' incubation, not two months. Is there some other way you could've got it?'

She looks guilty. 'I did go to the supermarket a couple of weeks ago, and it was an absolute free-for-all. People seem to think queuing outside gives them some kind of immunity. They go mental inside, shoving into one another, ten to an aisle. I felt like I was going to get trampled for salmon.'

She starts coughing and spluttering.

'Sorry, I think I need to lie down,' she says, carrying her laptop over to the sofa and throwing herself onto it. 'I should go,' she says weakly. 'I'm being boring. I'll be fine, women don't die from it, do they? Certainly not young, healthy women.' She thinks about this. 'OK, not *young* women. OK, young-ish.'

'You're not hanging up,' I say shortly, 'just keep me on screen; I'm not doing anything else so I'll stay with you. Long-term friendship is mostly about being boring together anyway. In nineteen years, I'd say we've easily spent at least a couple of those years lying around talking about nothing.'

I smile at her as she pulls a blanket over herself.

'Oh God!' I catch sight of the back of Natalie's head. 'Have you let Matthew give you a quarantine haircut?'

She pouts. 'Yes, and I know it's awful. I told him Carole Baskin had the right idea and I'm going to feed him to a tiger.'

'Absolutely fair.'

'Nineteen years,' she says now, thinking about it. 'I've known you more than half my life.'

I nod. 'Way more, even if you discount the couple of years we were in a huff with each other.'

'Isn't it funny,' she muses, stretching out her legs across the sofa now, 'how you can meet the love of your life out of nowhere. When you least expect it?'

'Who, Matthew?' I ask, brows furrowed. She snorts.

'No, idiot!' She laughs again. 'I mean *you*.' She pauses. 'Of course Matthew is also the love of my life – don't tell him I said it was you. But there are lots of kinds of love you can have in your lifetime. And let's face it, my one real, lifelong love has been a friendship. It's been you.' She smiles widely into the camera. 'Who could've guessed I would meet The One in the school loos on my fourteenth birthday.'

'It was fate,' I say, proudly. 'We were always meant to be friends. I don't know who I would've been without you.'

There is a long silence and I desperately wish I was holding her hand.

'Can I tell you a secret?' Nat says after a minute.

'I'm pretty sure I know all your secrets,' I smile wryly. 'These days, at least.'

'There is something I never told you.' She looks a little embarrassed. 'I never got my period that day.'

'What day?'

'That day we met, in the loos?' She is almost whispering. 'You were crying because you'd started your period?'

'Yes,' I confirm, 'And so were – wait, you weren't?'

'No.' She shakes her head. 'I was crying because I told a dinner lady I really loved Darius from Popstars and she said he was a creep, and I got upset because I really thought Darius was amazing and I couldn't believe she was being mean about him.' There's a long pause as the screen flickers. 'A lot of things made me cry back then.' She swallows and continues. 'Anyway, my period actually didn't start until about seven months later.'

'Oh my God, you little fucking weasel!' I shout. 'I can't believe our entire friendship is based on a lie.' I laugh. 'But we talked about periods so much in that first year,' I say in awe, remembering all the late-night chats about periods. 'Because mine were so sketchy – so all over the place – and so heavy.'

She shrugs. 'Yeah, I know. But I read *Sugar* magazine every month, so I knew all the things to say about it.'

'And, fucking hell, Nat, we spent ages talking about whether I should go on the sodding pill.' I shake my head, amazed. 'Because I thought it might help regulate my flow.'

'I know we did,' she says, cringing. 'And you just kept saying the word flow, which nearly ended our friendship. That was a very difficult time for us. Worse than when I had an affair with your brother.'

'STILL TOO SOON!' I shout into the mic and she covers her mouth with her hand, giggling.

'If it helps,' she says contemplatively, 'I was punished when my period did eventually turn up, because I still didn't know how to use a sanitary towel and couldn't ask you. I thought it was sticky side up. Like a plaster. I stuck the wings to the hair on my vag and it was very painful and very messy.'

'Nice.'

'Oh!' Natalie looks up, excited. 'I forgot to tell you. Guess who's just started working at my school? You'll never guess, so I'll just tell you.'

'OK,' I say agreeably.

'Andrea Allen!' she says, delightedly.

'Who?' The name rings a bell.

'*Andrea Allen*,' she repeats, exasperated. 'From school?'

'The graffiti,' I say, remembering.

'Yeah.' Natalie is nodding happily. 'I thought she looked familiar, so I asked and it's definitely her. We had a lovely chat and she gave me extra chips. It's funny, she said she had a bad time at school, too. Do you think everyone does, in their own way?'

'Probably.' I look down at my nails. 'I think everyone's dealing with their own thing, and growing up is fucking shit. Even the popular kids probably had their stuff going on.' I consider this for a moment. 'But I also don't think that excuses someone being a dick their whole life. Like Semen Stain clearly is.'

293

We nod wisely at each other.

'Oh, also,' Natalie looks solemn, 'it turns out Andrea didn't lose her anal virginity in a Café Rouge when she was eleven. It was in a Little Chef and she was fifteen.'

'RIP Little Chef,' I say automatically.

'RIP,' she repeats.

I hear Zoey screaming from off camera.

'Do you think Matthew's OK?' I try to sound concerned, but I don't want Natalie to go. Tomorrow's our birthday and I'm furious we have to spend it apart.

'Oh, he's fine,' she says, waving her hand dismissively. 'He can cope with her for one bedtime.'

'Is lockdown getting to you guys yet?' I ask carefully, but she laughs.

'Of course it is,' she says merrily. 'I hate him almost constantly.'

'I'm really sorry about your wedding,' I say, sadly. 'I guess that's looking less and less likely to happen in July now, right?'

Natalie nods. 'Yeah, we've already started calling round to cancel things. Maybe we'll do it next year instead. Or maybe we'll just run away to get married on a beach somewhere or with Elvis in Vegas. Then come back and throw a big party for you lovely idiots to celebrate with us.' She looks a bit dreamy. 'That would be fun.'

'Take me with you if you're going to a beach, please?' I beg. 'I've got such itchy feet these days. I think as soon as lockdown is over, I'm going to need a huge, epic adventure.'

Natalie nods, closing her eyes. 'Don't go too far away from me,' she murmurs, and she looks redder in the face than before.

'Are you OK?' I ask, feeling the pinch of worry.

'I think so.' She blinks at the light of the computer monitor.

'It's probably nothing, isn't it? I mean, getting it now means I'll be over it soon, and then I can be immune or whatever. My life can continue without worry because I'll have had my turn.'

'Sure,' I say, nodding a little too hard. 'But don't forget to test your eyesight with a visit to Barnard Castle before you're better.' She's quiet for a minute, her eyes closed again, and her breathing sounds a little bit ragged.

'I think it's human nature to assume you're going to die, every time you feel ill, isn't it?' she asks, her voice a bit high.

'Oh yeah.' I am still nodding aggressively. 'I think this is it every time I get a runny nose.'

'Ah well, you've still got my death video, right, Zo?' She opens her eyes a bit weakly and smiles to show she is joking.

'I'm right here,' I say again, wishing I could hold her hand. 'I'll always be right here with you, and you'll always be there for me, right, Nat?'

The camera cuts off suddenly and a message pops up.

'This meeting has now ended' – Zoom says, a bit shittily.

'Nat?' I say into the blankness.

19

Present Day: 2021

So then, why *do* women cry in loos?

Honestly, I don't fucking know. Hiding from the public humiliation? A fear of seeming fragile and broken? Even though that's exactly what everyone is, like, *most* of the time.

I spent so much of my twenties trying to seem strong. Trying to hide that fragility and all those broken parts. I was convinced my flaws were terrible – much worse than other people's – that they were impossible for anyone to overlook. So I had to hide them. All those bad things I saw about myself, I thought they made me a freak. I thought they made me unlovable.

And that was so, so stupid.

Because the truth is my flaws actually made me ordinary. Being scared and anxious makes me the same as every other woman out there. Every woman who's said nasty things about herself in the mirror or on the pages of a diary. Every woman who's doubted herself and hated herself and welcomed cruelty from others because it's what she believed she deserved.

Getting older has let me see myself better; to disassemble the pieces of me that felt wrong and put them back together in a way that is magical. I'm not so different from my fourteen-year-old self, but my perspective has shifted. I'm a magic eye that is only now coming into focus. And it turns out I am amazing.

I mean, don't get me wrong, it's still hard. I still doubt myself and hate myself and criticise myself. But it's getting easier. And it helps to know we're all doing our best – trying to, at least – and, fuck, I see now how hard it is for everyone.

I think that's why we need friends so much. It's why we need people who can keep reminding us it's OK to fall apart and to love us despite everything. To tell us it's OK to be weak and scared and rage against all those feelings of powerlessness. To cry in the loos next to us.

Like Zoe always did for me.

Of course, the real problem is that at some point we have to stop crying. We have to leave the loo and go out into the real world again.

Especially when some idiot's been banging on the door for half an hour.

ZOE

The problem with women crying in loos all the time is that it kinda takes ages and monopolises a space we all sodding need.

I've been trying to get in this bathroom for half an hour now but some moron is in there wailing. For God's sake, I think, banging on the door again, I just want to have one small, *quick* cry before the service starts. I just need a refresher, a soul cleanse, before I have to face everyone – and before I find Natalie to say how sorry I am for making her think I was letting her down – yet again.

See, I told her I wasn't coming today.

When she rang the other day with the awful news about Sue, I said I couldn't come back. I've barely been working in New York for a few months and I wasn't planning a return visit any time soon. I said I was sorry and Nat said it was fine, she understood. She said we could drink to Sue with Debbie when I was back next. But I could tell she was upset.

I hung up the phone and thought of all those times she was there for me, even when I was pretending I didn't need her or pushing her away. I thought of all the unconditional – and conditional – love she's given me over the past twenty years. I thought about our history and our shared lifetime of experiences and all our fights and all the stupid tears.

And so I made my first good decision in ages: I got on a plane in my mask and came to be by Nat's side. I just need to find her and tell her.

Finally, I hear a shifting from behind the door. The wailer is coming out, at last. The lock rattles and a pale, but oh-so familiar face appears.

'Oh my God,' I say because it's all I can say. 'It was you, you're the wailer.'

'I'm always the wailer,' she sniffs and then we're both wailing, and in each other's arms.

'I'm so sorry I wasn't here sooner.' The guilt pours out of me. 'I should've come right away but I had to get a test and I'm a selfish twat who's still trying to please everyone – even the idiot new bosses I don't care about. Please forgive me.'

'Don't,' she says through damp eyes. 'You're here, and I'm so fucking relieved. I really didn't think I could do this without you. I have to do the eulogy about Sue's life and it's going to be so horrible.'

'How's your mum?' I stroke her arm sympathetically.

'She's up and down . . .' Nat sniffs and then shakes her head. 'She just keeps saying how much she regrets that they weren't as close as they used to be. She says they let things come between them. They were still friends on the surface, but ever since that thing with your dad, and then with Sue dating Edgar, they drifted apart. They never had that big clear-the-air talk – they let stupid life get in the way and come between them.' She looks at me pleadingly. 'We can't let that happen to us, OK, Zoe? You're the love of my life and I know we've had our ups and downs, but that's the reality of a long-term relationship, isn't it? We have to keep constantly reminding each other that we love each other and are there for one another.'

'I know we do.' I nod solemnly and pull her in for another hug. 'I want you to know that I'm always here for you, even when I'm working five thousand miles away.'

'Fuck off, that sounds so glamorous.'

'You swear more than me these days.' I smile into her hair.

'I've grown up.' She pulls back, looking proud. 'I swear and I stand up for myself and I enjoy sex and I cry without being embarrassed – and I tell Nanny Surrey to fuck off when she makes comments about baby Zoey getting chubby.'

I roll my eyes. 'We've lost so many people. Can you believe that old witch isn't dead yet?'

'Unbelievable,' she agrees. 'Sue was no age and we lose *her*, yet Nanny Surrey is still stomping around being the same awful dick to everyone she always was.' She pauses. 'Poor Sue.'

'She was really happy in the end, though,' I say quietly. 'Edgar made her very happy. He restored her faith in love. And even if she and your mum weren't as close in those last few years, I think they both knew they had each other. Your mum was there with her in her last few minutes, wasn't she?'

Natalie nods, then frowns. 'I still think it was a bad choice. How they let things come between them like that.'

'I don't know about blaming bad choices for stuff,' I say and shrug. 'I think I've come to the conclusion that choices aren't really bad or good. Like, getting angry or regretting your decisions seems so pointless when you look back. We all fuck things up and we all also do wonderful, amazing things.' Nat looks confused. 'Like,' I take a deep breath, 'you made a choice back then with Matthew, and maybe that hurt people at the time, but it also helped people – and even *made* people!' I smile, thinking of how big Zoey's getting. 'And I made a choice that nearly fucked things up with you forever, but I can't regret that either, because I think it's made us happier and more balanced. It gave us the space to become our own people a little more and then we got to choose to come back together and value each other that much more.' I take Nat's hand and squeeze it. 'Choices sounds like such a finite, final thing. Like, we're meant to look at a path and pick one. But nothing is clear-cut like that. Every choice we make sparks another million choices and everything we do will hurt or help someone out there. When those paths are right in front of you, you realise there are fucking thorns in the way and grass and, like, dead bodies blocking your view. And maybe the paths end up in the same place anyway.'

Nat narrows her eyes. 'I think your analogy is getting a bit muddled.'

I laugh. 'Probably. But that's sort of my point, because life *is* muddled. All I mean, really, is that choices aren't necessarily bad or good. We do what we do in each moment, because we *have to* in those moments. I'm not sure there's that much choice in anything really.'

Nat side-eyes me warily. 'OK, well, you might want to remember that later when Mum insists on introducing you to the lesbian from her Zoom book club she *chose* to invite to the online wake, because she said it's high time you met someone.'

'Isn't that kind?' I say dryly.

We smile at each other for a moment in silence.

We're grown-ups, I think in awe, and I see the same horrible realisation in Nat's eyes.

'I suppose we better get out there, then,' she says at last, squeezing my hand. 'The service must be starting soon.' And a lot of people are live-streaming this from home.

I nod but don't move. We're grown-ups. I don't know how it happened, but we are. Twenty years of loving each other and we're still here, looking after one another.

I think that's pretty great.

'Just wait, Nat,' I say softly. 'Let's stay here for another minute. Just us, just one more minute.'

ONE DIRECTION fanfiction

Homepage>One Direction>Rated18>Archived fiction

What Makes Roxy Beautiful
By Anon

Roxy is shy and clumsy, and she has no idea how
really beautiful she is. She is modest and nice,
never noticing the admiring looks she gets, with
those huge green eyes and her long, red, lustrous
hair that ripples down her back like the tide.
She also has amazing curves, with a tiny waist
and large, ripe boobs with pink nipples that are
always erect.

She might not know her power, but men
everywhere notice her, and they WANT her . . .

One day, at her work as an HR rep - where she
is very undervalued and overlooked by her bosses
- a new girl walks in.

'Hello,' the stranger says, 'I'm the new girl;
my name is Zoella.'

Roxy looks up, surprised anyone would even
talk to her because she still doesn't realise how
attractive she really is to others. The new girl
before her is pretty - and somehow familiar, she
thinks to herself.

'Hello, Zoella,' Roxy says, smiling back,
showing off perfectly straight, white teeth.

'You're Roxy, aren't you?' Zoella says,
eyebrows raised.

'Yes, I am,' says Roxy, surprised at anyone knowing her name.

'I'm your new assistant,' Zoella informs her and Roxy is surprised.

'I didn't know I was getting an assistant,' she muses, looking around for her boss and wondering why no one ever tells her anything.

'Kenny told me to make sure you were well looked after,' Zoella explains. 'He's off this week on some executives team-building activity event thing.' She rolls her eyes so Roxy knows she thinks this is lame and Roxy warms to her new assistant.

'Well, that's wonderful,' Roxy replies, delighted she will finally get some help around here. Kenny lets her do everything and she is constantly buried under mountains of paperwork. She barely has time for a personal life and hasn't seen any of her friends in months.

I wonder if this woman could be a new friend, Roxy ponders, regarding the smiling Zoella.

'It's almost lunchtime . . .' Zoella checks her watch. 'Can I buy my new boss a burrito at the place across the road?'

'That sounds great!' Roxy replies, because she has a hearty appetite but never puts on any weight.

As the pair wander out of the building, Zoella asks her lots of questions about work and her life, which is unusual for Roxy. Most people just want to talk about themselves, she's found.

They buy their food and sit down in a quiet corner. Roxy ties her voluminous red hair up in a perfect scruffy bun without looking in a mirror, because she doesn't want to make a mess with her food and Zoella watches her admiringly.

'You know you're very beautiful?' she tells Roxy, taking a big bite of her food.

Roxy goes red and feels shy. She is very modest and not used to people being so nice to her.

'In fact, you're just my best friend Harry's type,' Zoella continues. 'Do you think I could set you up on a blind date with him sometime?'

'Oh my goodness!!' Roxy is still red-faced, but it suits her. 'That's very kind of you. But I have a boyfriend at home, his name is Simon.'

'Does he treat you right?' Zoella asks.

'Of course,' says Roxy immediately, but she is hiding a secret shame. Because at home Simon *isn't* treating her right. He is mean and unkind, saying lots of things you shouldn't say to a woman you love.

Zoella eyes her critically, as if she can tell the truth just from looking at her.

'OK. Well, how about we go for a drink tonight?' she suggests. 'And you can tell me all about Simon and the rest of your life. I want to hear *everything* about you.'

After an afternoon well-spent finally catching up on her work – mostly thanks to Zoella's brilliant help – Roxy is ready to go.

'Are you ready?' she asks her new friend Zoella.

'Not just yet,' Zoella replies. 'Can I meet you in the bar? I just need fifteen minutes to finish this.'

'Of course,' Roxy says and heads to the exclusive bar nearby where Zoella has booked them a table. Roxy has never been to this bar before, even though she's always wanted to. She always felt like she wasn't good enough for such a fancy place. Plus, she's been so busy with work and her boyfriend at home doesn't take her out - ever.

As she waits at the table with a glass of rosé, Roxy starts to worry Zoella is going to stand her up. She goes to message her, then remembers they haven't exchanged numbers.

'Excuse me,' a melodic voice interrupts her reverie, 'I hope you don't mind me interrupting you. I just have to tell you how extraordinarily beautiful you are.'

Roxy looks up, blushing prettily, and is faced with the most gorgeous man she's ever seen in her life. His eyes are deep and beautiful, pale green with flecks of yellow and brown. To Roxy, they are the most magical eyes she's ever seen. His light brown hair is big and wavy and he awkwardly pushes it off his face now as he waits for Roxy's answer.

'Um,' she stutters adorably. 'Thank you.'

'May I sit down?' he asks nicely, gesturing at the empty seat beside her.

'I'm actually w-waiting for someone.' Roxy swallows awkwardly, feeling lust like she never has before for this handsome stranger.

'OK.' He nods confidently, his large Adam's apple moving up and down as he speaks. 'Well, if you'd like to join me and my friends in the meantime, we're right there.'

He gestures behind him at a table full of the most good-looking men Roxy has ever seen. There's an angelic blond boy, smiling sweetly and waving. A sultry, smouldering dark-haired one, with stubble and piercing eyes. A handsome brown-haired boy with large shoulders, and a blue-eyed, hauntingly handsome slim guy, with tattoos on his fingers. They collectively shout hello and Roxy's heart drums hard in her chest.

'Who are these gods amongst men?' she thinks to herself. She can't help smiling at them, and - as if in a dream - she picks up her glass and goes over to join them. She's never been this brave before, but something spurs her on. It's as if she's powerless to resist these beautiful men.

They each greet her, introducing themselves one by one. As well as Harry, there's Niall, Zayn, Liam and Louis. They welcome Roxy excitedly, offering to buy her more drinks and complimenting her endlessly. They are all wonderful and gorgeous, but it is Harry who Roxy cannot tear her eyes away from. The pair of them can't stop staring at each other and, after half an hour of chatting about life and the world, the other boys make their excuses and head off back to their hotel room.

For a minute, Roxy and Harry just keep looking at each other in wonder.

'I've never seen anything so perfect,' Harry murmurs in her ear and for once, Roxy believes it.

'Are you real?' she whispers back.

'I am,' he confirms and leans in for a kiss. Roxy cannot help herself, she kisses him back, as if in slow motion. The world stops around them as they kiss and Roxy's head spins. This is unlike any kiss she's ever had before and she cannot believe the chemicals exploding in her chest and head. It's like magic and she never wants it to end.

They finish at last, breathlessly. Roxy draws back and they look at each other intensely.

'I think I . . .' she can barely speak, 'I think I need a moment in the bathroom,' she says and slips off the stool. 'I'll be back.' He grabs her hand as she leaves, pulling her back and into his chest, where he holds her still for a full minute. Their chests heave against one another as the smell of him fills her. She feels light-headed as she pulls away. This is terrifying and crazy and so, so incredible.

In the bathroom, Roxy stares at her beautiful reflection. 'What is happening?' she wonders out loud, confused. This is like a dream.

'There you are!' Zoella suddenly bursts into the loos dramatically. 'I thought you must've left! I'm so glad you haven't. Did you meet Harry and the boys?'

'Oh my goodness!' Roxy gasps. 'That's Harry, your best friend? The one you mentioned at lunch?'

Roxy is flabbergasted.

'Yes, and I'm sorry to stand you up earlier.'
Zoella smiles, unapologetic. 'I didn't mean to
trick you but I had to get you to meet him. I
arranged it so you'd be sitting next to each
other and I knew he'd fall for you the moment he
saw you. I just have this feeling about you two.'
She pauses. 'And I know you have a boyfriend but
- be honest, Roxy - are you truly, *truly* happy
with Simon?'

Roxy looks at the ground. 'No,' she admits at
last. 'He is cruel to me and I don't love him.
I've never felt anything for him like I already
feel for your best friend Harry.'

'I knew it!' Roxy exclaims happily. 'I'm so
happy. I know this is going to be good for you
both.' She pulls her coat tighter around her.
'Right, I'm going to head off home and let you
carry on your night together. I am so happy I did
this!'

She grins at Roxy and Roxy smiles back. 'Thank
you,' she whispers as Zoella leaves, and she
hears a 'You're welcome' float back through the
door.

When she returns to Harry's side, he stares at
her deeply. 'Will you come home with me tonight?'
he says, his voice deep and intense. He has the
sexiest look on his face and Roxy is suddenly
filled with shame.

'I have a boyfriend,' she whispers and Harry's
beautiful face falls. He looks devastated. 'But

I'm not happy with him!' Roxy adds quickly,
grabbing his hands. 'I'm going to message him
right now and end it!' She pulls her phone out
with a flourish and sends the message. She
doesn't wait for a reply before she throws it
back in her bag and takes Harry's hands again.

'If the offer still stands, I'd very much like
to come home with you,' she says sweetly and he
grins his cheeky, mischievous smile, looking like
himself again.

'I'd love that,' he says simply. Taking her
by the hand, he leads her out of the bar through
a back entrance Roxy never knew about. A sleek
black limo is waiting there and Harry opens the
door for her.

'This will take us to the hotel,' he tells her
as they climb in the back seat. He pulls out a
bottle of expensive champagne from a mini fridge
and Roxy gasps.

'This is so impressive,' she tells him as he
pours her a drink.

'No,' he says, shaking his head. *You're*
impressive.'

They kiss again, but this time it is sweet and
loving. When they come up for air they drink and
laugh, talking about every little part of their
lives.

It turns out Harry is in a band called One
Direction, although Roxy has not heard of them.
She's been too busy with work and Simon to listen
to music, even though it is one of her great
loves, and she secretly sings in the shower.

By the time they arrive at his room, the sexual
tension between them has reached fever pitch.
Roxy barely takes in the lavish penthouse suite
Harry is staying in, too focused on the beautiful
man taking off his clothes before her.

'Undress for me,' he says in a husky voice and
she slips her dress over her head. He stares at
her in awe, drinking her naked body in. She feels
no shame or embarrassment about her body and he
clearly loves it.

Naked together at last, they make love right
there on the thirty-thousand-pound rug. It is
hotter and sweatier than Roxy's ever experienced.
They swap positions loads and she orgasms several
times. When Harry cums after thirty minutes, he
looks deep into her eyes, groaning intensely.

'That was incredible,' he breathes into her
ear, holding her in his arms. 'The best I've ever
had. You are so beautiful and wonderful, I can't
believe I met you.'

They start to kiss again, and Harry's erection
is back already. This time the lovemaking is even
more intense and there are even more orgasms.

When they finish at last, they stare deeply at
one another.

'I want you to know, Roxy, this isn't just
about tonight,' Harry tells her earnestly. 'I
want you to be my girlfriend and be with me
forever. I know we haven't known each other
that long, Roxy, but I FEEL it. I think you're
my soulmate. I have never felt this kind of

connection with anyone before. Come live with me. We'll go get your belongings from your flat and if we see Simon I'll fight him if you need me to. After everything you've told me about the way he's treated you, I'd be glad to.'

'Yes, yes, yes!' Roxy shouts. 'I want to be with you, too. I feel the same, and I'm so happy. It's like magic!'

They kiss again, deeply. Fireworks explode and Roxy spontaneously orgasms, just from the kiss. She is happier than she's ever been in her life.

'Oh, Harry,' she sighs, when they finally stop kissing. 'I'm so glad your best friend Zoella set us up.'

'But, wait . . .' Harry pulls away, looking confused. 'Roxy, I don't have a best friend called Zoella!' He pauses, looking sad. 'I mean, I DID, but she died many years ago! Sometimes I still talk to her at night in my room. In fact, just the other day, I told her that I wanted to meet someone special. I asked her if she would help me meet someone wonderful just like you.'

Roxy gasps. 'Do you think . . . could it be . . .?'

They look at each other in wonder for a minute. And then they start to kiss again.

THE END

Click HERE to read the sequel: When Roxy Joins The Band

Acknowledgements

This is a book about best friends, and FUCK I have some wonderful best friends. I love them so much and – like so many people out there – I've spent the last year not being able to see them properly. And oh great, now I'm crying.

It's been a difficult time for everyone, I know, and writing a book in amongst the chaos was not an easy thing. I have relied on the love and generosity of so many more people than ever before – including strangers. And so I really want to thank you if you are someone who has messaged me, tweeted me, commented a nice thing on a stupid Instagram post of my stupid face, or reached out in any big or small way. It has helped lift me up in ways I never knew I needed until 2020 turned up with all its shit awfulness.

THANK YOU.

Of course I also have to thank my lovely, lovely family and friends. They've been amazing and I can never tell them how much their love and kindness means to me WHY DID I DECIDE TO WRITE THESE JUST WHEN MY PERIOD WAS DUE THIS WAS A TERRIBLE IDEA WEEEEEEEEEEEP.

Anyway, thank you so much Mum, Nigel, Dad, Liz, Dale, Lisa, Carey, Nick, Phil, Becky, Louise, Sam, Frankie, Charlotte, Ali, Sam, Leon, Charlie, Lola, Tilly, India, Flo, Ernie, Ros, John.

And also thank you to my new family, David, Claire, Paul, Lynsey, Lilly, Katy, Mavis and of course the light of my weekends, Amelia. You've all been incredibly warm and kind.

A couple of my friends really kept me together throughout all this, and I wouldn't have managed to write this book without encouragement from two in particular: Isabelle Broom and Daisy Buchanan. A I-can-never-thank-you-enough thank you to you two, as well as the rest of the Word Races gang.

Also thanks for being so brilliant to my best friends: Sarah Attrill and Lyndsey McDoris. As well as Fred Attrill, James Doris, along with Isla, Finn, Ciaran and Tara. Clair Green, Hayden Green, Abi Doyle, Emma Patterson, Jo Usmar, Kate Dunn, Katie 'Horse' Horswell, Daniel K, the Paw Walker gang, Karen Gill, Mike Townsend, Caroline Corcoran. A special snog for Abi – along with ES, DA, CC, MC, JG – who gave me some amazing music industry insight.

A thank you, as well, to my new Hemingford pals, Lucy Hocknell, Sarah-Jane Hilton, the squash fitness ladies and my excellent neighbours, Sally and John.

Probably the biggest thank you has to go to my wonderfully talented editor, Olivia Barber. Your plan for this book blew me away immediately and I've bloody LOVED working with you. Your insight and enthusiasm and talent when it comes to wrangling my words into coherence is astonishing, and I am in awe of you. Thank you. A huge thanks as well to Alainna Hadjigeorgiou for her incredible publicity work and cool glasses. To Yadira Da Trindade for her expertise and amazing gif game. To Rachael Lancaster for such an exciting, stand-out book cover. And to everyone at Orion for your ongoing love and support.

Diana Beaumont, you goddess, my queen. Thank you so much for your endless patience with my annoying emails. I'm obsessed with you.

Finally, before I go, I awant to take a moment to thank

the real life Hayley Wilson, for the use of her name in this book. Her dad, Richard Latham won this as a prize in CLIC Sargent's brilliant Get In Character campaign. CLIC Sargent is the UK's leading cancer charity for children and young people, doing vital and wonderful work. I urge you to find out more about them at www.clicsargent.co.uk.

Right, I'll shut up now. My biggest thanks goes to YOU for reading this book. You have no idea how much it means to me and I would love to hear from you with compliments. I'm too fragile for anything else, especially after this last year.

LOVE YOU BYE.